A Maiden's Honor

Book 1

The Woman from Eden series

Josanna Thompson

A Maiden's Honor

Honor

Book 1
The Woman from Eden series

Josanna Thompson

INKWELL BOOKS
Writing · Publishing · Printing

ISBN: 978-1-939625-64-9
Library of Congress Control Number: 2016921033

Shakespeare quote is from The Merchant of Venice.
Cover designed by Historical Fiction Book Covers

Published by Inkwell Books, LLC
10632 North Scottsdale Road, Unit 695
Scottsdale, AZ 85254
Tel. 480-315-3781
E-mail info@inkwellbooksLLC.com
Website www.inkwellbooksLLC.com

Printed in the United States of America

About the Author

I love a complex story with intriguing characters and an unpredictable, but satisfying ending. Those are the stories that I crave, and the stories that I strive to write.

A Maiden's Honor is my first published work. If I've learned anything from writing this book is that it's not in me to write a simple story. The characters from A Maiden's Honor are human, and the plot is filled with logical twists and turns. You won't see the ending coming. I have many other stories like A Maiden's Honor to tell.

I'm also a passionate historian who thrives on digging in and learning about the people and cultures from long ago. An avid traveler, I've been fortunate to visit many of the places in my stories. Exploring magnificent places like the Alhambra and the Topkapi Palace in Istanbul have helped me to bring my settings to life.

When I'm not writing or traveling, I live a quiet life with my husband. I also enjoy cycling and scuba diving.

Acknowledgments

For my husband and the love of my life, David, who encouraged me to pursue my dream. I couldn't have finished this project without his unwavering love and support. I would also like to thank my family for their support and their encouragement throughout this project.

Many thanks to my friend, Sue, for all the years she acted as my mentor and sounding board. As a fellow writer, her guidance and encouragement have been invaluable. I also appreciate the years of feedback and support from the members of my writer's group, Kathleen, Jenny, Cherie, Mike R. and Mike S.

CHAPTER 1

March 2, 1814 – The Barbary Coast

A warm breeze swept across the quarterdeck sending Emile Dumont's chestnut curls dancing around his leathery face. The chatty seagulls demanded his attention as their wings caught the wind, sending them swirling high above his three-masted clipper before diving to the water below. Not even the playful seagulls could distract his attention from the ominous dot lurking on the horizon, which was growing larger with every passing moment. Emile inhaled the last of the elixir from his wooden pipe. It was the only thing that calmed the uneasiness billowing inside him.

His captain approached him and leaned against the railing. "Report."

Emile tore his gaze from the horizon and gasped when he spotted the gleam in his captain's eyes. Gerard Rochelle looked like a rugged gentleman. His green eyes and casual smile engendered the trust of every man he met. The captain promised to take his crew away from Napoleon's war. He also promised them riches beyond their dreams. Desperately wanting to escape France, Emile eagerly signed on as the ship's surgeon.

"Your pirate ship is sailing straight for us, Captain." Emile looked back at the horizon, silently noting that the ship was now close enough to see its half green, half white Algerian flag waving proudly. "Do you think it's him, sir?"

"Of whom do you speak?"

"Hassan Aziz," Emile replied.

His eyes narrowed, the captain glared at Emile with pursed lips. "You've been obsessing about that savage since we reached the coasts of Africa," Gerard snapped.

"Perhaps we have a good reason to be concerned, sir. You've heard the sailors talk; Aziz has a reputation for being the most ruthless corsair on the Barbary Coast. Sailors claim that he is the devil himself. His ship appears out of thin air. God help you if your vessel catches his eye because there is no way of eluding him. If that happens, we can watch our freedom and possibly our lives sail away."

The corners of Gerard's lips curled into a mocking grin. "Don't be a gullible fool. Aziz is like any other man; he can be bought."

Emile turned away from his captain and raised his pipe to his mouth.

Gerard yanked Emile's arm, forcing the doctor to face him. "What?"

"What makes you so confident that these barbarians will seize our cargo and not sell us too?" Emile retorted.

Gerard took Emile's pipe and inhaled before handing it back. His eyes narrowed again, "I need to know that I can depend on you." Gerard's voice sounded almost sinister.

Emile forced his thin lips into a smile because he was sure that his captain would throw him overboard if he sensed the least bit of betrayal. "Of course, sir. Have I not proven my loyalty already?"

"You can prove your sincerity by administering Monsieur Campbell's medicine. Make sure it is extra potent this time. Prepare his daughter. I surmise that she will be meeting her new owners shortly."

Emile nodded and pushed past his captain.

Gerard grabbed the surgeon's arm. "Do not fail me."

"Why would I fail you? Or have you forgotten that I was the one who led the babes to slaughter?" Emile glared back.

"I've seen the way you look at that savage."

"Sarah Campbell is sweet, but I want my share of the prize as much as you do. Monsieur Campbell will be dead by the time the corsair ship arrives. I suggest that you prepare our ship to be boarded." Emile yanked his arm free and headed to the gangway leading to the middle deck. He scurried down the ladder and paused when he reached the deck below. Taking a few moments to let his eyes adjust to the darkness enabled him to collect his thoughts.

The beat of a drum stirred sailors into a flurry of activity. Emile took a deep breath and forced his way through the chaos to the surgery. He retrieved a vial of clear liquid and mixed it with the last of the red wine before heading to the ship's stern. Gerard initially placed the Campbells in the cargo hold. Because that area of the ship was prone to flooding, Emile offered them his quarters; he slept in a hammock in the surgery.

Mr. Campbell laid on his berth, which was nothing more than an oversized wooden shelf, attached to the bulkhead and covered with a thin layer of straw. Sarah knelt beside her father and wiped the perspiration from his forehead with a damp cloth. Emile's heart raced when he realized that this would be the last time he would see Sarah Campbell.

Hassan Aziz stood on the quarterdeck watching his prey through his scope. Every muscle in his face was tense as he stared at the ship's French flag waving back at him. A small merchant ship was legitimate prey even if he were flying under the British flag. Hassan knew his crew would have no trouble taking the ship. Still, the tension kept building inside him.

Amir Zamani sidled up beside Hassan. "The crew is ready." He paused as he studied his captain. "You seem nervous, Captain."

Hassan lowered his scope and glared at his second lieutenant. Amir Zamani was the only one among his seasoned crew who had naturally dark features. Amir was also the only one Hassan hadn't handpicked for his crew. "I am not weak," Hassan growled.

"I know you hate enslaving infidels. I see it in your eyes every time we attack another ship. It is the only way they will see the light," Amir stated.

"My crew and I do what is required of us. We have executed our duty with distinction, and I have made your employer a *very* wealthy man," Hassan reminded him.

"You mean *our* employer. Naa'il Dhar is the Dey of Algiers. Oh, I forget; you are a British subject, not a true Ottoman."

Hassan towered over Amir, his eyes narrowing. "Dhar would not have made me captain had I not renounced my allegiance to Britain, would he?"

Amir held his gaze. "His Excellency made you captain because your exploits are profitable." A smirk formed on his lips. "I am curious how it feels to sell your Western people into slavery?"

Hassan returned his attention to the French ship.

"I wonder; would you enslave your countrymen?" Amir queried.

Hassan looked his lieutenant in the eyes. "No. England pays Algiers a king's ransom in tribute money to prevent corsairs from attacking British ships. While other corsairs ignore this agreement, I will not."

"What about your Western women, would you sell them too?"

"I doubt I will ever have to make that decision. The people from Western countries will not bring women to this part of the world because they know they will be sold into slavery if they are captured."

"We get a few women from time to time," Amir countered smoothly. "I trust you will turn over the crew and whatever else you seize to His Excellency."

Hassan's knuckles turned white as his hand clutched the railing. "I have turned over the crew and the plunder of every ship that I have seized since I became a corsair. Why are you challenging my loyalties now?" His voice grew louder with every word he said.

"Because I know that you and your crew are still infidels. You all kneel on your prayer rugs, but you do not pray to my God. You drink your spirits; you play your games for money. We have strict punishments for these offenses."

Hassan gave his second lieutenant a murderous glare. "Dhar does not care what we do so long as we bring his prizes to him. That is *exactly* what I will do. Now report to your station."

Sarah Campbell stared helplessly at her father, who had been reduced to a hairless skeleton. At the beginning of their journey, Thomas Campbell was a strong and healthy man, but an illness seemed to have struck him a few days after they left their island. Each day he grew steadily worse, yet her father fought off death. He lost consciousness that morning; Sarah would do anything to make him well.

The crew had been kind to Sarah and her father during their journey. She was grateful that Emile gave them his quarters and medicine for her father.

"Sarah," said Emile in a gentle voice.

She wiped the tears from her Adriatic blue eyes and glanced up at her friend. "Da no better."

Emile squatted and tucked the cup under the berth. He took Sarah's arm, pulled her to her feet, and led her outside her cabin.

"I can see that. I brought more medicine for your father, but Sarah, you must be strong for him." Emile wiped a tear from her soft cheek and nudged closer. He slid his arms around her waist and pulled her against his chest, stroking her satin hair. Moments later, the ship shook after a loud boom.

Sarah yelped. "What is?" She pulled away, bracing herself when the ship shook from the impact.

"That? Oh, it is nothing. It is just … drills," Emile smirked.

Sarah knew that Emile was keeping something from her by the way he avoided eye contact with her. His widened eyes also hinted that he was scared. She heard another loud boom. This time, Sarah reached for Emile when the ship shook again and was followed by loud screams. "What is?" Sarah pleaded.

"Sarah, I am …" Emile pressed a kiss to her full lips. "Come with me to the quarterdeck."

"No, I stay with Da," Sarah insisted.

"It is better for you and your father that you join me on deck. I promise that the loud noises will end shortly," Emile reasoned.

"Why?" Sarah challenged.

"Trust me; it's a beautiful day. I think your father would want you to enjoy it."

Sarah was accustomed to the constant thundering of footsteps from the overhead, but her inner voice told her that these sounds were different, and something was very wrong. At the same time, Sarah couldn't deny that she missed the sun's warmth. Her father was sleeping, and Emile was right, he wouldn't miss her, providing that she didn't stay away for very long. "I come back soon?"

"Of course," Emile said convincingly.

Sarah bent over and retrieved the cup of medicine. The loud thud had caused half of the contents of the cup to slosh out. "Give him medicine now?"

Emile took the cup from her and carefully set it under the berth. "You can give it to him later."

Nodding to her friend, Sarah hovered over her father and kissed his forehead.

"Sarah, would you do something for me before we leave? Will you tie your cloth around your waist, like the way you wore it on your island?" Emile reached past her and retrieved her paru sitting on the edge of her father's berth.

"No, Da say he no want," Sarah countered. It was true that she wore only a cloth tied around her waist when she lived on her island. That was how the women dressed, but Sarah and her father left that life in what seemed to be a lifetime ago. Her father insisted that she remain covered for the duration of their journey, which meant wearing a shirt and breeches whenever she was on deck. *"It is for your protection, lass,"* her father counseled her. He was right; her western clothing seemed to lessen the sailor's hungry stares.

Emile gently tugged on a lock of her waist length hair. "Sarah, you look so beautiful when you wear your native cloth. Besides, your hair will protect you from the sun. Please, will you do this for me?"

"Da say no do; I no do," Sarah maintained.

"You must!" Emile snapped.

Sarah backed away from him when she spotted the anger in his eyes. "No," she maintained.

Just then, a man wearing loose-fitting trousers and a cloth wrapped around his head, ran towards them wielding a large saber in his hand. The invader stood at least half a head taller than Sarah. Although a pointed beard covered a third of the intruder's face, she could see that his skin was much darker than Emile's.

Emile slowly raised his arms over his head as he quietly and calmly spoke to the man in French. Fearing for her father's life, Sarah charged towards the invader, attempting to slap his face. The last thing Sarah saw was the intruder blocking her arm and striking her across her cheek.

Hassan's lips parted when he spotted Amir proudly carrying an unconscious naked woman over his shoulder with a French sailor walking beside him. He glanced over at the French captain whose smirk matched Amir's delight. Hassan wanted to rush over and kill his second in command for stripping a woman of her clothes, but his inner voice insisted that he wait. Amir reached the center of the mob and dropped the woman onto the deck.

Hassan squatted to take a closer inspection. He had known many women throughout his life, and he had never seen her equal. Her face, her curves, her long-flowing burgundy hair were absolute perfection.

"I am Captain Rochelle. It is my great pleasure to present a unique treasure. I assure you that she is the only one of her kind. We found this exotic maiden on an island in the South Seas. We will gladly give her to you … for a price."

Hassan studied the woman a little longer. He couldn't deny that the black outline of a single six-petal flower inked on each upper arm and the bands of matching flowers around her ankles gave her an exotic quality. Still, he wasn't ready to believe the captain. "Rochelle, did you say? I am not a fool. South Seas maidens are legendary. I know a person who enjoyed the pleasure of their company. He described their appearance to me, and I can ascertain by this woman's red hair that she is no more Polynesian than I am," replied Captain Aziz as he stood up.

"You have a keen eye, Captain. Sarah Campbell was born to Scottish parents, thus her red hair. Her father and mother lived on the island where she was born. Her mother died a few years later. The natives welcomed Sarah and her father into their village. Needless to say, the savages raised her as one of their own. In fact, we were the only civilized people that she's encountered, save her father of course. If you don't believe me, look at her markings. Surely a well-informed man such as yourself is familiar with the cultural trappings of the Polynesian women. Her arms are adorned with tattoos of flowers that are indigenous to her island. You can rub all you want, but the ink will never come off."

Sarah stirred when she heard the drone of an unfamiliar baritone voice. She slowly opened her eyes and gasped when she discovered Hassan crouching over her. He looked and dressed like the man who struck her, except he was even more intimidating. A short pointed beard covering his defined cheekbones and his chiseled jaw partially hid a scar on his left cheek. His muscular arms and chest looked like they could crush her with a single blow. Sarah would have been terrified had she not seen compassion in his brown eyes. Then he did the unexpected; he reached for her hand and pulled her to her feet.

One of Hassan's men began removing Gerard's coat. Emile stepped in and gave her paru to Hassan, who stared at the cloth with disapproval. Fearing he would throw her cover overboard, Sarah reached for the cloth. Hassan gave her a curious look before handing it to her. Sarah tied the paper-like cover over her shoulder. She knew her father wouldn't approve, but at the moment, it was better than wearing nothing at all. Sarah then gasped when she looked around and realized that she stood in the center of what seemed to be a legion of men. Half looked and dressed like the man who hit her. Each of them pressed a knife against a French seaman's neck. Fearing for her safety, she wanted to run, but Gerard locked his hands around her arms and pinned her back against the wheel.

Hassan and Gerard continued talking, although, Sarah only recognized a few words that Emile taught her. The rest of the conversation was nothing more than gibberish. Polynesian was the only language she spoke fluently; Sarah wondered if she would understand them better if they conversed in English. Her father attempted to teach his native language to her while they lived on their island. Learning English was difficult and a waste of time for Sarah because her father was the only person who spoke that language on her island. So, she saw no point in learning something that she would never use. In her defense, she honestly believed that she would never leave her island until the French ship arrived. Her father resumed her English lessons during their journey, but they were cut short after he became ill. Shaking herself from her regrets from past mistakes, Sarah attempted to focus on the current conversation.

"I see you still need more convincing, Captain Aziz. Her white teeth are another common trait to the Polynesians." The crew watching the spectacle erupted with laughter when Sarah snapped at Gerard's fingers as he attempted to part her lips. He forced her to obey by pinching her neck. "To my knowledge, the South Seas savages are the only ones who have teeth of this color. Perhaps the most prominent trait is her lack of shame." Gerard lifted the cloth to expose her front. "Do you see what I mean?"

Hassan chuckled when Sarah attempted to bite Gerard's hand. He didn't know what to think other than he couldn't take his eyes off her. His expression hardened a moment later when he spotted her humiliation after Gerard pulled back her cover. Hassan cocked his pistol, pointing it directly at Gerard's head. "That's enough. Now lower her cover."

Gerard grimaced as he released the end of her wrap. "That is not necessary." A sinister grin formed on his lips. "I see she pleases you; I will be happy to sell her to you for two hundred francs, or its equivalent in gold."

Hassan's eyes widened. "That is a high price for a maiden, even for one as pretty as this."

"As I mentioned before, she is unique. I assure you; this creature was raised to provide pleasure in a way that is worthy of commanding such a price. Do we have an agreement?"

Glancing to his crewmates on deck, Hassan signaled for them to take Emile and Gerard captive.

To Gerard, he replied, "No, we do not have an accord. Gentlemen, do not attempt to fight; every member of my crew is skilled at inflicting excruciating pain. I am seizing your ship and your cargo."

"Captain Aziz, I beg you not to do this. If you let me, I will return to the South Seas and will return with a ship full of these maidens," Gerard wheedled.

"Or you will flee from the Barbary Coast like cowards," Hassan countered.

A sheen of sweat beaded Gerard's brow. "No, I will return. I swear it."

"I do not do business with infidel dogs," Hassan nodded to the man holding Gerard hostage.

His captor thrust his fist into his ribs. Gerard collapsed and fell to his knees, gasping for breath.

"What do you intend to do with us?" Emile spoke up.

"I intend to sell you and your crew," Hassan replied. "Algiers is always in need of laborers."

Hassan glanced over at an older boy standing adjacent to Amir. Everyone surrounding the boy edged away from him when they heard and smelled the boy's waste trickling onto the deck, but Amir still kept his eyes focused on Sarah. "Are you frightened?" Hassan asked in French, even though it was plain to everyone that the boy's whole body was shaking.

"Please, I do not wish to become a slave," the boy pleaded.

"You seem to have no issue enslaving this woman," Hassan pointed out.

His comment was answered with silence.

"Answer me, boy," Hassan demanded; his tone was laced with anger.

"She is a heathen savage," the boy answered timidly.

Hassan leaned in and whispered, "We are all savages, including you." Straightening his body, he announced in French, "You are all the property of Naa'il Dhar. The only freedom you will have is the kind that comes from death." As he spoke the last words, Hassan's eyes rested on Amir with subtle malice.

"Is there nothing we can do to change your mind?" Emile spoke up.

Hassan looked at Emile with a menacing gleam in his eye. "No," he replied in an uncompromising tone. "Gentlemen, remove their clothes, take them below, and clap them in irons. They can travel like slaves to the Americas."

Hassan's crew screamed in unison like banshees as they ripped the clothing off the sailors' bodies.

The boy charged Hassan as another pirate tore his shirt from his chest. Their arms locked in a fight to control Hassan's knife. The corsair forced the boy's arm to his side and shoved him towards Amir. Hassan's second lieutenant gasped when the knife pierced his stomach. The pirate captain punched the boy's jaw several times, causing the seaman to fall to his knees. "Sorry, boy, you will not escape your fate so easily." Hassan nodded to one of his men to secure the prisoner.

"Take them below. The girl stays with me," Hassan commanded.

Sarah screamed as Amir collapsed onto the deck.

Hassan knelt beside him.

"You will pay for your treachery," Amir whispered.

"Your death was an accident. Your assumptions are correct; I am an infidel, and I will not sell a woman into slavery." Hassan pressed his fist against Amir's throat until he crushed his larynx. Gasping for breath, Amir stared at Hassan with bulging eyes.

Sarah watched Hassan with eyes, wide and dilated when he returned his attention to her. Her whole body trembled. Hassan raised his arms and tucked his knife under his maroon sash. "I will not hurt you," He said in a soothing voice.

Sarah leaped over Amir's body and raced to the nearest mast. She grabbed the closest ratline and began pulling herself up the rope. Hassan charged after her. He stood over six foot, two inches, yet Sarah was already beyond his reach. He gave the line she was climbing several good yanks. Sarah yelped as she lost her grip and fell into Hassan's arms.

"I won't hurt you," Hassan said more forcefully.

Sarah's athletic body writhed in Hassan's iron grasp. "Da," she shouted over and over again as she struggled to break free.

Hassan let go; Sarah landed on the deck with a thud. For a moment, she was immobilized. He locked his hands around her arms and pulled her to her feet. Just then, a salty breeze swept across the weathered deck like a storm tearing across a landscape. Hassan felt as though he had been thrust into a cyclone of absurdity. Sarah's wrap took flight as the wind passed under it. Her hair and her garment fluttered proudly like a banner in the wind as Sarah pleaded for help in her native language. Her tears flowed, and her movements became more animated with each word she spoke. During her entreating, she hadn't noticed that her body was completely exposed. All Hassan could do was smile and think, *my God, it's true.*

"Stop fighting, you little hellion. I am trying to help you," Hassan said with a distinguished English accent.

Sarah's lips parted, and her movements came to an abrupt halt. "You speak English?"

His hands remained locked around her arms. "Yes, and so do you," he replied with a hint of surprise. "Please, calmly tell me what 'Da' means."

"Da me da."

Hassan's brows snapped together. "Do you mean your father? He is still on this ship?"

"Aye, he ee ... eel," Sarah said as tears streamed down her cheeks.

"Do you mean that your father is ill," Hassan clarified.

Sarah nodded.

"Take me to him."

Sarah fervently led Hassan by the hand to the stern on the middle deck. Hassan was surprised to discover that this small merchant ship was large enough to fit a wardroom with six closet-size cabins surrounding the common area. There was also a long table with two benches in the center of the room.

"Da," Sarah pointed to the middle cabin on the starboard side of the ship.

Several of Hassan's crew had already discovered Sarah's father. Two of his men stood outside the room while another knelt beside the berth. All looked on with concern. The two men standing beside the door to her quarters made room for Hassan and Sarah to pass by them.

Hassan glanced at her father and then to the one examining him. "Is he dead?"

The lieutenant examining Sarah's father looked up at his captain with a grave expression. "He is still breathing, sir, but just barely."

Hassan's gaze drifted to the floor when he noticed a tin cup half-filled with red liquid peeking out from under the berth. He crouched down and picked up the cup. The corsair dipped his finger into the burgundy liquid and tasted the wine on his finger. Something had been added. Tilting his head to the side, Hassan issued a command to the Marine standing outside the cabin. "Get Rochelle and that helpful man who escorted Zamani to the main deck."

"It medicine for Da," Sarah piped up.

"Medicine," Hassan turned away before her hand could reach the cup. "I would like your captain to confirm the cup's contents before we feed it to your father."

Sarah replied with a puzzled look.

Several men appeared with Gerard and Emile. Their jackets and shirts had already been stripped from their bodies. Hassan was sure that his men allowed them to cover their lower bodies out of respect to Sarah.

"What is wrong with this man?" Hassan demanded.

"He fell ill during the journey," Emile said.

"Who are you?" Hassan studied Emile. Dressed in tattered breeches, he looked like a gentleman who was down on his luck, yet he still kept his sandy curls and beard neatly trimmed.

"I am the ship's doctor, Emile Dumont."

Hassan knew that the doctor was withholding details about Mr. Campbell's illness by his refusal to make eye contact with him. He held the cup to Gerard's lips. "What did you add to this wine?"

"Medicine," Sarah repeated.

The French captain rolled his eyes and looked away from his captor.

Hassan motioned to his Marines to pin Gerard against the bulkhead. Clutching the tin cup with one hand, he pressed a dagger against the captain's throat. "What did you add to this wine?"

Gerard stared back at the pirate captain with an enigmatic smile. "Medicine," he replied in a cool tone.

Hassan stood nose to nose with the French captain. "You may be able to fool the girl, but you do not fool me. For the last time, what did you give the girl's father?" he demanded in a hushed voice.

Gerard looked away.

"Very well. Tip the captain's head back and pinch his nose."

His Marines executed their captain's orders; Hassan returned his knife to his sash. When he raised the mug to Gerard's lips, the French captain jerked his torso forward, causing the wine to splash onto Hassan's face.

"I thought as much," Hassan grunted. "Very well, pin the captain's hand to the table in the wardroom galley."

Hassan's Marines locked their hands around Gerard's arms and escorted him to the table in the center of the wardroom. While the larger of the two held Gerard steady, the other pinned the French captain's hand to the table. Hassan pressed his saber against Gerard's pinky. "One last chance, Rochelle. Tell me what you added to the wine, or I will chop your fingers off, beginning with your fifth finger."

Gerard winced when he felt the blade piercing his skin.

Emile spoke up. "Arsenic. I added arsenic to the wine."

Hassan glanced back at his captive. Gerard's smug grin hadn't changed. Hassan lifted his crescent-shaped weapon and sliced off the French captain's pinky.

Gerard screamed as blood spurted out from his hand. "We answered your question!"

"No, your doctor answered my question, a question that I asked *you*," Hassan retorted. He released Gerard's arm and glanced over at Sarah, who looked on with interest. It was evident from her vacant expression that she didn't fully comprehend the point of the conversation. Hassan motioned to the Marines to pin Emile against the bulkhead. He moved in until the ends of their noses touched. Pressing the blade against Emile's neck, he said in a threatening tone. "Now you are going to tell the girl *in English* how you murdered her father."

Emile's gaze dropped to the deck behind Hassan. "No, I cannot," he whispered.

The corsair captain pressed the blade deeper into Emile's neck. "Tell her," Hassan shouted.

"Please don't slay me," Emile pleaded.

"Tell her," Hassan shouted over the doctor.

Emile looked directly at Sarah. "I poisoned your father's medicine."

Sarah rested her hand on her stomach. "I no understand," she said in a timid voice.

Emile refused to elaborate.

"Explain it in a way that she can understand," Hassan shouted. "I want her to understand your treachery. Tell her now, or I will cut off your ears, your nose, and every part of your body until you confess your sin." While several of his crewmen held Emile steady, Hassan pressed his saber against the doctor's ear. "This is your last opportunity to confess," he warned as he pushed his saber deep enough to draw blood.

Beads of sweat rolled down Emile's forehead. "I deceived you, Sarah." His voice quivered as he spoke in English. "We intended to murder your father when we decided to give you passage to France."

"What murder?" Sarah asked.

"Speak plainly," Hassan commanded.

"Captain Rochelle intended to kill your father. I poisoned the wine your father drank. That poison caused his illness, and it will kill him."

"I no understand," Sarah whispered.

Hassan released Emile and backed away.

The doctor reached for the cup and held it up. "This killed your father!" he shouted.

Though the lantern hanging from the overhead offered little light, there was just enough to see the color draining from Sarah's peach cheeks. She just stared at Emile with dismay. Her breathing became short and harsh. Hassan approached her and enveloped her in his arms. Sarah was trembling, yet there were no tears, no sobs. Without warning, she lifted the knife from Hassan's belt without his notice. Sarah pulled away from the corsair and lunged towards Emile, screaming in Polynesian. Hassan grabbed her waist with one hand and held her arm steady with the other.

"No princess, death is too good for these men. I give you my word that they will pay for their crimes," Hassan whispered in her ear as a

Marine pried the knife from her hand.

Sarah's body became limp, and her screams turned into sobs.

But Sarah heard another voice. It was the only one that had the power to soothe her anguish. He only needed to say one word, "Sarah."

"Da," Sarah whispered when she heard his voice. She glanced down and smiled at her father, who was looking directly at her. "Please," she said in Polynesian to Hassan.

Hassan nodded and released her.

Sarah knelt beside him. They talked quietly as though they were the only ones on the ship.

Hassan didn't know what her father said to her, but it was enough to stop her tears. He marveled at the tenderness displayed between this father and child. Her father's love, he reasoned, must have been fierce to allow him to return from the beginning of death's journey to comfort his child.

Hassan looked over Sarah's shoulder. "I am Captain Aziz. I am going to have you moved to my ship so that you can receive care from my surgeon."

"Grateful. Sarah?"

"Your daughter will join you. Do you have any belongings?"

"Trunk ... at feet ..." the man said with difficulty.

After uttering several words in Polynesian, Sarah jumped to her feet and pointed to a small wooden trunk sitting at the base of the berth.

"Return Rochelle and the doctor to the hold, transport the patient to the surgery and bring the trunk to my quarters," Hassan ordered.

"Aye, captain," they replied in unison.

After Gerard and Emile rejoined their crew, several more corsairs arrived to help. Two men carried Sarah's trunk out of the cabin while two others moved Sarah's father to a transportation plank and carried him into the wardroom. Sarah lingered in her cabin; Hassan didn't know why. "Shall we?" he asked after an awkward moment of silence.

Sarah started to answer. She shook her head and mumbled in her own language.

Hassan frowned when Sarah crawled across the berth. His brow furrowed when she retrieved a brown pouch concealed between the berth and the bulkhead. It was the size of a rounder's ball with pea-size divots bulging out the sides. "What is that?"

"It poe," she replied. "We go?"

Still puzzled by her cryptic behavior, Hassan extended his arm towards the wardroom and said, "After you."

Chapter 2

Hassan and Sarah caught up to her father on the main deck. He chuckled when he spotted Sarah staring at his much larger ship. Her mouth was open; her eyes widened, and yet she showed no signs of fear as she scrambled across the wooden plank connecting the two ships together. Hassan couldn't deny that the Zafirah was an impressive sight. Though it might have been considered a fifth-rate warship by English standards, this forty-four gun frigate was an intimidating sight, especially compared to Sarah's small cutter. While most corsairs instilled terror on their Xebec ships, Hassan preferred his man-o'-war. Of course, the Zafirah wasn't as fast or as agile as the Xebecs, but it was fast enough, and it carried twice the fire power and three-times the number of men.

Hassan led Sarah and the men carrying her father through the spacious gun deck and down to the surgery.

The ship's surgeon, Peter Hyatt, approached Hassan and his guests to inspect his new patient. "Careful," he cautioned as the corsairs carrying Sarah's father, gingerly transferred the patient from the transportation plank to a hammock suspended from the overhead. Peter glanced at Sarah, who was standing across from him, then at his patient before silently signaling to his captain that he needed to speak to him in private.

Peter was the only member of Hassan's crew that didn't try to conceal his Anglo-Saxon origin. Dressed in simple western clothing, he kept his face cleanly shaven, and his ash-blond hair fashionably short.

"Report to the main deck and assist with preparations for our departure," Hassan said to the crew members hovering around Sarah's father. He nodded to Peter to follow him into a small room adjacent to the surgery.

"I hope you are not expecting a miracle with this one, for that is the only thing that can save him," Peter said in English.

"The crew poisoned him with arsenic. I do not expect you to save him, though I would like you to try to make him comfortable. I would also appreciate it if you could wake him long enough to answer my questions."

"Who is the woman?"

"His daughter, Sarah."

"Why is she wearing a paru?"

Hassan frowned. "A what?"

"It's a kind of Polynesian dress," Peter clarified.

"The French crew assured me that they found Miss Campbell and her father on an island in the South Seas. It is a long and most certainly an interesting story."

Peter raised a brow. "Indeed? Polynesian women do not have red hair."

"That is because her parents were Scottish," Hassan explained.

Peter shuddered. "I see."

Hassan rubbed his chin with the back of his hand when Peter's lips twisted into a scowl. "Is something wrong, Doctor?"

"No," Peter said, looking past Hassan.

"Tend to her father. You will also need to bandage what's left of the French captain's hand," Hassan directed in a nonchalant manner.

"What happened to him?"

"I cut off his pinky."

"You cut off his pinky," Peter repeated with disbelief.

"Yes, I did," Hassan said defensively.

"What happened to your mandate that an officer of the Crown must conduct himself as a gentleman?"

"That blackheart deserved it. The good captain poisoned a British subject so that he could profit from selling this man's daughter into slavery. He showed no remorse for his actions," Hassan paused. "On another matter, Amir Zamani is dead."

"I can't say that I am sorry to hear that. What happened?"

"A boy was foolish enough to fight back; Zamani was killed during the skirmish," Hassan shrugged. "Please do what you can for her father."

"Of course." They headed back to the surgery. A faint smile curled on the doctor's lips. "If she truly is from the South Seas, watch your belongings. The South Seas natives make gypsy pickpockets look like novices."

"Yes, I know," Hassan chuckled. "Miss Campbell slipped my knife from my sash during my confrontation with the ship's surgeon."

Mr. Campbell was sleeping peacefully in his hammock. Sarah hadn't moved from his side.

Hassan approached Sarah while Peter inspected his patient standing on the opposite side of them.

"He's sleeping," the doctor said, breaking the awkward silence.

Hassan replied, "Carry on, Doctor."

"You leave?" Sarah's eyes pleaded with him to stay.

Hassan offered Sarah a reassuring smile. "I must work now. Stay with your father, and I will return as soon as I am able."

Captain Aziz left his guests and headed to the main deck. His crew was busy preparing both ships for their departures. Hassan's first lieutenant, Adam Boyle met Hassan as he strode across the plank to the Trésor.

Adam looked as though he could be Hassan's younger brother. He was the same build and height as his captain. They both had brown eyes and equally weathered faces with manicured-pointed beards. The only substantial difference was that Adam didn't have a scar on his cheek.

"The prisoners are secure, Captain. We transferred most of their cargo to the Zafirah. We also kept some of the food," Adam explained in

English. He and the captain dodged two seamen carrying an oversized crate. They moved to the quarterdeck to continue their conversation.

"Did you find anything else of interest?"

"Not much, sir. We found some clothes and spices. I also found these in the captain's quarters." Adam handed Hassan a small pouch. "It appears that the girl was not their only valuable cargo."

Hassan untied the drawstring and opened the pouch. He pulled out a small iridescent black pearl and admired its green tint. Up until that moment, black pearls were a mythical treasure that only royalty possessed. There weren't many in this pouch, but he was sure Naa'il Dhar and the jewelers in Europe would pay handsomely for them.

"What are your orders?"

Hassan closed the pouch and tied it to his sash. "You and another thirty sailors will sail the French ship to Algiers. Sell the prisoners upon your arrival and use the proceeds to buy supplies. We shall meet at our usual place within the fortnight."

"Very good, sir …," Adam paused.

Hassan sensed his first officer's hesitation. "Is something wrong, Mr. Boyle?"

Adam scratched the back of his head. "I would never question your judgment, Captain."

"But," Hassan demanded.

"I am surprised that you still intend to sell the prisoners now that Zamani is dead."

"I have my reasons. Besides, these men do not deserve mercy after what they did to the girl and her father. Carry on." Hassan paused and added, "And Mr. Boyle, don't go directly to the port. Delay your arrival for a week or so." Hassan weaved around his crew before crossing the plank to the Zafirah. Another crewman informed him that Sarah's father was awake. Sarah was still standing where he had left her.

Hassan looked into Mr. Campbell's weary blue eyes. "How are you feeling?" he enquired politely.

"Is there a safe place that you can send my daughter? Need to speak in private," he whispered in a faint voice.

"I will take your daughter to my quarters and will return as soon as she is settled. I promise I won't be long." Hassan understood her father's concerns without any need of an explanation. Sarah's visible long legs and small bare feet made her an alluring sight. Though the cloth covered her hour-glass figure, its gaping side still provided a clear view of Sarah's enticing curves.

Her father whispered something to Sarah, who still looked apprehensive after he passed along his instructions.

Hassan offered her a reassuring smile. "Come. It will be alright." Sarah released her father's hand and followed him. Hassan marveled at her obedience. He knew that she didn't want to leave her father again, yet she did so without raising any objections.

Hassan's personal bodyguards, Tristan Thatcher and Luke Finch, stood at attention on either side of the door to Hassan's quarters. Though Hassan was a half a head taller than most men, his bodyguards were even taller and larger. The two giants saluted their captain and then froze when their gaze fell on Sarah.

Hassan rolled his eyes and proceeded into his quarters with Sarah following behind him. Unlike the rest of his crew, he lived in a spacious suite behind the quarterdeck. His quarters took up nearly an eighth of the length of the ship and spanned the entire width. While most captain's quarters on the man-o'-wars used canvas curtains to divide the living space, Hassan's dividers were made of wood. To the untrained eye, his private chamber looked like a small four-room apartment. The walls separating his quarters from the quarterdeck, the dividers, and the furniture were configured in a way that made it easy to store them in case his chamber was needed for fighting. Battles rarely took place aboard his ship. That was fine with Hassan. His quarters were his sanctuary from his otherwise perilous life.

His crew had already delivered Sarah's trunk. She was too busy looking at the room's furnishings to notice her possessions. Hassan laughed to himself as she ran her hand over the polished table. While

Sarah continued inspecting his belongings, Hassan gave into his curiosity and reached for her pouch that was now sitting on the table. "May I see what's inside?" he asked.

"Aye," she replied before crouching onto his burgundy, black, and cream Persian rug covering the rough deck boards.

Hassan chuckled as she brushed her hand across the silk fibers seeming to inspect each color individually. While Sarah examined his Persian rug, Hassan peeked inside the pouch. His lips parted when he discovered black pearls almost filling the bag to the brim. There were at least two hundred of them, a small treasure.

Sarah stood up after completing her inspection. She picked up a pea-size pearl and said, "It poe."

"They are called pearls in my country." Hassan returned the jewel to the pouch and wrapped the string around the edges to draw it close. "I will keep these safe for you." Sarah had already moved on to inspecting the silver candlesticks. She seemed not to care that he hid her treasure in a secret compartment in his desk. Hassan glanced over at Sarah again and couldn't help smiling at her curiosity. He could have spent the entire day watching her make new discoveries of things that were commonplace to him. Remembering the urgency, Hassan ducked into his dressing room to find something appropriate for her to wear. She followed him into the room like a curious puppy.

Hassan opened a trunk and pulled out a dress. "I have been told that this is the latest Parisian fashion. I would like you to wear it." Hassan proudly held the dress up only to discover that Sarah wasn't paying attention.

She couldn't take her eyes off his gold pocket watch, which was suddenly in the palm of her hand. Her fingers traced the etched flower engraved on the cover. She opened the lid; the corners of her lips widened into a smile when the second hand moved.

"How the devil did you do that?" Hassan marveled how she could pick his pocket without him noticing. "I'll take that." He laid the dress on the trunk and snatched the watch from her just as she attempted to pull the hands off. "We must talk about stealing." Hassan grabbed her wrist and led her over to the table. "I know you are curious about everything," he said calmly. "You must not take things that do not belong to you without seeking the owner's permission first. People will take great offense if you do. That is doubly true if you steal from the people from this part of the world." Hassan knew by her vacant expression that Sarah had no idea that she had done anything wrong. "I hate to do this, but you need to understand the penalties for stealing." Hassan removed the saber from his belt and pinned Sarah's hand against the table. "This is what happens to people who are caught stealing in this part of the world."

Sarah cried out when Hassan pressed his saber against her wrist. After he released her hand, Sarah stepped back and held her arm against her chest.

Hassan returned his saber to his belt. "You need not fear me. However, it is vital that you understand the penalty for stealing. The people in this part of the world are unforgiving towards those who break their laws. The penalties for committing such acts are severe. I would hate for you to lose your hand for a crime you did not understand that you committed. Come." Hassan held his hand out to Sarah. "Let's find you something to wear."

Sarah slowly backed away without taking her eyes off Hassan's saber; her hand was still pressed against her chest.

Hassan winked and returned to his dressing room. "This is a very beautiful gown," he said, holding up the dress. It was a confection of white silk with intricate lace adorning the scoop neckline and skirt. Its short puffy sleeves were designed to be worn with long white gloves. The gown would have made any well-bred lady look like a princess.

Sarah mustered the courage to take a closer look. As she touched the garment with tentative fingers, her eyes glanced beyond the dress to a royal blue and gold silk cloth laid folded on top of the clothes in the trunk. Her hand dropped away from the dress. To Hassan, the two by three foot cloth was a useless gift from Naa'il Dhar, yet she stared at the cloth with twinkling eyes as though *it* were the latest fashion. Still, she dared not touch or take it, but held her hands close to her sides as if she were afraid of what would happen if she reached for it. Curious to see what Sarah would do next, Hassan gave the cloth to her.

Sarah looked at him as though he had given her a precious gift. Turning away from him, she removed her wrap and tied the fabric around her waist. She then surprised Hassan when she looked to him for his approval.

All he could do was interlace his fingers behind his back and nod. Hassan wanted to tell Sarah that he had never seen anything so beautiful. Her style of dress suited her better than the one he offered her. The blue cloth made the colors of her face, her eyes, and even her hair look more vibrant. If he had his way, Sarah would wear nothing else. "You are a temptress," Hassan mumbled. He glanced down at the white dress that was now draped over his arm. He already knew how Sarah would look in it – as ordinary as it would be possible to look with burgundy hair and blue eyes.

Hassan jumped when a knock on the door echoed through the room. He didn't need to answer it to know who it was, and what it concerned. "Stay here," he told her. Reluctantly, Hassan left the storage room to answer the door. Sarah ignored his order. Hassan chuckled and shifted her behind the door to keep her hidden from view. "Do not move," he whispered before opening the door just wide enough for his head and half of his body to be seen by the person waiting on the other side.

"I apologize for my interruption, Captain, but the girl's father is still waiting for you," Peter reminded him.

"Forgive my delay. I will be there momentarily," Hassan said.

"Sir, please do not delay much longer," Peter cautioned. "He does not have much time."

Hassan nodded and closed the door. "I need to talk to your father in private. I want you to stay here until I come for you. Do not leave my quarters or open the door to anyone except me. While I'm gone, I would like you to try on the gown. Do you understand?"

Sarah replied in Polynesian as she attempted to push past him.

"No, you must stay here until I come for you," Hassan said with a stern voice. He rested his hands on Sarah's shoulders and moved her to the center of the room. "I promise that you will see your father shortly. Please do as I say."

Tears filled Sarah's eyes. "No," she pleaded.

"I will have your father brought to you. You have my word. Please stay here until I return." This time Sarah remained still, even though her pouty lips made her objections abundantly clear. "I will return shortly. Until then, why don't you try on the dress?" He offered her a reassuring smile just before leaving his quarters.

Luke and Tristan snapped to attention as their captain passed by them.

"Do not let this girl out of my cabin," Hassan tersely commanded.

"Aye, Captain," they replied in unison.

Sarah's father was alert, yet the color was fading from his face. Peter stood across from him. He glanced at the captain and faintly shook his head to inform him that Sarah's father didn't have much time.

"Where's Sarah?" her father whispered.

"She is in my quarters. I have tasked her with trying on a dress," Hassan explained.

"A dress," her father grinned.

"Should I have given her something else to wear?"

"No ... she must learn ...." the patient said with shortened breath. "Sarah tried her mother's dress ... said too confining .... Captain, appreciate your kindness."

"I am happy to offer my assistance, sir. You may have guessed that I brought you aboard because I have questions that I think only you can answer. I would like to start by asking your name, Mr.?"

"Campbell. Thomas Campbell," he replied with a faint Scottish brogue.

"I understand that Captain Rochelle and his crew found you and your daughter on an island in the South Seas. Do I understand correctly that Miss Campbell was born on that island?"

"Aye, my Allie died when Sarah was young. Natives kind to us."

"Tahiti and its neighboring islands have a reputation for being a paradise. I'm curious why you left."

"Had no choice. Rochelle wanted Sarah from the first moment he laid eyes on her. I feared that he would abduct my daughter. I had no way to rescue her."

"If that is true," Hassan reasoned, "I am surprised they allowed you to come too."

"Rochelle is a smart man; he knew that my embarking on this journey was the only way that Sarah would go peacefully."

"I see." He silently concluded that Campbell knew that the French crew would assassinate him during their journey. Hassan wondered how far he would go to save the woman or child he loved.

"Captain, you know that I am dying, so I will be plain. What do you intend to do with my daughter after my death?"

"I appreciate your candor, sir; I will be equally plain. Captain Rochelle brought you to the Barbary Coast with the intention of selling your daughter into slavery. The men in this part of the world will pay handsomely for a woman with red hair. There is no telling what they will pay for the rarity of a European woman raised as a South Seas native. For the moment, your daughter is under my protection. She will remain so, as long as she does not cause trouble. It is clear that you have a powerful hold on your daughter. I encourage you to convey the gravity of her situation to her. You must make her understand that she will need to obey me if she wishes to remain free. Am I clear, sir?" Hassan explained.

"Not surprised at Rochelle's decision to come to the Barbary Coast. Appreciate your protection. You have my word that Sarah will obey you. You married?"

Hassan's brow furrowed. "No."

"Girls are raised to obey heads of their family. You will become the head of hers if you agree to become her husband. Polynesian marriages are formed by a simple agreement. Will that suffice, or should I give her to another?" Thomas asked.

"No, that will do," Hassan replied with seeming indifference.

Peter dropped his tin cup and looked at his captain as though he had witnessed his friend making a deal with the devil.

"Captain, I implore you not to exercise your husbandly privileges unless you decide to keep Sarah for yourself. She is still a virgin," Thomas continued.

"Indeed? It is my understanding that the Polynesians do not value a woman's virtue." Hassan frowned.

"You are right. Polynesian women are given in marriage. As head of her family, I could give my daughter to anyone I wished .... I never did. I am tired. I would like to be with my daughter now."

"Of course. I will have you brought to my quarters," Hassan replied. By this time, the color had completely drained from Thomas' cheeks.

Peter gave his captain a disapproving look and said calmly, "Captain, may I speak with you in private?"

Hassan nodded and followed the doctor into the adjacent room.

Peter waited for Hassan to close the door behind him. "With all due respect, what the devil are you doing?"

"I am trying to ease a dying man's concerns for his daughter's future."

"You know that keeping this woman is suicide. All captive women in this region are Naa'il Dhar's property. The penalty for withholding this kind of prize is death. You know this," Peter challenged.

"I know the penalty," Hassan growled back. "I will not sell a woman into slavery."

"I will not stand in your way if you want to sacrifice your life for this stranger. However, your decision affects all of us. I think I can speak for the entire crew when I say that I have no intention of returning to the quarries," Peter countered in a panicked voice. "Please, consider our well-being first, for we have made many sacrifices for this mission."

"I made my decision, Doctor." Hassan snapped.

"For God's sake, why?"

Hassan's lips twisted into a snarl. He grabbed Peter by his shirt lapels and pinned him against the bulkhead, "because I have had to do many despicable things since I came to this God-forsaken place. I will not sell a woman into slavery, and I do not care if it costs me my life."

Peter held his captain's gaze. "Zamani's death wasn't an accident, was it?"

Hassan unclasped his hands and looked him in the eye. "Of course it was."

"I know you, Captain. You had wanted to get rid of Zamani ever since he boarded our ship."

"Yes, I did. We all knew that he was Dhar's spy."

"What do you think Dhar will do if Zamani fails to report back to him?"

"Dhar will ask what happened, and I will tell him the truth; Zamani's death was an accident. I have a deck full of witnesses to confirm my story." Hassan turned to leave the room.

"And what if Dhar placed another spy on board?" Peter persisted.

Hassan looked back at his friend. "Sarah Campbell is under my protection," he said in an uncompromising tone.

"If she was truly raised in the South Seas, I can tell you from experience that those women are not worth protecting. Get rid of her, *now*."

Hassan stood over Peter. "I will say no more on the subject. I expect you to perform your duty," Hassan warned with threatening eyes.

Sarah paced the floor when Hassan returned to his quarters. She still wore the blue and gold cloth. He was sure that the dress was lying where he left it. He threw a blanket over her shoulders before several of his crew carried her father into the cabin.

Peter skulked off to the side as the sailors attached Campbell's hammock to hooks attached to the overhead's thick beams. Without saying another word to his doctor, Hassan approached Thomas' hammock and stood across from Sarah. Peter exited the room with the crew, leaving Hassan and Sarah alone with her father.

Thomas whispered to Sarah in Polynesian, marriage instructions, judging by the way she split her gaze between Hassan and her father.

It was unclear how she felt about his message. Sarah's face showed no emotion as she nodded. Thomas spoke a while longer. The only word Hassan understood from the entire conversation was "angels."

Hassan couldn't take his eyes off Sarah. She was an enigma to him. She looked like a genteel woman, yet her lack of modesty and painted body reminded him that she wasn't one. Needing answers, Hassan left Sarah with her father and stole away to the wardroom. Peter sat alone at the officer's table in the galley.

The doctor looked up from his book and said with a hint of sarcasm, "Having second thoughts about 'marrying' Sarah?"

"I apologize for being cross with you. Today has been most disturbing." Hassan took a seat across from his friend. "May we talk awhile?"

"Of course." Peter closed his book and laid it on the table. "What is troubling you?"

Hassan frowned. "Why do you call her Sarah and not Miss Campbell?"

"Because she will not answer to 'Miss Campbell.' The Polynesians do not have family names." Peter chuckled. "There were a few people in my village who changed their names on a whim, which proved to be quite confusing."

Hassan was too lost in thought to react to the doctor's light-hearted insights. "Miss Campbell is not Polynesian, and she has a family name."

Peter shifted in his chair until his lean belly touched the edge of the table. "Sarah Campbell may look like a genteel woman, but I assure you that her mannerisms prove that she was raised as a Polynesian."

Hassan shook his head and blurted out, "How could her father allow his daughter to run around like … like a wanton savage?"

Peter leaned back in his chair. "You know I can't answer that question. The only person who can provide those answers is dying."

"You're right." Hassan bit his lip with disgust. "Why would a man bring his wife to the South Seas?"

"The Duff, the ship that brought the first missionaries to Tahiti, transported whole families including women and children. You must understand that these missionaries weren't taking a long journey; they were sailing there to live. Of course, a man of honor wouldn't leave his family behind."

"Why didn't Mr. Campbell dress his daughter properly and teach her modesty? I would never allow my daughter to run around half-naked. Missionaries didn't go to the South Seas to assimilate; they went there to convert the natives. I am certain that teaching them modesty was a priority."

"Perhaps he didn't have clothes to give her. Campbell said that they lived on a remote island. It's possible that they lost their possessions during their journey. It's also possible that the Campbells were happy living on that island and made a decision to spend the rest of their lives there. If that is true, then it's likely that Campbell gave his daughter the freedom to adopt the Polynesian way of life because he wanted her to fit in.

"That is no excuse." Hassan leaned back in his chair and crossed his arms. "Campbell should have found a way to properly clothe his daughter."

"Basing my assumption on the theory that the Campbells' lost their belongings, what would Sarah wear? There are no textiles on the Polynesian islands. The closest cloth they have is a mash made out of bark, called tapa. It has the consistency of paper. Captain, you also must understand that the Polynesians don't have the same needs for clothing as the Europeans. Originally, people living in cold climates wore furs and clothing for warmth. It never gets cold in the South Seas."

"Have these people no shame at all?"

"They do, actually. Men cover themselves with a sackcloth and drape another cloth over their chest. Women dress in a similar fashion except they wear a cloth tied around their waist like a skirt."

"Sarah made it plain to me that she only wore a cloth tied around her waist." Hassan pointed out.

Peter shrugged again. "Well, fashion may differ from one island to another. That is true for the British Isles. Scottish men wear kilts; we don't."

"I suppose you're right."

"You must understand that 'sin and shame' are Christian beliefs. The Polynesian people do not consider running around scantily clad a sin – it is a way of life."

"How do you explain her father allowing Miss Campbell to ruin herself by imprinting ink on her body?"

"Again, I don't have an answer," Peter said with a twisted smile. "I surmise that her father was not pleased."

Hassan laughed. "Why didn't Campbell at least teach his daughter how to converse in English?"

"Her broken English is evidence that he tried, isn't it? Sarah would have been given to a Polynesian woman to raise if her mother had died at birth. Campbell would have had limited interaction with his daughter until she was five. At least that was how it was done in Tahiti. Sarah would have been fluent in Polynesian by that time. She would have considered English a second language when her father had the opportunity to teach her. If their village were anything like mine on Tahiti, Sarah would have spent most of her time with the women. I would not be surprised if Campbell decided that teaching English to Sarah was a fool's errand, especially if they intended to spend the rest of their lives on their island."

"I suppose you are right." Hassan stared thoughtfully at the table as he attempted to make sense of Peter's glimpse into the Polynesian culture. He tried to place himself in Thomas Campbell's situation. He was certain that he would have made different choices for Sarah. "Why didn't Campbell and his daughter live away from the village? That way he would have had more control over his daughter's education." Hassan reasoned out loud.

Peter shrugged. "I suppose they could have. They wouldn't have been safe had they done so. Westerners have the misconception that the Polynesians are peaceful people. The truth is that they are savages. They sacrifice people to their gods, and they eat their enemies' eyes because they believe the eyes will provide a glimpse into their enemy's soul."

Hassan massaged his temples and mumbled, "My God."

"Polynesians also worship the color red. I would not be surprised that the news of a child born with red hair spread to every island in the South Seas. Her village must have drawn a lot of unwanted attention. Living in a community as one of them was for the Campbells' protection. The natives will protect their own. However, they wouldn't protect a stranger. I am confident that Campbell understood this.

Hassan nodded and studied his friend. "Do you believe that Miss Campbell is a virgin?"

"It is not likely. The Polynesians do not value a girl's innocence," Peter chuckled. "They believe it's silly for a woman to save herself until her wedding night. I witnessed a man making love to a twelve or thirteen-year-old girl. The other women looked on and offered the girl instructions for pleasing the man. They proudly performed this ritual in front of all who wanted to watch. Call it a rite of passage if you will. It took my whole being to conceal my disgust."

Hassan shuddered at the thought of a child being taken by a man. "Thank you, your insights have been most helpful." He rose from the table and returned to his quarters.

Sarah's father lost his ability to speak shortly after Hassan arrived at his cabin. However, the love in Thomas' eyes did not fade until he closed them for the last time. A sliver of the faint morning light appeared on the horizon when Thomas Campbell drew his final breath.

Sarah whimpered when she realized her father was gone. She fought to maintain her composure, but her grief was too overpowering. Hassan was right there to catch her as she collapsed into his arms.

It had been a long twenty-four hours; Hassan was exhausted. Not wanting to leave Sarah alone, Hassan carried her to his berth. She didn't protest when he lowered her onto the feather bed, or when he laid beside her. Instead, Sarah buried her face against his chest and sobbed. Hassan felt helpless to comfort her. He wanted to tell her that she was safe and that she wasn't alone. But those were promises he couldn't make. All he could do was hold her, stroke her hair, and whisper, "I'm sorry."

Chapter 3

Naa'il Dhar opened his eyes to a feeling of an indescribable peace. The corners of his lips curled upward as he thought, *she is awake*. The first time he felt this peace occurred several weeks ago when one of his corsairs presented two American women to him. Ever since then, this feeling woke him about this time every morning. Naa'il now welcomed it as an old friend. The Algerian Dey glanced out the window at the fountain outside his room. There was just enough light to see its gold decorative plates against the white marble. His mind too active to go back to sleep, Naa'il donned a pair of brown salvar, or baggy Ottoman trousers that tied around his waist and cuffed around his ankles. He slid a bürümcük, or an embroidered crepe tunic, over his head. Naa'il released the ends of the cream shirt, sending the ends bouncing around his knees. The Dey reached for a rich-brown, brocaded kaftan and slid his arms through the sleeves. The floor-length robe's u-shaped neckline showed off the bürümcük's delicate lace around his neck. Finally, Naa'il placed a tall headpiece over his bald head, adjusting it until the large diamond, embedded in the base, faced forward. After slipping on a pair of leather slippers, Naa'il exited his quarters. His guards, dressed in royal blue Palace uniforms, snapped to attention when he appeared.

The Dey strolled down the corridor, silently reflecting on how much he loved this time of day. His mornings were usually peaceful, and the Palace was at its most beautiful. There were also only a few subjects or servants around to harass him. The only sounds he heard that morning were chirping birds and the soft scuffing of his leather slippers against the marble tile. His path was lit by flickers of light, dancing in the stained-glass oil lamps hanging from the ceiling. The morning sky was a grayish blue with pink clouds. Sometimes the dawn's rays turned the Palace's white walls to a soft pink, which grew whiter as the sun rose in the sky.

The call to prayer sounded; Naa'il dutifully headed to the Palace mosque where he said his prayers before continuing on his morning routine. Turning the corner, he nearly collided with one of the concubine bodyguards exiting the room where Naa'il was headed. Dressed in tan Ottoman trousers and a matching long shirt, Mamnoon's massive Sudanese body was an intimidating sight. Towering over the Dey, Mamnoon bowed to his master, but not before Naa'il spotted the scowl on his servant's lips.

"Mamnoon," Naa'il frowned as he surveyed the blood stains on his servant's tunic. "What were you doing in the infidel's room?"

The servant looked away to conceal his glares from his master. "I am worried about her, Your Excellency."

"Ah," Naa'il shrugged, "and here I thought that you found a way to take part in a woman's pleasure. Although, I did not think that was possible for eunuchs."

Forcing his arms to his side, Mamnoon rolled his hands into fists. "It is not, Your Excellency," he said through gritted teeth.

Naa'il led his servant to a vacant room further down the corridor. He opened the door and motioned to his servant to enter. Like the other rooms in the Palace, green and white mosaic tiles covered the lower half of the walls with long pillows lining the base of three out of the four walls. The only light in the chamber came from a small stained-glass window beside the door.

Naa'il closed the door and crossed his arms. "I sense disapproval from you." The Dey intentionally kept an arm's length distance from his servant.

Mamnoon's gaze remained fixed on the stone floor.

"I know you have something to say to me, so speak freely while you have the opportunity. You have my word that I will not punish you." Naa'il waved his hand above his head. "Speak."

"I have never before questioned your judgment, Your Excellency, but what you are doing to this woman is wrong." Mamnoon paused as tears filled his eyes. "Cora does not deserve to be treated with such cruelty."

"The infidel brought it upon herself," Naa'il shot back. "I would not have ordered this punishment had she converted and yielded to me. The infidel did neither," he said calmly.

Mamnoon stared at Naa'il in disbelief. "You command this suffering to continue because you want to break her spirit."

"How dare you?"

"Convince me that it is not true. You have had many infidel concubines, and you have never treated any of them the way you treat Cora. I escorted Cora and her cousin into the great hall. You looked at her with contempt from the moment you laid eyes on her."

"She is a whore. I could see that just by looking at her. She had no shame when I removed her clothes during our first meeting."

"Her hands and feet were chained to the wall," Mamnoon shouted back.

"You have no right to judge me. This infidel offered her body to me in exchange for her cousin's protection. If she were pure, she would not have done so. She did not care what I did to her. All that mattered was that her cousin was treated well. I kept my word; Cora did not." Naa'il clasped his hands behind his back and began to pace to offset the anger churning inside him. "I would have been contented having Cora in my bed, yet she came to me smelling foul." He turned his face away from his bodyguard and squeezed his eyes closed to shut out the memory of Cora pleading with him not to punish her cousin for her mistake. "I gave her to my guards to punish her for her insolence," he continued in a softened tone.

"That was not her fault."

"Did she tell you that?" Naa'il challenged.

"No. But I know the women in the harem. Many of them would kill if they believed that their rival had the potential of becoming your favorite."

Naa'il pressed his lips together. "If you can prove that someone sabotaged this infidel's first night, I give you my word that I will severely punish the one responsible for this treachery."

Mamnoon nodded, "I have already started making inquiries." He took a deep breath and continued, "Your Excellency, I have served you faithfully since the day you came into power. I have fought for you, and I would give my life for you. Please stop these attacks against Cora. I will gladly accept the torture in her stead. Please, I beg you to let her be. She is no threat to you."

"I already told you. She is a whore. My treatment is appropriate," Naa'il maintained.

"You are wrong about her."

"Mamnoon, Bashira informed me that only one of the cousins was pure on the day they were presented to me."

"Did she tell you which one, Your Excellency?"

"She did not need to; the infidel's dirty face and worldly demeanor made her true character abundantly clear."

"Why are you so certain that Abigail Randall is innocent? I have known many whores since I came to live here. I understand how they act; Cora is nothing like them," Mamnoon countered.

"No, Cora is difficult and unyielding, unlike her cousin who converted only a few days after she arrived." Naa'il insisted with his hands still clasped together behind his back. One of his hands squeezed the other, as though he wished that he could squeeze Cora into the same action as her cousin.

"That is all the more reason I do not trust Abigail Randall."

"Why?" Naa'il challenged,

"I have always been suspicious of anyone who is quick to change their faith. It makes me wonder who they truly are."

"Perhaps she saw the light."

"I doubt it. I think she converted to gain your favor."

"You know nothing about Abigail Randall. She is very sweet," said Naa'il defensively.

"I am pleased that you found happiness with her, Your Excellency. Since she gives you what you seek, please release Cora from her obligations. She is no longer any use to you. To persist in torturing her is cruel."

"Do you think hurting Cora gives me pleasure?" Naa'il shouted. "I am not evil. I give her the opportunity to convert every time I see her. Her answer is always no. If she does not come into the light willingly, then I must force her. Our laws are very clear."

"Yes, Your Excellency. The Prophet commands that infidels must either convert or die. Why not kill Cora? She has made it clear that she will not convert. Is death not more humane?" Mamnoon looked thoughtfully at his master. "Better yet, sell her to me. I have saved enough to pay the market price for your concubines. I will even pay double if that would please you, or you may take all that I have."

"What would you do with Cora? You cannot have children."

"I would look after her, Your Excellency."

Naa'il's lips parted as he studied his servant. "Why do you care about this infidel?"

A blissful smile graced Mamnoon's lips. "Cora is the rarest of all jewels, Your Excellency."

"You are a fool. I do not understand why you think so highly of her." Naa'il's eyes fell again to the stains on Mamnoon's uniform.

"We talk often. Cora has not thought about herself since the first day I met her. She has proven these many nights that she will do anything to protect her cousin. I am certain that she would not hesitate to give her life if she knew her sacrifice would save her cousin's life." Mamnoon looked away when he spotted his master's clenched jaw. "Many nights I stood watch outside her room while your guards ravaged her body. Her screams will haunt me for the rest of my life. Then I go to Cora after they finish with her," Mamnoon paused as he fought to control his anger. "I bring her food and water. I bathe her body, and then I comfort her as she weeps in my arms until she falls asleep. I remain with her throughout the night because she always wakes up screaming." The guard wiped a tear from his cheek. "Then she prays - every morning. I *feel* her prayers. That is why Cora is a pearl of great price."

Every muscle in Naa'il's face tensed. "Who told you to look after the infidel? Your duty is to guard the women in the harem," Naa'il demanded.

"That is true, Your Excellency. Cora lives in the Palace, and her needs are very great. Besides, I tend to her on my own time," Mamnoon answered

"She is *my* slave. You have no right to interfere." Naa'il rolled his hand into a fist. "The fact that she allows you to touch her should tell you that she is a common whore."

"Have you not heard what I said? The attacks leave Cora in great pain. She can barely move. Every night I contemplate slitting her throat to end her suffering. I have never known you to be a cruel man, yet what you are doing to Cora is barbaric. She does not deserve this treatment!" Mamnoon shouted.

"Get out before I have you put to death for treason! Never go near the infidel again!"

"Yes, master," Mamnoon said through gritted teeth. He bowed and backed out of the room.

Naa'il picked up one of the pillows and threw it across the chamber. "You are wrong about them," he mumbled. Just then, he felt her prayers again as though she were summoning him. The Dey headed to where his captive was being held. He cracked her door ajar and poked his head through the opening. Wrapped in a wool blanket, Cora Bradley sat perched on her pillow. He could see the anguish on her face, and yet he felt her serenity.

She opened her eyes when he closed the door and said with a doleful look, "Good morning, Your Excellency. Are you well?"

Naa'il marveled how Cora could be put through so much, and yet sit there so calmly, behaving as if nothing had happened. He shuddered when he spotted the dried blood on the floor. "No, I am not well. I am in a foul humor, and it is your fault. Do not press me this morning," he snapped, pacing in front of her.

"I am sorry to offend you," Cora replied, as her gaze remained fixed on the floor.

Naa'il picked up one of the cushions and laid it in front of her before sitting down. "Are you not going to ask me why I am cross with you?"

"No, it is not my place to ask," Cora winced. "How is my cousin?"

Naa'il visited Cora every morning since her arrival, and every morning without fail she asked about her cousin. Her initial question was always followed by: "Is she happy? How did she spend her day?" Cora wanted to know everything about Abigail's new life. Her eyes always sparkled as she eagerly received the little information that Naa'il provided.

"Will you please give Abigail my love and tell her that I miss her?"

"Huriyyah also sends her love," Naa'il lied.

"Who is Huriyyah?" Cora's crinkled forehead expressed her confusion.

"Huriyyah is my name for your cousin."

"What a beautiful name. Do your names have meanings?"

"Of course. Huriyyah means angel."

"I would say that name suits her. I am grateful that you have taken such good care of my cousin. Knowing that comforts me more than I can say." Cora tilted her face towards the floor and wiped a tear from the corner of her eye.

Naa'il replied with a sad nod. He didn't need Mamnoon to remind him that Cora's sacrifice was great. A nagging doubt made him question whether Abigail was truly worthy of the torture that Cora endured to ensure her cousin's protection. "Why do you give so much for Huriyyah?"

Cora looked at the wall to avoid his gaze. "Because I love her, and I want to protect her."

Naa'il pinched her chin between his two fingers and swiveled her face back towards his. "No, you feel guilty about something that happened to your cousin. What is it?"

"You are very perceptive, Your Excellency." Cora looked away with a pained expression.

"I command you to tell me."

Cora swallowed hard. "A friend gave me a mare before I went to live with my uncle and his family. My friend captured Ahyoka in the wild. We spent weeks breaking and training her. She was a beautiful black horse with four white socks and a star on her forehead. She was spirited too. Oh, how she loved to run."

Naa'il pursed his lips. "You rode this horse?"

"Yes, bareback," Cora said proudly. She closed her eyes before continuing her story. "Ahyoka was very temperamental; she hated when anyone but me rode her. One day, Abigail and I were down in the barn; she asked me to saddle a horse for her. The next thing I knew, Abigail climbed onto my horse's back in the ring. I tried to stop her, but Abigail didn't listen. She never had any sense around horses. Abigail did something to spook my horse, and Ahyoka threw her," Cora said mournfully. "My uncle shot Ahyoka that day; Abigail was bedridden for months. I prayed every day for my cousin. God answered my prayer on Christmas morning when she surprised us by walking across the room. That is why Abigail still walks with a limp."

"That is the reason you are so protective of her," Naa'il surmised.

"It was my fault that she was injured, Your Excellency."

"The responsibility belongs to the both of you. Your father should not have allowed you to own such a horse," Naa'il said disapprovingly. "Why did you go to live with Huriyyah's family? Or should I ask, what happened to yours?"

Cora stared at the stone floor with a haunted expression on her face; she bit her lower lip. "My parents and sisters were killed by an Indian war party. I was twelve."

Naa'il's lips parted with dismay. "Where were you during this attack?"

Cora let out a loud sigh. "I was the son my father always wanted.

While my sisters learned to cook and rear children, I spent my waking moments hunting, tracking, and fishing. I was a fair shot too. I rose early that morning to join my best friend and his father for a day of hunting. My father would have joined us, but he was ill at the time, or so he said. I came home later that night and discovered that my whole family had been slaughtered and our cabin had burned to the ground. The only thing that survived was my mother's Bible, which was a miracle in itself."

"Yes, your mother's Bible was delivered the same day you and Huriyyah were presented to me."

Cora's lips parted as she looked at him with a glimmer of hope. "Do you still have it?"

"Yes. I do not know why I keep it."

"Please, may I have it back? It is all I have left of my mother," Cora explained with pleading eyes.

"You know I cannot." Naa'il paused and looked away. "Cora, Mamnoon asked me to end the attacks against you."

"He is a good man."

"I will gladly end your suffering the moment you convert. The only other path is death. That is our law."

Cora leaned over and retrieved something hiding under her pillow.

"What are you doing?" Naa'il demanded when he spotted the knife in her hands. He recognized the ivory handle, and it belonged to Mamnoon.

"I made my choice," she laid the knife across the palms of her hands. "Please be kind; make it quick."

Naa'il wrapped his fingers around the handle. Cora didn't flinch when he pressed the blade against her neck. She just looked at him with pleading eyes. Naa'il threw the knife across the room. He sandwiched her face between his hands and punished her with a crushing kiss, his lips demanding a response. Her only reply was a whimper. Naa'il pulled away from her. "Even now you still defy me!" he shouted. "You vowed to do all that I asked!"

"What do you think I've done since I arrived?" Cora shouted back.

"You have never submitted to me, and you still refuse to convert. Yet, I have treated your cousin like an honored wife."

Cora dropped the blanket from her shoulders. Naa'il covered his mouth with his hand to conceal his consternation as he surveyed the injuries covering her body. Even though he knew that she had been tortured, he was not prepared for the severity of the damage that included: innumerable welts, cuts, and bruises that left very little of her pale skin intact.

"Cover yourself," Naa'il said gruffly. Standing, he picked up the pillow and threw it across the room. "Why can you not convert?"

Cora didn't answer.

"Very well, suffer. That is your choice, not mine. I am through trying to save you. I will not think of you after this day. I will not care that you are being tortured, nor will I feel guilty. You chose your fate; not me. You will die for a God who has forsaken you, and you will spend eternity in damnation for your whoring. Do not expect Mamnoon's help. No one can help you now," Naa'il warned.

Cora looked at him with fear and pleaded, "Please do not harm Mamnoon because of me."

Naa'il pursed his lips and shook his head. "Remember, taking your life will only endanger your cousin." He closed the door behind him and leaned against an adjacent wall with his face partially buried in his hands. It was ironic that while Cora was the one being persecuted, the strength of her resistance made him feel powerless to change or save her.

Chapter 4

Hassan stirred when he felt the morning sun warming his body, but it was the feel of a woman's breast cupped in his hand that brought him out of his deep sleep. He opened his eyes and glanced down at the woman sleeping in his arms. Then he remembered the corpse lying in the next room.

The corsair sat up, taking great care not to disturb his guest. Sarah didn't stir when he left his berth, or when he covered her with a blanket. The ship's bell sounded a few minutes later, and a soft knock on his cabin door followed. Not wanting to wake Sarah, he darted across his cabin to answer it. "Yes?" he whispered after cracking the door open.

"Good morning, Captain. How is our patient?" Peter whispered after Hassan put his finger to his lips.

Hassan opened the door wider. "Mr. Campbell died early this morning."

Peter entered the cabin and scanned the room. "Where's Campbell's daughter?"

"She's sleeping."

Hassan quickly dressed while Peter inspected Thomas Campbell's body.

"I should warn you that the Polynesians do not bury their dead.

They consider it taboo," Peter said as he examined the corpse.

Hassan raised a brow. "What is taboo?"

"Taboo is a practice or action that is prohibited by their customs. I call it superstition."

"I see." Hassan cracked a smile. "Just out of curiosity, how do the Polynesians dispose of their dead?"

"They prefer to leave a body with provisions in a hut. The body's odor is the worst stench you will ever smell," Peter explained with a hint of disdain in his tone.

"I appreciate your warning, but I will handle this matter myself. Of course, any suggestions on how to approach this delicate matter is always welcome."

"I am sure you will figure that out."

Still concerned about Sarah, Hassan requested, "May I task you to prepare Campbell's body for burial while Sarah and I eat breakfast?"

"Certainly, but Polynesian women do not eat with the men."

"Let me guess; it's taboo?" Hassan mused.

"Something like that."

"You need not worry; I will tend to Miss Campbell." Hassan went over to the door and summoned two seamen to take away Thomas' body. After they unhooked the hammock, Hassan held the door open while they carried the corpse out of the room. "Thank you, Doctor. Please inform me when the preparations are complete," Hassan said as Peter exited his quarters.

"Of course."

Hassan's stomach growled, reminding him that he hadn't eaten since early the previous day. He went over to Sarah. Though he hated to wake her, he sat down on the edge of his berth. "Miss Campbell," Hassan whispered.

Sarah didn't answer.

"Miss Campbell," he repeated several more times.

Sarah opened her eyes after Hassan shook her.

"La Orana," she said.

"Good morning," Hassan replied, flustered when she offered him a loving smile.

Sarah sat up and kissed Hassan sweetly before flicking the blanket off her.

Puzzled by her cheerful demeanor, he frowned, "Are you hungry?"

"Aye." She stretched, climbed down from his berth, and walked into the dining area. After scanning the cabin, she asked, "Where food? How I cook?"

"You do not need to cook. My servants will bring our breakfast to my cabin."

Sarah headed to the table; Hassan hooked his hand around her arm and said quirking a lopsided grin, "You must dress first." He led her to his dressing room. Hassan opened the lid of the trunk and searched for something appropriate for Sarah to wear.

She still ignored the white dress.

Hassan pulled out a formless gray gown. "This will have to do." He could tell by Sarah's frown that she didn't like his choice; she didn't complain either. "Hold up your hands." Hassan lowered the gown over her head and arms, and released the ends, sending the bottom tumbling to the floor. The dress looked like it belonged to someone during the Biblical era. It was plain, shapeless, and much too large for Sarah. Nevertheless, it was a perfect solution for camouflaging her figure. A knock on the door echoed through the cabin; Hassan led Sarah to the window. "That will be our breakfast. Please enjoy the view while the servants deliver our meal."

"I help?"

"It is not necessary." Hassan winked.

Sarah ignored the sun streaking across the water and looked on with interest as the servants paraded into his cabin carrying bowls and trays of food. Hassan's young staff froze when they spotted Sarah.

"I would like to eat this morning," Hassan gently prodded.

"Sorry, sir." A black-haired seaman simpered before setting a bowl of oranges on the table.

"Thank you, gentleman. That will be all," Hassan said when his men finished setting the table.

"Are you sure you don't want us to stay, sir?"

"Not today," Hassan said firmly.

"Enjoy your breakfast, sir," The crewman said with a hint of disappointment after tearing his eyes from Sarah.

She was already inspecting the white china by the time Hassan closed the door after his crew filed out of his cabin.

"Are you hungry?"

Sarah nodded. She stepped away from the table and knelt on the rug, tucking her feet beneath her with her eyes focused on the floor.

Hassan squatted in front of her. "I thought you were hungry."

"You eat; I eat after," Sarah explained.

"Would you not rather eat with me?"

"No, it taboo."

Hassan expelled a loud sigh. "Dr. Hyatt informed me that Polynesian women do not eat with the men."

"Aye."

Hassan stood up. "Men and women eat together on my island. I would very much like the pleasure of your company." He held out his hand and was relieved that she reached for it. He pulled out a chair and guided her to the seat. He then unfolded a white napkin, laid it across her lap, and took a seat beside her. Sarah's eyes were still focused on the china. Hassan chuckled as she traced the red flower in the center of the plate and then looked at her finger as though she expected to see red covering the tip.

"The red paint is baked into the ceramic; it should not come off."

Sarah turned her attention to the silverware. She picked one up at a time, examining each of them. Of the three, the spoon intrigued her the most. She poked at it several times, and then moved it back and forth without taking her eyes off the center.

It took a few minutes for Hassan to realize that she was staring at a small upside down reflection of herself. He couldn't help wondering if Sarah had ever seen her image before this morning. "This is a spoon, and this is a fork," he said, holding up one in each hand. "We use these to lift the food to our mouth." He placed his silverware on the table and picked up the knife. "We use this for cutting our food into smaller pieces.

Sarah placed her spoon on the table. Her stomach grumbled as she turned her attention to the food. Her eyes immediately rested on a matching small china bowl filled with oranges. She picked up an orange and rubbed the rough skin with her finger. Hassan threw his head back and burst into laughter when her face puckered after biting into the rind. She immediately spat it out onto her plate.

"That is an orange. As you discovered, the skin is very sour. The inside, on the other hand, is sweet." Hassan took the orange from her, peeled it and pulled the sections apart. He placed one section in his mouth and offered one to Sarah.

She sniffed the fruit before taking a bite. Her face was the epitome of bliss when the beads from the sweet juice burst on her tongue. Hassan placed the rest of the orange on her plate. He also taught her how to prepare and eat a soft boiled egg. She carefully scooped the gooey insides out of the brown shell until the egg was gone. Drinking tea, on the other hand, was another matter. Sarah stared at the steam rising from the brown liquid.

"This is tea, and it is very hot," Hassan warned. He held the cup by the handle and took a small sip.

Sarah sampled the tea and spat the beverage back into the cup after it burned the inside of her mouth. She returned the teacup to the table and didn't reach for it again.

Naa'il slowly opened the door and poked his head through the crack. He expected to see his American prize kneeling in prayer; all he heard was her soft snores as she slept on her pillow. After quietly closing the door, Naa'il went over and sat by her side.

Abigail Randall, now Huriyyah, was beautiful when she slept. *An angel.* She would be a perfect Algerian wife: quiet, submissive, chaste, and obedient - just like his other wives and concubines, he reflected as his lips formed a frown.

Abigail propped herself up on her elbows. "Your Excellency!" Her whole face lit up when she spoke his name.

"Good morning. Do you like your new apartment?"

"It is exquisite. I feel like a princess. I dare say that I am the envy of the harem."

"And so you should be." Naa'il's eyes fell on Abigail's partially exposed breasts peeking out from her vest. His brow furrowed when he silently noted that she made no attempt to cover herself.

"Will you show me how to pray again?" she asked as she fluttered her eyelashes.

Of course." Naa'il stood and offered his hand to Abigail. After he led her through the Morning Prayer, the servants delivered their breakfast. Abigail talked the entire time. She told him about her day, her experience in the harem, and even her life in America. Not once did she mention her cousin.

"Cora sends her regards," Naa'il said towards the end of their breakfast.

"Oh, how kind of her," Abigail smirked. "My lord, may I go to the Grand Bazaar? I understand it is a marvelous place."

"No."

Abigail's bottom lip jutted into a pout. "Why not?"

"It is not proper."

"I have not left the Palace since I arrived," she whined.

"You are young, and you do not understand our ways. I insist that you and the other women remain in the Palace for your protection. This city is a dangerous place. Why would you need to leave anyway? Do I not provide everything you require? You have food, clothing, and a beautiful apartment. What more could you want?"

Abigail crossed her arms. "I still feel like a prisoner."

"You are a well-provided prisoner," Naa'il countered with a hint of anger. "Be grateful for my generosity. The women in the harem would eagerly trade places with you." He stood and headed for the door. "Never forget that I can easily replace you. I would suggest that you contemplate how you can better please me."

"Good morning," Peter said to Sarah in Polynesian. The staff had just finished removing the breakfast dishes. The doctor gave Hassan a subtle nod and said, "Everything is arranged."

"Thank you, Doctor." Hassan dreaded the upcoming funeral. Saying goodbye to a fallen crew member was never easy. He couldn't imagine how Sarah was going to react to saying goodbye to her father. He knew he couldn't put it off forever. After a long pause, he said, "Miss Campbell, it's time to bury your father."

Sarah just answered with a vacant stare.

Hassan, Peter, and Sarah stepped out of his cabin. His officers were waiting for them on the quarterdeck. Sarah gasped when she discovered Hassan's entire crew had gathered on the deck below them. She hadn't noticed her father's body lying on the plank at the edge of the ship. In the traditional naval fashion, a seaman had sown Thomas' body in a hammock, though Hassan didn't have a British flag to cover the corpse.

Hassan scanned the crew staring back at him. He wished he had a Bible to guide him through what to say to Sarah. Their captors confiscated the ship's Bible when they captured Hassan and his crew. The corsair captain took a deep breath and said, "Mr. Campbell and his daughter came to us as strangers. I regret that I didn't have an opportunity to know him better." Glancing over at Sarah, he continued, "From the little I know of your father, he loved you deeply, and he would do anything to protect you from harm." Hassan paused as he observed Sarah yawning. "We commit his body to the sea, may he find eternal peace."

Several of Hassan's seamen tipped the plank up, causing Thomas Campbell's body to slide down the board and splashed into the water.

"I am very sorry for your loss," Hassan said to Sarah.

She looked at him as if she didn't understand why she was required to attend this ceremony.

Hassan glanced over at Peter for an explanation for Sarah's indifference. Peter just shrugged his shoulders.

Hassan and Peter escorted Sarah to Hassan's quarters. "Miss Campbell, I would like you to stay here for the remainder of the afternoon," Hassan explained.

"I go wit you, please," Sarah pleaded.

"Not today. I have much to do. I cannot perform my duties and worry about you at the same time. Please stay here, and I will have food brought to you." Hassan left Sarah standing in the middle of the room. Her pouty lips made him feel guilty for abandoning her so soon after her father's burial. As much as he hated leaving her alone, he knew in his heart that his cabin was the safest place for her. His crew hadn't seen many women since they came to the Barbary Coast, and Sarah was the prettiest woman he had ever seen. His crew seemed to agree with him by the way they leered at her. The only person that didn't outwardly lust after Sarah was Peter.

The doctor nodded to Sarah and followed his captain to the quarterdeck.

"I'm puzzled by Miss Campbell's demeanor. I must admit that I'm relieved that she is not overcome with grief. Though, I expected her to be a little sad," Hassan vented. "Do you have any explanation for her indifference towards her father's death?"

"Miss Campbell was raised in a pagan culture. Polynesians do not mourn as Christians do."

"But he was her father."

"Be grateful; you may get to enjoy your wedding night," Peter shrugged.

"Miss Campbell is not my wife," Hassan snapped. "At least not legally," he softened.

"May I enquire what you intend to do with her?"

"I intend to take her to her family of course."

"And how are you going to find her family?"

"Her father was from Scotland; Campbell is a prominent Scottish clan. I'm sure someone from her clan knew her father."

"You have to leave the Barbary Coast first."

"That is true." Hassan softly laughed. "Until then, Miss Campbell is under my protection. Carry on, Doctor."

CHAPTER 5

Naa'il had two primary duties as the Dey of Algiers: presiding over the affairs of the state and processing slaves. He liked his latter job because it was mindless work, and it made him *very* wealthy. His mornings usually began with saying his prayers in the Palace mosque and visiting his wives before starting his work, which usually began around 8:00. His visits with Cora and Abigail had delayed him this morning. It was already 8:00, and he still hadn't visited his wives and children. Naa'il would have liked nothing more than to begin his work in the slave yard. As a servant of habit, the Dey headed to the wing where his wives resided.

His first wife, Mariam, sat in a gilded chair in the center of her apartment while her attendant arranged her knee-length black hair into an elaborate bun. During their twelve years of marriage, Mariam bore him four daughters. Her countenance had changed from an impressionable young girl to a matron. Though Naa'il was two years older, he couldn't help straightening his posture whenever he visited her, and yet he couldn't deny that his first wife was still a stunning woman.

An incurable traditionalist, Mariam dressed similarly to Naa'il, except she preferred bright colors. Today, she wore peacock-green Ottoman trousers and a white chemise, or gömlek that hung loosely from her shoulders to her mid-calf. Once her servant arranged her hair,

Mariam stood up while her attendant slid a brocade hirka or fitted jacket over the first wife's arms. The calf-length hirka was made of the finest silk and studded with sapphires and emeralds and embroidered with gold thread to resemble peacock feathers. The royal-blue jacket was a perfect complement to her brightly-colored salvar. Mariam adjusted the embroidered cuffs while her servant fastened the gold buttons from her waist to the underside of her firm breasts, leaving her lace bodice exposed.

"Blessings be upon thee, husband." Mariam held out her arms while her servant fastened a jeweled belt around her waist while another attached an emerald necklace around her neck. She slid her feet into her gold and sapphire slippers and said, "Bring tea, then leave us."

Naa'il studied his wife and frowned when he spotted her worried look. "What is troubling you?"

Mariam hesitated to answer.

"What has my second wife done this time?" Naa'il demanded.

"She was dancing with the harlots in the harem yesterday afternoon."

Naa'il pursed his lips. "Are you certain of this?"

"Yes, I am certain. I saw Samina myself. I would not bring it up except that I thought her behavior was not suitable for a Dey's wife."

"You were right to tell me. Dancing with harlots is improper conduct." Naa'il's brows bumped into a scowl. He wandered through an arched doorway leading to her courtyard and stared mindlessly at the fountain as the water spilled from the top tier to the one below it.

Mariam followed him into her garden and rested her hand on his shoulder. "What is troubling you, husband?"

Naa'il looked over his shoulder and shook his head. "The American infidel vexes me."

"I thought you had two Americans."

"Yes, they are cousins. I named the light-haired one Huriyyah."

"You like her."

"Why do you feign interest in my Americans when I know you disprove of my keeping infidel women?" Naa'il snapped.

"I do not care about them; I care about your happiness," she said with a coy smile.

"Lying does not become you."

"Forgive me, husband. You are right; I worry about bringing infidel women into our home. They are filthy and immoral. That is doubly true of the American women." She looked down at the floor. "I fear they will taint our way of life."

"No, you worry about my shaming our family by becoming an apostate! I am not weak!"

She jumped as his shouts thundered throughout her chamber. "I have never believed you were," she countered in an almost obsequious tone.

"I take my responsibilities to my faith very seriously. Not even the most beautiful infidel can turn me from my faith or cause me to dishonor my family." "Forgive me for doubting your honor." Mariam pressed her lips together and looked away.

"You may be pleased to hear that Huriyyah converted."

"Indeed? Were her vows sincere?"

"Of course," Naa'il said unconvincingly. He knew by the way Mariam pursed her lips that she didn't believe him.

"I would be happy to test her sincerity."

"You will stay away from my Americans. Repercussions will be severe if you disobey me," Naa'il growled.

"I merely wished to assist you," Mariam countered smoothly. She lowered her gaze to the red flowers planted at the base of the fountain. "Naa'il, may I offer a suggestion?"

"You may."

"Why not sell the one that vexes you and keep the one that you like? This infidel is not worthy of the frustration she causes you."

Naa'il crossed his arms again and faced the fountain. "You are right; this infidel is not worthy of my attention." All he could think about was losing the peace that Cora's prayers brought him each morning. As angry as Cora made him, he dreaded the thought of never feeling that peace again. He looked back at his wife and said, "I will leave you now."

Mariam pressed her lips together. "Your daughters will be here momentarily," she protested.

"I do not have time to visit with them this morning. I must tend to the matter of Samina's indiscretion." With a curt nod, he turned around and strode out of the room.

Naa'il came to an abrupt halt as he stood in the doorway to his second wife's apartment while he waited for her attendants to finish dressing their mistress. Samina's servants arranged her raven hair in an elegant bun. She only wore a brocade entari or a floor-length robe that Ottoman women usually wore on formal occasions or when visiting friends. Samina's maroon dress was made of silk and embroidered with gold thread. While traditional entaris were worn open from the waist to the floor, the lower part of Samina's resembled a three-paneled skirt. Traditional entaris were only buttoned at the waist and worn open the whole length of the bodice; Samina's dress was buttoned from her waist to the high neckline. Naa'il couldn't deny that the tailored bodice complimented her V-shaped figure. Still, Naa'il's frown deepened as he surveyed her from head to toe. "What are you wearing?"

"It is called an üçetek." Smiling proudly, Samina held her arms out to her side and slowly turned around so that her husband could inspect her. "It is beautiful, is it not? My friends told me that my üçetek resembles the gowns worn by women from Paris.

Naa'il shook his head without realizing that he was doing so. Samina was a traditional Arabian beauty who had no equal, not even in the Sultan's Palace. Naa'il always liked her oval face and delicate features. She also had a way of making him feel loved when she ran into his arms whenever he visited her. His wife's clothing choice this morning reminded him that she still had much to learn about being the wife of the Dey of Algiers.

"I do not like it," he said with pursed lips. "It looks too much like a Western dress. We have been married long enough for you to know what is considered an appropriate dress for your rank."

Tears flooded Samina's onyx eyes. "My Lord, I have worn salvars, gömleks, and hirkas my whole life. I thought an üçetek would be a pleasant change. My friends outside the palace wear üçeteks that are similar to mine."

Naa'il entered her apartment and closed the door behind him. His face turned from a frown to a scowl as he approached her. "Your friends are not the wives of the Dey of Algiers; they can wear whatever they wish. As the second wife of the Dey of Algiers, you must be held to a higher standard than your common friends. That brings me to the purpose of my visit.

Samina held her arms close to her middle when she spotted the anger in Naa'il's eyes. "Did I do something wrong, my lord?" she asked in a timid voice.

"I understand that you were dancing with the harlots in the harem."

Samina backed away and hugged herself when she heard the disapproval in his tone. "It was innocent amusement, my Lord."

"You are the wife of the Dey of Algiers, not a common harlot!" Naa'il shouted.

"I danced in the harem, not in public, my Lord," Samina meekly countered.

"That does not matter. Women talk, and not just among themselves - they talk to their lovers. Those men serve me." Naa'il removed a short whip from his belt.

"My Lord, please have mercy on me. I meant no harm!" Samina backed away from him.

"Your youth does not excuse your behavior, Samina. You brought shame to our family and me. You must be punished." Naa'il tore her üçetek from her body and threw her onto her pillow bed. When he finished flogging her back, he calmly went to the door and rested his hand on the doorknob. "You will dress appropriately from this moment forth, and you will sever ties with your friends," he commanded before leaving.

Servants had just delivered tea and refreshments when Jamal entered his sister's apartment.

"Ah, there you are." Mariam admired how handsome her brother looked with his recently trimmed pointed beard. As the Vizier of Algiers, Jamal was the second most important official in the country. He always dressed like a prince. His long–flowing robes were made of the finest silks, and he covered his bald head with headpieces worthy of the Sultan. Mariam always felt pride whenever she saw him.

"I was concerned that your duties detained you," Mariam continued.

Jamal greeted his sister with a warm smile. "It was a busy day. There were many slaves to process this afternoon." His voice trailed off when he spotted the worry on her brow. "Are you ill? Did something happen?"

"Come, let us talk over refreshments." Mariam wrapped her hand around Jamal's arm and led him to the cushion where the food was set up. After sitting down, Mariam poured her brother some tea while he helped himself to a date.

Jamal took a sip and asked, "What is troubling you?"

Mariam looked thoughtfully at her brother. "I had a disturbing conversation with Naa'il this morning. Is he in love with the American infidel?"

"Naa'il visits the light haired one every day."

"Naa'il calls her Huriyyah. He cares nothing for her. I am concerned about the other one - the infidel. What can you tell me about her?"

Jamal laid his empty teacup on the floor. "You need not worry about her." He told his sister about Cora's captivity.

Mariam covered her mouth with her hand to conceal her consternation. "That is barbaric. Why does he not simply execute her?"

"I do not know. Naa'il does not confide in me about such matters because of my relation to you."

"We must help her in some way."

"I thought you hated the infidel."

"I do. As a woman, I cannot condone these attacks against her. It is inhumane. I would much rather slip poison into her water than allow this violence to continue."

"Do not interfere, Mari. Naa'il keeps the infidel alive for a reason. You will make an enemy of him if you try to help this woman."

Mariam lowered her cup to the floor and crossed her arms. "I think about our sister. That is all."

"Our sister was flogged to death because she lost her innocence to strangers."

"She said she was taken by force, and I believe her."

"Our sister put herself in danger."

Mariam shot her brother a murderous glare. "Perhaps. I say there is no excuse for men violating a girl or woman. If anyone attacked me, I would seize his sword and slay him where he stood. I will do exactly that if I meet our sister's attackers."

Jamal shuddered. "I believe you would." He studied his sister. "I am curious; what did Naa'il tell you about this American?"

"He did not say much. I believe the infidel torments him. She could not affect him in this manner unless he has feelings for her."

"What if he does? You of all people should know that Naa'il has always been drawn to women from other lands. They amuse him for a while until he finds another."

Mariam sighed. "You know I do not care about my husband's lovers. He can have as many as he wishes. I dread the day when he falls in love with one of them. My heart tells me that this American infidel is different. That frightens me."

"I think you worry for naught."

"What if she bewitches him, and he becomes an apostate?"

Jamal wrapped his arm around his sister's shoulder and leaned against the wall, pulling her close to him. "It has not happened yet. Even if it does, you have my word that I will always take care of you and your children."

"You are too kind to me; I do not know what I would do without you."

"You would be lost, my dear sister," Jamal teased.

Mariam replied with a faint laugh.

"It is a good day; I made you laugh," Jamal said with a grin.

Chapter 6

Abigail lifted her head off her pillow when she heard a knock at the door. Her heart raced with a fool's hope that Naa'il returned to apologize for quarreling with her. She bounded off her pillow, ran towards the door, and opened it. She frowned when she discovered Mamnoon standing on the other side. "Oh, it's you. What do you want?"

"His Excellency asked me to escort you to the harem for your bath," Mamnoon announced.

Abigail held her chin up and stared down her nose at him. "I will bathe here today. Have hot water, soap, and servants brought to my chamber."

Mamnoon wedged his foot in the door before she could slam it in his face. "All women, including His Excellency's wives, bathe in the harem."

"I don't want to go," Abigail hissed.

"You have no choice. You can walk with me freely, or I will drag you," Mamnoon said in a menacing tone as he reached for her arm.

Abigail pulled away and slapped her bodyguard's cheeks. "You filthy slave, how dare you lay a hand on me? Do you know who I am?"

"You are a lowly concubine," he said, undaunted by her attack.

"I am *not* a concubine!"

"You are not the Dey's wife either. That makes you his slave."

"I have Naa'il's ear. He will not be pleased to learn that you mistreated me!" Abigail shouted.

"You want to stay? Stay. I will inform His Excellency that you refused to go to the harem, and I will bring you nothing. You can explain why you are not clean. I should warn you; there is nothing His Excellency despises more than an unclean concubine."

Tears filled Abigail's eyes. "I don't like the harem. Can't you bring me what I need for my bath? Please? I would be most grateful if we can come to an understanding." She leaned in and fluttered her thick eyelashes.

"I cannot. Come with me now, or I will leave you. This will be your only opportunity to go to the harem today."

"Very well," Abigail consented grimly. She followed her bodyguard. Every muscle in her back tightened with each step she took.

The guards standing by the harem's entrance opened the arched doors. The music and the activity ceased the moment Abigail stepped inside. Bashira, the overseer of the harem, greeted her with several servants standing behind her. Dressed in Ottoman clothing and covered with a long green Kafka, Bashira was a shadow of the Arabian beauty that she once was. Half of her raven hair was white, and permanent wrinkles had settled into her brow. Still, she was beautiful. Abigail couldn't help straightening her posture every time she felt Bashira's all-knowing brown eyes watching her.

Mamnoon and Bashira spoke briefly in a language that sounded like gibberish to Abigail. The bodyguard offered his friend a weary bow and left the harem.

"Come with me," Bashira said curtly.

Abigail felt the eyes of every person in the harem focused on her. Holding her head up high, she looked straight ahead and followed the servants through the doors leading to the bathing room. Like the main gathering room, the concubines' conversations stopped abruptly. Abigail ignored their unwelcoming glares while the servants undressed her. She headed to the only vacancy at the far edge of the pool. Soaking in the warm water was the perfect distraction from her predicament until her mind fell upon her first day in the harem.

Abigail's jaw dropped as she took in the opulence of her new home. Harems were part of an exotic world in a distant land. Never did Abigail imagine that she would set foot in one during her lifetime. It was even more majestic than she ever imagined. The palatial quarters housed over fifty concubines, servants, and children. The main gathering room was larger than her ballroom at her parent's Virginia home. The harem's high ceiling made the room seem even larger. Rope-marble dividers and raised platforms lined with pillows against the tiled walls partitioned the corners of the chamber into alcoves. The center of the room was large enough to fit a table covered with bowls of fruit and other food. Nearly every inch of that room was occupied with women and children.

Cora charged across the room. "Are you hurt? I was so worried about you," she said, hugging her cousin.

"Yes, I am quite well. I had a private meeting with Naa'il Dhar himself. He was very kind to me." Abigail studied her cousin, silently noting that her peach cheeks were paler than normal.

"I am grateful." Cora grinned and hugged Abigail again.

Abigail pushed her cousin away and stepped deeper into the harem. "Isn't this a beautiful place? Can you believe that we're in the Algerian Palace? I feel like a princess."

Instead of answering, Cora held her hand over her mouth and ran in the opposite direction.

"Where are you going?" Abigail chased after her cousin to the back of the great hall. They passed through an arched door leading to a hallway. Abigail halted her pursuit to peek inside the rooms. The chamber to her left had a pool taking up nearly two-thirds of the floor. There were clusters of naked women scattered around the edges of the water. Some laid on the marble benches while their personal slave rubbed their backs. Others gathered by the basin's edges, some in and some out of the water while discussing the latest gossip.

Cora came out of another door, wiping her mouth with a wet cloth.

Abigail's face puckered. "What is wrong with you?" She covered her nose with her hand to block the stench of vomit.

"It's nothing; I am going to lie down for a while," Cora replied.

Abigail followed her cousin into the main hall to a nearly vacant alcove. No sooner had they sat down when two screaming women charged towards them. Abigail and Cora covered their heads with their hands to block the attacks. Bashira heard the commotion and raced across the room, pulling the women away from the cousins.

"Come with me," said a woman with a mild Irish brogue.

The American cousins studied this striking woman. Her hair and eyes were as dark as the Algerians. She also wore the concubine uniform. Her skin, however, was as light as Abigail's.

"You're Irish!" Cora exclaimed.

"Aye, what was your first clue?" she said in a haughty and slightly irritated tone. "Follow me, unless you want them to attack you again."

Abigail and Cora left the alcove and followed their rescuer to another corner of the room.

Cora was the first to sit down. "What did we do wrong?"

"You laid your head in the wrong place. You belong over here," she said. "The one you were in is for the Dey's favorite concubines."

"All the spaces on the pillows are taken in this one," Abigail complained.

"Then you stand or sit on the floor," the woman countered.

"I'm sorry that I mistook you for Persian. I thought everyone here was from this part of the world," Cora said.

"Most are, but there are a few of us who aren't. I'm Tess O'Shea. Madame Bashira sent me to instruct you."

"I'm Cora Bradley. This is my cousin, Abigail Randall. I'm pleased to meet you."

Abigail was too annoyed to offer Tess a curt smile.

"Don't let Ula and Rana get to you. They think they are better than the rest of us. Everyone hates them. Ula is one of the Dey's favorite concubines - or at least she was. It has been over a week since she was last with him. She knows she's fallen out of His Lordship's favor. Thus she feels particularly threatened by any new additions to the harem. We also heard the rumors that His Lordship hand-picked you both today."

Cora's brows snapped together, "Are you referring to Naa'il Dhar?" she asked after a few thoughtful moments.

"Aye," Tess impatiently answered. "Who else would I be referring to?"

"It's just that we were instructed to address the Dey as 'His Excellency,'" Cora explained.

"And so you should. 'His Lordship' is my name for him," Tess clarified.

Abigail's lips parted when she spotted Cora's green eyes glistening with a floodtide of tears spilling onto her cheeks. Ever since her cousin came to live with her family, never once had Abigail seen her cousin cry.

Tess rested her hand on Cora's shoulder and offered her a sympathetic smile. "I know it is hard to see it right now, but His Lordship has given you a great honor."

"Honor?" Cora retorted. "Do you consider becoming a slave an honor?"

"'Tis a far better life than being taken to market and sold to the highest bidder. If that happens, you're better off slitting your throat and explainin' your suicide to St. Peter. The women sold to common Ottomans live hard lives. You will live very well here if you are invited to stay. You must understand the rules if you wish to survive."

"What is this about slaves?" Abigail asked. "No one told me that I was a slave. Naa'il Dhar was quite kind to me."

"His Lordship is kind to everyone during their first meeting with him. Make no mistake; you are both his property now."

Abigail swallowed hard.

"The harem is like a small city. It is ordered by a strict hierarchy. The Dey's first wife is the Queen. She and His Lordship's other wife live in their own apartments."

"How many wives does the Dey have?" Cora asked.

"Two at the moment. Mariam is his first wife; Princess Samina is his second."

"How many wives can he have?" Abigail asked.

"The men in this part of the world can have as many as four. His Lordship had three. His foolish third wife was stoned to death after getting caught committing adultery, or so it was rumored."

"You can be stoned to death for adultery?" Abigail gasped.

"Oh aye. You will find that the punishments here are quite harsh. You will lose a hand if you are caught stealing, and you can get flogged one hundred times if you leave the Palace or are caught with a man other than your husband or relative," Tess explained.

"Thank you for the warning," said Cora.

"It is a little different for us. As Naa'il Dhar's concubines, we are not held to the same standards as his wives, although you can still lose a hand for stealing," Tess cautioned. "Bashira asked me to explain the ways of the harem to you. You know about the 'Queen' and the 'Princess.' You will never see them because they enter through a private door when they come to bathe. No one is allowed in the bathing area when they are here. Bashira is the valide, and she is the third most important person in the harem. The Sultan in Constantinople gave Bashira to His Lordship. Her sole purpose is to oversee all that goes on in the harem. You do not want to anger her; she can decide your fate just as easily as His Lordship. The next in rank are the mothers of His Lordship's children. The mothers and his sons gather in one alcove; mothers and his daughters assemble in another. Then come His Lordship's favorite concubines - the kadins. They gather in another alcove. The rest of the young women are the odalisques. They are used as servants and entertainment."

"What are we?" Abigail demanded.

"You both are odalisques," Tess answered, "and so am I."

"How do we improve our standing?" Abigail asked.

"That is simple. Please His Lordship and learn as much as you can," Tess said.

"Then it is true, the harem is just a brothel," Cora mumbled.

"Not quite. Our small community acts somewhat like a brothel with a few significant differences. Men are not allowed in here; we are sent out to entertain His Lordship and other Palace guests. All the women, except for the wives, live here."

"But there are men in here." Abigail pointed to Mamnoon.

"Aren't you observant?" Tess said with a hint of sarcasm. "His Lordship keeps several guards in here to maintain the peace. Otherwise, there would be a bloody war in the harem. We're all in a fierce competition with each other. As you discovered, some women can be downright cruel. The guards are here to make sure that no one kills each other. You don't have to worry about them; they are eunuchs."

"What is a eunuch?" Abigail asked.

"It means that they've been gelded."

"Oh," Cora said in a faint voice.

Abigail erupted into giggles.

"Unlike the brothels at home, we are not free to come and go as we please. As I mentioned before, all the women in this room, including the Queen and the Princess, are the Dey's property. Some of us came from ships that were seized by His Lordship's pirates. Others were bought from the slave market. We all live at the Dey's mercy. Cora, I understand that you will be spending tonight with His Lordship. He has particular requirements. You must do exactly as I say."

Abigail's eyes narrowed. "Why do you get to spend the evening with Naa'il Dhar? He liked me better, and I'm prettier than you are."

Cora looked away.

Tess rolled her eyes and continued. "Be grateful that you are not. Most of us have several years to train to be a proper concubine." Tess shook her head. "I have never heard of His Lordship summoning a concubine on the day she arrives."

Cora pressed her lips together.

"This is what you will need to do." The volume of Tess's voice dropped so that only Cora could hear her; Abigail crossed her arms and sulked, yet she still looked on with mild interest. Cora's cheeks drained of color as she listened to Tess's instructions.

"Do you understand?" Tess pressed her.

"Yes." Cora turned away from her new friend with her head tilted toward the floor.

Tess grabbed Cora's arms, forcing Cora to face her. "Now you listen to me; you have one chance and one chance only to convince His Lordship that you are worthy of being part of his harem. I already told you what happens if you fail. Living in the Algerian Royal Palace is not so bad. Many consider living here a great honor. This harem is much like that of the Royal Palace in Constantinople. The women are given a good education. If you learn well and work hard, you can improve your place in the harem. Many women here go on to marry. If you are lucky enough to bear the Dey's son, and your son is chosen to take his father's place as the Dey of Algiers, you will rise superior to even the Queen. So, you can view your new situation as a curse or an opportunity. How far you go is up to you. Never forget that you can be replaced. His Lordship is a very fickle man. As Ula and many others discovered, one moment you are his favorite, and the next moment you are being taken to the slave market to be auctioned off to the highest bidder. His Lordship acquires new concubines every day."

A loud knock on the door thundered throughout the primary living quarters. Every person in the great room looked on with interest as Bashira strolled over to answer it. No one made a sound as they attempted to hear the whispers between the valide and the guards. Tess left her new friends to join a group of women standing nearby; Cora and Abigail nudging their way beside her. Bashira scanned the room with a grave expression on her face.

"Oh God," Tess mumbled.

"What's wrong?" Abigail whispered.

"His Lordship is selling one of us," Tess replied.

"How do you know that?" Cora asked.

"Because Bashira always gets that same look on her face when she delivers bad news, and the only bad news she ever delivers is when His Lordship orders one of us to be sold at market."

Other women, including Tess, ducked behind a cluster of women when Bashira approached the group where the three women stood. The valide turned slightly and approached a girl who looked like she was *around sixteen years old. She was a traditional Persian beauty with a sweet smile and doe eyes. When Bashira delivered the message to her, the girl's knees buckled, and she let out a loud cry. The valide embraced the girl and whispered something in her ear, but nothing could console her. The overseer and a woman standing beside the girl escorted her to the exit and delivered her to the guards. A quiet hum of whispers replaced the silence. Every woman in the chamber looked unnerved. Even Ula looked pale.*

Tess glanced over at Cora. "That girl spent almost two years preparing for her night with His Lordship. She was so proud when she received word that she had been selected to spend the night with him. That blackheart threw her away like an old shirt after spending one night with her. Poor lass; I liked her too. Don't think for a moment that His Lordship won't do the same thing to you."

Cora's legs weakened as she came crashing onto the floor. Tess took a seat beside her.

Moments later, a little girl ran up to Tess. She couldn't have been more than four years old. "Mama!"

"Where the devil have you been?" Tess snapped.

"I was playing with my friends," the little girl whimpered.

"Very well." Tess sighed. "This is me daughter, Molly."

"Hello, Molly," Cora said.

Abigail greeted her with a curt nod.

Molly rubbed her eyes. "I'm tired."

"Then take a nap."

Tears filled Molly's eyes; she looked up at her mother with quivering lips.

Tess took a deep breath. "Come here," she softened as she hoisted the little girl onto her lap. Molly nuzzled against her mother and buried her face in her mother's chest. "She's a wee bit shy." Tess rocked her daughter and combed her hair with her fingers until Molly was asleep.

Abigail studied the little girl's face. Though she had light skin, she didn't look like her mother; she didn't look like Naa'il either. Giving in to her curiosity, she inquired, "Who is Molly's father?"

Tess's lips curled into a dreamy smile. "Oh him. He is a scalawag that I met in the Palace."

"Go on." Abigail nudged Tess's shoulder with her own.

"Well …" Tess sighed. "I met her father shortly after I arrived at the Palace. He was the first man who I was … you know. Nathan was a prisoner like I was, except His Lordship treated him like an honored guest. I was sent to entertain him."

"Where is he from?" Abigail asked.

"He's an Englishman, and now he's a bloody corsair," Tess volunteered.

"Wait. An Englishman is a corsair? I thought the corsairs were Ottoman," Cora challenged.

"Most of them are. There are a few exceptions. Nathan was a legendary English captain, who turned pirate. He goes by a different name. He told me once," Tess frowned. "He said his name was …." She sighed, "Oh, I forget."

"Do you see him very often?" Cora asked.

"Aye, I see him whenever he comes to stay at the Palace. We always have the grandest time together." Tess paused. "Although, I haven't seen him in a long while."

"Why doesn't he take you and Molly away?" Abigail asked.

"Because he's an important man. He promised to take Molly and me to England one day," Tess said, hugging her daughter. "Then we will start a new life together."

"May I ask how you came here?" Abigail asked.

"Oh, that." Tess sighed. "I was born and raised in Ireland. I met a man who promised to take me to an exotic land. He brought me here. It's not the life I thought I'd have, but it's better than the one I left. I suppose I would never have met Nathan had I not come here."

"You have a beautiful little girl to watch over," Abigail pointed out.

"Aye, I do," Tess said with a rueful smile.

Cora stole away to the only empty corner in the room. She clutched her waist and looked sick to her stomach.

Abigail followed Cora and sat down beside her. "Are you afraid about tonight?"

Cora couldn't answer.

"I wouldn't worry too much. You will let Naa'il have his way with you, and then he'll dismiss you. I think tonight will be a blessing in disguise."

Cora glared at her cousin. "And how do you figure that?"

"I think we both know that you will not please the Dey; he will not fall in love with you, nor will he marry you."

"Can you please leave me in peace? I don't want to talk about this right now," Cora snapped.

"I don't want you to have the same illusions that you had with Jordan Donnelly."

Cora's lips parted. "What does Mr. Donnelly have to do with tonight?"

"You've always had a bad habit of reaching for the things you don't deserve," Abigail countered in an angry whisper. "Jordan Donnelly is the son of the wealthiest landowner in the state. You could never be more than a servant in his world, yet you made a fool of yourself when you threw yourself at him. Naturally, he rejected you. The same thing happened with Stephen MacDonald. At least he was closer to your station."

Cora grimaced at the mention of Stephen's name. "First of all, I did not pursue Mr. Donnelly; he pursued me. I was never in love with him." Cora's voice trailed off. "As for tonight, I do not wish to discuss it. Please leave me alone."

"Fine." Abigail got up hastily. "Do not expect a marriage proposal from Lord Dhar."

Later that evening, Abigail stood off to the side, watching a group of servants dressing Cora for her night with Naa'il. Cora looked unusually stiff as the servants slid a green silk vest onto her shoulders.

"Cora looks nervous," Tess observed, balancing Molly on her hips.

Abigail smirked. "Don't let my cousin's innocent demeanor deceive you. Cora had at least five lovers since she came to live with my family. Each one cast her aside once they discovered what she truly is."

"That's a wee bit harsh," Tess said.

"Forgive me; I know my cousin better than you do."

"Well, we can't all be as perfect as you. Let me know if you need any

pointers for pleasing His Lordship. You'll need it."

"I think I know how to capture a man's heart," Abigail said with an air of confidence.

"If you say so." Tess turned on her heels and walked away.

Abigail spotted Ula and Rana whispering in the corner of the room while watching Cora prepare for her night. They ducked into the chamber pot room.

"The guards are here for you," Bashira announced.

Cora answered with a nervous nod.

Ula and Rana appeared a few minutes later. Rana held a chamber pot; both had a mischievous gleam in their eyes. Abigail and the rest of Cora's observers covered their noses to offset the stench coming from the pot. The only person who didn't seem to notice was Cora. Bashira escorted Cora to the door; the rest of the residents in the room followed behind them. Abigail kept back, watching as Ula and Rana closed their distance to Cora. Abigail grimaced as she watched Ula slip her hand into the pot.

"Cora," Ula called out. "I wish you success tonight," she said in a falsely bright tone. As she hugged Cora, she wiped the brown waste on Cora's back.

The women who were close enough to see what happened cackled at Cora's horror. Even Abigail shared their amusement.

Cora attempted to return to the bathing room, but Bashira blocked her path. "You must leave," the valide barked.

"Can't I wash this off?" Cora pleaded.

"No, you must not keep His Excellency waiting." Bashira pushed Cora out the door. Everyone in the room laughed at Cora's predicament, except Bashira. With fury in her eyes, she slapped Ula. "That is for your insolence."

"It was a harmless joke," Ula said innocently.

"Do not let her wash her hands," Bashira said to the guards.

"What if His Excellency sends for me?"

Bashira pursed her lips and said to the servants, "Get her ready in case she is needed."

"Thank you." Ula bowed with a triumphant grin.

Ula's prediction was right; Naa'il sent for her just as she finished getting ready. Cora didn't return to the harem.

Exhausted from her day, Abigail headed towards her designated corner to look for space to sleep. One of the first lessons newcomers learn is that there are few comfortable places to sleep. If you wanted to sleep on a pillow, you would have to claim your spot early. Abigail silently noted that there was only one vacant space left. Rana was already several steps ahead of her. Abigail's casual stride turned into a sprint across the room. Her blue eyes locked on her target; she exclaimed, "This space is mine!" as she knocked Rana off her feet.

Rana jumped up and tackled Abigail. The two women rolled around on the floor in a battle of clawing, kicking, hair pulling, and screeching while on-lookers cheered them on. Guards latched onto each of their waists and pulled them apart. Neither of them got to sleep on a comfortable pillow that night. Instead, Bashira made them sleep on the floor of the chamber pot room under guard.

"You are meeting with the Dey this morning," Bashira announced to Abigail the following morning. "These girls will prepare you."

The dark room and the lighted lanterns hinted that it was still early. For Abigail, her first night in the harem felt like a lifetime. Abigail nodded to the matron as she struggled to stand. Every muscle in her body ached. Moving was all the more painful. Finally, the servant girls had to pull her to her feet.

Abigail glanced across the room at Rana who stared back at her with a dark look on her face. Rana didn't dare move while a guard stood over her. Abigail welcomed a steam bath, a massage, and a warm bath. By the time the servants covered her in Jasmine oil, most of the kinks in her body had relaxed. A few women in the main room stirred as Bashira led Abigail to the exit.

A guard escorted Abigail past the room where she met Naa'il the previous day. She gasped when she spotted several bare-legged men staggering out a room behind her. They paused just long enough to put their legs through the trouser legs before running away as though they were fleeing a crime.

Abigail pointed to the room from which the man fled. "What is happening in there?"

Instead of replying, the guard led her in the opposite direction to a room at the end of the corridor. He handed her a lantern before ushering her into the chamber and locking the door behind her. Despite her exhaustion and the presence of an oversized pillow, Abigail paced the floor because she was too nervous to sleep. Sunlight was just starting to filter into the room when she heard a key turning the lock. Her heart racing, Abigail formed the most confident smile she could muster.

"Good morning," Naa'il frowned. He held up his lantern and studied her face. "What happened to you?"

Tears flooded her eyes. "I was attacked last night."

Naa'il's brow furrowed in anger. "What happened?"

Wiping the tears from the corner of her eye, Abigail explained, "I was trying to lie down for the night, and this woman attacked me without warning. It was horrible. I have never been attacked before."

Naa'il twisted her head from side to side. "Who attacked you?" he demanded without taking his eyes off the bruise on her face.

"I believe her name was Rana. Please, I do not want to get anyone in trouble. I promise you; my injuries are not as bad as they look," Abigail said with a brave smile.

Naa'il pursed his lips. "You are not hurt otherwise?"

"I assure you; I am well," Abigail insisted.

"Rest for now; I will take care of this matter."

Abigail's stomach made a loud gurgle. "Forgive my stomach, Your Excellency." She blushed.

"When was the last time you ate?"

"I think it was yesterday evening."

"I will have some food brought to you. Rest until then." Naa'il turned towards the door.

"Your Excellency, thank you for your kindness. I don't know what I would do if you hadn't come to my rescue. You are truly a noble man."

Naa'il's hand slid off the doorknob as he turned and faced her. "You are most welcome." He returned to her and gently kissed her lips. "Rest; I will visit you later."

"Thank you."

Later that afternoon, guards escorted Abigail back to the harem. Rested and well-fed, she felt as if her situation was improving. Her buoy of hope sank when she realized that she had earned the contempt of every woman in the harem. Each one looked as if they wanted to attack her, yet all but one kept their distance.

Handing her daughter to another mother, Tess approached Abigail with the same contempt as the others. "You've got a bloody cheek coming back here," she said.

"I can't help that His Excellency favors me."

"I'm not talking about that. His Lordship's guards came for Rana this morning. She's to be sold at market. Apparently, His Lordship decided to sell her after her fight with you."

"He asked me what happened, and I told him. It's not my fault he chose to sell her," Abigail said defensively.

"I supposed you didn't tell him that you started the fight."

Abigail grimaced. "I asked His Excellency not to punish Rana. I wouldn't have said anything if I knew how he intended to punish her."

"If you say so. You must understand that whatever happens in here never leaves this room. Not keeping a tight rein on your tongue will only earn you enemies here. Never forget, you may be His Lordship's favorite now, but your circumstance can change without warning. Then you will live at our mercy."

"I don't wish to make enemies. I'm new here. I don't understand this place. Please, don't abandon me; you're the only friend I have," Abigail pleaded in a sweet and pitiful voice.

"Speaking of allies, have you heard any news about Cora?" Tess asked.

Abigail's lips parted. "She hasn't returned?"

"No. We usually hear something; I find it strange that there is no news of her whatsoever."

As Abigail sank into the pool of water, she rested her head against the edge and closed her eyes as she pondered Cora's fate. Though she lost track of the days of her captivity, Abigail at least knew that several weeks had passed. There was still no news of her cousin. The women in the harem speculated that Cora was either dead or had been sold. Abigail couldn't bring herself to risk her good standing to find out what happened to her cousin.

Tess slid into the water beside Abigail. "I understand that you have a new apartment."

"Yes," she replied, not wanting to volunteer any more information. "Tess, I did not ask Naa'il to place me in an apartment. You have to believe me."

"So it's Naa'il now," Tess said with a hint of sarcasm.

"He has been very kind to me." Abigail's voice trailed off.

"But it is not perfect."

Abigail shook her head. "He treats me like a little girl. The only thing he hasn't done yet is pat the top of my head."

"Would you rather His Lordship treat you like a whore?"

Abigail lowered her gaze to the water and shook her head again before looking back at her friend. "I love him so much. I just wish I knew how he felt about me."

The muscles in Tess's face tightened. "Perhaps you should give His Lordship some encouragement. Men are witless oafs when it comes to love. It could be as plain as the sun on their face, yet they are blind to a woman's feelings towards them. Sometimes you need to take matters into your own hands."

Abigail's hand clutched her belly. "Then you think he loves me?"

"I can't say for certain because I have never seen him with you. The fact that he visits you every day and does not treat you like a whore should be encouraging. You have an apartment now. That alone should tell you that he cares for you. I wouldn't be surprised if he were considering adding you to his family."

Abigail cupped her mouth with her hand. With a twinkle in her eyes, she asked, "Do you think so?"

"My God, you're as blind as His Lordship." Tess rolled her eyes.

Abigail hugged her friend with a beaming smile. She left the harem still grinning and her heart beating with excitement. All she could think about was getting married in a chapel and becoming a queen. Her life was going to be perfect, Abigail thought. Her smile turned to a grimace when her limp reminded her that she wasn't as perfect as she should be.

A Maiden's Honor

Chapter 7

Hassan returned to his cabin just as the sun began to set after a long and busy day. He was about to open the door when he heard muffled voices coming from inside his cabin. Hassan shot a quizzical glance to his guards standing by the door.

"Doctor Hyatt has been with Miss Campbell for almost an hour, sir," Tristan reported.

Hassan frowned and answered with a silent "Ah," while wondering how Peter slipped into his cabin without his notice. He entered his quarters without saying anything further to his guards. Sarah and Peter were seated at the table with a plate of untouched food in front of each of them.

Hassan looked disapprovingly at Peter for his unannounced visit. "Good evening."

"Good evening, Captain," Peter replied.

"Good evening, Cattin," Sarah said with admiring eyes.

"Sarah was telling me about her journey from her island," the doctor explained.

Hassan raised his brows. "In English?"

"No, we converse in Polynesian. You may recall that I speak this language fluently."

"Yes, you told me – several times." Hassan glared at his friend.

Peter stood up and brushed past Hassan like a servant who had been rudely dismissed. Sarah looked on as though she was unaware of the silent confrontation taking place between the two friends.

Hassan followed Peter to the door. "What are you doing in here?" he whispered.

"I thought I could assist you with ascertaining details about her life," Peter said defensively.

"Very well." Hassan sighed. "What did you learn?"

"Sarah told me that you are her husband. She's also quite smitten with you," Peter said with an undertone of sarcasm.

"And you disapprove because you want the girl for yourself."

"God no. If she were mine, I would do to her what we do to rats."

"You would drown her? I find that hard to believe."

"You don't know the South Seas women as I do," Peter said bitterly. "Have a pleasant evening, Captain."

"Good night, Doctor." Hassan opened the door and motioned to Peter to leave. *A wife from the South Seas.* The only thing that Sarah was missing was a mermaid's shimmering tail. Like most sailors, Hassan spent many nights fantasizing about the pleasures these exotic women offered their guests. Never did he imagine that his dream would become a reality. Hassan returned to the table and sat down beside her. "How was your day?"

"It … was good," Sarah replied, hesitantly. "I say right?"

"Yes." Hassan chuckled at Sarah's insecurity over her ability to converse in English. He could almost hear his mother, the ultimate grammarian, mercilessly correcting Sarah for every tiny mistake, just as she had done to him when he was a boy. He was grateful that she could communicate with him – even in a small way. "Do you have all that you require?"

"Aye. Do you? I help?"

"Thank you, but I do not need anything at the moment." Hassan and Sarah studied each other as an awkward silence grew. Each was curious about the other, but neither knew what to say next. Hassan couldn't help thinking about the South Seas maiden's reputation. Legends described the Polynesian women as eager whores, but Sarah was unlike any whore he had ever met. Giving in to his curiosity, he leaned over and pressed a kiss to her lips. Hassan expected her to answer with wanton enthusiasm; Sarah trembled uncontrollably instead. "Come here," he said in a sensual whisper. He held out his hand and pulled Sarah onto his lap. She was still trembling when Hassan wrapped his arm around her waist while caressing her cheek with his free hand. His inner voice screamed that he should treat Sarah like a lady, yet he couldn't let go of her.

With her eyes focused on her lap, Sarah lifted her gown to her knees.

Hassan's conscience screamed even louder. Finally, he yielded to his inner voice and lowered her dress. "We should not continue at this time."

Sarah looked Hassan in the eyes. "Why?"

Hassan caressed her cheek, "Well, our dinner will be here shortly. More importantly, I would like to get to know you better. You see in my country, a man and woman go through a courting period before they are joined as husband and wife."

"What courting?"

Hassan paused as he stared at the overhead. He looked back at Sarah and explained, "Courting is a period when a man and a woman get to know one another before they wed."

Sarah's eyes widened. "What you do?"

"Well, we attend balls together; we take long walks. Mostly, we compare the sizes of our fortunes, our family's influences, and our family's connections to ascertain if the match is advantageous."

Sarah stared at her lap. She looked back at Hassan and asked, "Why you marry me if you not want me? We not be married if you not wish." She dropped her gaze to her lap again.

Hassan swiveled her face towards his. "I agreed to marry you because I am fond of you, Miss Campbell. You showed great courage yesterday. I want to know you better."

"Cattin, why you say me 'Miss Campbell'?"

"That is the proper way to address you. We do not address people in the familiar until we know each other well," Hassan explained. "In our case, it is not appropriate for me to address you as 'Sarah' until we are married."

"We married," Sarah pointed out.

"I suppose we are," Hassan laughed.

A knock on the door prompted Hassan to lift Sarah from his lap. "Dinner," he said.

Three men wearing gray tunics and Ottoman trousers entered. All nodded to Hassan and looked hungrily at Sarah until they met their captain's disapproving glare. Without a word, Hassan's servants removed the plates from lunch and arranged two sets of white china plates and silver wine glasses. They left again and returned carrying trays of food.

"Thank you, gentlemen," Hassan said once the servants had finished setting the table. Sarah waited for his invitation to join him.

"Are you hungry?"

Sarah replied with a nod.

"Good, let's eat." Hassan extended his hand to his bride, who took it and sat down in her usual chair.

Hassan unfolded a gray napkin and laid it across her lap. It didn't surprise him that she reached for an orange. This time she peeled it herself.

Once Sarah finished the orange, she turned her attention to her fish. She peeled back the skin and picked up a piece of the fish before placing it in her mouth. Sarah picked off another piece, lifted the meat to her lips and froze when she noticed Hassan watching her.

"I suppose you don't have silverware on your island," Hassan teased. Sarah looked as though she were afraid to move. "You need not be embarrassed, little one. I recognize that you do things differently than I do. Let me show you how we eat fish in my country." He stood directly behind her. "First, wipe your hands and face with the napkin in your lap."

Sarah did so. She glanced up at Hassan and back down at her plate.

"As I explained this morning, we eat most of our meals with either a fork, a knife or a spoon. You will need a fork and a knife to eat your fish. This is a fork." Hassan picked up the fork and placed it in Sarah's left hand with the prongs facing downward. "This is a knife. Be careful; this edge is sharp." He pointed to the knife's sharp edge. "You will use a knife to either cut away the fish's skin or cut the meat into smaller pieces." He covered her hands with his and showed her how to slice off pieces of fish with her knife while holding the meat securely with her fork. "Now the fish is ready to eat," he said as he shifted the fork to her right hand with the prongs facing upward. "Would you like to try on your own? I know I shouldn't need to tell you this, but be careful to avoid the bones." Hassan returned to his chair.

Sarah followed Hassan's instructions, however, using the fork was clearly awkward for her. He was grateful that she was at least willing to try. She only ate a few bites more before turning her attention to the other food.

Hassan spent the rest of the meal teaching Sarah about the foods on the table. Never had he enjoyed a meal more than watching her discover each new delicacy. She approached them with a childlike wonder. Sarah enjoyed the dried figs, but her face puckered when she tasted the French wine, which Hassan gladly finished for her; she drank water instead. For a person who preferred to eat her meal with her hands, Sarah ate with the grace of a lady.

"You are adorable." Hassan filled an empty bowl with water and placed it in front of her. "Use this to clean your fingers."

Sarah dunked her fingers into the water and dried them on a cloth that Hassan provided.

After dinner, Hassan decided not to call his servants to clean up the remains of their dinner because he didn't want to give them another opportunity to ogle at Sarah. Instead, he stacked the dishes and most of the food. Hassan decided to leave the bowl of oranges in case they wanted something to eat later that night. After cracking the door open, he passed the various dishes to the startled guards standing watch.

"May we assist you, Captain?" Luke asked, looking past Hassan.

"I appreciate your offer, but I can manage tonight. I could use an oil lamp, though."

"I'll get one straight away, sir." Luke left his post and returned carrying two glass oil lamps. "Here you are, sir."

"Thank you." Hassan took the lamps from his guard. Just as he was about to close the door, he spotted his quartermaster approaching him.

"I apologize for interrupting you, Captain. May I have a word with you, sir?" his officer asked.

Hassan glanced back at Sarah, who was still sitting at the table. "One moment." He closed the door with his foot. "I need to leave you," Hassan said, hanging the lamps from hooks attached to the overhead. "I promise that I won't be long."

"Aye, Cattin," Sarah shyly replied.

Hassan returned to his quarters a half an hour later with a perfect sunset unfolding outside his window. Streaks of fuchsia danced across the water as the orb slowly sank into the horizon. Sarah was oblivious to the setting sun, even though she was sitting beside the window. Instead, she sat naked with her feet tucked under her. Her discarded garment lay folded on the floor beside her. She had emptied the oranges from the bowl and neatly stacked them on the table. The china bowl sat beside her, filled with water, untouched. She just stared at the trunk in front of her with her hands resting on the latches.

Hassan felt a fire in his belly and quickly tore his eyes from the soft curves of Sarah's waist. He forced himself to focus on her tousled hair hanging loosely down her back before retrieving a silver brush from one of his plunders. "I thought you could use this." Hassan knelt beside her, restricting his gaze to her eyes. He could tell by Sarah's tentative movements that she was uncertain about the evening ahead of her. He couldn't tell if she was feeling sadness or fear.

Sarah smiled politely and said something in her language before taking the brush from him. Instead of combing her hair, she traced the floral design engraved on the back of the brush.

"This is for your hair." Hassan took it from her and demonstrated how to use it before handing it back to her. Sarah patiently brushed out the tangles; Hassan couldn't take his eyes off her. "No, you keep it," he insisted when Sarah attempted to hand the brush back to him.

Sarah laid her gift on the floor beside her before returning her attention to her trunk. Once again, she reverently rested her hands on the latches.

"Do you miss your home and your father?" he asked.

"Aye," Sarah quietly admitted. There was unmistakable sadness in her voice.

"Why don't we open your trunk together?" Hassan placed his hands over hers as they lifted her trunk's domed lid. The inside smelled of flowers and coconuts. It didn't surprise him to discover a chest filled with worthless treasures. Sarah removed a straw mat, a sponge, a flat shell, a triangular tooth, and a shiny stick. He picked up the stick and discovered that the inside was hollow. Sharp-narrow spears were cut on one end of the tube, and the other half, he reasoned, was used as a handle. Giving into his curiosity, he asked, "What is this?"

"I show." Sarah took the primitive tool from Hassan and ran the spears through her hair.

"That's very clever." Hassan marveled at the Polynesians' ingenuity. He picked up the tooth. It was gray and took up nearly a third of his palm. "What is this?"

"It fish." Sarah pointed to her teeth. "It sha … sharp?"

Hassan rubbed his thumb across the serrated edge. "I noticed. What purpose does this have?"

"I show." Sarah took the shark tooth from Hassan and bent a lock of her hair over her finger. She slipped the tooth's sharp edge through the loop and pressed it against the inner edge.

"Don't you dare," Hassan gasped when she began slicing through her hair.

Sarah released the lock and looked at him with wide eyes. "What I do wrong?"

Hassan's cheeks warmed unexpectedly. "I don't want you to cut your hair for me. It is lovely the way it is." He knew that it was not his place to dictate how she wore her hair, but he hated the thought of her shortening it just the same.

"Aye? You like?"

"Very much."

Sarah bit her lip. "Umm women, hair ... wear here." She placed her hand on her shoulder to indicate that the women wore their hair cut to their shoulders.

"Why did you not cut your hair to that length?" he asked with a mild curiosity.

"Da not like."

"Your father preferred that you wear your hair waist-length."

"Aye."

Hassan surmised that her father had other reasons for keeping his daughter's hair long. Sarah's hair was thick, and it provided a natural cover for her chest. He was sure her father's requests to keep her hair long was a subtle way of enforcing his daughter's modesty. Hassan leaned in and whispered, "Your father was right; your hair is perfect the way it is. I would not change a single hair on your head."

Sarah blushed. She rummaged through her trunk and pulled out a thick parcel wrapped in stiff paper. She peeled back the edges.

Hassan's eyes widened when he discovered the images drawn on paper identical to the cloth that wrapped the bundle. To his amazement, they weren't primitive images, but complex black and white drawings that were worthy of hanging in a fine art gallery.

Sarah picked up the first picture in the stack and handed it to Hassan. "My friend, Temoe. She ... beautiful, aye?"

Hassan frowned as he studied her drawing. If he had to guess, her friend looked as if she were Sarah's age, perhaps a little older. She wore her hair cut to her shoulders with flowers tucked behind her ears, just as Sarah described, but she was not the Aphrodite goddess from his fantasies. Her flat nose and angular jaw gave her a slightly masculine quality. Dressed only in a cloth tied around her waist, her full breasts provided the only proof that she was a woman.

"She beautiful, aye?"

"Well, um." Hassan didn't know how to answer her. "Do all the women on your island look like this?"

"Aye. You not like?"

"I am certain that your friend is lovely. Honestly, it's hard to ascertain her beauty from this portrait."

"Temoe have … um … many sweetheart."

"I see." Hassan grinned as he studied the expression on her face. "I imagine you had many sweethearts of your own."

Sarah looked down at her lap as her trembling hand fidgeted with a lock of her hair. "No. I not beautiful."

Hassan lifted his brow. "You must be joking."

"No, my." Sarah pointed to her nose.

"Nose," Hassan offered.

"Nose. It not like Temoe nose."

"What do you mean?

Sarah pointed to her friend's nose. "Beautiful women have nose like Temoe."

"Do you mean that men esteem women who have flat noses?"

"What esteem?"

"Um." Hassan thought for a moment. "In other words, your people consider flat noses as a sign of beauty."

"Aye."

Hassan wished he had a mirror to show Sarah just how exquisite she truly was. Then again, he wondered if it would make a difference considering that she measured beauty by the Polynesians' standards. In this part of the world, Sarah would be regarded as the rarest of all beauties, for he had never seen her equal. Hassan caressed her cheek with the back of his finger and said, "I cannot speak for your countrymen, but I can speak for mine. They will esteem you as a lovely young woman."

"Aye?" She looked at Hassan as if this was the first time someone had told her that she was beautiful.

"Yes," he whispered. Hassan glanced back at her sketches and asked,

"May I see your other drawings?"

"Aye," she said, handing the stack to him.

He silently studied the sketches of people bathing in a pool with a waterfall spilling into the pool in the background, a warrior holding a tall spear, island landscapes, and an exquisite portrait of her father portraying his rustic demeanor. Unlike the warriors in her drawings, who didn't seem to have a single hair on their chest or face, her father sported a carpet of hair on his chest and a thick beard on his face. What stood out to Hassan was an unmistakable tenderness in his eyes.

"Did you draw these?" he asked without taking his eyes off her father's portrait.

"Aye," Sarah shyly replied as she stared at the images. Looking up at him, she asked in a hesitant voice. "You like?"

"They are extraordinary, Sarah," Hassan said just as she looked away. "Did your father teach you how to draw?"

"Aye." Sarah took the stack from him and flipped through each one until she came to a drawing of her. She explained in broken English that her father had drawn this portrait a few days before the French ship arrived. It had been a perfect day. While the people in her village gathered at the pond for their midday bathing, she and her father slipped away to a different part of the pool.

Hassan's breath hitched as he studied her portrait. Sarah sat on a log beside the pond with a waterfall spilling into the water in the background; the flowers in the foreground seemed abundant. His imagination filled in the scents and the colors that the black and white sketch denied him. It wasn't hard to imagine that her island was a paradise. Sarah wore a cloth tied around her waist. Her hair, adorned with a crown of flowers, hung loosely over her chest. Her lips wore a playful smile. Above all, Sarah looked like a girl who didn't have a single care.

"You like?" Sarah asked after a few awkward moments of silence.

"It's exquisite," Hassan whispered without taking his eyes off her portrait. He didn't want to give it back to her. If he had his way, he would display it so that he could look at it often. Being a man of honor, he handed the portrait back to her.

"You keep," she insisted.

"I couldn't possibly, Sarah. This belongs to you."

"You keep," she said, pushing his hand away.

"Thank you. I shall treasure it, always." Hassan studied her. "Tell me more about your people."

Sarah used her illustrations to teach Hassan about her people. Cleanliness was an important part of her culture. Everyone in her village, including men, women, and children, gathered at a fresh-water pool to bathe three times a day throughout the year.

That was a stark contrast to his people, who ironically, were regarded as the epitome of "Polite Society". Englishmen, including women, bathed privately once a month if that. Their hands, necks, and arms were the only parts of their bodies that his countrymen washed with regularity. Hassan was no exception. Although, he and his crew took full advantage of the Turkish baths whenever they were in the city of Algiers. In their defense, fresh water in England was not as abundant as it was on Sarah's island, and it was often too cold to stand in for longer than a minute. Everyone, including Hassan, hated using lye soap because it burned their skin. So far, no one had come up with a suitable alternative. Lastly, the water quality made bathing unsafe. Hassan knew a few people who died from ailments contracted from swimming in a lake. As a result, no one swam in England, and people only bathed when necessary.

Sarah told Hassan about her people's bathing ritual. Bathing was always a social time, a happy time for everyone. Sarah's melancholy voice and downturn lips made it abundantly clear that she missed her people.

Hassan wiped a tear from her cheek. "I'm curious," he said with a playful grin, "did you bathe today?"

"Aye." She held up two fingers.

"Indeed," Hassan said, wondering when she fit in her baths. He couldn't help wondering how bad he smelled to her. Not wanting an answer to his question, Hassan studied her with narrow eyes and picked up a flat shell. "What purpose does this have?"

Sarah's somber demeanor brightened. "I show," she said with enthusiasm.

"If you wish." Hassan chuckled.

Sarah reached for his arm and pinched a few hairs between her fingers. Placing the flat shell against his skin, she used the edge to slice off the hairs.

Hassan frowned as he wondered why she didn't cut off the hairs from her body.

Sarah answered his unspoken question by guiding his hand across her arm. "No hair. We say, hair here not clean."

"Ah," Hassan mumbled. The skin on her arms, her legs, and even her armpits were completely devoid of hair. Sarah had also sculpted her brows into perfect thin arches. The only other hair on her body was what covered her head.

Hassan tilted his head to the side and asked in a thoughtful way, "Does that mean you believe that I am unclean by wearing a beard?"

"No. You like Da. Da not take off hair."

"I see," Hassan traced the outline of her cheek with the back of his finger.

Sarah got quiet again, and her demeanor somber. Without saying another word, she twirled her hair into a bun. After dipping the sponge into the bowl of water, Sarah began washing her body as if she were alone.

Hassan moved to the table, hoping he was at a safe distance from her. He knew that he couldn't resist making love to her if he remained sitting beside her much longer, for he had never wanted any woman so badly. Everything about this creature fascinated him - her perfect figure, her graceful movements, but it was much more than that. Sarah was sensual, yet innocent, and Hassan found that combination irresistible.

It would be so easy to make love to her tonight, he mused. Sarah was willing. Moreover, she thought of him as her husband. Hassan shook his head in a futile attempt to dismiss the unbidden images filling his mind. Feeling his loins tighten, he jumped to his feet and fled his quarters.

Tristan and Luke stood at attention as Hassan rushed past them. The captain welcomed the salty breeze and the clear night sky that seemed to loosen the knots of tension gripping him. He once again reviewed the day's events. For some reason, his thoughts returned to Peter Hyatt.

Peter looked up from his book when he heard a knock on the door. "You're the last person I expected to see tonight."

Hassan entered the small room and took a seat at a square table before being invited. "My Christian upbringing got the best of me. It's wrong to consummate a marriage the day after her father's death, especially since Sarah and I aren't legally married."

Peter closed his book and looked at his friend intently.

"Sarah …" Hassan paused, "is not the person I expected. She is the embodiment of Eve before the fall. She has no consciousness of being naked. I keep expecting her to behave like the women described in the South Seas legends. But …."

"Ah, the legends. I am particularly fond of the ones about wanton-naked women who keep the sailors captive until they fulfill the maidens' desires. Then there is the British rendition of the Tahitian Love Fests, in which men and prostitutes run around like lust-addled animals, making love to one and all, a frightening spectacle if I do say so myself." Peter chuckled.

"The South Seas maidens aren't like the legends, are they?" Hassan asked with a thoughtful expression.

"Let's just say the sailors' tales are a bit exaggerated, but not entirely untrue. You must understand that the Polynesians do not share the same values as you or I. That is doubly true for the women."

Hassan knitted his brows together. "In what way?"

"Well, I already told you about the girls' training."

"Yes." Hassan shuddered.

"You must understand that women in this society are raised to give pleasure; moreover, it is a Polynesian custom for a man to offer unmarried women, including their daughters, to their houseguests."

"And the women agree?" Hassan asked with mild consternation.

"Yes, the women consider it their duty."

"My God." Hassan shook his head.

"Do not pity the women; they enjoy doing their duty."

"Is that why you spoke with disdain about Sarah just before you left my quarters this evening?" Hassan asked with dawning awareness.

"You must understand the person that you have taken for your wife. From my experience, South Seas maidens are incapable of being faithful to only one man," Peter said with a hint of disgust.

"Perhaps that's true about Polynesian women, but I find it difficult to believe that about Sarah. She's very innocent." Hassan sighed, in spite of the dread growing inside him. "What are your other observations?"

Peter stared at the table with a pained expression and was reluctant to continue.

"I know it pains you to speak of your experience in the South Seas, yet I feel compelled to ask, what happened to you?"

The doctor swallowed hard. "I was a guest of one of the villagers. They esteemed me because I had things of value to offer them. I lived with the village's leader and his family until they could build me a hut of my own," Peter explained.

"Did the village's leader offer a relation to you?" Hassan postulated.

"Yes, he offered me his niece, Tiari. I loved her from the moment I first saw her. Her presence was nothing less than intoxicating. Tiari knew how to please. I could have made love to her night and day – at least in the beginning." Peter stared at the flame in the lantern as though he had fallen into a trance.

A moment of awkward silence passed. Hassan was about to ask what had changed when Peter roused himself to continue.

"I learned a lot about their customs. I cannot deny that the people and their simple way of life are beautiful, but there are some traditions that I will never understand. Even though I knew that Tiari belonged to me for the length of my stay, I could not help feeling that we loved each other. I offered to marry Tiari. She refused without hesitation, informing me that she loved her freedom more than me. I discovered early in my stay that it was common for the unmarried people to frequently switch lovers.

Tiari enjoyed that way of life so much so that she took lovers whenever I was elsewhere. After a time, I noticed that she showed signs of being with child. I kept pressing her and her family for marriage, but they refused despite my offer to care for her and the child. Months later, Tiari bore me a son." Peter's voice cracked as he wiped a tear from his eye. His voice took on a harsher tone as he continued. "Then she smothered him. My son had not even lived an hour. Tiari showed no remorse, no sadness. Her only explanation was that she did not want the responsibility of raising a child." Peter looked into Hassan's eyes and added bitterly, "Tragically, smothering infant children is an age-old custom in their society. Tiari had already taken a new lover before I left."

Hassan stared at his friend in dismay for a moment before dropping his gaze to the table. His mind searched for the right words to say, but they altogether eluded him.

"Now you understand my contempt for Sarah and her South Seas *civilization*." Peter practically spat out the last word.

Hassan rested his elbow on the table and covered his eyes with his hand.

"I don't know what advice I can offer you about Sarah, other than to be careful. The South Seas people have a talent for stealing, and stealing hearts is no exception. Occasionally, they will return the items they take, but I can assure you that the maidens will always return your heart broken."

Hassan lowered his arm and looked at his friend. "Sarah may have been raised in the South Seas, but you saw how close she was to her father. Can you honestly believe that he had no influence over her life?"

"Are you certain that Sarah and her father were truly close? Her cheerful demeanor today strongly suggests that she cared nothing for him," Peter challenged.

"I think Sarah loved her father very much. She demonstrated that on the day he died by her refusal to leave his side. That night, she cried in my arms until she fell asleep. Even tonight, she was subdued after dinner. She even admitted that she missed him, and I believe her."

"Be that as it may, it still doesn't mean that Sarah will be a good wife to you," Peter insisted.

"I believe that Sarah is a virgin. Her father made a point of telling me that she is."

Peter chuckled. "I'll wager a bottle of port that she isn't. Her father may not have given Sarah to another, but that does not mean that she did not give herself to one or more without her seeking her father's permission first. Regarding her fidelity, you can easily test it by commanding her to give herself to either me or to another member of the crew."

Hassan's knuckles turned white as he gripped the arms of his chair. He took a deep breath and said, "I will consider your suggestion." He rose from the table and headed for the exit. "Thank you for telling me about your experience."

Peter nodded an acknowledgment. "Good night, Captain." He reached for the bottle of wine.

Although Hassan felt that he should return to his cabin, he stood by the railing on the quarterdeck for a long time staring at the moon's reflection dancing across the water. Peter's description of the Polynesian customs unnerved him. His friend was right; Sarah was a stranger, and it was too soon to ascertain her true character. All Hassan knew was that he was drawn to this exotic creature. He felt his self-control slipping away every time he was with her. Hassan yawned and decided that he was too tired to reach any conclusions tonight. "Is something wrong, gentlemen?" Hassan asked as he spotted the concern on Tristan's and Luke's faces as they guarded the door to his quarters.

"Well, Captain," Tristan started. "We heard Miss Campbell weeping after you left."

Luke continued, "Then her weeping stopped … and … well … er … we were concerned that she might have harmed herself …."

"Oh dear God!" Hassan rushed into his quarters before Luke could finish. Sarah sat up, startled when the door flew open. Hassan breathed a sigh of relief when he noted that she hadn't moved from her trunk. He was grateful that she had covered her waist with the blue cloth.

"Do you need our assistance, Captain?" Tristan asked.

Hassan glanced at Sarah, then at his guards and said, "Thank you, gentlemen. That will be all." After closing the door in their faces, he approached Sarah and squatted beside her, "I apologize for abandoning you tonight," he said softly. The thoughts of Peter's story began to fade after inhaling Sarah's delicate scent. "Shall we retire?"

Sarah nodded without meeting his eyes. Hassan stood and pulled her to her feet. She shyly took his hand and followed him to his berth. While Hassan folded down the covers, Sarah remained standing before him. Her gaze remained fixed on his chest as she untied her wrap.

Hassan's heart was beating so hard that he thought it would burst. They had only known each other for less than forty-eight hours. Sarah had already given him her love, and now she was prepared to give him her body. Hassan grabbed her hand before she could loosen the knot. "You don't have to give yourself to me tonight."

Sarah's gaze met his. "You husband," she said shyly.

Hassan's inner voice screamed at him to tell her the truth about their marriage, but all he could muster was, "We're still strangers."

"You not want me?"

He wanted to tell her that he had never wanted any woman as much as he wanted her, but he couldn't bring himself to reveal his true feelings. He just caressed her cheek and said. "It has been a long day. I can't speak for you, but I'm exhausted. Why don't we sleep tonight and figure out our future later." Tucking one arm around her waist and the other behind her knees, he effortlessly lowered her onto his berth. Hassan removed his shirt and his slippers and laid down beside her.

Nestled in the crook of his arm, Sarah placed her delicate hand on his chest and murmured something in her native language.

"Good night, little wife," Hassan whispered before closing his eyes.

Chapter 8

Naa'il took a different route to Abigail's apartment to avoid passing by Cora's quarters. He wished he didn't feel so conflicted about what to do with her. He desperately wanted to stop thinking about Cora so that he could focus entirely on Abigail. He quite liked her, Naa'il reminded himself. Abigail had all the qualities he desired in a wife, and there was nothing to prevent him from marrying her. His pursed lips curved into a subtle smile as he contemplated making Abigail his third wife. Then his footsteps slowed as his thoughts drifted back to the peace that Cora's prayers brought him. Suddenly, Naa'il visualized Cora's intoxicating lips and her figure's athletic curves, and he winced as his thoughts swirled darkly when the dilemma over Cora's fate commanded his attention again. Moments later he heard Abigail's melodic voice, and his heavy thoughts faded.

Quietly, he opened the door part way and peeked inside. Abigail was dancing with an invisible partner to the melody she hummed. Her feet light and agile, she moved with an elegance that he had not seen before. The tension on Naa'il's face relaxed; he entered the room and closed the door.

"Your Excellency!" Abigail said with a radiant smile as she ran into his arms.

Naa'il welcomed her into his embrace. He was relieved to see her cheerful face that showed no trace of her petulant attitude from the morning. He then realized what was different about her. She was moving freely with no indication of a limp. He stiffened slightly, and Abigail pulled away and looked into his eyes.

"I am so sorry for the way I behaved this morning. You have been so kind and generous. I acted like an ungrateful wretch. Can you forgive me?"

"Give it no more thought." Naa'il studied Abigail as a seed of doubt sprouted in his mind. "Did something else happen today?"

"Yes!" she said enthusiastically. "I discovered this afternoon that I no longer need to walk with a limp. The pain is gone! It's what we call a miracle." Abigail stepped back and twirled in front of him. "Isn't it wonderful?"

"How fortunate for you." Naa'il couldn't help wondering if Abigail could walk normally all along. "Cora told me why you walked with a limp."

Abigail turned away from the Dey and hugged herself. "Cora had no right bringing that wretched horse to our home." She looked back at Naa'il. "Father was justified to put it down."

"I see." Naa'il crossed his arms. "Why do you hate Cora?"

Abigail stared at the floor. "I don't hate her."

Naa'il pursed his lips again when he heard her haughty tone. "It is puzzling. You have never once asked about your cousin. Are you not even a little curious about what happened to her?"

"Of course, but I didn't think it would be polite to question you. I assumed that you sold Cora until you mentioned her this morning," Abigail answered quickly and smoothly.

Naa'il's jaw tensed as he circled Abigail. "I have not, but I am considering it. How would you feel if I sold her?"

Abigail peeked up at him from beneath her thick eyelashes and replied, "I would never presume to tell you what to do, Your Excellency. All I will say is that you must do what you feel is best. If Cora does not please you, then perhaps it is best that she live somewhere else."

"I see." A sickly feeling growing inside him made him wonder if Mamnoon was right about Abigail. "I will leave you now," Naa'il said, heading for the door.

"You don't need to leave, Your Excellency," Abigail cooed softly, yet with a hint of desperation in her voice.

Naa'il looked back in time to observe Abigail sliding her vest off her shoulders. Giving in to his curiosity, he turned around and inspected her with eyes sharpened by emotions he hadn't fully acknowledged. Though she lacked the curves of a woman, the loose curls of her pale hair grazing her firm breasts made Abigail Randall an irresistible sight. Naa'il moved in close enough to slide his arms around her waist. He covered her thin lips with his own, unsure whether he was doing so out of passion or anger. He quickly pulled away and stated with a frown, "You have been kissed before."

"A few times," Abigail blushed as she reached up to kiss him again.

"Are you certain you want to continue?" Naa'il coolly asked. Whatever affection he felt for Abigail was turning to loathing. Despite his increasing inner turmoil, Naa'il's body was keen to discover what Abigail had to offer.

"Show me how to please you," she entreated in a throaty whisper.

His eyes narrowing, Naa'il tore her trousers from her body and loosened his own. Abigail locked her legs around his waist as he abruptly lifted her and shoved her against the wall. He thrust inside her, finding none of the resistance he still half expected. Abigail cried out with joy, clearly eager for more. Prying her legs from his waist, Naa'il released her, causing her to fall to the floor as she was unable to unclasp her legs fast enough to catch herself. He stepped back, breathing heavily and staring at Abigail with a gaping jaw. He no longer saw a sweet innocent girl, but something quite ugly.

"What's wrong, My Lord?" Abigail exclaimed in a frightened tone as she picked herself up off the floor.

"Cora!" Naa'il gasped. Without sparing another look at Abigail, he quickly dressed and ran out of the room. From the other end of the hall came the sound of cheering men followed by Cora's screams. Mamnoon was already charging to her rescue. When he spotted his master, the bodyguard stopped and looked at him defiantly. "Go!" Naa'il shouted, picking up his pace. When he arrived, Mamnoon had already started throwing men out of the room. Naa'il was taken back by the number of men who had lined up to force themselves on Cora. He hadn't realized he had so many guards within the Palace wall. "Get out, all of you!" the Dey shouted, shoving his men towards the door as he forced his way to the front of the line. The cheering stopped abruptly at the sound of Naa'il's tenor voice. With frightened faces, the mob rushed out of the room. Her body bruised and bloodied, Cora lay on the floor with her arms and feet chained. Seeing the defeated look on her face and unable to cope with the sudden flood of guilt that beset him for his hand in Cora's torture, Naa'il sought refuge outside the room.

The Dey squatted by the door and buried his face in his hands, not caring who was around to witness him in despair. Naa'il knew what was happening to Cora, but it wasn't until this night that he understood her terror. He was close enough to the room to hear the clanking from Mamnoon removing her shackles.

"It is alright. I am here," Naa'il heard Mamnoon say in a soothing tone.

"You came," Cora mumbled.

"You should know by now that an army could not keep me away from you. Now permit me to clean you," Mamnoon said tenderly.

"Please," Cora pleaded.

Naa'il gasped when he heard Cora's plea. He turned to look inside the room and saw Mamnoon pressing his knife against her throat. "No!" Naa'il softly exclaimed though he made no attempt to save her. Part of him believed that she deserved the freedom death would bring, yet he breathed a sigh of relief when Mamnoon returned the knife to his belt.

"I cannot. I love you too much to part with you, but I promise, this is the last time you will be violated." Mamnoon's voice was choked with emotion.

Cora began to sob wretchedly. It continued for what seemed an eternity to the Dey. Each cry felt like acid burning Naa'il's heart while he remained frozen in place, unable to move either towards or away from Cora. Finally, Mamnoon left the room. Naa'il stood and asked, "How is she?"

"Cora is sleeping, Your Excellency," his servant said with a cold stare. "End this. Please, I beg you. Cora is strong, but I fear that she is not strong enough to survive another attack."

Naa'il nodded, feeling sudden respect for his servant's courage.

"Thank you." The bodyguard bowed his head.

"You rest; I will tend to Cora tonight," said Naa'il. "That is a command, Mamnoon."

His servant didn't move.

"I give you my word that no harm will come to Cora ever again," Naa'il vowed.

"Thank you, Your Excellency." Mamnoon bowed and backed away.

Entering Cora's room was painful. Though it looked like the other rooms in the Palace, Naa'il knew that after what he had witnessed tonight, this room would always feel like a torture chamber. He knelt beside Cora and combed her hair with his fingers. "Cora," he crooned.

Her eyelashes fluttered open revealing bloodshot eyes that struggled to focus. "Your ..." Cora said in a breathless whisper.

"Can you stand?" he asked, haunted by the memories of their first meeting and her torture resulting from his critical mistake.

"I ...."

"I will help you," Naa'il said tenderly. Taking hold of her hands, Naa'il stood and pulled Cora to her feet. She teetered towards him because she lacked the strength to stand on her own. Naa'il wrapped one arm around Cora's waist, tucked the other behind her knees, and carried her to his apartment. She didn't make another sound as he dressed her in a cream tunic and laid her in his bed. She was asleep again the moment her head touched the pillow. Naa'il surrendered to his own exhaustion and slipped into bed beside her.

Sarah woke to a dark room. Her husband had left her alone again. In all honesty, she couldn't blame him.

She swung her feet over the edge of the berth and climbed down. As quietly as she could manage, she peaked around the divider. The main room was mostly dark, save the flicker from a lantern sitting on a table. Hassan was also seated there with a brown bottle and a pewter mug in front of him. The flame's light bathed his face with its yellow hue as he stared at his cup, taking periodic sips from it.

"Cattin?" Sarah said hesitantly.

Hassan tilted the bottle and poured more liquid into his cup. He took another sip and looked over at Sarah. "You could not sleep?"

"I woke; you not with me."

"We must talk." Hassan used his foot to slide the chair out from the table. "Please join me."

Sarah couldn't move.

"Come here, Sarah. It's alright," he said in a softened tone.

It wasn't that she feared him so much as that she dreaded hearing what he had to say. His demeanor could only mean that he was going to tell her something that she didn't want to hear. Sarah forced herself to take one step and then another until she reached the table. Bracing her hands on the smooth surface, she lowered herself onto the chair.

"Cattin, I know I not good wife. I wish. Da no let me have wife…." The words tumbled out of her mouth only to stop abruptly as her mind frantically searched for the next word.

Hassan's brows knitted together. "What do you mean?"

"Girls … we learn ….," Sarah stared at the ochre beams above her for a moment. When she was unable to find the right words, she shook her head. "I not know how say." She smiled apologetically.

"I am surprised that your father didn't teach you to speak English."

"He try. I not want then. I listen, no speak," Sarah said with a frustrated sigh.

Hassan tilted his head to the side and looked thoughtfully at Sarah. "You thought that you would never leave your island."

"No," she said sadly.

"That's damn unfortunate." Hassan looked at her thoughtfully. "Dr. Hyatt informed me that your people teach girls how to make love when they are young. Is that the training to which you are referring?"

Sarah nodded, "Aye, I want. Da not want."

"You chose to obey your father," Hassan surmised.

Sarah looked down at her hands, embarrassed to admit her failing. "Aye."

Hassan chuckled. "You made a wise decision. In my country, it is the husband's duty to train his wife to be a proper lover. There is no greater offense than for a woman to lose her virginity before she is married."

Sarah felt the knot in her belly loosening as she began to grasp that Hassan was not upset by her ignorance. "What virginity?"

"A virgin is a person who has not made love before. People in my society believe that the only time that making love is appropriate is when two people are married to each other." Hassan's gaze dropped to his mug.

"You ... you virgin?"

"No, I am not. Not everyone follows the rules. Men can get away with such behavior; a woman cannot."

Sarah frowned. "You say husband teach wife. You not teach me."

"No, I did not. That is why I wanted to talk to you." Hassan shifted uncomfortably as he took another sip of his drink.

Sarah bit her lip. "You not want me."

Hassan shook his head. "That is not the reason. I understand that marriages on your island are formed by a simple agreement. Formalizing a marriage in my country is more complicated than on your island. Therefore, the laws in mine will not recognize our marriage. That is why we cannot behave as though we are."

Sarah struggled to understand Hassan's explanation. "We not married?" she clarified in a timid voice.

"No, we are not."

"You say we married," Sarah said, after recalling Hassan speaking of it even though she remembered little of the whirlwind from the last few days.

"Yes, I did. I was wrong to say so. I told your father that I agreed to our marriage to ease a dying man's concern for your future. He understood that it would take time for us to marry formally. When I realized that you believed that we already were, I felt it was inappropriate to correct you in your time of sorrow. However, I concluded last night that allowing you to believe a lie would only cause you additional pain. That is why I am being honest with you now. Please forgive me for any pain I have caused you."

"Cattin, what ..." Sarah's voice trailed off.

"You are concerned about your future."

"Aye." She frowned as she struggled to recall how her father died. He was dead – that was all she knew.

"Your father informed me before he died that he hoped to bring you to live with your family in Scotland. I intend to honor your father's wishes, providing we leave this god-forsaken place. Until I reunite you with your family, I am your guardian. Do you understand what 'guardian' means?"

Sarah shook her head.

"It means that I will watch over you. Do you understand now?"

"Aye," Sarah said with worry still on her brow. "You find me husband?"

"In my country, young men and women choose their own husbands and wives, with the approval of their parents of course. As your guardian, I will approve a match for you. You need not worry; I will provide for you, I promise."

Sarah stared at her bare thighs as she tried to imagine what Hassan's life was like at home. Then the unthinkable occurred to her. "Cattin?"

"Yes?"

"You have wife?"

"Not anymore. She died shortly after we were married."

Sarah sensed his reluctance to discuss his life with his wife, yet she wanted to know more. "You have no woman?"

"Only you," Hassan said. "Do you have any other questions for me?"

"Say about home?"

"Only if you will tell me more about your life on your island," Hassan said with a wink.

"Aye," Sarah grinned.

The ship's bell rang, and Hassan stood up. "We will have to talk about these matters later. I must start my day. Breakfast will be here soon. We should dress."

This morning Hassan dressed Sarah in a pair of brown Ottoman trousers that enveloped her petite body. He pulled the drawstring tight and tied a double bow to keep the trousers from falling.

"One moment," Hassan called out when he heard a knock on the door. Sarah mindlessly turned and headed for the door. "Come back here. You need to wear a shirt." Hassan grabbed her arm and yanked her back to him. "Hold your arms up." He lowered a tan peasant shirt over her head. The shirt fit about as well as her trousers. "I'm afraid this will have to do," said Hassan as he ripped the ends of each sleeve to make them shorter. He was about to rip the bottom of the shirt, but Sarah spared its ruin by rolling up the bottom and tying the ends around her waist.

"Better?" she asked as her eyes sought his approval.

"Much better," Hassan admitted.

After his crew had cleared their dirty breakfast dishes, Hassan turned his attention to concealing Sarah's hair. "Tie your hair up the same way you wore it when you bathed last night." Sarah bent over and twirled her hair into a bun on the top of her head; Hassan pulled out a long muslin cloth. Holding one end against the bun, he wrapped the thin cloth around her head and tucked the end under the mound. He frowned at his handiwork. "Well, this isn't perfect, but it is good enough I suppose. Sarah, you will need to wear this turban for as long as you are on the main deck. Do you understand?" Hassan glanced down at her bare feet. His frown deepened when he realized that he couldn't provide shoes for her little feet. "I regret that I do not have shoes for you."

"It not matter," she said. "We go?"

"Not quite, I must do a little work before we can leave." Hassan retrieved a book and a brown leather pouch from a secretary before sitting down at the table. He withdrew a wooden stick from the bag and began moving it across the blank page.

Sarah's lips parted with fascination. The stick left marks on the paper, yet his fingers remained clean.

Hassan's brow snapped together as he watched Sarah rubbing her finger over a word on his page and looked surprised when it didn't turn the tip black. "What is the matter?"

"It not come off," she said, showing him the tip of her finger. She got up from her chair and retrieved a picture of her friends bathing in the pond.   Sarah rubbed another finger over a tree in her drawing and showed him the black tip. "It come off."

"I'm curious. What did you use to draw your picture?"

"It wood, after fire."

"Hmm, charcoal. That is clever." Hassan held up his pencil. "This is a little different. It can also dirty your finger if you are not careful, but it will not come off as readily as your charcoal."

"Oh," Sarah muttered when her gaze fell on her friends. Seeing this picture still brought tears to her eyes. It was hard being reminded of all the things that she had lost, and the people she had left behind. With her future now uncertain, the pain only dug in deeper.

Hassan slid his chair out and retrieved another book and a handful of pencils from his desk. He returned to his seat and said, "I can see why you miss your island. Do not let your sadness blind you to the good that is present." Hassan handed her the items. "These are for you to record many happy memories to come."

Sarah took the book from him and opened the cover. She picked up one of the wooden sticks and drew a line at the top of the blank page. She couldn't believe how easy it was to draw. Sarah pressed the book against her chest and said, "Thank you!" in Polynesian. She was so pleased with the gift that she didn't realize what she said until Hassan asked, "Do you mean 'thank you'?"

"Aye." Sarah nodded.

"Say 'thank you' in English," Hassan encouraged her.

"Tank you, Cattin," Sarah repeated.

"You are welcome. Be warned that I expect many masterpieces from you," he teased.

Sarah nodded, even though she had no idea what a masterpiece was.

Once Hassan finished his business, they stepped onto the quarterdeck. Hassan asked a seaman to bring up a bench so that Sarah could pass the day observing and drawing while he carried out his duties. Hassan was more productive than she was that day. Captivated by the activity taking place on deck, Sarah was too distracted to draw more than a few lines on a single page. What intrigued her the most was watching the sailors adjusting the sails while balancing on a thin rope. She wanted to join them, yet she wondered if Hassan would allow her to learn how to tend the sails.

CHAPTER 9

An insistent knocking on his apartment door woke Naa'il from a deep sleep. He sat up sharply and glanced down at his guest. "Cora," he gasped when he spotted the beads of sweat on her forehead. She didn't stir. Naa'il jumped out of bed, covered himself in a maroon robe, and ran to the reception room. He opened the door and discovered Mamnoon standing in the hall with a distressed countenance.

"Your Excellency, Cora is missing!" the bodyguard announced breathlessly.

Naa'il held up a hand for silence and turned to the guard standing outside his apartment. "Send for a healer." He looked back at Mamnoon and explained, "I brought Cora to my chamber after you left." Naa'il swallowed hard. "I fear she is ill."

"Ill?" Mamnoon stared at his master in disbelief. "May I see her? Please?"

Naa'il wanted to say no. Instead, he opened his door and invited his servant to enter. The Dey's hands squeezed the edges of his robe as Mamnoon sat on the edge of the bed. He combed Cora's hair with his fingers while murmuring to her. "Please, do not give up - not now. You have endured so much, and the worst is over. You have too many happy years ahead of you."

Never before had Naa'il felt more uncomfortable in his bedchamber than as he watched Mamnoon tending to Cora the same way a loving husband might by holding her hand and wiping the perspiration from her forehead. When the healer arrived, it was clear that the only reason Mamnoon stepped aside was to allow the elderly woman to inspect her patient.

"Will she live?" Naa'il asked, clasping his hands together so tightly that his knuckles turned white as he helplessly looked on.

"I do not know, Your Excellency," the elderly healer replied.

"Can you explain her illness?" Naa'il pressed.

"She has a fever. I cannot tell you the cause. All I can say definitively is that she has been through a great ordeal. With rest, she may find her way back. I will stay as long as you wish."

"Thank you." Naa'il nodded in gratitude for her presence.

"What can I do, Your Excellency? Please, I will do anything," Mamnoon pleaded.

Relieved to have an excuse to remove Mamnoon from Cora's bedside, Naa'il said, "Escort Abigail Randall back to the harem. Explain to her that she will reside there from now on."

Mamnoon's face lit up. "May I ask why you changed your mind?"

Naa'il winced and escorted his servant into his reception room. "Your observations about the cousins were accurate. It is time to correct my error."

"You are a wise Dey." Mamnoon bowed his head. "I must advise you that Abigail is not welcome in the harem."

Naa'il let out a loud sigh. "Inform Bashira and the other women that Abigail is still under my protection," he said, feeling distaste for the words as he spoke them.

Mamnoon nodded. "Of course. I will convey your wishes, Your Excellency." His brow furrowed and he looked at his master thoughtfully. "Should I tell Abigail about Cora?"

"No, say nothing. I am still hopeful that Cora will find her way back to us," Naa'il answered.

"Very good, Your Excellency." Mamnoon bowed and left just as

Jamal arrived.

"Good morning, Your Excellency." Jamal bowed. "May I speak to you in private?"

"Enter," Naa'il said, tightening his sash.

"I apologize if I came too early. We can discuss this matter later," Jamal offered.

"No, I would rather talk now." Naa'il closed his bedchamber door as well as the door to his apartment. He held out his hand, inviting the Vizier to sit on the red couch.

The ends of Jamal's blue robe took flight behind him as he glided into the room.

Naa'il waited long enough for Jamal to take a seat before lowering himself onto a matching chair.

"Are you certain that you would not prefer me to return in an hour or two?"

"I would rather discuss this matter now," Naa'il said tersely.

"Did something happen last night? Is your family well?"

"State your business," Naa'il snapped.

"Very well," Jamal said, disconcerted by the Dey's enigmatic demeanor. "The British Ambassador contacted me yesterday. He said it is urgent that he speak to you."

"Yes, I know. I have read the letters from his government."

Jamal's brow furrowed. "What did they say?"

"Is it not obvious? The British are displeased that my corsairs are seizing their ships and selling their countrymen into slavery."

Jamal bit his lip. "Do you think they will seek retribution?"

"What can they do to us?" the Dey said sardonically. "They are already at war with the French and the Americans. They cannot afford another one. That is why they pay tribute money to our country."

"Perhaps you should meet with the Ambassador."

"No, I will not, but I will have John answer their correspondence. Please send him here after we finish our meeting."

"Of course, Your Excellency."

"I would also like you to oversee the slave yard today."

"I will be happy to assist you in any way I can." Jamal bowed his head.

Naa'il groaned in exasperation when he heard another knock on his apartment door. "Excuse me." He stood and went to answer.

Another advisor bowed to his master. "Forgive my intrusion, Your Excellency; there is a matter that requires your attention."

"Very well," Naa'il let out a loud sigh and stepped out of his apartment to keep the conversation private from Jamal. Naa'il was only out of the room for a few minutes, yet upon his return, he caught the Vizier closing the door to his bedchamber. "What are you doing?" Naa'il demanded, silently noting his advisor's flushed cheeks.

"I ... I was concerned that something was wrong with my sister."

"No, you were meddling in something that is not your concern. You will not speak of what you saw to anyone. Now leave my apartment," Naa'il shouted.

"Your Excellency." Jamal nodded and backed out of the room hurriedly.

Abigail had been unable to sleep. She spent the entire night tossing and turning. When she tired of laying in her bed, she rose and paced back and forth across the room. She glanced over at the door every few minutes, hoping Naa'il would return. He was so angry last night, and Abigail had no idea what she did wrong. Her disappointment turned to concern as the darkness gave way to the dawn's first light. A knock on her door set her heart racing - only, Naa'il never knocked. Abigail's heart sank, and tears filled her eyes when she discovered Mamnoon standing outside her door.

"What is it?" Abigail snapped.

"His Excellency asked me to escort you to the harem," Mamnoon said calmly.

Her breath catching, Abigail whimpered, "But Naa'il always comes for breakfast."

"His Excellency asked me to pass along the message that he will not come to you again. You will reside in the harem from this moment forth."

Mamnoon's sense of satisfaction with her situation was clear, in spite of Abigail's small world suddenly spiraling out of control. Her chest heaving with unchecked sobs, Abigail pleaded, "Can I talk to him, please?"

"No, His Excellency's word is final. Come with me now." Mamnoon's voice was unyielding and offered no sympathy.

She knew that he didn't care what happened to her. A new sudden fear gripped her. "Is he going to sell me?" she asked in a panicked voice.

"Not at this time. Come with me now."

Abigail knew there was nothing she could do but to follow him.

By the time they reached the harem, Abigail was shaking uncontrollably. Everyone in the room knew that her appointed bath time was in the afternoon and not the morning. Abigail could almost hear the whispers of speculation among the women, yet all but Tess kept their distance from her.

Her friend slid into the bath beside Abigail and asked, "Did something happen?"

Tears welled up again in her eyes, "Yes! I took your advice. I thought it was going well, but then Naa'il rejected me!" Abigail sobbed as she recounted the details of the evening. "He called out Cora's name as he made love to me. I think he loved her all along."

"I told you to encourage His Lordship, not seduce him."

"You advised me to take this matter into my own hands," Abigail said defensively.

"Encouraging and seducing are two different things," Tess retorted. "Did His Lordship take away your apartment?"

Abigail nodded, sniffling miserably. "What am I going to do?"

"There is nothing you can do. I told you when you first arrived that you would only have one chance to impress His Lordship. You've had your chance. Now your fate lies with him."

"His wretched guard said that Naa'il has no intention of selling me."

"That is something. The only other thing that could save you is if you are now carrying His Lordship's child." Tess sighed. "Be comforted. It appears that you are not going anywhere today."

Mariam passed several women carrying bloodied bandages from Samina's apartment. The second wife laid on her bare stomach waiting for the servant to deliver fresh water and bandages that arrived in the hands of another servant woman who followed on Mariam's heels. After directing the placement of the items on a table beside Samina's bed, Mariam waived her hand in the air. "Leave us."

The servants bowed to the first wife and scurried out of the room, closing the door behind them.

Samina turned her head and gave Mariam a murderous glare. "How dare you come here? I know you told Naa'il about my dancing in the harem."

"Yes, I did," Mariam confirmed, undaunted by the second wife's attack.

"How could you betray me that way?" Samina bitterly asked.

"Dancing with the harlots was inappropriate."

"It was innocent fun. Besides, I was in the harem."

"You are the Dey of Algiers' wife, not an odalisque!" Mariam shouted. "Your imprudent behavior damages our family's honor. Did it ever occur to you what would happen if people learned that you danced with whores? That would destroy Naa'il's honor. He would lose the respect of his advisors, not to mention the Sultan's. If I were you, I would be grateful that Naa'il only gave you fifteen lashes and not fifty."

Samina shuddered and then whimpered when a wave of pain

followed. "I will not do it again. Please leave me."

Mariam knelt beside her pillow bed. She dipped a clean muslin cloth in the water and rung out the excess before blotting Samina's bloodied back. "I know you think I do not like you, but I am not your enemy," she murmured.

Samina looked skeptically at the first wife. "Aren't you? I know you were bitterly against Naa'il marrying me."

"Yes, I was. I believed you were young and reckless. I was right, but I accepted our husband's decision. That does not make me your enemy."

"Doesn't it? We both compete for our husband's attention."

"Yes, that is true, but you are my sister-wife first. I do not need to tell you that our lives are difficult. One small mistake, however innocent, could result in our execution." Mariam shifted around until her back faced Samina. The first wife removed her lavender hirka and lifted her white gömlek to expose her back.

Samina gasped at the flogging scars crisscrossing each other. "What happened?"

Mariam lowered her gömlek and moved around until she faced Samina. "I was imprudent too when I was first married," said Mariam as she resumed cleaning Samina's wounds. "It does not matter what I did."

"How many lashes did you receive?"

"Forty. It took me weeks to recover. I reported your impertinence with the hope that you would learn from this punishment to avoid making a worse mistake."

Samina closed her eyes and sobbed, "I hate it here. I know I should be grateful that I am the Dey's wife, but I am so lonely. Naa'il forbade me from visiting my friends outside the Palace. I am not allowed to interact with the women in the harem. My son is dead. There is nothing to look forward to." Samina paused as she fought back her tears. "Sometimes I wish I were a lowly odalisque. At least I would not be so lonely."

"Do not say such things. Naa'il bestowed a great honor upon you by making you his wife. Do not be deceived; odalisques lead very hard lives. Few ever marry," Mariam said. "The lives of Ottoman women are difficult and painful. I wept each time I learned that I gave birth to a daughter. But this is the life to which we are born, Samina, and complaining about our lot will not help us. I will share the advice that my mother gave me. No one, not our husband, our father, or our children can take away our dignity. That belongs to us and us alone."

"What gives you the will to keep living?"

"I live for my children. Someday you will have your own to care for."

"Naa'il has not sent for me since Labeeb's death. I think he is bored with me." Samina sat up and covered her chest with a blanket.

Mariam laid the bloodied cloth beside the bowl. "Naa'il still needs an heir. I can tell you that he would prefer that one of his wives bear that child than a concubine. Be patient with our husband; he will send for you again - once his anger diminishes."

"Are you and Naa'il still intimate?"

Mariam winced. She hadn't been with Naa'il in months. "That is not your concern."

"I heard rumors that Naa'il is in love with an American," Samina frowned when Mariam grimaced again. "It is true?"

"I do not know."

"Do you think he will marry her?" Samina pressed.

"I do not know, Samina." Mariam snapped. "Naa'il does not discuss these matters with me."

"Would you tell me when you learn something?"

Mariam rested her hand on Samina's shoulder. "Do not trouble yourself with this matter now. What is most important is that you rest. Let your wounds heal. We will talk at another time."

"Will you visit me again?"

"Of course." Mariam gave Samina's shoulder a gentle squeeze before leaving the room.

"Where have you been?" Naa'il shouted. "I sent for you hours ago."

Dressed in tan-Ottoman trousers and a cream tunic, John Montgomery bowed to the Dey while focusing his olive-green eyes on the marble floor in front of him. "Forgive my tardiness, Your Excellency. I came as soon as I received your summons."

Naa'il pursed his lips when he realized that the fault must lie with the messenger. "You should have come sooner."

"Your Excellency, how may I assist you?"

Naa'il had always liked John ever since he first set eyes on him in the slave yard. A prisoner from the United States, he was drawn to John's humble demeanor. The Dey chose him to answer his English correspondence after learning that he was an educated man. John had thus far proved to be a dutiful servant throughout his four years of service.

"You have been neglecting your duties. I have a large stack of correspondence from England and America." Naa'il glanced over at his bedchamber door. His desk and the unanswered letters were in the room with Cora and the healer.

"I apologize, Your Excellency," John bowed his head. He glanced up and studied his master. "Are you well?"

Naa'il stared blankly at his servant. "What?"

"Forgive me; you seem upset. I asked if you were in health."

"Of course I am well!" Naa'il snapped. Frowning, he glanced at the door again, then back to his servant. "You are a Christian, are you not?"

"I …."

"You do not have to answer. I know that you are."

John confirmed Naa'il's suspicions with a subtle nod.

"Do you still pray?" Naa'il's question was met with silence. "I will not punish you for your answer – so long as you answer truthfully."

"Yes, Your Excellency. I pray every morning," John replied with hesitation.

"Does your God comfort you? Does he answer your prayers?"

"Yes. Becoming your servant is evidence of God's mercy."

Naa'il swallowed hard. "I acquired an American woman about a month ago. She is also a woman of faith, and she is very ill. Will you pray for her?"

"Of course." John's face expressed surprise by the Dey's request.

"You may go."

"Would you like me to answer your correspondence?"

"Not today. You may leave now."

John bowed and backed out of Naa'il's chambers.

Naa'il remained motionless on his couch. Once again, he felt powerless to save Cora. There was no antidote to cure her, and Naa'il doubted that his servant's prayers would help her either. Deep down, he knew that Cora's will to live was the only way she would return to him.

Jamal entered his sister's apartment. Mariam was seated on her favorite cushion with her youngest perched on her lap, and her other three daughters seated around her while the servants and nurses looked on. The girls, ranging in ages from three to nine, featured a perfect blend of their parents' physical traits. Each child was as lovely as the other. Jamal looked on with tenderness at the sight of his sister and her little girls. He thought to himself that he would do anything to keep them safe.

"Uncle!" The youngest, Zeba, climbed off her mother's lap and ran into Jamal's arms.

"Good morning, little one." Jamal kissed his niece's cheek and lowered her to the floor. He gave his sister a serious look and said, "We need to talk."

Mariam nodded subtly and smiled at her daughters. "Go with your nurses." Expanding her gaze to include all the other servants, she added, "Leave us."

Jamal held the door open as the group filed out of his sister's chamber.

Mariam remained seated after her brother closed the door. "What happened?"

Jamal hadn't moved from where he stood. Instead, he shifted his weight from one foot to the other because he was unsure how to proceed with explaining this delicate matter to his sister. He stared at the floor for a few long moments, his lips moving without making a sound. Finally, he raised his eyes to his sister and said, "Naa'il asked me not to speak of this, but I think it's important for you to know."

"What?" Mariam asked with a pained expression.

Jamal crossed the room and stood before her. "I had a meeting with Naa'il this morning, during which I noticed that he was behaving secretively. He also seemed anxious. He kept his bedchamber door closed. So when the opportunity presented itself, I peeked into the room and spotted the American infidel sleeping in his bed. I now believe you're right about Naa'il's feelings toward her."

Mariam rested her elbow on the table beside her and buried her face in her hand.

Jamal laid his hand on her shoulder. "Mari, I do not believe that all is lost yet."

Mariam shook her head sadly. "Mark my words, that woman will bring ruin upon our family." She chuckled darkly. "It is ironic; I was raised to believe that it is the woman who holds her family's honor in her hands. In reality, it is my husband who will bring about our family's destruction."

Jamal squatted in front of her and enveloped her hand in his. "Naa'il has done nothing to dishonor our family yet. If it is a comfort, I believe the infidel is very ill. Allah willing, perhaps she will die before Naa'il makes a mistake. Either way, you have my word that I will never let it come to that. Now, I must go to work." Jamal kissed his sister's cheek and strode out of the room, leaving Mariam sitting alone with a furrowed brow.

Chapter 10

The bell rang, signaling the watch change, just as the sun began to set. The clouds surrounding the red sphere glowed a pinkish hue. Sarah couldn't take her eyes off the sailors descending the ratlines with a cat-like grace. During her day in the sun, she spotted the perfect perch - a ledge attached to the tallest mast. It looked like an ideal spot from which to watch a sunrise or sunset like the one currently taking place. Sarah decided that the ledge would be her viewpoint for viewing the sunrise the next morning.

You didn't draw much." Hassan sat down beside her and stared at the few lines on the page.

"I like here," Sarah said, her eyes beaming.

"Did you spend much time on the deck of your other ship?"

"Um, a wee bit," Sarah remembered how she treasured the brief visits to the quarterdeck that her friendship with Emile had afforded her.

"Are you hungry?" Hassan asked. Sarah nodded. They rose together and entered his quarters. The empty dining table hinted that their dinner was still a few minutes away. Hassan pulled out a chair for Sarah while he changed into tan breeches and a white peasant shirt.

Hassan sat in the chair beside her. "Dinner will not be ready for at least another hour. What would you like to do until then?"

"What you do?" Sarah asked with genuine interest.

"I usually take care of personal business."

"You have business?"

"Not tonight," Hassan replied. "You told me this morning that you have many questions for me. What shall we discuss first?"

"Say your family?"

"You want me to tell you about my family," Hassan clarified.

"Aye."

"Well, my father, mother, older brother and younger sister live in England. Am I correct to assume that you do not have any siblings?"

"What siblings?"

"Siblings are brothers or sisters."

"No siblings. My people family."

"Does that mean you have many brothers and sisters and aunts and uncles?" Hassan teased.

Sarah laughed. "Aye, but only one da. Say about home."

"I also live on an island."

"It … beaut … I no remember word." Sarah blushed.

"Beautiful?"

"Aye, beautiful. Home beautiful?"

"Yes," he said with a rueful smile. "My country offers something for everyone: big cities, seaside towns, farmlands, and small villages."

"Where you live?"

"I lived with my family in the country. I must admit that my home is quite beautiful. There are lush green pastures, quaint villages, castles, and farms." Hassan paused when he spotted her vacant expression. "You do not understand my descriptions do you?"

"No," she smiled apologetically.

"Perhaps one day you will."

"You help my English?"

"Of course I will. What else would you like to know?"

"You like country?"

Hassan frowned. "Do you mean, do I like living in the country?" he replied after a long pause.

"Aye."

"It's a very different life from the one I am currently living. England is quiet and peaceful. Each day blends into the next without any significant changes. My countrymen are born; they grow to adulthood; they marry, and they raise their children. So continue the lives from one generation to the next. What was your life like on your island?"

"It same," Sarah paused. "Why you leave?"

"Well, I did not appreciate the quiet life when I was younger. I longed for adventure and perhaps finding treasures along the way. My country life could not provide the life I sought. So, I became an officer in the Royal Navy." Hassan sighed. "I was a fool."

"You not find adventure?"

"No," Hassan laughed faintly. "I found plenty of adventures. I also acquired enough treasure to live comfortably for the rest of my life. Both came at a great cost."

Sarah placed her hand over his and looked at him tenderly. "You miss home and family."

"Yes. Not a day passes that I don't think about them, especially my sister. We were very close. I don't even know if she is married. It has been so long since I last saw them. I hope they are well and happy. I hope to see them again."

"You see family, Cattin. You good man. You find wife. You have children. You be happy," Sarah stated confidently.

Hassan caressed her cheek. "My God, you are sweet."

Sarah and Hassan talked through dinner and late into the evening until they were too tired to form a complete sentence. At her insistence, Sarah slept in a hammock in the dining area. Hassan retrieved several more blankets to keep her warm.

Sarah woke just before dawn. Still intent on watching the sun rise from the top, she dressed in the clothes that Hassan gave her the previous day. She also twirled her hair into a bun and wrapped the cloth around her hair. Finally, Sarah placed a few oranges in a cloth shoulder bag she found hanging in the dressing room. The only thing she didn't know was how to slip out of the cabin without Hassan's notice. To her knowledge, there was only one exit, and it was guarded at all times. Still, she hated the thought of missing another sunrise.

Sarah quietly opened the door. Her heart raced when she discovered that no one was guarding Hassan's quarters. She closed the door and headed to the main deck. A ban of red light was just starting to appear on the eastern horizon. Sarah scampered to the tallest mast because she knew her time was limited. She glanced up to her goal. It was higher than she remembered. A small part of her warned her to return to Hassan's quarters. It had been too long since she had seen a sunrise that the thought of watching one beckoned her irresistibly. Sarah reached for the ratline that Hassan's crew used. Climbing the rope ladder was far easier than she ever imagined. It wasn't long before she reached the top. Sarah poked her head through the hole in the platform. With a little effort, she climbed aboard.

Sarah couldn't believe the view from her perch. The folded sails made it easy to take in the 360-degree view. The sky continued to grow lighter, turning the black water to dark blue as the light filtered through it. The only thing interrupting the edges between the water and the sky was a faint sliver of land on the horizon. Sarah took out an orange and peeled it as she faced east. Her heart soared like the seagulls flying above her when the red orb appeared.

Half asleep, Hassan reached for Sarah. His eyes fluttered open when he didn't find her. He then remembered that he tucked her into the hammock before retiring to his berth. He marveled at how he could miss lying beside a woman who had only slept with him for two nights. Yet, sharing a bed with Sarah felt natural. He missed her warmth, her touch, her smile. Hassan swung his legs over the edge of the berth and went to check on his guest. "Sarah?" he called out when he discovered the empty hammock. There was no answer; he called her name again. This time there was panic in his tone. Hassan quickly dressed.

"Have you seen Sarah?" he asked the guards standing outside his quarters.

His bodyguards looked at each other before looking back at their captain. "We thought she was with you, sir," said Luke with genuine surprise.

"I would not be asking if she were." Hassan darted out to the quarterdeck. "Sarah!" he called in a frantic voice as he scanned the deck. He then spotted the end of her turban waving proudly like a banner. "I'll be damned," he muttered to himself. Hassan raced over to the mast, reached for the ratline, and went aloft. "What the devil are you doing up here?" he demanded as he climbed onto the top.

"I wake; not sleep," she said sweetly.

"You should never leave my quarters without me. It is not safe for you to roam around the ship alone. Climbing up here is dangerous, Sarah. Do not come up here again. Do you understand?" Hassan growled. "We will climb down this instant."

"We stay? It almost here. Na?" she pointed to the horizon.

Hassan realized that she was looking at the half-risen sun. He could tell by her pleading eyes that watching the sunrise was important to her. "Very well," he conceded.

"You like?" Sarah offered him half of her second orange.

"Yes, please." He took the sections from her.

They ate in silence. Sarah watched the sunrise; Hassan watched Sarah. He couldn't take his eyes off her. Her face glowed with the sun's radiant light. What he loved most was seeing the peaceful expression on her face as she took in this majestic view.

"Beautiful, aye?" she asked without taking her eyes off the eastern horizon.

"Yes," he whispered, still watching her.

They were both disappointed when the sun had finally risen above the horizon. It was time for them to start their day. Neither of them wanted to leave their perch.

"We should return to the quarterdeck, but how do I get you down safely?" Hassan mumbled as he contemplated carrying Sarah over his shoulder while descending the line.

"I do it," Sarah said cheerfully.

"It's not as easy as it looks."

"I do it, Cattin. I not fear."

"Very well, we shall do it together. I will go first." Hassan ducked through the top's hole and balanced on the ratline and waited for Sarah to join him. They both descended their lines slowly and steadily. Hassan was pleasantly surprised at how effortless the descent was for Sarah. She climbed down with the same ease as the abled seamen who had scaled the lines for years. Hassan landed on the deck in time to lower Sarah the rest of the way. "You did very well," he said with genuine amazement.

"Cattin, we go there to see sun sleep?"

"I will consider it. I meant what I said. Do not roam around this ship or go up to the top without me. Do you understand?"

"Aye."

"I do not mean to be cross with you. I am only saying this for your protection. I want you to promise me that you will not roam this ship alone again."

"I promise," Sarah said, with a hint of sadness.

"In my country, people do not break their promise once they have given it."

"I promise, Cattin," she insisted.

We shall see. Hassan had never met a woman who kept her promises.

Tristan and Luke greeted them on the quarterdeck. Hassan knew by their worried looks that they felt guilty about leaving their posts. "Would you wait for me on the bench, please?" he asked Sarah.

"Aye," she replied, taking a seat.

"I will only be a moment," Hassan said before ushering his bodyguards into his cabin.

"Sir, we are submitting ourselves for disciplinary action for abandoning our posts this morning," Luke began.

Hassan closed the door. "Why did you leave your posts?" He crossed his arms.

"It was only for a moment sir. I needed to make a trip to the head. I was only gone for a minute," Tristan explained.

"Sir, I was …," Luke continued.

Hassan raised his hand to silence them. "You should never abandon your post. If we were on a traditional naval ship, you would face disciplinary action. You of all people know that our mission is anything but traditional. I was grateful when you volunteered for this mission, and you have both served with distinction. Moreover, your valor is unparalleled to anyone with whom I've ever served. I will excuse your negligence this one time. Do not let it happen again," Hassan said sternly. He chuckled under his breath as he observed their expressions turning from worry to relief.

"Thank you, sir. You have our word that it won't happen again," Luke vowed.

"Dismissed."

It was a beautiful day – the sun was shining, and the air was warm. Everyone wanted to be outside. Sarah spent the entire day on the quarterdeck with her sketchbook lying open across her lap. Unlike the previous day, her pencil moved rapidly from one part of the page to another.

"Good morning, Doctor," said Hassan.

"Good morning." Peter sidled up to the captain with his back to Sarah. "I see your wife has already ensnared you."

Hassan stared at his friend with dismay. "I beg your pardon?" He glanced over his shoulder to see if Sarah had heard the doctor's comment. She was still drawing and seemed oblivious to the people around her.

"I saw you two sharing a moment on the top this morning. You appeared to be in love."

Hassan heard unmistakable disapproval in Peter's tone. "First, I have done nothing improper." Hassan glared at his friend. "I told Sarah the truth about our marriage yesterday morning."

Peter raised his brows. "Indeed? How did she take the news?"

"Quite well. I conveyed my intentions to deliver her to her family in Scotland. Sarah also understands that she is free to choose a husband."

Peter smirked. "She chooses *you*. Have you also told her that you cannot offer her marriage?"

"Do not burden yourself with this matter any longer. Sarah and I are not your concern. If I want your council, I shall seek it," Hassan said with a growl.

"Please forgive me, Captain. I do not mean to pry. I see that I have upset you; I will take my leave." Peter leaned over so that he was close enough that no one else could hear him. "When the day comes that your Tahitian prize breaks your heart, and she *will* tear your heart apart, do not say that I did not warn you."

Hassan towered over the doctor, squaring his shoulders. His nostrils flaring, he whispered through clenched teeth, "I am warned. Do not speak of this matter again."

"Good day." Peter bowed and walked away.

Hassan glanced back at Sarah, who was watching him with concern. He offered her a polite smile, which was all he could do. The last thing he wanted was to share Peter's concerns about her.

The rest of the day passed as quietly as it began. When the bell rang, both Sarah and Hassan looked towards the late afternoon sky. The sun had already dipped below the horizon. Sarah left her sketchbook on the bench and walked to the west facing railing. Hassan stood beside her as they watched the setting sun in silence, each a prisoner of their own thoughts. They returned to his quarters at twilight. Hassan had just enough time to change into breeches and a peasant shirt. The servants delivered their dinner; Sarah and Hassan ate in silence.

Halfway through dinner, Sarah looked at him thoughtfully and asked, "What women like on your island?"

Hassan bit his lip. "That is a very complicated answer. English women are as diverse as the regions in my country. I am not certain that you would understand my descriptions even if I told you."

"What good wife?" Sarah queried.

"That depends on the man. Men of my social standing treasure a woman who comes from a good family and provides a handsome dowry. She is well mannered and excellent company. She is accomplished in dancing, drawing, and sewing. She is also well-read. She is a loving mother and a good manager of the home. Above all, she is a lady." Hassan stopped and noted the blank expression on Sarah's face. "You do not understand me, do you?"

She shook her head. "What you say good wife?"

Hassan sighed heavily. "Honestly, Sarah, I have not given this subject much consideration. I have been at sea for a long time. I never thought it was fair to marry only to leave her for months or years at a time. More importantly, I have not met anyone who has given me a reason to change my profession. Perhaps I will feel differently one day. At the moment, I am content with the life that I am living."

Sarah bit the inside of her lip and looked away.

"That is not the answer you expected to hear," Hassan surmised, after spotting the disappointment in her eyes.

"I wish you happiness. I sad you not have love."

"Have you been in love?"

"No." Sarah insisted. "I wish marry man like Da. Men not like Da on island."

"I understand that you were very close to your father. It makes sense that you prefer to marry someone like him. What if you do not meet a man like your father? Would you choose not to marry?"

Sarah's forehead crinkled. "I not know. I wish marry. Da say ... he and my mother. He loved her so much. I want that. You think men in Scotland like me?"

"That's a silly question. Of course they will. You are a beautiful young woman. You are sweet; you are innocent, and you are one of the most accomplished artist I have ever known."

"I not like women on your island. I not know how do things you say," Sarah pointed out.

"Neither could they when they were younger. Girls learned those skills from their mothers. And so will you. It is never too late to learn. I am confident that you will find a husband who will love you."

"Why not you?"

"You do not want me, Sarah. How older are you? Sixteen, seventeen?"

"I no understand."

"Your age," Hassan clarified.

"What age?"

"Your age," he repeated. "Um. It is a measurement of time during which a person has lived. You have no idea what I am saying, do you?"

Sarah shook her head.

"The people in this part of the world celebrate the day of their birth. Each birthday we celebrate represents another year that we have lived." Hassan paused. "Your people do not celebrate their birthdays?" He surmised when he spotted her vacant expression.

"No."

"Your people do not record months or years?"

"What months?" Sarah frowned.

"January, February, March." Hassan laughed at the irony. "Your father never spoke of those?"

Sarah shook her head.

"Did your father ever talk about the day of your birth?"

"Aye, he say it hot, not rain."

Hassan laughed. "So, your island has no seasons ... um, different weather patterns. England has four." He held up four fingers. "They are winter, spring, summer, and autumn. It is cold during the winter, rainy during the spring. It can be hot during the summer and cool during the autumn. I imagine your island has never experienced winter. Does your island have different kinds of weather?"

"Aye, it rains; we have lot food; it hot."

"I see," Hassan laughed again. He looked at her warmly and said,

"The point I was trying to make earlier is that we just met. You do not know me well enough to love me. All you know is that I rescued you and your father from a dangerous situation."

Sarah reached for a lock of hair and flicked the ends across her thumb. "You good man," she said after a pause.

"I am flattered that you think so. I caution you to be careful not to fall in love with the first man you meet. The world is full of noble men. It is likely that you will soon meet someone who you will prefer above all others." Hassan reached over and covered her hand with his. "Be patient. Let love happen naturally. Trust me to guide you through what will seem to be a confusing new world."

CHAPTER 11

Naa'il shifted in his chair to offset the pain shooting down his back. For the third night in a row, Naa'il nursed Cora, which mostly consisted of wiping the perspiration from her forehead and feeding her water through a wet cloth. Her condition hadn't improved. His only comfort was that she was still breathing. The notes and the passages underlined in her Bible made him feel close to her. The majority of them were about love and forgiveness. Naa'il couldn't help wondering if Cora could forgive him for the torture he inflicted on her.

He nodded off again and woke a few hours later to the peace he hungered for since the last time he felt it. Naa'il opened his eyes and glanced over at his bed. She was gone. He closed her Bible and laid it on the table. "Cora!" he called out in a frantic voice. He jumped up from his chair when no one answered his call. Naa'il ran into his reception room. He opened his mouth to call her name again when he spotted her standing in his garden. Dressed in a knee-length tunic, Cora Bradley looked like an angel standing in her bare feet with her auburn hair hanging loosely down her back as she gazed up at the night sky. All that was missing were wings and a halo. "Cora," Naa'il crooned as he wrapped a blanket around her shoulders.

She looked at Naa'il with twinkling eyes. "Of all the things I miss at home, I miss seeing the stars and feeling the sun's warmth on my face the most. I've forgotten how beautiful the stars are." She pointed to the sky. "Look, they're performing tonight."

Naa'il spotted a shooting star out of the corner of his eye. "How are you feeling?"

Cora shrugged her shoulders. "A little confused. I feel as if I woke from a terrible, terrible nightmare where men attacked me, and I couldn't do anything to stop them." She tilted her head towards the fountain positioned in the center of the courtyard and wiped a tear from the corner of her eye.

"You are safe now." For the first time in Naa'il's life, he had no idea what to do next. He wanted to hold Cora. In his heart, he knew that he was the last person she wanted to comfort her. Still, he held his arms out and said, "Come here, Cora." To his great surprise, she welcomed his embrace as she buried her head in his shoulder and sobbed. Naa'il couldn't remember a time when anything felt more natural than holding the woman he loved. It was as if she belonged there.

In Cora's usual fashion, she pulled away and wiped the tears from her cheeks as if she were ashamed of weeping in front of a stranger. "Thank you. I am sure you will find this offensive, but you answered my prayers. May I ask why you ended the attacks? I did not convert."

"No, and I doubt you ever will." Naa'il stared at the marble floor. "I suppose you have earned an explanation." His Adam's apple bobbed up and down as he swallowed. "As you may recall, Bashira examined you and your cousin when you first arrived at the Palace. She informed me that only one of you was pure."

Cora knitted her brows together. "What do you mean by 'pure'?"

"I believe the proper English word is virginity."

Cora covered her lips with her finger and stared blankly at the Dey. "Are you saying that between my cousin and me, only one of us was a virgin? How can that be?"

"Those examinations never lie."

Cora struggled to take a breath; her body shook uncontrollably. "You thought I was not a virgin," she clarified.

Naa'il glanced at the fountain and hung his head. "Yes."

Her lips, wrenching in anger, Cora slapped his cheek. "I'm sorry; I shouldn't have struck you," she gasped in horror a moment later.

Naa'il grunted, covering his cheek with his hand. "No, you should not." His frown curled into a playful grin. "Do not strike me again."

"How could you think so poorly of me? You never met me," Cora hissed.

"You told me that your cousin was innocent. You said you would do anything to protect her, including offering your body to me. What was I supposed to believe?" Naa'il shouted back.

"How … how did you learn the truth?"

Naa'il swallowed hard again and bit his lip. "Abigail offered herself to me on the night I ended your persecution."

Cora's eyes narrowed. "You took advantage of my cousin?"

"Cora," Naa'il said with a nervous laugh. "Abigail and the rest of the women in the harem are my concubines. She also made me angry when she said some unkind things about you."

"Oh." Cora looked down at the fountain. "Does she know what happened to me?"

"No, I did not think you wanted her to know."

"Where is she?" She asked in a timid voice.

Naa'il tucked his finger under her chin and tilted her face towards his. "Abigail lives in the harem. She has not been harmed, just as I promised you."

As Cora turned away from Naa'il, her shoulders rapidly rose and fell as she wept. Naa'il slowly spun her around. "I made a great error in judgment. I do not expect your forgiveness. I am terribly sorry for all you suffered at my command."

"That must have been difficult for you to say, Your Excellency."

"More than you will ever know. One moment, please." He dashed to his bedchamber and returned with her Bible. "A peace offering."

Her lips parting, Cora took her Bible and embraced it like a long lost friend. "I don't know what to say."

"I do not know why I am returning this to you," he said with a lopsided grin. "Perhaps this will bring you peace."

"I thought you wanted me to convert to your faith."

"I do, and you should. I will not stop encouraging you to do so - if only to save your immortal soul. I will make an exception for you, so long as you do not try to influence the others with your beliefs."

"You have my word." Cora hugged her book again. "Thank you for keeping my Bible safe. I know you could have burned it."

"And so I should," Naa'il winked. His smile faded to a somber expression. "You have my word that you will never be persecuted again."

"Thank you."

"You should rest now."

"But I've slept for days, Your Excellency."

Naa'il scooped Cora up in his arms and carried her to his bed. "You do not have a choice." He took her Bible from her and laid it on the table. "Sleep now." He kissed her forehead.

"My mother used to sing me to sleep," she teased.

"Trust me when I say, you do not want me to sing to you." Naa'il's heart was buoyant when he heard Cora laugh for the first time. It sounded like the sweetest melody he had ever heard.

"Thank you for looking after me these past few days."

"Rest, sleep, pray. I will come to you later." Naa'il paused when he spotted her concern. "Do not worry. I will not make love to you unless you ask me. You have my word. Now sleep."

Cora's mind was too active to sleep. Now that she no longer had to worry about her safety, she sat up and admired the Dey's quarters. Naa'il's private suite was a blend of the East and West. The room maintained the Persian architecture with arched doorways and walls tiled with black and white mosaic designs. Naa'il seemed to prefer the ease and comfort of the European furniture. Though she had never been inside a European palace, Cora recognized the French furniture. Abigail spent most of her life boasting that her furniture was built in Paris. The curves in the gilded chairs and the silk upholstery looked as if they were made by the same people. Only Naa'il chose red fabric, Abigail preferred pastels.

Still feeling restless, Cora climbed out of bed and wrapped a blanket around her shoulders. She followed the light until she found Naa'il sitting at his desk with a perplexed look on his face. "Are you alright, Your Excellency?" she asked, resting her hand on his shoulder.

"What are you doing out of bed?"

"I could not sleep." She blushed. "I'm sorry; I can see you are busy. I didn't mean to interrupt you."

"I must answer these letters." Naa'il pointed to the stack of folded parchment on his desk. "The man who usually answers my English correspondence has neglected his duties as of late." Naa'il paused. "That is not true. My concern for your health caused me to neglect my duties."

Her cheeks burned. "I am sorry. May I assist you with this task? I will say whatever you wish."

"I do not need your help," Naa'il snapped.

"I am certain you don't. Forgive my intrusion; I will return to bed." Naa'il halted Cora's retreat when he locked his hand around her arm.

He stood up from his gilded chair. "Sit."

"Are these the letters?"

"Yes. You will write one letter for all of them," Naa'il instructed.

"May I read them first? It would help me to understand what I am writing."

Naa'il waved his hand above his head. "Yes, read."

Cora gasped when she read the first letter on the stack. "This is from the King of England. Is it true that your government enslaves British subjects in spite of the tribute money their country pays you to leave the British subjects alone?"

"This is not your concern. Write this down." Naa'il paced back and forth with his fingers interlaced behind his back.

> *"I am writing in response to your February 24th letter. By the treaty between our countries, I write to say that we do not prey upon your ships or enslave your citizens. I resent you accusing me of violating our accord."*

"What?" Naa'il demanded when he noticed that Cora hadn't written a single word.

"Your Excellency, I would not presume to challenge you, except a ship containing British subjects was processed on the same day that I was. How you conduct your state affairs is your concern, but I admonish you to be very careful about breaking your treaty with the British. They are a powerful country."

"I am surprised you defend the British after they attacked your ships and pressed your people into duty. Is that not the reason your country is fighting a war against them now?"

"I know what the British did, Your Excellency, and I do not condone their actions. Be that as it may, the British are still a powerful force."

"Your country defeated England in your war of independence."

"We did, but we could have just as easily lost that war."

"But your country did not." Naa'il paused. "Is it true that your country's current war with England is not going well?"

One end of Cora's lips curled upward. "I heard those rumors too. The English haven't defeated us yet." She gently squeezed his hand. "Please be careful of the British, and do not underestimate the Americans either. Thomas Jefferson was a guest in my uncle's house several times. On more than one occasion, Mr. Jefferson expressed his outrage over Algiers and other Barbary Coast states' practice of seizing US ships and enslaving our citizens. The United States will go to war with the Barbary Coast states if you continue to do so."

Naa'il kissed the back of Cora's hand. "I thank you for your concern. These matters are my concern, not yours. Please, write my letter."

Cora dipped the quill in ink and scribbled Naa'il's message with an elegant penmanship. She sprinkled a little dust across the parchment to prevent the ink from smudging. "Is this satisfactory, Your Excellency?"

Naa'il's lips quirked a grin. Cora's letter was better than anything that he or John had ever written. Her letter expressed the exact message he wished to convey, yet it was written with a diplomat's eloquence. "This is sufficient. You will write my English letters from now on."

"I am happy to serve you." Cora laughed.

"That is the second time you have laughed." Naa'il smiled affectionately. "It pleases me to hear it." He kissed Cora's forehead and extended his hand to her. "Come to bed."

Even though Cora cringed at the thought of sharing a bed with Naa'il, let alone any man, she took his hand and followed him to his bedchamber.

"What is wrong?" Naa'il asked when Cora froze, looking intently at his canopy bed.

"Do I need to crawl under the covers at the foot of the bed? That was the instruction I received in the harem."

Naa'il pulled the covers back and climbed onto the far side of the bed. "Come here, Cora." He patted the space beside him.

"I have nightmares."

"Yes, I have heard them, and I do not care." Naa'il patted the space again.

Cora reluctantly obeyed. Naa'il was true to his word. He kissed her tenderly and held her throughout the rest of the night. For the first time since she arrived in Algiers, Cora felt safe.

Chapter 12

Naa'il stirred during the early morning. He reached for Cora and opened his eyes when he didn't find her lying beside him. There was just enough light to make out Cora kneeling beside his bed with her head bowed in prayer. The Dey propped himself up on several pillows and studied her. "After all you have been through, why do you still pray to a god that failed to protect you?" he asked when she didn't stir.

Cora rose and sat on the edge of the bed after Naa'il tugged on her arm. "God didn't fail me."

"Of course he did; he allowed you to be violated," Naa'il pointed out.

"My mother used to say, 'God is not found in the problem, but in the solution.' You're right. God did not spare me from the attacks, but He gave me the strength to endure them." Cora's voice quivered. "He showed me compassion when He sent Mamnoon to care for me after I surrendered to despair, and God showed me mercy when you ended the attacks. How can I turn from Him now?"

Cora glowed with an inner conviction as she spoke of her experience despite cuts and bruises covering her body. Naa'il had never seen a more beautiful woman. "Your God should have spared you," he whispered as he hung his head in shame.

"God didn't spare Jesus from the crucifixion. Look what he accomplished after he died on the cross?" Cora gently squeezed Naa'il's hand.

"I feel your prayers."

Cora's lips parted. "You do?"

"Yes. I have felt them ever since the day you arrived." Naa'il kissed the back of Cora's hand. "How did you learn to pray like that?"

Cora pressed her lips together. "No one taught me if that is what you are asking. All my inspiration came from reading the Bible. It was the only thing that comforted me after losing my family. It has comforted me every day of my life."

"I read your notes."

Cora's brow arched over her eye. "All of them?"

"Most of them. You wrote a lot. Many are about forgiveness. Can you forgive your enemies?" Naa'il paused and continued in a timid voice. "Can you forgive me?"

Cora bit her lip. "Not today, but I know I must."

"Why must you?"

"Because forgiveness is the only path to peace. My mother used to say that bad things happen to good people. How we react is our choice. We can either spend our lives feeling bitter about a past injustice, or we can forgive, put the past behind us, and move forward. I want to be free."

"Forgiving is that simple?"

"No, on the contrary, it is the hardest thing to do in the world."

"Can you forgive all the men who violated you?"

Cora's teeth clamped down on her lower lip. "Not today."

"Can you forgive the people who murdered your family?"

Cora looked the Dey in the eyes and said, "Not today, but I am no longer bitter either."

"What happened to them - the people who slew your family?"

"I don't know. Perhaps nothing at all. That is the danger of living in the wilderness. The only form of justice is revenge. I wasn't old enough to take on a war party."

"I am sorry you lost your family at such a young age."

"Do not pity me, Your Excellency. I led a good life after I went to live with my aunt and uncle. I met extraordinary people," she said with a warm smile. "I was given free access to read any book in my uncle's extensive library. I have no complaints about living with my cousin's family."

Naa'il looked thoughtfully at Cora. "Why are you not married? I do not understand."

"Oh that," Cora blushed. "I was asked by two men on separate occasions. I almost said yes to the latter."

"Go on."

"The first was a wealthy landowner. His name was Jordan Donnelly. He was the perfect suitor. He was handsome, and he could have any maid he wanted. For one reason or another, he chose me." Cora shook her head. "I have no idea why. I had absolutely nothing to offer him, least of all a dowry. I doubt his parents would approve of me had we courted when they were alive."

"That is not difficult to understand. Why did you not love him?"

"I didn't respect him; I didn't like the way he treated people that were beneath him. He was arrogant and even cruel at times. I always felt that he didn't respect me whenever we were together." Cora shrugged. "More importantly, I had given my heart to another - a man who worked in my uncle's stables. He was a Scotsman named, Stephen MacDonald," she said with loving eyes. "We shared a passion for horses. I lived in the attic room. It was frigid during the winter and unbearably hot during the summer. I used to sneak out at night and sleep under the stars in the garden during the summer. I encountered Stephen every night. We stayed up for hours talking."

"Talking?" Naa'il raised a brow.

"Yes. Talking. Mr. MacDonald was a perfect gentleman."

"Why did you not marry him?" Naa'il asked with unmistakable disapproval in his tone.

"I wanted to say yes. Stephen is a good man."

"Why did you refuse him?" Naa'il pressed.

"My uncle arranged for Abigail to live with her family in England.

He wanted me to go with her. We came here instead."

"Did you not tell your uncle that this Stephen asked you to marry him?"

"No," Cora said with a heavy sigh.

"I see. You agreed to escort your cousin because you felt guilty about her limp."

"I ruined her life."

"You did not ruin your cousin's life, Cora," Naa'il paused. "There is something I must tell you, and I fear it will be difficult for you to hear."

"What?" Cora asked in a quiet voice.

"I caught Abigail dancing when I entered her apartment on the night I ended your attacks. She walked to me without a hint of a limp when she greeted me." Naa'il hesitated. "I believe she could walk freely all along."

Cora shot up from the bed and stood with her back to Naa'il. The Dey approached her and rested his hands on her shoulders. Cora looked back at him with tears streaming down her cheeks. "Why would Abigail do such a despicable thing? She knew that Stephen had proposed to me."

Naa'il's heart ached when he spotted the devastation on her face. "I do not know. Cora, I did not mean to cause you additional pain. I thought you deserved to know the truth, especially after all you sacrificed for her."

"No, I am glad you did. It all makes sense now. I heard rumors of Abigail's indiscretions. I didn't believe them. Abigail always had a way of making me pity her. I suppose that explains why my uncle arranged for her to live with her family in England." Cora shook her head. "I am a fool."

Naa'il spun her around and swiveled her face towards his. "You are not. You have a kind heart. I promise that your cousin will not profit from her lies here. I kept my word to you. No harm will come to her, but she will spend the rest of her life in the harem."

Shaking uncontrollably, Cora struggled to breathe as the permanence of her captivity sunk in. Though she knew that she was a prisoner, it wasn't until that moment that she understood that she would never leave Algiers or set foot on her homeland again.

"Cora, what is troubling you?" Naa'il carried her back to bed.

Cora spotted his concern, but she couldn't speak.

Naa'il brushed the hair from her eyes and gently entreated, "Cora, please talk to me."

"I'm alright," Cora said, once her breathing returned to normal.

"What is troubling you?"

"It does not matter. What is important is that I am safe. I am hungry, though," she added after her stomach gurgled.

"You are very brave, but you are not convincing. Come, I will have breakfast brought to us."

Servants carried in several trays of food and placed them on a table in the reception room. "Leave us," Naa'il commanded his servants who stood at attention beside the table, waiting for orders. They bowed in unison and backed out of the room. Naa'il closed the door, took a seat across from Cora and grinned as she stared at the feast with wide eyes.

"My goodness, I have not seen this much food since I left home." She held up the small brown oval fruit. "What is this?"

"That is a fig," Naa'il said. "Try it."

Cora took a bite of the fruit. "Umm, that is very good," she said before tossing the other half in her mouth. "What is that?" She pointed to the pie cut into six wedges.

"It is called M'shewsha. It is a traditional Algerian breakfast," Naa'il said proudly.

"What is in it?" Cora picked up one of the wedges and smelled it. The pie's yellow color hinted that eggs were a primary ingredient, but the rest of the contents was a mystery to her. All she knew was that it smelled sweet.

"I do not know, but it is topped with honey. Try it."

Cora closed her eyes; her face was the epitome of bliss. "Oh my goodness. I think this is the best thing I have ever tasted."

"I am pleased that you like it." Naa'il's smile widened.

Cora blushed and lowered the other half of her slice onto her plate when she realized that Naa'il hadn't touched his breakfast. "Forgive me; you must think my manners are appalling. May I pour you some ...." She glanced down at the light brown liquid. "Is this tea?"

"Your manners are not appalling. And yes, I would like some tea." Naa'il picked up a slice of M'shewsha and took a bite. He spent the rest of the meal teaching Cora about Algerian cuisine. She asked questions about almost every food on the tray, and then she got quiet again. "What upset you just before breakfast?"

Cora took a deep breath. "I was thinking about the women in the harem. What happens to them once they outlive their usefulness?"

"I sell them. I cannot afford to keep people who have no purpose." Naa'il pursed his lips. "You disapprove."

"It is not for me to judge. All I can ask of anyone is that they do what they believe is right."

Naa'il drummed his fingers on the table. "You are not convincing. What would you have me do with them?"

Cora shrugged. "I would grant them freedom; perhaps allow them to return to their homes - at least for the ones that served you faithfully."

"What would a woman do with her freedom? Her place is to serve, whether it is her master or her husband. Her husband or master provides for her needs in return for her service. That is the way of it here, Cora. Sending the Americans or the Europeans home is not possible."

"England and the United States would capture your ships if they got too close to their land," Cora surmised.

"Yes." Naa'il reached across the table and covered her hand with his. "You need not worry about your fate, Cora."

"What if I fall out of favor?" she asked, half teasing. "I seem to have a proclivity for making you angry."

"Yes, you do." Naa'il sighed. "Perhaps, we can work together to make the lives of the women in the harem more comfortable."

"Thank you ... and thank you for not being angry when I expressed my opinion."

"You have a kind heart. You are always thinking about everyone but yourself." Naa'il's lips curled into a tender grin. "I should not say this, but Mamnoon offered to pay me all that he had for you."

"He did?" she asked with genuine surprise.

"Yes. I am not ready to give you up. I like talking to you. I like feeling your prayers again. They comfort me." Naa'il reached across the table and gently squeezed her hand.

"I like talking to you too. My pa taught me that sometimes the best way to conquer an enemy is to talk to them. You discover that you are not as different as you think. My Ma believed that people live on borrowed light. All people, regardless of their race or nationality, can be noble, kind, compassionate, strong, loving, and a host of other qualities."

"How did your parents explain immorality and evil?" Naa'il challenged.

Cora shrugged. "Not everyone chooses to be good. That is their choice … and their curse."

"Yes, I have heard of your Christian philosophy concerning eternal damnation," he said with a hint of condescension.

"I'm not talking about hell. I've known immoral people, and they do not live happy lives. Some pay dearly for their sins. That is why I pity them, and why I pray for them."

Naa'il knew he didn't need to ask her if she prayed for him. It was the only logical explanation for feeling her prayers. Still, he asked, "Do you pray for me?"

"Of course. I pray for everyone, including my persecutors," Cora said without hesitation.

Naa'il hung his head when he heard, "persecutors," because he knew that she justifiably considered him as one of them.

"I'm sorry I upset you again," she grimaced when he made a sour face.

"No." He forced a smile and paused. "I am not accustomed to talking to women," he said in a desperate attempt to change the subject.

"Is it as terrible as you imagined?" Cora teased.

"Most of the time, yes. I like our talks." Naa'il kissed the back of her hand. "We will talk often. I must work today. You will spend the day in the harem."

Cora cupped her mouth with her hand. "Really?"

"Yes, I imagine you have much to say to your cousin. You will return tonight. We will talk more."

"May I ask you a question?"

Naa'il motioned with his hand. "Ask."

"Why are you being so kind to me?"

Naa'il let out a loud sigh. "Because Mamnoon was right about you; you *are* the rarest of all jewels. He has always been a keen judge of character."

"I don't know what to say," Cora whispered.

Naa'il laughed. "You can think about your answer in the harem. I must prepare for my day." He led her to the apartment exit and kissed her before opening the door.

"Mamnoon!" Cora's eyes lit up when she discovered him standing in the hallway.

"My lady," Mamnoon bowed.

"Take Cora to the harem. Keep an eye on her and bring her to me this evening."

"Yes, Your Excellency." Mamnoon bowed.

Cora waited until they turned the corner, and Naa'il was nowhere in sight when she turned and hugged her protector. "It is so good to see you, my friend. I missed you."

"I was so worried about you. Are you well?" Mamnoon hugged her back before examining her from head to toe then back again.

"No, but I will be." Cora wrapped her hand around his arm. The two meandered to the harem. She came to a sudden halt when she spotted sunlight streaming into a courtyard.

"What are you doing?" Mamnoon demanded when she broke away from him and walked to the center of the courtyard.

"This." She stood in the open space with her arms stretched out and her face tilted towards the sun. "It feels like a lifetime since I felt the sun's warmth." She grinned at her friend. "I feel reborn."

"You should have told me. I would have arranged for you to feel the sun's warmth."

Cora squeezed his hand. "You're too good to me."

Mamnoon allowed her to remain in the courtyard until the shadows overtook the sunlight.

"I suppose we should go to the harem," Cora said sadly.

"Yes, you will see the sun tomorrow," Mamnoon promised.

They continued meandering down their path. Neither was in a hurry to reach their destination.

"His Excellency said that my cousin is in the harem," Cora said.

"Your understanding is correct."

"How is she?"

"Humbled." Mamnoon stifled a laugh.

Cora stopped and studied her friend. "Oh?" she raised her brows. "What happened?"

"His Excellency gave your cousin an apartment. He took it away several days later," he said with a pleased grin.

"Oh dear. How is she getting along in the harem?"

"I think she will be glad to see you. You may be her only true friend."

"I see," Cora sighed. They stopped, and Mamnoon knocked on the Harem door. "Bashira!" she exclaimed with a toothy grin when the valide answered the door.

"His Excellency sent word to me this morning that you would be returning to the harem. I have been so worried about you. Are you alright?" Bashira asked as she inspected Cora.

"No, but I will be. I am confident that my wounds will heal."

The valide leaned in and whispered, "I was relieved to hear that His Excellency ended the attacks against you. They were not right."

"Thank you for all you did for me during that time. I think I would have surrendered to despair had you and Mamnoon not helped me the way you did," Cora said as tears flooded her eyes.

"You are most welcome. Come, you shall be pampered all day."

"May I see my cousin first?"

"She is inside." Bashira nodded to Mamnoon to open the door.

CHAPTER 13

The day began with a clap of thunder. The waves tossed the ship around as if it were a small toy. Hassan dressed and reported for duty as if the sun were shining; Sarah spent the day in his quarters at the captain's insistence. He eased her captivity by promising to bring her a bucket of water, food, and a day's supply of oranges. Sarah had no choice but to accept her fate.

Sarah hated being alone; she always did. There was a constant supply of friends to keep her company on her island. This was the first time that she could remember that she was completely alone. The guards standing outside Hassan's quarters made sure that she could not escape, or that anyone could enter except for Hassan. To make matters worse, there was nothing to do except draw in her sketchbook, which was not enough to entertain her for an entire day. Sarah sunk in her chair and stared at the blank page. Her hand moved across the parchment, sketching an image of her friends preparing food for one of the village's celebrations. It was a painful reminder that life with her friends was never dull. Had she been at home, she would have gone swimming, made tapa cloth, gathered food, and prepared meals. She couldn't do any of those things on the ship.

Sarah sighed with relief when she heard a knock on the door.

"Sarah," Peter's muffled voice called out after knocking a second time.

She poked her head through the crack. "Good morning," she said with a warm smile.

"Good morning," he replied in Polynesian. "Captain Aziz asked me to bring a bucket of water to you. May I come in?"

"Please." Sarah opened the door. Though he wasn't Hassan, she liked being able to converse with someone in her native language. Holding a conversation in English was still difficult for her.

Peter entered carrying a bucket of water into the cabin. "Where shall I put it?"

"There." She pointed to her trunk.

Water sloshed on the floor with every teetered step he took.

"Can I help?"

"No, I can manage." Peter insisted. He took a few more steps and lowered the bucket beside her trunk. He straightened his back and faced her. "How are you and Captain Aziz getting along?"

"I like Cattin." Sarah tilted her face towards the floor and sighed.

"But?"

"He confuses me."

"How so?" Peter extended his hand, inviting her to sit at the table with him.

Sarah sat in her usual seat; Peter sat in Hassan's chair with his legs and chest squarely facing her.

"He said we are not married."

"Yes, he told me," Peter confirmed. "He was right to tell you."

Sarah's lips parted. "Why?"

"Would you prefer him to make love to you, only to discover that your whole marriage was a lie? You must understand that he can never marry you."

"Why?"

"Because his parents would never allow it."

"Why? I do not understand."

"You have nothing to offer him. Captain Aziz was born into a privileged family. They will not allow him to marry just any girl. His future wife must come from a family that is at least the equivalent to his social rank. She must also be able to provide him with a handsome dowry. You can offer him neither of those things."

"I do not understand," Sarah said timidly.

"Nor do I expect you to comprehend what I just told you. You and Captain Aziz were raised in very different worlds. All you need to understand is that Captain Aziz can never offer you marriage."

Fighting back her tears, Sarah looked away.

Peter covered her hand with his. "That doesn't mean that you can't have love with another. I am not bound by such obligations. I think you would be very happy with me."

Sarah slid her hand out from under Peter's and laid it in her lap. Her eyes blinking more than usual, she shifted her gaze from Peter to the table when she felt his brown eyes boring into her. "You are very kind, but I belong to Cattin."

"You're in a different part of the world now. Women are free to choose their lovers."

Sarah responded with a glower. "I was free to choose my mate at home. My father did not approve of me giving myself to the men in my village. I loved him too much to betray him. Cattin is the head of my family now. I will honor his wishes the same way I honored my father's."

Peter's eyes flashed with anger, "I can assure you, now that your "Cattin" has refused you, he will not care if you take another lover."

"Perhaps, I am not ready to give myself to another." With tears streaming down her cheeks, Sarah jumped up from the table and ran behind the screen. She laid down on the berth, hoping that Peter wouldn't follow her.

The sounds of the harem turned to silence the moment Cora and her friends entered the room. Mamnoon hovered near Cora, shooting menacing glares at anyone who meant to harm her. Cora anxiously scanned the room for her cousin.

"Where is . . ." her voice trailed off when she spotted Abigail hobbling through the doorway leading to the bathing area. Cora charged across the room and embraced her cousin. "Are you hurt?" she asked, inspecting her cousin for signs of abuse.

"No! I am quite ill. While you have been God knows where, doing God knows what, I have been trapped in this horrid place. The people here are so unkind. How could you abandon me during my hour of need?" Abigail whined.

Cora stared at her cousin with disbelief. "I have not seen you in weeks, and this is how you treat me?"

"I can treat you any way I want. I wouldn't be in this predicament had it not been for your wretched horse," Abigail said, squaring her shoulders.

Cora mirrored her cousin's stance, except her arms were crossed. "His Excellency informed me that you no longer need to walk with a limp." Cora leaned in and whispered, "I agree with him; I think you have walked normally for a very long time."

Abigail leaned back and glared at her cousin. "How dare you? Why would I lie about something like that? Do you think being a cripple gives me pleasure?"

"Yes, I do. I think your lie has served you remarkably well by the way you manipulated everyone to pity you and do your bidding. If you want to continue walking with a limp, walk with a limp. My sympathy has come to an end. I've sacrificed enough for you," Cora said bitterly.

"How could you be so unkind?" Abigail sobbed.

Her face looked as if she were weeping; even her voice was convincing. For the first time, Cora noticed not a single tear shed from her eyes. "Watch out," she shouted when Ula approached Abigail from behind with a chamber pot in her hand.

Abigail scampered out of the way without a trace of a limp.

Mamnoon took the chamber pot from Ula before she could throw its contents. He nodded to several guards standing nearby to restrain Ula and take her away.

Cora broke free from Abigail and led Mamnoon to a nearby corner. "What are you doing?" she whispered.

"Is this the woman who covered you with filth on your first day in the harem?"

"Before I answer, I want to know what you intend to do with her."

"I told His Excellency that I did not believe that you spread filth on your back the night you were sent to him. He commanded me to find the person responsible for this mischief. I am going to take her to His Excellency for punishment," Mamnoon explained.

Cora rested her hand on his arm. "My dear friend, I thank you for watching over me. You can't fight all my battles. If I may, I would like to fight the ones in the harem."

"What are you going to do with Ula?"

"Nothing for now."

"Cora, you would not have been violated had this woman not covered you with filth," Mamnoon said angrily. "She deserves to be punished."

"I know what she did. Ula fell out of His Excellency's favor, and she will never get him back. She knows this, and she will spend the rest of her life as a slave. That is punishment enough." Cora's lips curled into a mischievous grin. "That doesn't mean that we can't let her fret over her future."

"You are a better person than I. I will respect your wishes, but I will not lie to His Excellency if he asks me to report on the progress of my investigation."

"Thank you. You're a good friend." Cora rose up on her toes and kissed his cheek.

"What do you want to do about your cousin?" Mamnoon asked without taking his eyes off Abigail.

"Again, this is my battle. Keep her away from me for now. I'm likely to strangle her."

"Very well," Mamnoon conceded.

"Thank you." Cora glanced at her cousin who was staring at them with disgust.

"Are you in love with that … that …." Abigail's face puckered.

"His name is Mamnoon, and he's a better friend than you ever were," Cora shot back.

"I was going to tell you," Abigail bit her lip.

"No, you weren't. Your only regret is that you were caught. The trouble with lying is that once people discover your deception, they will no longer believe anything else you say. Stay away from me." Nodding to Bashira, Cora turned on her heels and walked away.

"I did not deceive you. You owe your life to my family and me. You would have been a homeless orphan had my father not taken you in."

Cora returned to her cousin. She leaned in and said in a menacing tone, "There is no question that your family was generous to me. Perhaps I was even a burden. This I know; I would be married had you not manipulated me with your deceit."

"Why would anyone want to marry you? You are no …" Abigail's voice trailed off when Mamnoon shoved her against the wall with his hand cupping her throat.

"Mamnoon," Cora said calmly.

"She is not worthy of all that you sacrificed for her," he said bitterly.

Cora rested her hand on Mamnoon's arm. "She is still my cousin. Please, let go of her."

Mamnoon yielded to Cora's will; Abigail hunched over gasping for breath.

"Thank you, my friend. Perhaps it's best that you have someone else guard her today. You can keep me company after my bath."

Hassan returned to his quarters later that day. His rich brown hair and his clothes were soaked. His face was flushed and his eyes glazed over. He hadn't noticed that Sarah had been crying. All he said was, "Dinner will be ready shortly." He then left her lying on his berth.

Sarah pulled herself off the feather bed and followed a trail of Hassan's clothes to his dressing room. "Cattin," she called out when she spotted the back of him standing motionless in the darkness.

"I am changing out of my wet clothes. I will join you shortly." He called back in a faint voice.

Sarah turned away to give him privacy. She couldn't help noticing that his movements were slower than usual. Hassan ate only one bite of his dinner. He spent the rest of the meal staring at his food. "Cattin, you ill?" she asked when she spotted beads of sweat covering his forehead.

"I am a little tired. I apologize for not being good company tonight."

Sarah reached over and touched his arm. "You rest."

"Thank you for understanding. I think I shall." Hassan stood up. His legs teetered as he took a step.

Sarah lunged towards him, catching him before he could fall over. "I help," she said, wrapping her arm around his waist. Hassan rested his arm on her shoulders. Together they walked to his bedchamber. She carefully lowered him onto his berth, removed his slippers, and covered his trembling body with every blanket that she could find. Fearing for his life, Sarah ran to the door.

"Please. Cattin ill," she said frantically to one of the guards.

"I will get the doctor," said Tristan.

Sarah returned to Hassan's side. Peter ran into the cabin a few minutes later.

"Leave us," Peter barked to Sarah.

Sarah returned to her chair with her pencil and her sketchbook. All she could do was stare at the blank page. She glanced over at the bucket of water sitting beside her trunk. She had forgotten about her bath after her conversation with Peter. Bathing still sounded appealing. She looked back at Hassan's bedchamber and sighed. Peter offered her no hint as to when she could see Hassan again. Sarah undressed and knelt on her straw mat in front of her trunk. She dipped her sponge into the water and stared at the ripples. *Cattin would be alright, wouldn't he? Peter wouldn't bother helping him if he were going to die.* Sarah dressed in the formless gown and took a seat in Hassan's chair. She rested her feet on the seat's edge and wrapped her arms around her shins. Her eyes stared blankly at the lantern as her thoughts returned to her conversation with Peter tumbled in her mind until they tangled into a giant knot of confusion. She had feelings for Hassan; she was certain of it. Her brow furrowed, but was it love? More importantly, did she love him enough to set him free so that he could honor his family's wishes? She didn't have answers that night. The only thing that mattered to her was that Hassan would be alright. Shivers spiked up and down her spine when she heard Peter's footsteps. She jumped up from her chair and faced the doctor. "How is he?"

"The captain is resting," Peter said gravely. "Have you thought about my offer?"

"No, I cannot think about that now," Sarah said, hugging herself. "What can I do to help Cattin?"

"There is nothing you can do except prepare yourself for the possibility of his death."

"No." Sarah shook her head, fighting back her tears.

Peter ambled towards her and attempted to envelop her in his arms. He leaned down to kiss her, but Sarah squirmed out of his arms before his lips reached hers.

Sarah squared her shoulders and said with conviction, "I cannot do this. Cattin is not dead yet, and I will not betray him."

Peter answered her rejection with the kind of smirk that hinted that he knew a secret. He leered at her and said, "Your '*Cattin*' is undeserving of your love. He came to me this afternoon and offered to give you to me."

"I do not believe you," she whimpered.

"But what if he did? Would you obey your master?" Peter challenged.

"I would do my duty," Sarah answered through gritted teeth. "Until those words come from Cattin's lips, my loyalties remain with him. Please leave."

"Very well." Peter headed for the door.

Sarah returned to the bedchamber to check on Hassan. He looked so cold as he clung to his blanket. She gathered all the jackets that she could find and placed them on top of him. After retrieving the bucket of water, she knelt by the berth and wiped the perspiration from his forehead; his condition hadn't improved. "I may not be able to heal you, but I can at least keep you warm." Sarah removed her gown, tied her paru around her waist, and laid beside him. Though he was unconscious, Hassan wrapped his arms around Sarah and pressed his body against her. In time, his shivering stopped.

Gerard Rochelle stared into the abyss of darkness. Every part of his body ached. He lost track of how long he had been there. All he knew was that his pinky's bleeding had finally been reduced to a dribble. None of his crew said anything since settling into the hull of the ship. Gerard would have sworn that he was alone had he not felt the warmth from the bodies of the two men sitting on either side of him. He was strangely grateful for his crew's silence because it gave him time to think.

Gerard grimaced when his pinky throbbed again. The pain fueled his rage. He couldn't understand how his plan had failed. He knew his plan wasn't perfect, yet he was confident that it would succeed none the less. He was equally certain that the corsairs could be bought, and that he would profit from selling his Tahitian prize. Had his plan truly failed? Hassan Aziz wasn't the only corsair in the region. Gerard was equally sure that Aziz wasn't without enemies. All he needed to do was find one.

The overhead thundered with rapid footsteps. Moments later, the lock clicked, and the hatch creaked when it opened. Gerard and the others lifted their heads to see the outlines of the stream of corsairs descending the ladder. Several of them carried lanterns and hung them from the hooks on the overhead.

"Get up," said one of the corsairs in French. Gerard and the others were slow to obey. The pirates yanked them up by their hair when they didn't move. Each winced in pain as they stood for the first time in several days. The prisoners trudged to a symphony of clinking chains as they ascended to the main deck. The sun's punishing rays beat down on the prisoners, forcing their eyes to close until they adjusted to the light. They knew they were in a strange land when they heard the call to prayer echoing from a tower on shore. Gerard's and his crews' steps grew heavier and their stomachs tighter when their eyes landed on their white walled prison.

Gerard studied the captain talking to a member of his crew. The pirate kept pointing to Gerard's men.

Emile leaned forward and whispered. "What do you think they're saying?"

Gerard just shook his head and scanned his crew. "Several members of my crew are missing. What have you done with them?" he demanded.

"Silence infidel dog," a corsair hissed as he thrust his fist into Gerard's stomach.

"They are dead," Adam replied.

"How did they die?" Gerard demanded.

"They took their lives while they were below deck," Adam explained. "I would be more concerned about your own neck."

The corsairs shoved Gerard and his crew forward after Adam barked an order. Glaring at his captor, the French captain cooperated. His pinky throbbed as he descended the rope ladder to the jolly. Once they were settled, he scanned the blue-green harbor and silently noted that he and his men were not alone.

Xebec ships, frigates, merchant ships and fishing boats filled the harbor, all converging to barter or sell their treasures. There were dozens of small boats carrying men, women, and children of every race and nationality. Every captive wore the same expression of dread regardless of their nationality or skin color.

The city of Algiers was an ominous sight with its towering walls staring down at the harbor. It was an impenetrable fortress that looked strangely serene from the outside looking in. The buildings in the city resembled tan building blocks with windows, one stacked on top of the other. Curious spectators stared down from their arched windows, screaming like banshees when Gerard and his men entered the city. Moments later, the Algerines spit and threw rotten food at them in addition to their high-pitched screams. Adam and his corsairs led them across the uneven cobblestone street unaffected by the residents' reception. Gerard and his crew were relieved when the fickle crowd turned their attention to a group of prisoners containing women.

Adam escorted his prisoners through an arched doorway directly beneath the tower. The doors closed behind them, cutting off the fresh air and the natural sunlight. Their captor escorted them down a stone staircase lit with torches lining the wall. The muffled voices coming from below grew louder with each step they took. The narrow passageway eventually opened up into a larger room filled with slaves and Algerine soldiers. Then, they waited.

A distinguished officer sat at a small table, writing down basic information. He was an older man with defined lines grooved into his copper face. What impressed Gerard was his ability to speak whatever language that was required. "Give me your name," the Algerine said in perfect French when Gerard reached the front of the line.

"Rochelle, Gerard Rochelle," said a man with a tenor voice coming from the back of the room.

"Back so soon, Captain?" The Algerine soldier continued in French.

"I had good fortune," the voice replied.

Gerard looked straight ahead as his lips curled into a faint smile.

Chapter 14

Claude Fornier approached the table. "Gerard Rochelle is my cousin."

The Algerine soldier studied the two men. Their body structure and faces were similar enough to come from the same mother. They shared the same pencil-thin mouth and the same weathered face. The only difference was their attire: one was naked, and the other dressed like a corsair. The infidel's hand was also bandaged and looked as if it was missing a finger.

"That changes nothing. The infidel is the property of Naa'il Dhar. He must be processed with the rest of the new slaves," the Algerine maintained.

Claude pursed his lips and acknowledged with a nod. There was little that he could do to help his cousin for the moment. Claude and Gerard waited off to the side of the room for the rest of Gerard's crew to be processed. While they waited, Claude studied Adam Boyle, who stared back as if he were a former adversary. The details of their meeting eluded Claude.

Claude leaned over to Gerard and whispered without taking his eyes off Adam. "Is that the one who seized your vessel?"

"No, Hassan Aziz captured us. He left us in that man's care. Do you know of whom I speak?" Gerard whispered back.

"Only by reputation." Claude frowned. "Did Aziz sever your finger?"

The Algerine guards ushered Gerard's crew into another room before he could answer. They blocked the door, prohibiting Claude from following his cousin. Gerard lingered long enough to answer. "Yes, I have more to tell you. Find me," he shouted before the guards shoved him out of the room. They were taken to a bathing area where they were scoured from head to toe with soap and water. Once clean, they were each given a pair of Ottoman trousers, a matching sleeveless shirt and a coat that reached the middle of their calves. Though Gerard wouldn't admit it, he welcomed the bath and fresh set of clothes. He couldn't remember the last time he had either. After everyone had been cleaned and dressed, their captors herded them into a metal holding cell where they received instructions for their meeting with the Dey, which would take place the following morning. Finally, Gerard and his men were each given a piece of brown bread and a cup of water for their dinner. Then it was quiet. While his men sat in silence, Gerard paced across a small section of the cage, his eyes glancing at the door every few minutes.

A guard called his name almost two hours later. Gerard grinned as he darted to the iron door while ignoring his crew's inquisitive stares. He followed the Algerine guard down a narrow corridor to a small room off to the side of the main hallway.

"You have ten minutes," the guard said to Claude, who surreptitiously slipped him a gold ring. "I will return for the infidel in a half an hour," the guard amended after tucking the ring into his pocket.

The cousins embraced after the heavy iron door clicked shut. "You were a fool to come to the Barbary Coast, but it is good to see you none the less. What happened?" Claude asked.

Gerard recounted his tale, beginning with acquiring Sarah. However, he left out murdering her father.

"I don't care about the harlot; I want to know about Aziz. I don't need details about his attack. I want to know about *him and his crew*," Claude interrupted.

"Aziz and his crew looked and dressed like you. They spoke in English when they talked amongst themselves - when they thought no one else could hear them," Gerard explained.

"Was their accent American or British?"

"British, I am certain of it."

"Tell me about Aziz. Can you remember anything that distinguishes his appearance?"

Gerard stared blankly at a small scar on his cousin's neck. "Yes, Aziz had a scar on his cheek."

"Shelby!" Claude punched the stone wall.

"Who is Shelby?"

"The man matching your description sounds like Nathan Shelby. He was a captain in the British Royal Navy. We met in battle several years ago, a battle I should have lost, but by sheer luck, we defeated them. I should have let them go, but selling them to the Dey of Algiers was profitable," Claude explained in an almost trance-like state.

"Claude, are you sure that Aziz is Shelby?"

"Yes, I cut Shelby's cheek when we faced each other in battle."

The guard poked his head around the door and motioned for Gerard to follow him.

Claude reached for his cousin's arm and said, "I will try to arrange a private meeting with the Dey. I am certain that he will be interested in hearing about your prize. Until then, try to rest; you will need your strength."

It had been almost three days since Naa'il visited Mariam and nearly five since he visited Samina. Though he had a hectic day ahead of him, Naa'il decided to visit his second wife first. He would keep his visit short; he told himself as he headed to Samina's chamber. Naa'il posted guards outside his wives' apartment day and night. It was early morning, and no one stood guard outside Samina's door. His second wife wasn't an early riser either. Even at a distance, he could tell that the door was slightly ajar.

"You, come with me," Naa'il barked at the two soldiers guarding another room.

They snapped to attention and followed their master. Naa'il burst into the room just as his second wife yelped, followed by laughter. Dressed in a yellow robe, her head and her face were completely uncovered. Samina stood behind a guard who was crouching on the floor. "My lord." She covered her mouth with her hands when she spotted her husband standing in her doorway with an angry look on his face.

The guard assisting Samina jumped to his feet. He looked as terrified as his wife.

His eyes narrowing, Naa'il commanded, "Take him. Have him executed tomorrow morning."

"No, he was just trying to help me." Samina cried as the soldiers led the guard away.

Naa'il waited until he and his wife were alone. "You wretched whore!" He backhanded Samina across the cheek.

She fell to the floor, crying. "I screamed because I found a mouse in my room. He came to my aid to capture and dispose of it."

"A mouse," Naa'il scoffed. "You were caught alone with a man in your bedchamber, improperly dressed and uncovered!"

"Yes, that is true, but we did nothing wrong," Samina pleaded.

"You brought shame on my family. You will receive one hundred lashes," Naa'il said in a murderous tone. "Put her in irons," he said to the additional guards, who led her out of the room screaming. His knees buckled; Naa'il collapsed onto the bed and closed his eyes when Samina shouted, "I am innocent!" The morning light filtering into the room gently encouraged him to continue his morning visits.

Mariam had just finished dressing when Naa'il entered her apartment. "Leave us," he barked.

Mariam's attendants bowed to Naa'il and glanced back at their mistress, who nodded for them to leave.

"Good morning, my husband," Mariam said curtly as she adjusted her green hirka before slipping her gold bangles onto her wrists.

"Are you in health?" Naa'il replied in a like manner.

"Yes, and so are your daughters." Mariam lowered her gaze to the floor.

"Forgive my absence." Naa'il laced his fingers together behind his back.

"You have many demands on you," Mariam paused as she studied her husband. "You seem troubled, my Lord." Her statuesque expression didn't change as Naa'il informed her of the events from that morning.

"It is just as well." Mariam shrugged. "I always knew Samina's recklessness would bring shame on our family. So she has. I trust her punishment will be discreet."

"Of course. If you will excuse me, I have work to do."

"Would you not like to see your daughters?"

"Not today." Naa'il walked out of the room.

After a relaxing morning of being pampered by servants, Cora spent the rest of the afternoon talking to Mamnoon. Every woman in the harem seemed to be aware that she would be spending the night with the Dey. No one made an effort to sabotage her this time, especially with Mamnoon watching over her.

Naa'il was sitting in the garden with his head bowed when Cora arrived. "Good evening, Your Excellency." Cora curtsied to him. "You seem troubled. Would you like me to leave?"

Naa'il held out his hand. "Come, sit by me. It has been a trying day," he said once Cora was seated.

Cora covered her mouth to masque her horror as she listened to Naa'il's story. "I'm so sorry," was all she could say. "Are you certain that they are guilty of the crime of which they have been accused?"

Naa'il stood, facing away from her with his fingers laced behind his back. He glanced over his shoulder and said, "I do not expect you to understand our ways. It is a crime for a girl or woman to be alone with a man who is not a member of her family. Her punishment is appropriate for the offense."

Cora bit her lip as she attempted to form an answer. "You're right; we come from two different worlds that couldn't be more opposite from each other. Your culture embraces polygamy; mine does not."

"What is polygamy?"

"It means that a man is married to more than one woman at the same time."

"I never understood why men in your country cannot have more than one wife. What if his wife does not give him a son? Do men in America not need an heir?"

Cora stifled a laugh. "I believe that is true for some affluent families. Most parents in that predicament, like mine, love the children that God gave them. Is that not true for your people?"

"Yes. I have four daughters. I love them very much." Naa'il smiled tenderly. "Why do your men allow their women to be alone with men who are not part of their family? Are they not concerned about their family's honor?"

"Of course they are. In my culture, men choose to trust women."

"Women are weak," Naa'il scoffed. "They can easily be tempted."

Cora raised a brow. "Is that what you think of me?"

"No, you are different. You are strong and honorable," Naa'il softened.

Cora shifted beside Naa'il and sat down on the edge of the fountain. "It may surprise you that we women take our marriage vow very seriously. Marriage in my country is sacred, as it is in yours. I freely admit that not all men and women honor the promises they make to each other. Those that are fortunate enough to join in union out of love - real love, will live for each other for the rest of their lives. They would rather kill themselves than betray the other by taking another lover. Likewise, there is no greater betrayal than when a woman discovers that her husband was unfaithful to her and vice versa."

Naa'il's eyes narrowed. "Are you rebuking me for being intimate with my concubines?"

"I am not passing judgment, Your Excellency; I am merely defending the people of my gender." Cora studied Naa'il. "May I ask you a personal question?"

"That depends on the question." Naa'il's posture stiffened.

"Do you love your second wife?"

"Yes," Naa'il said without hesitation.

"Don't you owe it to her to investigate whether or not she was telling the truth?"

"I know what I saw. Our laws are clear, Cora. Samina must be punished," Naa'il said bitterly.

"Then I suppose that I should be put to death too."

"This is different," Naa'il snapped.

"Why? We are not related, yet we are alone. We have even shared a bed."

"You are my slave; you must obey me."

"I see." Cora grimaced. "Regarding your wife, permit me to give you something to ponder."

"Continue." Naa'il flicked his hand in the air.

"Why do you post a guard outside your wife's door?"

"He is there to protect her."

"Precisely. When a soldier hears a scream from the person that he is assigned to protect, he is not going to hesitate to ascertain why, for he fears that delaying, even for a moment, may kill her. Likewise, when a woman is frightened, she is not going to delay her scream long enough to cover herself, especially if an intruder is attacking her. My point is Your Excellency, if you love your wife, love her enough to try to confirm her story. If she is truly innocent, then perhaps she and her guard deserve mercy."

"Mercy is for the weak. Changing my mind is a sign of weakness."

"Perhaps. I agree with a playwright named William Shakespeare:

The quality of mercy is not strain'd,
It droppeth as the gentle rain from heaven
Upon the place beneath. It is twice blest:
It blesseth him that gives and him that takes.

Naa'il shook his head. "Samina said that she screamed because of a mouse. Why would anyone be afraid of a little mouse?"

"I am afraid of rats," Cora admitted. "I scream every time I see one."

"You surprise me. I did not think you feared anything," Naa'il grinned.

"We are all afraid of something." Cora stood and rested her hand on his arm. "Regarding your dilemma, you must do what you believe is best. I caution you because I don't want you to live with the guilt of putting two innocent people to death, should you discover later that they were innocent. If it pleases you, I will take my leave so that you can ponder your dilemma."

"Thank you for your counsel. You will return tomorrow so we can talk more." Naa'il leaned over and kissed her.

"I look forward to our next meeting. Good night, Your Excellency." Cora stood and curtsied.

Everything that Cora said resonated with him, moreover, he shared her concerns. Cora was proof that he had been wrong before. She was right; he couldn't live with himself if the guard was simply doing his duty. Yielding to his conscience's insistence, Naa'il returned to Samina's apartment. It was strange being in her chamber when she wasn't there to greet him. Ever since the day they married, Samina ran into his arms, smiling at him as if she hadn't seen him in years. In spite of her impetuosity, she never gave him a reason to doubt her love until this morning.

Just then, a tiny gray mouse scampered across the floor, heading to the place where he found Samina and the guard that morning. Naa'il lifted her bed, sending feathers flying into the air. Three baby mice toppled out of the bottom. "Samina." Naa'il dropped the feather pillow and ran to the dungeon where his wife was being held.

His child bride laid on the stone floor. Her sobbing ceased; she sat up and looked at Naa'il as if she didn't know what to say. She wasn't the only one who was at a loss for words.

"I found your mouse. You were sleeping on a family of them," Naa'il said, entering her prison cell with hesitant footsteps.

"Then you believe me?"

Naa'il nodded and crossed his arms. "Do you love me, Samina?"

"Yes, with my whole heart, my Lord," Samina replied, staring at the floor.

"I cannot condone your being alone with a guard in your chamber. I can admit that he was doing his duty to protect you, even if it was from a little mouse."

"Then you will spare his life?"

"Yes, I have already commanded him to return to duty. He will no longer be assigned to guarding your apartment," Naa'il said with a sheepish grin. "I will look past your indiscretion this one time. Know this; I will not hold back punishment if you are caught in another compromising situation."

Samina bowed her head and wept even harder.

Naa'il squatted in front of her and wiped the tears from her cheeks. "No more tears, Samina. You will spend the night with me while I rid your apartment of your mice. Perhaps we can make another child." He toppled over when Samina threw her arms around his neck, this time crying with joy. Naa'il personally escorted his second wife to the wives' private entrance to the harem. "Come to me after you are clean."

"I look forward to it." Samina smiled sweetly.

Naa'il waited until his wife was inside the room before saying to the guard, "Have Mamnoon bring Cora Bradley to Abigail Randall's apartment. He will understand my message." He ran back to his apartment and retrieved Cora's Bible before heading to her new home. They arrived shortly after he did. "Thank you, Mamnoon. Bring food and drink to Cora. You are dismissed after that."

"Yes, Your Excellency," Mamnoon bowed and left, closing the door behind him.

Naa'il couldn't help smiling as Cora surveyed her new apartment with a gaping jaw. He couldn't deny that it was a beautiful room. It was more than twice the size of her torture chamber. Blue, white, yellow and green tiles arranged like six-petal flowers covered the lower half of the walls of her new home.

"This must have taken years to carve," she said, tracing the intricately carved upper wall with her finger. Cora wandered over to the alcove directly in front of her. The bed consisted of an oversized pillow with smaller ones lining the wall. The yellow silk curtains hanging from the ceiling created a canapé above the bed. Cora knelt down and ran her hand over the lemon-color pillows. "It's beautiful," she cooed.

After exploring the main room, she meandered through the arched doorway, leading to a small courtyard filled with flowers in raised beds in each corner. A four petal flower bed surrounded a three-tiered fountain in the center of the garden. Naa'il turned a knob at the base. Cora's eyes lit up as she watched the water trickle from the top tier to the bottom.

"Now you can feel the sun's warmth on your face or look at the stars in peace whenever you wish."

"Do you mean this room is for me?" Cora asked with genuine surprise.

"Yes, you have earned it." Naa'il handed the Bible to Cora. "May these both help you find peace. You have my word that no one will enter your apartment unless they receive your permission first."

"I don't know what to say, except, thank you." Cora wiped a tear from the corner of her eye. "Did I understand correctly that your second wife was delivered to the harem a few minutes ago?"

"Yes, you and a little mouse saved her life."

"And the guard?"

"He is free too. I am grateful for your counsel."

Cora bowed her head, expelling her breath. "Thank you for listening to me."

"You are a wise woman, Cora Bradley." Naa'il gently squeezed her hand.

"And you are a good man. I hope this means that you are going to spend some time with her."

Naa'il raised a brow. "Yes, tonight." He said with a hint of regret in his voice.

"I am pleased to hear it."

"Are you tired of my company already?" Naa'il teased.

"No, of course not. You should spend the night with your wife."

Naa'il sighed, "But I want to be with you."

"I'm fond of you too. Being with your wife is the way it should be, Your Excellency. Now off with you."

Naa'il sadly nodded. "Would you like me to send your cousin to you?"

"No, I'm cross with her right now. I confronted her about her limp today. I think a night to myself will do me good. Thank you for my new home." Cora escorted him to the door.

Naa'il rested his hand on the doorknob and looked at her thoughtfully, "Cora, we are better, yes?"

"Yes. Enjoy your evening, Your Excellency."

"And to you." Naa'il kissed her.

Passing the night with his second wife felt like a lifetime. After making love to Samina, Naa'il tossed and turned until the dawn's first light. He grinned when he felt the familiar peace covering him like a warm blanket. Naa'il slid out of bed, taking extra care not to disturb his wife. He dressed in the dark, not caring if his clothes didn't match. All that mattered to him was seeing Cora again.

The guards stepped aside as he poked his head through the door like a parent looking in on his sleeping child. It didn't surprise him to find Cora sitting in the courtyard with her Bible perched on her lap. Naa'il quietly closed the door behind him and leaned against a roped pillar like a person having nowhere to go while he watched the woman he loved. Her eyes were closed, and a peaceful smile graced her lips. "Good morning," he said when he couldn't wait any longer.

"Your Excellency." Cora jumped to her feet, sending her Bible toppling to the ground and scattering her notes everywhere.

"Forgive me for startling you." He crouched beside her. "How was your evening?" he asked as they gathered her papers. He picked up her book and stuffed the notes between the pages.

"Peaceful. How was your night?"

"It was not good, not good at all." Naa'il invited Cora to sit while he remained standing.

"I'm sorry."

"Are you not going to ask me why?" he asked, impatiently.

"It is not my place to pry into your affairs."

"It concerns you."

"Oh dear," Cora mumbled.

"I could not stop thinking about you. All night, thoughts of you filled my head." Naa'il let out a loud sigh. "I called your name when I made love to my wife - twice, or perhaps even three times."

"No!" Cora covered her mouth with her hand.

"Samina cried herself to sleep. I spent the rest of the night lying in bed thinking about you." His face relaxed. "You should have been lying beside me, not Samina."

Cora opened her mouth without making a sound.

Naa'il took a seat beside her. He reached for her hand and continued, "I came to a decision last night. I know what you will say; I want you to listen to me first. Please."

Her head bowed, Cora rested her hand on her stomach.

"I want you to be my third wife. I do not expect to make love to you immediately. I hope we will someday - when you are ready. I can be patient, but I do not want to delay our marriage."

Unable to answer, Cora stared at the Dey with a slack jaw. "I don't know what to say, Your Excellency. Why do you want to marry me even though I refuse to abandon my faith?"

"Yes," he caressed her cheek with the back of his finger. "You are very obstinate. I think that is why I love you. You are an extraordinary woman, Cora Bradley. I have never met anyone like you. I suppose that is why you consume my every thought." Naa'il took a necklace from his pocket.

"Oh my goodness!" Cora stared wide-eyed at the band of white stones. "May I ask what these stones are?"

"They are diamonds. Consider them a token of my love."

Cora hung her head to conceal her tears. "I don't know what to say to your gift or your proposal, Your Excellency."

His breath hitched when he spotted the sadness in her eyes. "I believe the appropriate answers are 'thank you' and 'I would be honored,'" he suggested, knowing that her reply was already no.

Cora stood and faced the fountain. "I am not worthy of you, not after what happened. I am no longer a virgin."

Naa'il approached her and spun her around to face him. She stiffened when he kissed her cheek tenderly. "I do not care."

"It does not bother you that at least half, if not all your guards have had their way with me?" she asked as tears streamed down her cheeks.

"They took you by force at my command. I still love you, and I want you to be my wife," Naa'il maintained. "You have not given me an answer."

"May I have some time to consider your proposal? Please?"

Naa'il sighed. "What are your concerns?"

Cora wrapped her hand around her wrist and squeezed for fear of letting go. "My recent ordeal has left me more wounded than I can begin to tell you. I fear that I can't be a good wife to you or anyone else. It is hard for me to be touched without recoiling. That is not fair to you."

"I told you that I can be patient. All you know of intimacy came by force. I believe you will discover that making love is different. I promise." Naa'il paused. "I think we will be very happy together."

Cora's shoulders straightened as she gained control of her emotions. "And what of your wives and daughters? Though I do not know them personally, I have to believe that they love you. I do not want to be the person that takes you away from them."

Naa'il sighed again. He looked into her eyes. "I love my wives and daughters. I always will. I can be a good husband to all of you. Mariam and Samina have shared me for several years now, and I have never neglected either of them. I will not neglect them after we marry."

"May I have time to think before I give you my answer? Please?"

"If you must; I will come to you on the third day; I will expect your answer then." Naa'il tucked the necklace into his pocket.

"Thank you for your patience." Cora forced a smile.

"I will leave you now." Naa'il walked to the door in his usual confident strides. As soon as he turned the corner and with no one around, Naa'il sagged against the wall, sinking into a sitting position and resting his forehead on his knees.

CHAPTER 15

It was still early when Naa'il headed to Mariam's apartment. She usually rose before her attendants. "Is my wife awake?" he asked the guard standing outside her door.

"I heard her rustling around her chamber, Your Excellency." The guard bowed.

Naa'il knocked on the door. "Mariam."

"Enter," her muffled voice called back.

Mariam had just tied her silk robe's cream sash. Her hair was still in a single braid draped down her chest. "Good morning, husband. You are up early," she said in a conversational tone.

"Good morning." Naa'il stepped into the room and closed the door behind him.

"Shall I send for some tea?"

"Not this morning," he said, intentionally looking past her.

"Would you care to sit?" Mariam sat down on a cushion and invited her husband to sit beside her. Naa'il remained standing. "I imagine you have much on your mind this morning, preparing for the guard's execution and Samina's punishment. I trust you will be present for both?"

Feeling a sudden thirst, Naa'il went over to a small table against the wall. He poured a glass of water and drank his beverage in a few gulps. "I granted them clemency." Naa'il glanced over his shoulder.

Mariam stared at him with a gaping jaw. "You did what?"

"I granted them clemency. It was the right thing to do this time." Naa'il explained his reason for changing his mind.

The consternation on Mariam's face didn't change. "The circumstances do not matter. I like Samina, but she brought shame on our family. She must be punished for her indiscretion, or she will never learn from her mistakes."

"How dare you question my judgment? I could flog you for your insolence!" The Dey shouted. "I made my decision. It is not your place to challenge my rulings." Naa'il threw a bowl of fruit against the wall.

Mariam jumped when the bowl shattered. Still, she stared at him with contempt.

Naa'il took several deep breaths. "I also came here to inform you that I made a decision to marry Cora Bradley," he said in a calmer tone.

"Marriage," Mariam gasped. "Did she convert?"

"No. I am the Dey of Algiers, and I am free to do as I wish."

"You are not above our laws," Mariam protested with a shrill. "You can be put to death as easily as any of us."

"There is no law forbidding me from marrying a Christian woman."

Mariam stood and approached her husband. "Naa'il, I beg you; please do not do this."

"I love her. I *want* to marry her," Naa'il said calmly.

"That woman is going to bring destruction upon our family, and you are too blind to see it. Please leave." Mariam turned her back to her husband.

Naa'il could tell that she was crying by the way her shoulders bobbed up and down, and he was too angry to care.

Cora hadn't moved from her bench when Mamnoon came for her. She was so deep in thought that she hadn't noticed him standing in front of her, or that the mid-day sun was shining on her face.

"Cora," Mamnoon gently prodded. "It is time for you to go to the harem."

Cora didn't move from her bench. "May we talk first? I need to confide in someone. Please?"

"Of course." Mamnoon sat beside her.

"I don't know where to begin," she said with a weary look. "His Excellency asked me to marry him this morning."

Mamnoon hung his head and closed his eyes. "That does not surprise me," he said, looking down at her.

Cora bit her lip. "Why not?"

"For a long time, I thought His Excellency hated you. I recently realized that you tormented him because he was in love with you. He could not admit it to himself until a few days ago. How do you feel about him?" He paused when he spotted her hesitation. "I will not repeat what you say to anyone."

Cora took a deep breath. "I cannot deny that I find myself caring for him; I believe that he cares for me too." She shook her head. "I fear that our feelings towards each other do not outweigh my concerns."

"What are your concerns?"

"My recent history is one of them. The wounds on my body will heal; I fear that my inner wounds will always torment me. You may not know this, but I can't sleep anymore. When I do, I wake up screaming. I worry that I will never feel comfortable having a man touch me again. That is not fair to His Excellency, especially if he wants me to give him children." Cora stood and walked over to the fountain. Her hands clutched her arms as her shoulders hunched over. "I feel so dirty, all the time. As hard as I try, I cannot get clean," she said, fighting back her tears. She looked over her shoulder at her friend. "What if I am already with child? How … how can I love a child that was born out of force?" Cora shuddered and took another deep breath. "Then there is the issue of being part of a polygamous marriage. I know your laws permit men to have up to four wives, but it is a sin for a Christian. I cannot imagine how wives competing for their husband's affections benefits anyone. That is doubly true for the children. I do not want to come between His Excellency and the family he already has. Those are just a few of my concerns."

"Did you express them to His Excellency?"

"No. I only asked for time to consider my answer."

"I think you already know your answer."

Cora nodded and looked reflectively at her friend. "May I ask you a question?"

"Of course."

"Do I have a choice in this matter?"

"No, you do not," Mamnoon said grimly.

"I agree."

"Marrying the Dey is not terrible, Cora. Naa'il Dhar loves his wives and his children; he would give his life for them."

"Does he? How much time does he spend with them beyond his morning visits?" Cora challenged. "I come from a world where marriage is defined between one man and one woman. I, like most girls, dreamed of marrying a prince. None of those dreams included sharing my husband with other wives, not to mention with a room full of concubines. The thought of not having a husband to myself makes me cry. What is my alternative, spending the rest of my life in a room filled with women who want to kill me?"

"Cora, His Excellency *is* different with you; he listens to you. He talks to you more than he talks to his wives. That should give you hope. As his wife, you would have the ability to influence him. Perhaps, you can persuade him to improve the lives of the women in the harem."

"That is encouraging." Cora crossed her arms and studied her friend. "You like His Excellency, don't you?"

"I served his predecessor. The previous Dey was a very cruel man. He had three out of four of his wives stoned to death."

Cora covered her mouth with her hand to conceal her shock. "My God."

"As you witnessed, Naa'il Dhar can be equally cruel. You do not want him for an enemy. Unlike his predecessor, His Excellency is a fair man. It took great humility for him to admit that he misjudged you. He must love you deeply to want to marry you in spite of your recent history. I am certain that he understands that you may never want him to touch you. That alone should convince you that there is good in him."

"You're right," Cora admitted as the tension drained from her face. "I suppose that we should go to the harem."

"Yes, we should."

"Thank you, my dear friend." Cora kissed Mamnoon's cheek.

Mariam brushed past the guards, waving off Samina's attendants. "You wanted to see me?"

Samina sat up when she spotted Mariam standing like a statue, glaring at her with unforgiving eyes. Swallowing hard, Samina asked. "Did Naa'il tell you his news this morning?"

"Yes, he informed me that he intends to marry the American infidel," Mariam replied in a matter of fact tone.

"Why would Naa'il want to marry an infidel? They are dirty people. She will bring shame on our family."

Mariam remained standing in the center of the room with her arms crossed. "She would not be the first. I understand our husband granted you clemency for your indiscretion."

"I was innocent; I swear it," Samina hissed.

"Be that as it may, you brought shame upon our family. Had I been your husband, you would have been flogged one hundred times. There is no excuse for what you did," Mariam said with a stony glare.

Samina pulled herself off her bed and glowered at the first wife with her back arched. "Of course you would think that. You are a rigid old hag," she sneered. "Compassion is not in your nature. You would have had me flogged even if I were being attacked by an intruder."

Mariam slapped Samina's cheek. "You brought shame on our family. You do not deserve mercy."

The guards rushed into the room when they heard Samina scream. One guard grabbed her just as she charged Mariam with her claws drawn, "I hate you; I hate the American. I hope you both die a long and painful death." The other guard grabbed Mariam and forced her to leave the apartment.

Cora took a deep breath as she stood outside the Harem with Mamnoon by her side.

"Are you sure you want to go in?" Mamnoon teased.

"No, but I should spend time with my cousin."

"You have done enough for her."

Cora leaned in and whispered, "Now, now." She sighed. "I suppose I cannot delay this any longer."

"Cora, you are braver than many soldiers I know. If you can survive what you have endured these past few weeks, you can survive being with your cousin and the other women in the harem."

"How can I not be when you're watching over me?" Cora nudged her friend with her shoulder. Abigail and Tess were huddled together playing with Molly. It still surprised her how she could make a room full of people stop what they were doing, just by stepping into the room. "Excuse me," she said to Mamnoon before breaking away from him.

"Can you watch Molly for me tonight?" Tess asked Abigail. They glanced at Cora and continued their conversation as if she weren't there. "I am entertaining a guest."

"Of course," Abigail replied.

"Thank you. I should be back by morning."

Cora sighed when they didn't acknowledge her presence. "May I join you?"

"If you must," Tess rolled her eyes. "I understand that you are His Lordship's new favorite."

"If you say so." Cora shrugged and sat down on the floor.

Tess looked down her nose at the intruder. "You must have done something right to get your own apartment."

"You will have to ask His Excellency," Cora countered.

"Then it's true; you are his mistress," Abigail surmised.

"No, it's not. His Excellency and I are not lovers; we never were," Cora plainly stated.

"What is your relationship to His Lordship, exact ...?" Tess's voice trailed off when Samina and her attendants entered the main harem. "What is she doing in here?"

"Who is that?" Abigail whispered.

"That is Princess Samina, His Lordship's second wife. I don't understand why she didn't use the wives' private entrance."

Samina stood at the door, scanning the room as if she were searching for someone. Bashira approached her from across the chamber and bowed when she reached the second wife. They spoke only for a few moments. Arching her back, Samina marched over to Cora. Cora did her best to duck out of Samina's way as she screamed and hit her. Mamnoon charged across the room. Samina's screams continued as he grabbed her waist and pulled her away from Cora. Samina didn't stop screaming until the bathing room door closed.

"What did you do to her?" Tess asked Cora.

Cora stared at the bathing room door with a gaping jaw. "I don't know."

"You must have done something to offend her," Abigail insisted.

"We've never met."

"I don't believe you," Abigail countered.

"I don't care if you believe me or not. I have no reason to lie," Cora snapped.

"Oh God, you're going to be His Lordship's next wife, aren't you?" Tess postulated. "That is the only reason the princess would be that bitter."

Cora looked away.

"It's true. Naa'il asked you to marry him, didn't he?" Abigail said with a dazed stare.

Cora scanned the women surrounding them, who were all watching her with interest. Her lips subtly formed a mischievous grin. She leaned in and whispered, "Yes, His Excellency asked me this morning. I have not given him my answer."

Tess stared at Cora as if she were mad. "Why not? It gets you out of here."

"I hate you!" Abigail screeched. "I hope you and Naa'il will be miserable together." She stood up and stormed off.

"Abigail," Cora called out. Her cheeks burned when she heard the whispers about her pending marriage spreading throughout the room.

"If you want my advice, marry His Lordship. It is better than living in this prison," Tess said.

"Thank you, Tess, I will consider your advice," Cora replied angrily.

"Good! I hope you will make me one of your attendants."

"I'm certainly not going to ask Ula," Cora stood up. "Please excuse me."

"What the devil is taking her so long?" Tess groused as she plopped herself down beside Abigail and shifted Molly onto her lap. "How am I supposed to prepare for tonight when I can't take a bath?"

"Do you mean Samina is still in the bathing room?" Abigail asked.

"How am I to know that? The door has been closed for hours. Some of us have to entertain clients!" Tess shouted at the bathing room door.

Abigail scanned the room. "Where is Cora?"

"I don't know," Tess shrugged. "Perhaps she left. She was talking to Mamnoon the last time I saw her."

"Good riddance," Abigail said as she watched the servants setting food on the table in the center of the room.

"Will you watch Molly? Bashira has finally come out of hiding."

"Certainly." Abigail held her hand out. "Come to Auntie Abigail," she said in a baby voice. "We are going to have lots of adventures tonight, aren't we?"

"Let me know if any of them involve escaping this prison." Tess rolled her eyes. "I will find you before I leave." Bashira was talking quietly to a group of servants when Tess approached her. "Are we going to be able to get into the bathing area any time soon?" Tess silently observed Bashira sliding a small green vial into her pocket. "I am part of His Lordship's entertainment tonight."

"Yes, yes. I am aware of your needs," Bashira said to Tess and the small group of women gathering around her for the same reason. "You may go in now." She pointed to the bathing room door which was now open.

"It's about time," Tess huffed.

"You will have plenty of it. Now, off with you."

"Are you ready to return to your apartment?" Mamnoon asked.

Cora was too focused on the scene unfolding in front of her to answer. Dressed in an orange silk concubine uniform, Tess headed to the front door with a few other women wearing similar clothing. It was dinner time. The slaves were busy serving food to their mistresses. The servant that drew Cora's attention was the one Ula was beating. She was a pretty girl that couldn't have been more than ten years old. It broke Cora's heart seeing cuts and bruises on the child's sweet face. Cora ran up to Ula and blocked her hand before she could hit the girl again. "Leave her alone."

"What are you going to do, report me to the Dey?" Ula sneered back.

"No, I'm perfectly capable of fighting my own battles." Cora punched Ula's jaw. The concubine toppled into her friends who steadied her enough to charge back. Cora darted and grabbed Ula from the side. She forced Naa'il's former paramour to hunch over and kneed Ula in the stomach before breaking a bowl over her head. The concubine collapsed to the floor, unconscious. "Does anyone else want to challenge me?" Cora shouted, staring defiantly at the women surrounding her. "Anyone who attacks another child will answer to me."

"That's enough!" Bashira shouted as Mamnoon grabbed Cora's arms from behind. "The rest of you return to your assigned places, or you will not get any dinner tonight." The women scattered and returned to their normal activity upon seeing the valide's uncompromising glare. "Cora, come with me. Mamnoon, send word to His Excellency that there has been an incident involving Cora. She will wait for him in the box."

Winking to Mamnoon, Cora turned on her heels and trotted back to the discipline room with two guards struggling to keep up. One opened the door to the room, which was nothing more than a small closet. Cora stepped inside and slid to the floor with her knees pressed against her chest.

Naa'il pushed past the guards into his wife's apartment. "Leave us." He barked to her attendants. He stepped aside and waited for them to exit before closing the door. "You wanted to see me?" He demanded, glaring at Mariam. "State your complaint plainly, for I do not have much time to spare tonight."

The first wife glared at her husband and said angrily, "I was in the harem today. I left in time to witness your beloved infidel attacking another woman."

"Indeed." Naa'il groaned.

"My Lord, I know you care for this woman. Keep her as your

mistress, if you care that much for her. I implore you; do not marry her. She is not a suitable wife for the Dey of Algiers."

"I will tend to this matter." Naa'il nudged in until the ends of their noses touched. "Never tell me what to do."

Mamnoon opened the door twenty minutes later. "His Excellency wants to see you." He offered his hand to Cora and pulled her to her feet.

Cora bit her lip. "Is he angry?"

"Yes." Mamnoon paused. "His Excellency already knew about your altercation."

"Oh dear." Cora sighed. She found Naa'il pacing back and forth across the floor in her apartment with his fingers interlaced behind his back. He looked as angry as she had ever seen him. Cora kept her distance when she spotted the scowl on his lips. "Good afternoon, Your Excellency. I did not expect to see you today," she said casually.

"I understand that you got into an altercation this afternoon."

"Yes, I did. A woman attacked a little girl; I made her stop," she proudly explained.

"That is not acceptable behavior for my wife," Naa'il shouted.

"What was I supposed to do; allow this woman to beat the child to death?" Cora shouted back.

"She is a slave." Naa'il's voice boomed over hers.

"She is an innocent child. We may be your property, but we are all God's children and are therefore precious to Him. We laugh, we cry, we love, and want to be loved. There is nothing more offensive than mistreating children. I will not apologize for stopping that attack, and I will fight for every child that is mistreated in the harem!" Cora looked away and bit her lip. "Your Excellency, I am honored that you want to marry me," she continued in a calmer tone. "I care enough about you not to want to do anything to dishonor your family. If you are concerned that

I will embarrass you in some way, perhaps it is best that we not marry. Either way, I will not stop protecting mistreated children."

Naa'il pursed his lips. "Who attacked the child?"

"I would rather not say."

"You would rather not say," Naa'il angrily repeated. He held his hands by his side, forming them into fists. "You are going to tell me."

"This matter is settled. Bashira took the servant away from the woman, and I doubt she will give her another one. That is why you need not be involved."

Naa'il headed towards the door. He rested his hand on the doorknob and looked back at her. "This matter is not settled. I will return to you during the morning of the third day; until then, you will remain here. I will inform you of my decision concerning your fate the next time we meet. I would encourage you to ponder your future while I am away."

Chapter 16

Hassan's eyes fluttered open when he felt the warmth of a person lying beside him. He crinkled his forehead as he tried to recall Sarah entering his berth when he distinctly remembered informing her that they couldn't be lovers. They slept separately ever since then, or so he thought. Hassan never drank enough to get drunk. The last thing he recalled was standing in the rain and feeling miserable by the end of the day. Now, he lay on his berth under a thick layer of coats and blankets.

Hoping to find clues, Hassan flicked the layers off him and lifted the remaining cover. He was wearing breeches, but someone had removed the rest of his clothes. Sarah only wore the blue cloth tied around her waist. Hassan glanced over to the other side of him and frowned when he spotted a chair and a bucket with a wet cloth draped over the bucket's edge sitting beside his berth. He had no idea how they got there, or why they were even needed. The sun looked like it was sinking below the horizon, and he wondered how long he had been asleep, or why no one woke him for his watch.

Sarah rolled over and sat up. "Cattin." She looked at Hassan as if she was relieved to see him.

"What happened?" Hassan asked in a groggy voice.

"You ill."

"Ill? How long was I unconscious?"

Sarah pressed her lips together. She looked up at the ochre rafters before answering. "You sleep this day." She held up her first finger. "This day," she extended another finger. "You wake this day," she held up a third one.

"I have been unconscious for two days?" Hassan gasped.

"Aye."

"Have you been here this whole time?" he asked.

"Peter helped. I get him." She climbed down from the berth and entered the main cabin.

"Cover yourself," Hassan called out when Sarah passed beyond his view.

"Aye," Sarah peered around the divider before disappearing again.

Hassan chuckled seeing Sarah dressed in a white tunic with a proud grin. She still didn't care that her legs from her knees to her feet were fully exposed.

"Look who is awake," Peter said a few minutes later. He sat down on the chair. "How are you feeling, Captain?"

"Weak and confused. Sarah said that I was unconscious for over two days?"

"You were very ill. We were not sure if you would survive," Peter said with a hint of amazement.

"You should know me by now; I am not that easy to kill. What happened?"

"There isn't much to tell other than you were delirious for several days. Do you remember anything?"

"Hmm." Hassan looked intently at the coats and blankets piled at the end of the berth. Just then, cryptic images flashed into his mind. "I remember Sarah lifting my head and feeding me water. I remember her wiping the perspiration from my forehead." His smile widened. "I remember Sarah using her body to keep me warm." He looked at his friend. "She never left my side."

Peter grimaced. "Sarah took good care of you."

"I am grateful for your care as well," Hassan said with sincerity.

"Of course." Peter stood up. "I will let you rest."

Sarah peered around the divider. "You like food?"

Hassan's stomach growled. "I would." He threw the remaining blanket off him.

"You stay. I bring food." Sarah covered him again.

Ordinarily, Hassan would have insisted on eating at the table. His only ambition tonight was to sit up enough to lean his back against the bulkhead.

Moments later Hassan spotted a flicker of light growing brighter as it neared his chamber. Sarah climbed onto a chair and hung the lamp from the overhead. She scampered down and left him before returning with Hassan's dinner. She carefully laid the tray on his lap and walked away.

"Are you joining me?" he called out.

"Aye," Sarah called back. She reappeared carrying her dinner. Holding the tray steady, she lowered herself onto the chair.

Hassan pulled back the fish's skin and sliced off a piece of meat. "Thank you for looking after me," he said before stuffing it into his mouth.

Sarah's blue eyes widened in astonishment. "You remember?"

Hassan reached over and gently squeezed her hand. "I don't remember much, except that you were part of every memory I have of the past few days. I am grateful for your caring for me."

"You welcome." Sarah smiled back and peeled an orange.

"I thought we agreed that you would not sleep with me unless we are married," Hassan teased before slicing off another piece of his fish. "Or did I imagine that conversation."

Sarah bit her lip. "You say I not sleep here; we not married. You cold. I put those on you; they not help. I sleep with you; you keep warm. I do wrong, Cattin?"

"No, on the contrary, you saved my life. I thank you for that," Hassan said with genuine gratitude. He laughed to himself. "I suppose I will have to marry you now." He stared at his plate and realized that he was comfortable with the idea of their union.

"You no have to marry me," Sarah insisted.

"No?" Hassan lifted a brow. "Why not?"

"Peter say why we not marry."

Hassan dropped his fork on his plate. "What exactly did Dr. Hyatt tell you?"

"He say you important on island ...."

Hassan's lips parted as he listened to Sarah's summary of her conversation with Peter. Reeling from her child-like revelation, he closed his eyes and shook his head. He didn't know what bothered him more, that Peter talked about his private life behind his back, or that Sarah wasn't angry. "And you still kept me warm," he said at the conclusion of her report. "You are not angry with me?"

"I sad .... When you ill. I thought, you friend; I wish you happiness. You say you help me. I trust you." Sarah peeled off a slice of orange and lifted it to her mouth. She looked at Hassan thoughtfully. "You loved wife?"

"No, as I said, I married her out of duty to my family," Hassan explained, looking Sarah in the eyes.

Sarah rested her hand on his and said tenderly. "I sorry."

"It is all in the past. Now I am free to be with whomever I please."

Sarah stared at her plate with a scrunched up brow. "Peter not say this."

"Perhaps he did not know. Moreover, it was not his place to tell you about my private affairs."

"What woman's name?"

"Her name was Lydia."

Sarah peeled off another section of her orange and set it on her tray. She looked at him thoughtfully, "I hope you find love. It right you have love."

"Thank you." Hassan stared at his wine with a scowl on his lips. What he held back was that men and women in his world often married for money and position, but not always for love. He couldn't help wondering what marriages were like on Sarah's island. He forced a smile and asked.

"So, how can I repay you for saving my life?"

"I repay you. You save life too." Sarah reminded him. "We friends now, aye?"

"Of course."

Sarah slept in the other room that night, he on his berth. Hassan woke early the next morning thinking about Sarah. He hoped that she would find a reason to crawl into bed with him. She didn't. Hassan finally gave up sleeping at the first sign of the dawn. He tiptoed into the dining area and grinned when he spotted Sarah curled up in a ball on his table with her blanket covering her head. Carefully, Hassan peeled back her blanket.

Sarah sat up and looked at him with concern. "You ill?"

"No, I am in health, but you look cold."

"Aye, a wee bit."

Hassan wrapped her blanket around her. "You should tell me when you are cold; I will find a way to keep you warm." He rubbed her arms vigorously with his hands. "Better?"

"Aye."

"The dawn is approaching. I wondered if you would care to join me on deck to watch the sunrise."

"You ill?"

"I assure you that I am well. However, I doubt that I am strong enough to climb to the top this morning."

"We watch from deck."

Sarah and Hassan quickly dressed and stole away to the quarterdeck. A cool breeze and the promise of a glorious day greeted them when they reached the railing. Hassan stood behind her with his arms wrapped around her shoulders. Sarah snuggled against him, all in the name of keeping warm this time. They watched in silence as the giant red ball rose above the horizon. The sun's glow turned the blanket of clouds pink. Hassan noticed a change in Sarah. She no longer looked at him as a suitor. She was relaxed and seemed to be at peace with their friendship. Hassan pulled her closer to him.

With his strength returned, the captain of the Zafirah took his place beside the helm for the first time in three days. It was just in time to steer his ship into his private hideout, a secluded inlet off the coast of Africa. He and his crew discovered it by accident shortly after he became a corsair. The inlet proved to be a perfect trap for attracting unsuspecting ships. His hideout was positioned in a way that Hassan's ship could hide from his prey. The inlet's lush landscape always lured ships through its narrow passageway with the promise of providing needed food and water. When their enemy least suspected it, Hassan ordered the attack. He freely admitted that attacks didn't happen often. Truth be told, it only happened once. For Hassan and his crew, this private beach provided a place where he and his men could escape from the war.

Hassan watched the horizon as they navigated into the bay. He always loved this view. The sun was at its highest zenith, bathing everything it touched with its warmth. Sarah, who was still standing by the railing, made the view even lovelier. Hassan wandered over and stood beside her. "This will be our home for the next few days."

"Aye? We no sleep on ship?" Sarah's voice rose with surprise.

"Only if you wish. I thought that you might enjoy sleeping on the beach."

"Oh aye!" Sarah said with a beaming grin.

"I imagine it has been a long time since you slept on shore. We will have to change that, won't we?"

"Aye!"

"Pardon the interruption, Captain. I wanted to let you know that we dropped anchor," reported one of his lieutenants.

"Very well. Continue preparations for going ashore." Hassan escorted Sarah to his quarters. "Collect your belongings. I will come for you later." Hassan went looking for Peter. He didn't have to go far when he spotted him watching them from the main deck. Hassan could almost feel the doctor's disapproval from across the ship. Peter turned and headed below deck; Hassan followed his friend to the surgery. The doctor was already seated at his table reading his book by the time Hassan caught up to him.

"I understand that you and Sarah had a conversation about my private life the other day." Hassan stood over his friend with his chest held high.

Peter closed his book and glared at his captain. "Sarah asked me questions about you; I answered them."

"Tell me, where did my family obligations fit into your discussion?"

Peter's lips parted. "Sarah needed to be told the truth!"

"I told her the truth, and you know it. Lydia died shortly after we married. I am free to marry whomever I please," Hassan shouted.

"Well, I was mistaken," Peter said without a trace of regret in his tone.

"No, you weren't. You said those things deliberately to hurt Sarah. More importantly, you made me look like a lying fool," Hassan retorted.

"May I have your permission to speak freely, Captain?"

"Please do."

"Even if you are not married, Sarah has a right to know why you cannot offer her marriage. You know that your family would never allow it, and they will reject Sarah if you do."

"I have not seen my family in years," Hassan countered. "Moreover, I am not certain that we will ever set foot on our homeland again."

"We can leave any time you wish. You remain here to settle your vendetta."

Hassan raked his fingers through his thick hair. "I stay here because those are our orders. We will leave this region at the completion of our mission." He rested his hands on the table, hovering over his friend. "I am only going to say this once," Hassan said in a menacing tone. "Do not meddle or speak of my private affairs ever again. If I learn that you did, I promise you, ship's doctor or no, we will cross swords."

Chapter 17

Sarah was seated at the dining table when Hassan returned to his cabin. He silently admired how beautiful her hair looked after she brushed it. He surveyed her belongings which included: a straw mat, a wool blanket, a brush, a sketchbook, and a few pencils. Hassan half-expected Sarah to insist on bringing her trunk. "Is this all that you wish to bring with you?"

"I need more?"

Hassan did a double take when he spotted the edge of her paru sticking out from under her mat. "No, I imagine you have all that you require. We can always return to the ship if you forgot something." Hassan retrieved a clean shirt, a bottle of wine, several goblets, and a cloth bag to hold their belongings. Sarah offered him a playful grin and went over to her trunk. She retrieved a large conch shell, a wooden flute, and a drum.

Hassan examined the drum with a pigskin top. "This is beautiful," he said, appreciating the drum's intricate carvings. "What the devil are you going to do with these?" Hassan handed the drum to her and picked up the shell.

"I show." Sarah placed the drum beside her belongings and took the shell from Hassan. Lifting the pointed end to her lips, she took a deep breath and blew through a small hole.

Hassan covered his ears to muffle the shell's strange and deafening sound. "Hmmm, that may be useful. May I?" Hassan stuffed the conch and the drum in his bag. He picked up her flute and admired the swirls engraved in the bamboo wood. Hassan had no idea what Sarah planned to do with her instruments, but he was sure that she would use them to teach him a little more about her Polynesian heritage.

Hassan climbed down to the jolly and looked up as the crew lowered Sarah on the bosuns' chair. He grabbed hold of her waist and shifted her into the boat.

Sarah stared at the water in the bottom of the jolly as if it were her nemesis. She lifted her skirt to keep it out of the water before taking a seat. Her forehead furrowed when the bottom edge of Hassan's Ottoman trousers got wet. He took a seat beside her; Sarah didn't take her eyes off the wet part of his pant leg.

"What are you doing?" Hassan demanded as she pulled the wet pant leg above his knee.

Sarah spoke to Peter in Polynesian with an animated voice.

"Would you care to explain why Sarah is concerned about my wet trousers?"

"Certainly, Captain," Peter said with a subdued laugh. "Sarah was concerned that your cloth would disintegrate if it gets wet. You may recall that Polynesian tapa cloth is similar to paper."

"I see." Hassan rested his chin between his thumb and forefinger. "So," he said after a few thoughtful seconds, "when it rains, the Polynesians go?"

"Yes," Peter finished Hassan's thought. "You can imagine the missionaries' reaction when it rained."

"Can I ever." Hassan and his crew erupted in laughter as they envisioned the Christian missionaries lecturing the puzzled natives about going naked during a rainstorm. He turned to Sarah and said with a wink, "You need not worry about my trousers. Water will not destroy our fabric."

Sarah blushed and sheepishly lowered Hassan's pant legs below his shins.

Hassan leaned over and whispered, "You will not be able to rid yourself of your clothing so quickly."

Sarah's face turned even redder.

Hassan's horseshoe shaped hideout afforded his crew and him a perfect escape from their otherwise treacherous life. Like most pirates, Hassan concealed his treasures in a secret place in the caves behind the white sandy beach. Besides a few jewels, food, and other luxuries, there was an abundant supply of wine and spirits confiscated from seized ships. He and his crew also took advantage of the rainy season by planting a small orchard of fruit trees. They also set up a water collection system so that they could have fresh water whenever they needed it.

Sarah bounded out of the jolly just before it reached the shore. Hassan's crew were already enjoying their time on the beach. Their activity came to a sudden halt as they watched Sarah splashing in the water. Hassan and the other people in the jolly were no exceptions. She darted in and out of the water as the waves ebbed and flowed around her shins. Hassan's lips curled into a smile when he heard her melodic laugh for the first time.

"Captain?"

Hassan's breath hitched when he spotted a lieutenant standing in the water beside him. "Did you say something?"

"Yes, Captain. We are waiting for your orders, sir," the lieutenant said patiently.

Hassan glanced over his shoulder and noticed that most of his crew were already engaged in activities on the beach. Some carried baskets of food while others waited for his orders. "Coordinate the men to set up camp."

"Yes, sir." His lieutenant nodded.

Hassan knew he had duties as well, which meant leaving Sarah's side. Allowing her to stay on the beach unchaperoned wasn't the same as letting her sit on the bench on the quarterdeck. Each crew member worked at a station on the ship. When they weren't working, they were below deck either resting or eating. All but a handful were on shore, each eagerly looking forward to enjoying a well-deserved shore leave. Hassan knew by the way his crew leered at Sarah that they all wanted to enjoy her company. He doubted that any of them were bold enough to hurt her when they were sober, yet he worried what they *would* do after they got drunk, and they would get drunk this evening.

Hassan smiled back when Sarah's gaze met his. "Are you enjoying being on shore?" he asked when she waded over to the jolly.

"Aye," she replied with joy beaming from her eyes. "You come?"

"Yes." Hassan stood and tossed his bag over his shoulder. A crew member held the boat steady as their captain climbed out. No sooner had he reached the beach when his officers swarmed him. They each politely demanded answers to their questions. Sarah backed away without his notice. Twenty minutes later, Hassan spotted her talking with Peter and a small group of his crew. Unconsciously, he rolled his hand into a fist when she and her admirers laughed in unison. "Please excuse me," he said to his lieutenant. The group had disbursed by the time Hassan reached them. A handful of his crew took the jolly into the bay while another group dug a pit; the rest headed to the cave.

"What are you two conspiring to do?" Hassan gently demanded.

"We …" Sarah struggled to find the right words. "I no how say."

"Allow me," Peter offered. "Sarah suggested organizing a Polynesian feast. Of course, we do not have the South Seas boars or their vegetation, but there is plenty of fish. We also have plenty of provisions to add to our feast."

"I see." Hassan frowned as he watched his men burrowing in the sand. "Why are they digging a pit?"

"Cook fish," Sarah replied.

"The Polynesians have a scrumptious cooking tradition," Peter explained. "They dig a pit and fill it with rocks heated in a fire. The fish or pork are tucked between woven palm leaves and are placed on the hot rocks to cook the meat. The result is a delectable meal. The best part about this cooking method is that it's an effective way to feed a lot of people at once."

"Carry on," Hassan said.

While the crew assisted Peter, Sarah turned her attention to collecting low-lying palm leaves. Hassan cut enough to make a medium size pile and handed them to Sarah one at a time as she wove them into mats. Once Sarah completed her project, they wandered over to inspect the rest of the preparations for their meal. The crew started heating the rocks in the fire pit. Other seamen finished digging a long and narrow hole.

Hassan leaned over and quietly asked Sarah. "Do you approve of the way my crew is preparing our meal?"

"Aye," she replied.

The crew completed their fishing duties while others carefully moved the heated stones to the pit. Sarah laid a layer of palm mats directly on top of the hot stones. She placed the fish on top of the first layer of mats and covered them with another. The crew piled on a layer of sand. While the food baked, the cooks turned their attention to preparing the rest of their dinner, which consisted of oranges, peaches, figs, grains, and of course, wine and spirits.

The festivities started shortly after sunset with the unveiling of the main course. Everyone, except Sarah and Peter, was surprised to discover the fish thoroughly cooked. Sarah and a few others handed a plate of food to each crew member. Everyone, including Hassan, devoured their meal.

A few men entertained the group by singing a lively tune after finishing their meal. One of the officers pulled out a fiddle and a bow from a narrow case. Sarah retrieved her flute and handed her drum to the sailor standing beside her. The musicians interrupted their playing when Sarah accompanied them on her flute. Soon, everyone joined in with singing and clapping their hands. A few even danced a jig. The entire crew watched Sarah and Hassan during the next few songs. They exchanged glances with each other as if they wanted to make a request, but were too timid to ask.

Finally, Tristan summoned the courage to enquire. "Miss Campbell, would you care to show us how you dance in the South Seas?"

"What is dance?"

"Timorodee," Peter explained.

"Oh aye?" Sarah's face brightened with a smile.

Hassan glanced over at Peter, who subtly shook his head. He darted behind Sarah and rested his hands on her shoulders just as she lifted her arms. "Not tonight," the captain replied before she could begin her dance.

"Oh," Tristan said with an unmistakable disappointment in his tone.

Sarah, Hassan noted, looked just as disappointed as his bodyguard.

"Captain, would you care to teach Miss Campbell how we dance in England?" Tristan suggested.

Ah, Hassan thought when he understood what his crew wanted. "Would you like to learn how we dance in my country?"

"Aye," she replied with downcast eyes.

"Are you certain? You can decline their request if you wish."

"I not know how."

"I will show you." Sarah placed her tentative hand in Hassan's; he led her into the center of the group. The pirate captain wrapped one arm around her waist and enveloped her other hand in his. "Ready?"

The fiddle player picked a slow melody for their first dance. Hassan masterfully guided Sarah, twirling her around and around. Sarah followed his lead with surprising ease and gazed into his eyes as though he had bestowed a great honor upon her. The crew clapped and cheered when they finished their dance. Hassan leaned down and whispered, "Would you be willing to dance with the members of my crew?"

Sarah replied with a reluctant nod.

"You will make them very happy." Hassan spun Sarah around, pressing her back against his chest. "Gentlemen, the beautiful Sarah Campbell has graciously agreed to dance with you." The crew whistled and cheered. Hassan raised his hand to silence them. "These are the rules: no slow dances, no *island* dances." He gently squeezed Sarah's shoulder. "The dancing ends when I say so. And gentlemen, remember that I will be watching." The crew replied with a less enthusiastic applause. Hassan offered Sarah to Tristan first.

The Marine signaled to the fiddle player, who opened with an Irish jig. Sarah paused long enough to learn the steps. A few steps later, she was dancing almost as well as her partner. The sailors then cheered Tristan and Sarah on, and soon all but the musicians lined up to dance with this exotic maiden. Peter stood back and accompanied the fiddle player on Sarah's drum. She welcomed each sailor with a warm smile. Hassan nodded to the musicians to stop when the last member of the crew had danced with Sarah. Everyone acquiesced with sighs before disbursing into smaller groups. Many laid down and went to sleep because they were too drunk to do anything else.

"We should retire too," Hassan suggested.

Sarah looked around the beach. "Where I sleep?"

"We shall retire to my private beach." Hassan led Sarah to an opening in the boulder wall.

"Good night," Sarah said to Luke, who was guarding the entrance to Hassan's secluded beach.

"Good night, Captain, Miss Campbell," Luke nodded back. "And thank you for the dance."

"Good night, Mr. Finch." Hassan had always preferred sleeping separately from his men. One of the primary reasons he chose this cove was because the beach was divided into two sections. Hassan gave his men the larger of the two, and the freedom to spend their time doing whatever they pleased, within reason. He preferred the quiet solitude of his own private beach at the end of the day. The boulder wall offered a natural barrier from his crew's activities, which were often loud and lasted throughout the night. For the most part, no one bothered Hassan after he retired. The nearby cave provided a dry place to store a tent, a feather bed, and a few other belongings while they were away at sea. His crew had already set up his camp by the time he and Sarah arrived. Hassan's only complaint about this beach was the cold nights.

Feeling the chill in the night air, Sarah charged towards the bonfire. Hassan caught up to her a few minutes later. He added a few more logs and looked over at Sarah. Her arms extended above the flames, she stood as close as she could to avoid catching her gown on fire, or so Sarah thought.

Hassan darted behind her. "Step back from the flames." He wrapped his arms around her waist and nudged her back to a safe distance. "Are you still cold?"

"Aye," she said, rubbing her arms.

After ducking into the tent, Hassan returned with a blanket and wrapped it around Sarah's shoulders. "Better?"

"Aye." Sarah pulled the blanket tightly against her.

"Would you care to sit by the fire?"

Sarah nodded and took a seat on a log next to the fire pit; Hassan sat beside her.

"Thank you for what you did for my crew today. Living in this region is very difficult. We were all forced to leave our families behind when we embarked on this mission. It has been an age since I last saw mine. It pleased me to see my crew's spirits soar today. That was because of you."

Sarah studied him. "Why you come here?"

"That is a question with a complicated answer." Hassan sighed. "I cannot tell you why my crew and I are on the Barbary Coast. I will say that I came here for a specific reason. My crew and I will leave once our mission is over."

The fire popped, sending a burst of luminescent embers into the air.

Hassan looked thoughtfully at her. "Dr. Hyatt told me about some of your South Seas traditions. May I ask your opinion of them?"

She replied with an uncertain nod.

"Dr. Hyatt informed me that South Seas maidens take many lovers. In my country, most husbands and wives remain devoted to each other for the rest of their lives. Are you capable, I mean, could you love one man for the rest of your life?"

Sarah looked at the sky, then back at Hassan. "Aye, that true …. My friends be with …." Sarah's voice trailed off. She let out a heavy sigh when she couldn't come up with the right words.

"Many lovers?"

"Aye. Not all like that. Lot of my people like your people." Sarah looked at the sky again.

"You mean, a man and a woman spend their whole lives devoted to each other," Hassan clarified.

"Aye." she nodded with relief. "Um, me Da ... loved ... me ... wife?"

"Do you mean your mother?" Hassan offered.

"Aye, he no have wife after her. He say he love her. I see love in his eyes when he talk of her. I want that." She paused after saying each word as she carefully chose the next one.

"I see," he grinned.

"You know what I say?"

"Yes." Hassan nodded. "My next question."

Sarah clutched the edge of her blanket.

Hassan chuckled when he spotted the dread in her eyes. "I will try to help you find the correct English words if you cannot come up with them yourself. My next question. Dr. Hyatt said it is custom for unmarried girls to offer themselves as lovers to the male guests in their home. Do you understand what I am saying?"

"Aye."

"Is that true of the women on your island?"

"Aye," Sarah said timidly. "Friends important. We wish they feel ... what is word ... wel ... welcome?"

Hassan tilted his head to the side and bit the inside of his lip. "So, if I commanded it, would you give yourself to another?"

Sarah stared at the sand and hugged herself tighter. "I obey," she murmured.

Hassan caressed her jaw with his thumb and tilted her face towards his. His heart throbbed when he spotted the sadness in her eyes. "You would obey my command, but you would hate doing it."

"Aye," Sarah confirmed in a little voice.

"You need not worry, sweet one," Hassan smiled tenderly. "I would never share you with anyone if you were mine." His hand dropped to his lap; the muscles in his face tensed again. "My next question. I understand that it is customary for women to kill their children immediately after giving birth to them," he said in a hardened tone.

"Aye, it true my friends kill child. Da say they … fear … they love child if they keep …. Fear right word?"

"Yes, fear is the correct word."

"They fear they be …" Sarah looked at the sky again, "bad mother. They say it best for child to kill. You understand?"

"Yes, but how do *you* feel about having children of your own?" Hassan prodded. "Would you kill our children?"

Sarah looked him in the eyes and said emphatically. "I could not. Da say it wrong. He say it …. I no remember word."

"Murder?" Hassan offered.

"Aye, murder," she confirmed. "I like children. I want … this." she held up five fingers.

"Five children," Hassan's gasp turned into laughter. "We shall see about that," he mumbled. "My last question." With a playful grin, Hassan pulled her blanket down to expose the tattoo on her arm. "Did it hurt when you had this done?" he asked, tracing the outline of the six-petal flower.

Her eyes widened as she nodded vigorously. "Aye."

Hassan laughed at her animated reply. "How did your father feel about you painting your body with permanent ink?"

"Da not like; he understand."

"I see. So you were following your people's customs," Hassan offered.

"Aye. You like?"

"Well, I wouldn't want you to add any more to your body," Hassan admitted. "I must say, yours are in good taste. They suit you," he said, covering her exposed arm. "Tell me more about life on your island."

In her broken English, Sarah told Hassan about the life she left behind. A man by the name of Tupia governed her village. Everyone loved and respected this beneficent chief who ruled his village like a democracy. Her father and the other men would gather around the fire to discuss important matters before making a decision. Hassan couldn't help wondering if Sarah's father gave them the idea for using that form of government. There was no money, no commerce, no land ownership. Their island provided all the food they required, which was free for the taking. War and crime had never plagued her people. Though there were a few disputes here and there, for the most part, Sarah and her people lived in peace.

"I envy you for coming from such a place," Hassan said, marveling at the idea of living in a world without money, where poverty was unknown, and the people were free to marry whomever they pleased.

Sarah got quiet after she finished telling Hassan about her life on her island. Her eyes drifted to the night sky, darting from one constellation to another. Her mouth moved without making a sound as she scanned the stars.

Hassan rested his hand on her shoulder. "What is the matter?"

"They ... not same."

Hassan frowned when he spotted her concern. "What are?"

"Those." She pointed to the night sky.

"Do you mean the constellations?" Hassan clarified.

"What is const ...?"

"A constellation is a grouping of stars." Hassan nudged closer to her. "That is Orion." He pointed to the group of stars outlining a smaller string. "He is a hunter in ancient mythology. See the three stars across the center?" He pointed to a row of stars crossing the rectangular formation.

"Aye."

"That is Orion's belt. The three stars below the belt are his sword." Hassan looked back at Sarah. "I trust you are not familiar with Orion."

Sarah shook her head.

"To answer your question, the southern hemisphere has a different set of constellations. You need not worry; your stars are still there, even if you cannot see them."

Sarah mumbled something in Polynesian.

Hassan frowned. "Would you care to tell me what you just said? I still do not understand your native language."

Sarah looked at him with teary eyes and said, "How I find home?"

Hassan glanced at the fire. He didn't have an answer for Sarah; nor did he have the heart to tell her that it was likely that she would never see her island again. Hassan added another log to the fire and returned to his place beside her. "I am confident that someone can help you find your way home if you so desire. Sarah, I spent many years at sea. If my life has taught me anything, it's that you carry your home inside you. I know that may not be very comforting, but that is the only advice that I can offer you."

"You miss England?"

"Sometimes. I like spending time on this beach. It is very peaceful here."

"I too." Sarah stared at the fire. "I miss doing timorodee with friends."

"Why don't you dance for me?"

"You say you not want me do timorodee."

"No," Hassan clarified, "I said I do not want you to dance for my crew. I never said that I did not want you to dance for me. Will you?"

"Aye," she said eagerly. "It better if I wear paru."

"Your cloth is in my bag. You should find the bag in the tent.

"Mauru'uru," she said, heading into the tent.

"What does that mean?"

She stopped at the edge of the doorway and looked back. "It mean, 'tank you.'"

"I see. Go change into your cloth."

Hassan watched the tent, anxiously waiting for Sarah to reappear. Anyone looking on would mistake his calm demeanor for boredom. What they couldn't see were his sweaty palms. Ever since Sarah's arrival, Hassan looked forward to retiring to his cabin with her at the end of the day. As soon as their dinner ended, and he was sure that there would be no more interruptions, Sarah would cast aside her ugly turban and formless gown and transform into the most exotic creature he had ever seen. Hassan still marveled how Sarah could spend an entire evening with him wearing only a narrow swath of cloth tied around her waist with her thick hair hanging loosely down her front and back. Yet she was the least sensual person he had ever known. "What is the matter?" he asked when she walked out with a disappointed look on her face.

"It back there." She pointed to the wall.

"What is?"

"The ...." Sarah pumped her hands up and down.

"Do you mean the drum?" Hassan guessed.

"Aye, - drum."

"Shall I retrieve it for you?"

"No, I do timorodee." Sarah moved close to the fire. She closed her eyes and sung a Polynesian melody. Lifting her arms in front of her, Sarah's body began to sway, and her hips gyrated as her feet danced to her song. Hassan's hand covered his mouth as he took in this exotic sight. He understood Peter's caution for not allowing Sarah to dance for his crew. Most Christians would consider her dancing lewd. But to him, it was a beautiful sight that would burn in his memory forever.

Sarah studied Hassan after she finished her dance. He hadn't moved since she started it. "You no like?" she asked after a few awkward moments.

"No, on the contrary," he said, feeling as if his breeches would burst.

"I no understand," Sarah said with a scrunched up forehead.

"I liked your dance very much," he clarified in a throaty whisper.

"I dance more?"

"Yes, please." Hassan felt a sense of heaviness as he watched Sarah dance around the fire. He knew that the Polynesian culture was different from his own. It wasn't until their talk that he understood that no two cultures could be more opposite. Moreover, Sarah was completely unprepared for life in England. She had no idea of the scandal she would cause if she danced like that in front of his countrymen, or even worse, his family and friends. His hand clutched the corner of his shirt as he contemplated Sarah giving up the very part of her that drew him to her. She would be required to do precisely that once they reached England. Hassan just hoped that Sarah was strong enough to adapt.

CHAPTER 18

The sun beat down on Gerard Rochelle's head as he lifted the stone block into the cart. His hands and back ached with every load he carried. It had been almost a week since his cousin promised him a meeting with the Dey. Instead, he and his crew were processed in the square the morning after they arrived in Algiers. Having no relevant connections and no money, Gerard and his men were sent to the quarry in chains. According to their Algerine captors, the only thing they were deemed fit for was hard labor. Gerard did his best to avoid his crew. However, he couldn't avoid their glares. They hated him for the promises that he had made and broken to them. He couldn't blame them either.

The guards came for Gerard late that morning. Without a word, they escorted him to a room where he bathed. His captors surprised him with a fresh set of clothes. Afterward, they escorted him to a small room. Gerard gasped when he discovered his cousin waiting for him. "Where the devil have you been? I thought you had abandoned me," he exclaimed.

"Arranging a private meeting with the Dey is not a simple task. Be grateful that he favors me; he is interested in hearing about your prize. Now listen carefully. Naa'il Dhar thinks of himself as a demi-god. If you wish to win your freedom, you will treat him like one. This is what you will need to do …." Claude spent the next few hours grooming his cousin for his upcoming meeting. Once Gerard was prepped, they boarded a coach that took them on a bumpy ride to the Palace.

"We're here," Claude said when the carriage came to a stop. "Sorry to do this." He covered his cousin's head with a black hood.

"Why do I have to wear this? I can't see a damn thing."

"I am following the Dey's instructions. Do not speak unless someone asks you a question," Claude warned before getting out of the coach. He reached for his cousin's hand and helped him to the cobblestone street. "His Excellency is expecting us," Claude announced to the guards.

Gerard gasped when he felt a hand locking around his arm. "Will you remove this hood? My head is baking."

"Sorry cousin, your head must remain covered until we reach the Great Hall. Let's go." Claude tugged on his cousin's arm.

The guards cackled when Gerard tripped on the marble step. A sharp pain shot out from his knee when he landed with a hard thud.

"Get up." Claude pulled his cousin to his feet. "Watch the ground if you don't wish to fall again."

Gerard tilted his head towards the floor as his cousin led him through a series of mazes. He silently cursed Claude for not allowing him the opportunity to take in the Palace's beauty. His imagination, however, filled in the details that his mask denied him. He could almost see the lavishly decorated rooms and the nobility that occupied them. He also envisioned slave girls creeping through the hallways to entertain the Dey's guests. His black hood reminded him that he couldn't be certain of anything except that they had two more escorts, one walking in front of them, and the other behind.

It was only when they reached their destination that Claude removed his cousin's hood. Gerard blinked several times to allow his eyes to adjust to the light. Even though there were no harem women in sight, the Palace was even more exotic than he imagined. They stood in a hallway, lined with two stories of whitewashed arches. Blue and white mosaic tiles covered the base of the walls. To the left of the corridor was a square courtyard that had plenty of sunlight for the flowers and shrubs surrounding the three tier fountain positioned in the center. The sound of the fountain's gentle trickle comforted Gerard's nerves, but it wasn't enough to ease his concerns about his meeting with the Dey.

"His Excellency is expecting us," Claude announced to the two Algerine soldiers guarding the door with their legs splayed shoulder width apart. Each held a spear that was almost a head taller than they were and a saber tucked under their belts. One of the guards entered the room on the other side of the giant-intricately carved doors they protected. He reappeared a few minutes later with a distinguished looking gentleman.

Claude clasped his hands together in a prayer position and bowed to the lean man dressed in silk Ottoman clothes. "Blessings be upon thee, Vizier Rahmani," Claude said, staring at the stone floor.

Jamal surveyed Gerard from his feet to his head, then back again. "Is this the prisoner?"

"Yes, Vizier."

Jamal and Claude whispered as if Gerard wasn't there. The Vizier then said in French, "Follow me."

"Remember what I told you," Claude warned in a low voice.

"I will make you proud." Gerard offered his cousin a confident grin.

Claude just rolled his eyes.

Gerard followed Claude and Jamal through the doors and paused to take in the splendor of this opulent room. The two-story walls and spacious floor looked like it was built for a giant. Intricately carved walls and false arches adorned the second floor. Gerard admired the colorful tapestries and ornate hutches lining the walls on the floor below. Clusters of men dressed in lavish robes talking quietly among themselves filled the main floor, many of them were seated on oversized pillows. Gerard surveyed the people, hoping to spot the Dey, but none of them stood out as the leader of Algiers.

"Keep moving," Claude tugged on Gerard's arm. Moments later the cousins were standing in the center of the great hall.

Gerard's eyes drifted to a balcony overlooking the room. The arched opening looked like delicate lace dangling from the ceiling; only it was carved out of marble. What caught Gerard's attention was the man lounging on an oversized maroon pillow at the edge of the balcony. Gerard knew that he was the Dey of Algiers because he was dressed like a king in a silk robe, studded with diamond buttons. His advisors treated him with reverence and perhaps with a little fear. One advisor cowered to their leader as he whispered something in his ear. Then the counselor backed away until he was beyond his master's line of sight. Naa'il Dhar kept a watchful eye on the activity taking place below him. Everyone seemed to be on their best behavior.

Claude tugged on his cousin's arm again when Jamal reached the platform. Like the other advisors, Jamal cautiously approached the Dey. They spoke quietly for a few moments, and then Naa'il turned his attention towards them.

"Kneel," Claude commanded in a firm whisper.

Gerard's knees buckled beneath him when he spotted fear in Claude's brown eyes. For the first time, Claude's caution began to sink in. The Dey wasn't just a means for gaining freedom and wealth, he was a powerful man who could take a man's life just as easily as he could spare it. Claude took a huge risk arranging a private meeting with Naa'il Dhar. It was evident by Claude's insistent behavior that he didn't just fear for his cousin's life, he feared for his own.

Like a toad, Gerard sat with his feet tucked beneath him. He stretched his arms in front of him and bowed his face to the floor. Though he stared at the ground, he felt the Dey's full attention on him. Naa'il asked Claude questions in a language he didn't recognize, and Claude answered him with an obsequious respect. The Dey and his advisors laughed among themselves. Gerard wasn't sure what they said, but he was sure that they speculated about his missing finger.

"Move ten paces forward," Claude whispered.

Gerard slithered towards the platform on his hands and knees, all the while staring at the gray and white marble floor directly in front of him. His approach pleased Naa'il Dhar - at least until he attempted to look directly at the Dey.

A guard with ebony skin, standing off to Gerard's side, cracked his whip and barked, "Do not look directly at His Excellency, infidel."

Gerard winced when the leather whip sliced through his shirt and into his skin. He snapped back into the froglike posture. His back stung, but the humiliation was excruciating. The laughter stopped suddenly. It was as though the cackling was contained in a box and only made the sound when the lid was open.

"Tell us about this prize of yours," Naa'il Dhar said in French with a tenor voice.

Gerard refused to move. The pain in his back made it impossible for him to think, let alone speak.

"Sit up, infidel and answer His Excellency's question," the African guard barked again.

Gerard's jaw clenched when the whip cracked across his back again. He obeyed and glared at his cousin for not intervening. Claude just stared at him like a wooden soldier. He could see the guard raising his arm to strike him again. "Sarah Campbell is the rarest of all flowers, Your Excellency." The words tumbled out of his mouth. "I was willing to risk my freedom so that I can present her to you," Gerard spoke as his eyes remained fixed on the cream lines embedded in the floor directly in front of him. He spent the next half hour telling Naa'il about Sarah. He described her appearance, her history, how he came to acquire her, and finally how Hassan Aziz wrongfully stole her from him. Naa'il and his advisors listened in silence. It was torture not being able to see the Dey's reaction. The silence following the conclusion of his story was even worse.

"I have heard of the South Sea maidens. They are known for their abilities to give pleasure. I understand why she would be highly prized in your country, but she would be worthless here. You see, the people in my country treasure a woman's purity above all else," Naa'il explained.

"If I may be so bold, Your Excellency, my country also treasures a maiden's innocence. Sarah Campbell's father assured me that she is still a maid."

Naa'il leaned forward and covered his mouth with his hand. "Are you certain of this?"

"I am, Your Excellency," Gerard insisted.

"Are you willing to wager your freedom on your prize's innocence?"

"I am, Your Excellency."

"Very well." Naa'il waved Gerard off.

Gerard stood and glanced at Naa'il before heading to the exit with his cousin. The Dey whispered to Vizier Rahmani, who bowed before backing out of the balcony. Claude and Gerard had reached the hallway by the time the Vizier caught up to him.

"His Excellency wants you to return at 7:30 tonight," Jamal said to Claude while ignoring Gerard altogether. He remained long enough for Claude to give the Vizier his answer.

"Why can't I return tonight?" Gerard complained.

Claude glared at his cousin to keep silent before returning the hood to Gerard's head. The two climbed into the carriage. They rode in silence during the first part of their trip back to the quarry.

"You fool, never question the Dey's wishes, especially while inside the Palace. The walls and the streets have ears, and His Excellency hears everything, even when you think he's not listening. You will spend the rest of your life working in the quarries for uttering statements like that. Now listen to me carefully. Your Tahitian wench intrigues him; else he would not have granted you an audience. My guess is that I am meeting with him tonight to discuss a plan to retrieve her."

"Why can't I be part of making the arrangements? She is my prize after all."

"Be grateful that Dhar granted you a meeting. I will inform you of his decision. Until then, pray that you did not offend His Excellency."

Claude returned Gerard to the quarries. Having several hours before his meeting with the Dey, he stole away to his apartment. Like most Algerian residences, his was nestled in the heart of a cluster of block buildings.

A cool breeze greeted Claude when he opened the door to his apartment. Though his abode wasn't lavishly furnished like the Dey's Palace, it was comfortably decorated with red Ottoman rugs, large tan pillows, and a few short tables, topped with bowls of figs and oranges scattered throughout the room.

Claude ambled towards the sweet scents lofting from the potted flowering trees on the balcony. He leaned against the doorway and watched his wife, Janna, hanging his wash on a line. Though she wore a blue and gold entari that barely covered her bulging belly and a matching veil, all Claude could see was her cream hands seemingly moving independently from the rest of her. Janna was a gift from Naa'il Dhar. Claude was drawn to her sweet face and doe eyes. Above all, he liked her gentle demeanor. He approached her and wrapped his arms around her waist.

"Claude," she squealed as she felt her husband's warmth pressing against her back. "You are home early. Did your meeting go well?"

Claude reached for her hand and led her into their apartment. "My meeting went as well as could be expected. I will need to return to the Palace in a few hours. I thought it would be pleasant to pass the afternoon with you." Claude peeled away her veil and entari, revealing his adoring wife dressed in lavender Ottoman trousers and a tan gömlek. She threw her arms around his neck and greeted him with a kiss. Claude answered her in kind and lowered her onto the pillows by his feet. "How is my son today?" He asked, rubbing his hand across her belly.

Claude returned to the Palace just after sunset. A golden hue illuminated the whitewashed Palace walls. The guards greeted him with their usual curt nods and instructed him to follow the escorts that were waiting for him. Flames dancing in stained-glass lanterns hanging from the ceiling compensated for the fading light. After making a few turns, Claude heard the faint sounds of belly dancing music spilling into the hall from the room directly ahead of him. The music grew louder as he approached, so did the smell of the feast that awaited him. The guard opened an ornate door and said, "His Excellency is expecting you."

Naa'il was perched on a small stage, covered with a gold canopy. He lay on a pillow and feasted on grapes. He was so engrossed in his conversation with his advisors that he hardly noticed the dancers competing for his attention.

"Captain Fornier." Naa'il motioned to Claude to approach him.

Claude bowed and entered the room. At Naa'il's insistence, the captain took a seat on a red cushion beside his master.

"Have some food." Naa'il motioned to a woman to serve Claude figs and lamb. Another brought him a cup of water in a gold goblet.

"Thank you, Your Excellency," Claude said, welcoming his master's food, even though he would have preferred a glass of wine to accompany his dinner. He plucked a grape from the cluster and popped it into his mouth. Claude could tell that Naa'il was distracted by his pensive stare as he watched the evening's entertainment.

Naa'il glanced over at his friend and said, "I want you and your cousin to bring his prize to me."

Claude just stared at the flickering candle as the dancers blew across the floor.

Naa'il pursed his lips. "I thought you would be pleased."

"I am, Your Excellency," Claude replied in a stoic demeanor.

"What is troubling you?"

"May I have your permission to speak freely?"

"Speak." Naa'il waved his hand in the air.

"I recently learned that Hassan Aziz is Nathan Shelby. Your Excellency, I would never question your judgment, but Nathan Shelby is your enemy. I was surprised to learn that you allowed him to become a corsair." Claude spoke as if the words tumbled out of his mouth.

"Nathan Shelby is *your* enemy, Captain Fornier. Captain Shelby offered me the same thing that you did, and he has served me well … until recently." Naa'il nodded to his Sudanese guard to bring in a prisoner.

Claude's lips parted when he spotted Adam Boyle in chains.

"This prisoner is for you. You may use him to find Shelby. I want it understood that you are to bring him to me alive," Naa'il said with a cold stare.

Chapter 19

Cora's Bible was her only companion during the next two days. Mamnoon brought food, water, and a few other provisions to her. He never stayed long because he told her in confidence that Naa'il was having him watched.

She shuddered when Naa'il walked through her door on the morning of the third day. Dressed in black and various shades of gray, his somber countenance matched the color of his clothes. Cora had no idea how to interpret his demeanor. Still, she rose to her feet and curtsied before approaching him. "Good morning, Your Excellency."

"Good morning," Naa'il said warmly.

"I trust you reached a decision."

Naa'il led Cora into her courtyard; both remained standing by the fountain. "I do not approve of your behavior in the harem the other day. I also understand that you were protecting an innocent child." Naa'il paused and reached for her hand. "You are always protecting the innocent. That is one of the things I love most about you. I want you to be my wife, Cora. As my gift to you, I issued a decree to the harem. All of the servant girls are under my protection; anyone caught mistreating them will be sold at the slave market.

Cora covered her mouth with her free hand and gasped. "You did that, Your Excellency?"

"Yes, I concluded that it is the only way to keep you out of trouble.

Will you be my wife?"

"Yes," Cora said, choking back her tears.

"Then I am pleased." Naa'il forced a smile. He looked thoughtfully at the fountain without saying anything further.

"Your Excellency." Cora gently touched his arm. "Are you certain that you want to marry me? I understand if you changed your mind."

Naa'il looked at her with a vacant expression. "What?"

"You seem troubled. Are you certain that you want to marry me?"

"I made my decision. We will marry tomorrow."

"You still seem troubled."

Naa'il kissed the back of her hand. "Yes, I am. It has nothing to do with you. I learned the other day that one of my servants betrayed me."

"How awful."

"My corsairs are required to bring all captured women to me."

"One of your corsairs didn't do that."

"No. Since meeting you, I would not care. This one is unique. It is my understanding that she is the only one of her kind."

Cora tilted her head to the side. "In what way?"

"It was explained to me that this woman is of Scottish descent. She was born and raised in the South Seas. It is said that she is very beautiful," Naa'il said with a subtle smile.

Cora bit her bottom lip. "She intrigues you."

"Yes. I ordered the woman's and the corsair's capture."

Cora stared at the water spilling to the tiers below. "What will you do with them?" she asked in a quiet voice.

"If the woman is pure and worthy of the Sultan, I will send her to Constantinople; if she is not, I will add her to my harem, and will execute the corsair for his crime."

"I see." Cora grimaced.

Naa'il wrapped his arms around her waist and looked into her eyes. "This will not change us. You will be my third wife, and I will love you. In time you will give me sons."

It was evident by the way Naa'il gritted his teeth that he was holding something back from her. She knew he sincerely cared for her, but Naa'il Dhar was still a son of his culture. He would never give up his concubines, nor would he stop searching for the next beauty to give him pleasure in his bed.

"I must leave you now." Naa'il kissed her forehead.

Cora nodded, "May I go to the harem? I have grown fond of the pampering, and I promise that I will stay out of trouble."

"Yes. We will talk tonight." Naa'il kissed her again. "I must tell our news to my wives."

Cora forced a smile, fighting back her tears until he closed the door behind him. Mamnoon arrived with breakfast later that morning.

"You saw His Excellency this morning?" her bodyguard prodded.

"Yes," Cora said quietly, "Congratulate me; I am going to be his third wife."

Mamnoon placed the tray at the base of the fountain and sunk onto the bench beside her. The disappointment on his face mirrored her despair. They sat in silence while holding hands.

"This is my choice," Cora whispered. "It is best for everyone. Now, kiss me and take me to the harem."

Mamnoon caressed her cheek and looked at her tenderly. "I love you, Cora Bradley, with my whole heart."

"And I will love you, always," Cora whispered. Their lips touched and moved as one. Though she wanted their kiss to continue, Cora was the first to pull away. "We should go," she whispered.

They walked in silence, both fighting the urge to exchange loving gazes, hold hands, or show any hint of affection towards the other. To the person looking on, Mamnoon and Cora resembled a guard escorting his prisoner to her execution. The only thing that was missing was shackles.

"You do not need to go inside if you do not wish. I can bring you what you need," Mamnoon offered.

"I think we both know that I must. Besides, I want a massage and a hot bath." Cora winked at her friend. She expected to feel a little animosity, but not even she was prepared for the wave of hatred emanating from the women of the harem.

Bashira was the only one to approach them. All the others, including Abigail and Tess, remained in their little clusters as they whispered among themselves while glaring at Cora. Ula was lurking in the corner with her friends. Even the child slaves kept their distance. Cora offered her friend a subtle nod.

"You made a lot of trouble for us," Bashira said coldly.

Cora grimaced when she spotted the bruise on Bashira's face. She squared her shoulders and said, "I am not sorry for what I did. Ula had no right beating that child."

Bashira leaned in and growled. "You knew the rules, and you broke them. Everyone knows it."

"If your rules include beating children, I will gladly fight to change them." Cora's eyes narrowed to slits. "As for your rules, things are going to change in here." She added with a menacing grin. Cora scanned the room and held her head high before making her announcement. "I agreed to be the Dey's third wife. You will all treat me with the respect I deserve."

Bashira stepped back and gave Cora a curtsy worthy of a king. "Of course, your Maaaajesty."

"That is better. I will take my massage and bath now, alone," Cora said in a haughty tone.

"Of course." Bashira clapped her hands, sending a small group of slaves running towards her.

Cora emerged from the bathing room. Though her body was relaxed, the worry on her face lingered. Tess, Abigail, and Molly hadn't moved from where they were sitting. Cora could tell from their glares that they didn't want her to disturb them. She approached them anyway. "May I join you?" Cora asked, with Mamnoon standing off to the side of them.

Abigail stuck her leg over the place where Cora attempted to sit. "This seat is taken."

Cora exhaled a loud sigh. "How about here?" She shifted to her left.

"That seat is taken too. They are all taken. There is no room for the likes of you," Abigail retorted.

"Very well," Cora's voice cracked. She turned away and wiped a tear from her cheek. Mamnoon started to lunge towards her cousin but stopped when Cora subtly shook her head.

"That was harsh," Tess snickered.

The servants were already busy setting up a table for the noon meal. The women and children gathered around, ready to swarm as if that meal were the only food they would get that day. Other servants passed out cups of water. Cora and Mamnoon waited until there was a clear path to the table. The little girl that Cora fought for the other day brought Cora a handful of figs.

"Thank you," Cora said to the girl, who looked back at Cora as if she were a hero. Care for some?" She offered Mamnoon.

"No thank you," Mamnoon said quietly.

Another servant handed Cora a ceramic mug and moved on without offering one to Mamnoon.

Tess strolled up from behind. "So, when are you and His Lordship getting married?"

"Tomorrow," Cora replied, before taking a bite of a fig.

"Abigail and I were curious about who you will pick for your attendants," Tess continued.

Cora studied Tess and her cousin, who now looked at her as if she were their dearest friend. "I haven't thought that far ahead. Can I assume that you are kind to me because you want to be my attendants?"

Abigail sidled up to Cora. "Oh come now, cousin, it will be amusing."

"Of course you, Abigail, and Molly will be my attendants. I wouldn't want anyone else." Cora smiled back. Her trembling hand lifted the mug to her lips. She took one sip of her water. A moment later, her ceramic mug slipped from her hand and shattered when it hit the floor. Her knees buckled; Cora's eyes rolled into the back of her head.

Abigail screamed when her cousin collapsed.

"Cora!" Mamnoon pushed the women away in an effort to reach her. "Send for a healer!" he shouted as he lowered her to the marble floor.

Mamnoon shook Cora and did everything in his power to bring her back. In the end, all the bodyguard could do was hold his charge in his arms as she fought to breathe.

"Tell … him … I forgive him … I forgive them all … take care of her." She whispered with a peaceful expression on her lips. "We'll see each other again."

"Soon," Mamnoon whispered with a brave smile.

"Don't be sad … I'm free now," Cora smiled before closing her eyes.

"Be at peace, my beloved." Mamnoon closed his eyes and let out a loud cry.

"Stand back." Bashira pushed the women and children aside. Tears filling her eyes, she covered her mouth with her hand to conceal her quivering lip. "Send a message to the Dey. Tell him that Cora Bradley was poisoned."

Abigail, who was looking down on Cora's exchange with Mamnoon, turned to walk away with her nose in the air, but not before mumbling "Good riddance" under her breath.

"You ungrateful whore." Mamnoon sneered at Abigail. Had he not been holding Cora, he would have strangled the life out of her. "Night after night Cora was violated and tortured, not by one, but by many," he said with tears streaming down his cheeks.

"She brought it on herself." Abigail stared defiantly at the bodyguard.

"Cora sacrificed herself to protect *you*!" Mamnoon shouted. "Even now, during her dying moments, she was still protecting you. I will never understand why she sacrificed so much after seeing the way you treated her!"

"I don't believe you." Abigail turned her shoulder's sideways, glaring down at him as if he were her slave.

Mamnoon slid Cora's white gömlek up to her breasts exposing what Cora fought so hard to conceal.

Abigail and the women surrounding Mamnoon gasped in horror as they surveyed the welts, the cuts, and the bruises on Cora's stomach. It was evident to everyone that her wounds covered her entire body. Even Tess and the other mothers shielded their children's eyes from the spectacle.

"You should all be ashamed of the way you treated Cora." Mamnoon lowered Cora's gömlek and stared at Ula. "One word from her to His Excellency, and he would have sold you. Cora protected all of you. Oh, how she suffered by keeping silent about your mischief. Had she lived to marry His Excellency, she would have made your lives better. May Allah help you now; I will not conceal the truth from your master."

Ula lowered her eyes and slithered away.

"All of you return to your respective areas," Bashira ordered, shoving the women away.

Chapter 20

"Your Excellency, I must speak to you in private," Jamal whispered in Naa'il's ear.

"Jamal, you complain that I have been neglecting my duties for weeks. Now that I am finally here, you want me to leave the slave yard. As you can see, there is much to do today," Naa'il said, pointing to the yard filled with people.

"I would be happy to deliver your message here, but I think you would prefer to hear this news in your private office."

Naa'il pursed his lips when he spotted the somber expression on his Vizier's face. "Very well." He got up from his pillow and walked with Jamal to a small room. Located off of the slave yard, Naa'il's private study was big enough to fit a desk and three chairs. He chose this room for its view of the harbor. Once they were inside, the Dey closed the door. He pressed his lips together to form a thin line. "Well, what do you have to tell me?"

"I received a message from Bashira." Jamal's Adam's apple bobbed up and down as he swallowed. "Cora Bradley is dead."

Naa'il's lips parted. He reached behind him and clutched the doorknob to brace himself. "What? I just saw her a few hours ago."

"She was poisoned in the harem. Bashira said that she died instantly. I am sorry. I know you cared for her."

Naa'il straightened himself and shoved his advisor deeper into the room. "No! You Lie!"

"I am sorry."

"Where was Mamnoon during Cora's assassination?"

"He was standing beside her. Bashira said the inf … the American died in his arms."

Naa'il's knees buckled. Bracing his hand on the desk was the only thing that prevented him from collapsing onto the floor. "I want to see Mamnoon at once."

"You failed me!" Naa'il cocked his fist back and punched Mamnoon in the jaw, causing his servant to stumble backward. "How could you allow this to happen?"

Mamnoon straightened himself and removed the saber from his belt. "You are right, Your Excellency; I failed you. I will gladly accept my punishment." He offered his saber to his master.

"Put your saber away. I am not ready to kill you, but I am very disappointed." Naa'il glanced at the green and white tiles at the base of the wall. "Do you have any idea who is responsible?"

"I cannot give you a definitive answer. Cora had many enemies in the harem."

Naa'il approached the arched window and rested his arm on the wall above his head while he watched the birds swirling above the harbor. "I do not understand how anyone could hate Cora. She was a kind person."

"Yes, she was," Mamnoon answered with a faint smile. "The women in the harem hated her because she won your love."

Naa'il looked back at his servant. "Were they aware that Cora and I were to be married?"

"Yes, Your Excellency. The truth was revealed the other day," Mamnoon hesitated.

Naa'il frowned. "What happened?"

"Samina attacked Cora in the harem that morning. Tess O'Shea guessed correctly that your wife was angry because she had learned of your intention to marry Cora."

Naa'il let out a loud sigh. "No, that was not the cause of Samina's anger. I will talk to her. This is what I want you to do …."

Naa'il decided to talk to his wives separately. This time he had them brought to his private study. Staring at the azure Mediterranean Sea with this hands clasped behind him, Naa'il turned slightly towards the room when the door opened.

Dressed in various shades of green and gold, Samina entered his study with heavy footsteps. Instead of running into Naa'il's arms, she remained standing by the door. "You wanted to see me, my lord?" She bowed to him with her gaze fixed on his desk.

"Sit." Naa'il waited until she was seated before sitting in the chair behind his desk. "I wanted to inform you that Cora Bradley was assassinated this morning."

"Dead?" Samina's eyes widened with genuine astonishment. "How?"

"She was poisoned in the harem."

"Oh." She pressed her lips together to suppress her delight.

"I understand you attacked her a few days ago."

Samina grimaced. "Yes." She rested her hand on her stomach.

He glowered at his wife. "Why? What did Cora do to make you hate her?"

Samina looked away and wiped a tear from the corner of her eye. "You called her name twice when you made love to me. How can I feel anything but bitterness for that wretched woman?"

Naa'il's cold stare softened. "I will not deny or apologize for loving Cora. You should not hate her either. Cora saved your life."

Samina bit her lip. "I do not understand."

"I confided in Cora about your indiscretion. Of course, she didn't understand our ways. Cora encouraged me to reconsider the circumstances under which I found you," Naa'il smiled faintly. "She made an argument with which I could not disagree. Cora was the reason that I returned to your apartment. Had she not advocated on your behalf, I never would have found your mice; you would have received one-hundred lashes, and your guard would have been executed. You may not believe this, but Cora also encouraged me to be with you the other night. She wanted me to be a good husband to you and Mariam. Though she was too polite to admit it, she did not want to be my mistress," he paused, "or my wife. She believed that I should only have one wife."

Samina folded her hands in her lap and bowed her head. "If you could only have one wife, who would you choose?"

Naa'il answered with silence; his lips formed a faint smile as Cora's peaceful continence filled his thought like a light beaming through the window. "You may go."

Samina bit her lip to stifle a cry. "What is to happen to me, my lord?" she asked in a timid voice.

"My heart is too heavy to answer you right now."

"You loved her, the American, I mean?"

"Yes." *With all my heart.* "Return to your apartment and reflect on what I told you."

Samina ran out of the room with tears streaming down her cheeks. She paused in the doorway as she passed Mariam, each glaring at the other. Naa'il looked on, pretending not to notice their exchange.

"Close the door," Naa'il said to Mariam.

"Certainly, my husband." The first wife obeyed and took a seat across from him. "You summoned me?"

"Yes." Naa'il rested his elbow on the arm of his chair and cupped his chin between his fingers.

"I heard that your American was poisoned this morning," Mariam said with genuine sympathy.

"Of course you heard," Naa'il replied in a tone laced with annoyance.

"One of my attendants was in the harem at the time of her death. Jamal also sent word to me. I am sorry, Naa'il."

"Are you? I was under the impression that you hated Cora more than Samina," Naa'il bitterly challenged.

Mariam stared at the desk. "We have never met." She returned her gaze to her husband before continuing. "Yes. It is true; I disapproved of her because I believed that she was a threat to our way of life."

"Cora was never a threat," Naa'il countered through gritted teeth.

"If you say so, but she changed you."

His hands clutching the arms on his chair, Naa'il jumped to his feet. "Yes, I have changed; I loved her! I loved Cora with my whole heart, and I will love her until I draw my last breath." His voice broke. "Do not be deceived; I am still the ruthless man you married, and I am as devoted to our faith as I ever was. Know this, I will find Cora's killer, and I will not show her mercy. Leave me," Naa'il said in a threatening tone.

Swallowing hard, the color in Mariam's cheeks faded. She rose from her chair and rushed out of the room, closing the door behind her.

Mamnoon placed Cora's body on a table in a small room a few doors down from the harem. The only other adornments in the room were the stained-glass lanterns hanging from the ceiling. Servants had already delivered buckets of water.

"I found this." Bashira held up a white dress. She closed the door behind her and strolled into the room. Standing across from her friend, the valide looked down and admired Cora's face. "She looks so peaceful."

"Yes, she does." Mamnoon combed Cora's hair with his fingers.

"I am relieved that Cora did not die at the hands of her attackers."

"I know. There was a time when I feared that she would. Thankfully, I was wrong."

Bashira dipped a white cloth in the water and began cleaning one side of Cora's body. "I suppose this is the last time that we will clean Cora again."

"I suppose it is," Mamnoon offered his friend an appreciative smile. "I am grateful for your help each night after the attacks. I could not have managed without your assistance."

"I was only too happy to help." Bashira smiled back at her friend.

Once they finished bathing her, Mamnoon lifted Cora up while Bashira slid the dress onto her body.

"Cora looks so beautiful." Bashira stood back and admired her handiwork. "Would you like me to help you wrap Cora's body?"

"Not yet; I want to give His Excellency an opportunity to say goodbye."

Bashira looked down at Cora and said, "Goodbye, my friend. I shall miss you, but I am certain that you have gone on to a better place." The valide leaned down and kissed Cora's forehead. "May you find eternal peace. I hope we will meet again someday." Bashira glanced up at her friend and continued, "Please let me know if I can assist you with anything else."

"Thank you, Bashira." Mamnoon nodded. He waited until his friend left the room before returning his attention to Cora. He sat with her reflecting on the little time they had together and the future that fate had denied them. With tears streaming down his cheeks, Mamnoon kissed Cora's lips. "Oh, how I will miss you. I wish we could have made a life together."

Mamnoon returned to Naa'il's office just as the sun was setting. Naa'il stood at the window watching the activity in the harbor. Though the fuchsia orb wasn't in plain view, the bodyguard could see its reflection dancing on the azure water. "Your Excellency." Mamnoon bowed to his master before entering the office. "I placed Cora's body in a private room in case you wish to say goodbye to her."

"Thank you, but that will not be necessary." Naa'il gave a cursory glance to his servant before returning his attention to the harbor. "I do not know what to do with her body. I cannot give her a traditional burial."

"I will dispose of Cora's body, Your Excellency." Mamnoon paused. "May I ask what you intend to do with Cora's cousin?"

Naa'il sighed. "I do not know. I would rather sell Abigail, but Cora's sacrifice forbids me from acting upon my wishes. I think she would never forgive me if I did."

"Cora forgave you. She said so just before she died. Please accept my apology for not conveying her message to you sooner. I forgot until now."

Naa'il stared at his servant with parted lips. "Thank you for telling me. That will be all." He forced a smile.

"Very good, Your Excellency." Mamnoon bowed and backed out of the room. "I will delay burying Cora until tomorrow - in case you change your mind."

"You are a good servant." Naa'il went to Cora's apartment long enough to retrieve her Bible before returning to his own. All he could do was sit on his couch and stare at the Bible's black cover. With rage building inside him, Naa'il threw the book against the wall. Hours later, his eyes fell on the trail of handwritten notes surrounding the book. He went over and gathered the Bible, the notes, and the letters. Naa'il thought he had read all of them, yet there was still one that remained concealed from him. He had no idea when she wrote it. He ripped the parchment into pieces and went to toss it into the fire, but he couldn't bring himself to burn them. Instead, he knelt on the floor in front of the hearth and reassembled the letter.

Your Excellency,

> *You once asked me how I pray each night. This is my prayer for you. I pray that all will see you as the honorable man that I know you are. I pray for God to give you King Solomon's wisdom to rule your country. I pray that one day that you will find the kind of love that will sustain you through your darkest hours. I pray that you will find joy in your life. Above all, I pray...*

Her letter ended abruptly. Tears flooded his eyes as his heart yearned to read the rest of her message. He sobbed, knowing that Cora's message would remain forever unfinished, and he would never know how it ended. Naa'il pulled himself up from the floor sometime during the early hours of the morning. Instead of retiring, he wandered through the halls with heavy footsteps. He told himself that he didn't want to see Cora Bradley, but his feet still led him to the corridor where Cora's body was being kept. Mamnoon stood guard outside the room as if he were expecting his master.

"What are you doing?" Naa'il demanded.

The servant bowed. "Cora's body is in here, Your Excellency."

"I command you to retire. Report to me tomorrow morning," Naa'il barked.

"Thank you, but I would rather stay." Mamnoon bowed again.

"Do as you wish," Naa'il said before entering the room. The lanterns and the torches hanging on the wall bathed Cora's body with a golden hue. Even a few hours after her spirit left her, all that remained of Cora Bradley was a shell of the woman he loved. She still smelled like Jasmine. Her cream cheeks had turned to a silvery white. Someone had dressed her in a gown. As much as Naa'il hated Western clothing, this dress suited her. Though her body was stiff and unresponsive, the peaceful smile on her lips reminded him that she was still the woman he loved.

"Tell Naa'il that I forgive him."

Anger building inside him, Naa'il paced back and forth beside the table. "What a pair we make. I set out to conquer you, yet I stand before you conquered." Naa'il's steps became more deliberate. "I am so cross with you," he shouted. "How could you leave me? You knew that I loved you.

I was going to make you my wife; you were going to give me sons," he continued, his voice cracking. "It no longer mattered to me that you had not converted because I believed we could be happy together. I believed you could love me as I love you." Naa'il swallowed hard to regain his composure. "Now you are gone. You left me to go to your Paradise, leaving me behind to console my heavy heart. Do you know why I wanted you to convert? It was not just so that it would save your soul from eternal damnation; I wanted us to be together always. I do not care about spending eternity in the land of milk and honey. All that mattered to me was that we would always be together. Now, I will never see you again." Naa'il's voice trailed off when he spotted the bruises on her chest.

They were still a painful reminder that Cora had suffered greatly at his command. Now she was beyond his reach, and perhaps that was his punishment for persecuting one of God's own. Naa'il was sure that Cora would spend eternity in her Paradise, which his faith prohibited him from entering. Even worse, he would be forced to live with the guilt of torturing the only woman he had ever loved. Caressing Cora's cheek with the back of his fingers, the mighty Dey fell to his knees and looked up to Heaven. "Please tell Cora that I am sorry for the pain I inflicted on her. Watch over her." He pulled himself to his feet. His tears spilling onto her face, he kissed her tenderly and said, "I love you with my whole being, Cora Bradley. May you have joy and peace for all eternity."

CHAPTER 21

Hassan and Sarah stole away from the group at the end of the evening, just as they had done for the past few nights. They both looked forward to this time of day, each joyfully anticipating the new adventure that awaited them. They danced, they swam, and they talked while strolling down the beach.

"We swim tonight?"

Hassan couldn't deny that the warm air and calm wind made it a perfect night for a moonlit swim. Still, he didn't divert from their path. "I would rather walk on the beach if you don't mind."

Sarah groaned, "I speak English?"

Hassan raised a brow. "You do not enjoy our conversations?"

"No, I like; you talk."

"But?"

"English hard."

Hassan laughed. "I know you struggle through our conversations. You are right; English is a difficult language to learn. I thank you for trying." He gently squeezed her hand to convey his appreciation for her effort. "I promise that I will try to be more diligent about teaching you to speak proper English. I would also like you to teach me your language." With a playful gleam in his eyes, he asked, "How do you say 'hello' in your language?"

"La orana."

"Ya rana," Hassan repeated. "Is that correct?"

"Aye."

"How do you say, 'goodbye'?"

"Nana."

"Nah Nah," Hassan repeated, emphasizing each syllable. "How do you say, 'please'?"

"Na."

"Na? That is simple enough, providing I don't confuse the two. And 'thank you'?"

"Mauru'uru," Sarah replied.

"Ma roo roo," Hassan slowly sounded out each syllable. "I've heard you say that before. I think you will need to remind me of that one."

"Aye," Sarah laughed.

"Yes."

Sarah's round eyes tossed him a puzzled look. "Yes?"

"That is the proper English word for 'aye.'"

"Yes," Sarah repeated.

They strolled down to the end of the beach and returned to camp when the air turned crisp. Hassan stoked the fire and covered Sarah with a blanket. He took a seat on the log beside her and said in a serious tone, "I found a husband for you."

Sarah squeezed her eyes shut; her whole body trembled. Fighting back her tears, Sarah stood and ran towards the water. Her knees buckled, and she collapsed onto the sand, gasping for breath.

Hassan chased after her. "Sarah!" He knelt in the wet sand as the water surged and retreated beneath his knees.

"I do duty," she whimpered with her gaze fixed on the sand.

Hassan tucked his thumb under her chin and swiveled her face towards his. "Please, look at me. Sarah Campbell, you have shown great courage during an impossible situation. I would like to know what you want." Shivers spiked up and down his spine when he spotted tears surging into her eyes. "Please tell me."

"I ...," was all she could say.

Hassan could almost see the frustration building inside her as she fought to summon the right words. Her lips moved without making a sound, and tears streamed down her cheeks. Hassan rested his hands on her shoulders and said calmly, "Breathe."

Her bottom lip quivering, Sarah took a deep breath.

"I will start your answer. I want ..."

"You," Sarah said in a small voice.

"Good," Hassan smiled tenderly. "If you had let me finish, I was going to tell you that I think we should formally marry."

"You wish marry me?" Sarah's tone rose, mirroring her surprise.

"Yes, I do. Will you agree to marry me, Sarah Campbell?"

"Cattin, your family. Peter say we no marry."

"Do not worry about my family. I have not seen them for a long time. As far as I am concerned, I did my duty. Now, I am free to marry whomever I please." He enveloped her hand in his and kissed it.

The muscles in Sarah's face tightened. "You marry me like first wife - for duty?"

"Look at me." Hassan caressed her cheek and looked her in the eyes. "You have given me a happiness that I have never known during my lifetime. I want us to spend every day together as husband and wife for the rest of our lives. That is why I want to marry you. So, I ask again. Will you marry me, Sarah Campbell?"

Sarah studied Hassan with a slight gap between her lips. "You certain, Cattin?"

Hassan caressed her cheek with his finger. "Yes, I am certain. You still have not given me your answer."

"Yes, I marry you," she said eagerly.

"I am pleased. Come here, Sarah," Hassan said in a throaty whisper as he guided her down to the sand. He kissed her cheek softly and slowly moved to her lips. Sarah answered, unhurried. Hassan groaned as their kisses deepened. His mouth opened, and his tongue traced the outline of her full lips. Sarah used her own to encourage his tongue to continue their dance, circling and darting in and out of each other's mouths. She didn't flinch when his hand slid under her gown and explored every curve on her perfect figure. His hand playfully squeezed and traced her firm breasts and then slid down to her waist. Sarah parted her legs, inviting him to explore her. Hassan pulled away and looked at her with surprise. "My God, you *are* a virgin."

Sarah sat up and lowered her gaze to her dress. "I no please you?" she timidly asked as her hands fidgeted with the ends of her gown.

Hassan also sat up and opened his mouth without answering her.

"We no marry if you no want. I wish happiness," she whispered.

Even though her hair blocked a clear view of her face, Hassan heard a tear splash onto Sarah's skirt. His fingers tucked her hair behind her ear before pressing a kiss to her temple. "It is not that. You continually surprise me. Just as you did tonight when you demonstrated your skill at kissing."

Sarah looked back at him with parted lips. The tension on her face began to fade. "I do wrong?"

"Only if you kiss another man the way you just kissed me."

"No, you only one." She studied him with eyes, round and dilated. "You like?"

"Um hmm."

"We do more? We married now, yes?"

Hassan kissed her again, "As I mentioned before, the marriage laws in my country are more complicated than the laws on your island. I cannot begin to tell you how tempting it is to carry you into my tent and make love to you for the rest of the night," he said, interlacing her fingers with his own. "That would not be fair to you, it is abundantly clear that your father did not prepare you for living in the world from which he came. The things I speak of have no meaning for you." He kissed her hand. "Someday they will. I don't want you to resent me, or feel as though I took advantage of your innocence. That is why I won't make love to you until we are properly wed. You must understand that there is no more important day to a woman than her wedding day." He grimaced. "I want to give you such a day."

Sarah tilted her head to the side and pressed her lips together as she looked at her fiancé in a thoughtful way. "Say about weddings."

"Wedding days can be very special. The bride, the woman, will wear the prettiest dress that she can afford. The groom, the man, will wear his best clothes. The bride and groom and their family and friends will congregate, meet in a church, where the bride and groom exchange their wedding vows. A vow is a promise that people make to each other. They promise to love and take care of each other for the rest of their lives. After the ceremony, people will gather at one of the parent's home for a celebratory breakfast, a morning feast." Hassan's voice trailed off. "Then the bride and groom begin their new life together on their wedding night." He paused and studied his fiancé. "Do you have any marriage traditions on your island?"

"Aye," she said in a matter of fact tone. "If woman no like husband, she leave."

"I see." Hassan chuckled. "You can't rid yourself of me so easily, Sarah Campbell. Ending a marriage on my island is seldom done. A person must have a legitimate reason for annulling their marriage if he or she chooses to do so."

"You still wish marry me?"

He caressed her cheek and kissed her tenderly. "Yes, I still want to marry you."

"We wait to England?"

Hassan stared at the moonlight dancing on the water. The ends of his lips curled downward as he contemplated delaying their marriage until they reached England.

"Cattin?" Sarah said sweetly.

Hassan exhaled a hard sigh. "I was thinking about delaying our wedding until we reach England. I wish I could tell you that we'll leave this god-forsaken place soon, but it would be a lie if I did. In all honesty, I have no idea when that day will take place. We could sail home tomorrow, or several years from now. Sarah, I was sincere when I said that I want to give you a proper wedding. You deserve that, but I do not want to delay our life together as husband and wife either."

Sarah bit her lip. "We say vows here? We say vows in England?"

Hassan's lips parted. "Is that enough for you?"

"This say," she rested her hand on her chest, "I wife now. You same?"

"Yes, except *my* heart tells me that I am already your husband," he admitted. "Are you certain that you want to exchange our wedding vows tonight?"

Sarah kissed him tenderly.

"Very well," he smiled back.

Sarah's hand clutched the brown muslin dress. "This best dress I have. It wet."

"Hmm," Hassan frowned. With a gleam in his eye, he kissed her again. "I have a better idea."

"Aye?"

"I do. Come with me." Hassan stood and pulled Sarah to her feet.

They returned to their camp. Sarah added a log to the fire while Hassan stepped into his tent. She giggled when he came out with her paru dangling from his hand.

He handed the cloth to her. "Wear this."

"It not dress."

"This is *our* wedding. We may wear what we please."

"We ask Peter and men come?"

"No, let's limit our celebration to just us. Besides, you could not wear this cloth if my crew were present. Would you care to change into your wedding …?"

"Paru."

Hassan held the tent flap open. "Change in here."

"Mauru'uru," She rose up on her toes and kissed him.

"Get dressed." Hassan patted her bottom. He couldn't stop grinning at the thought of exchanging wedding vows with Sarah. Marrying her tonight was the last thing on his mind, yet having Sarah for his wife felt as natural as drawing breath. Hassan lit a torch and went to cut some flowers growing near the cave. He had just finished picking a modest bouquet when he looked up and spotted her standing before him. Hassan's heart raced when he felt her love radiating from her whole being. "I found some flowers for you. They aren't as pretty as the ones we have at home."

"Na, I like." Sarah broke off the largest white flower from the cluster and held it up to her left ear. "This say, 'I married.'" She moved the flower to her right ear. "This say, 'I no married.'" She turned her head to the side and held the flower against the back of her head. "This say, foll …."

"Follow," Hassan offered.

"Aye. This say, follow me."

"I see." Hassan laughed. "You don't need to wear a flower on the back of your head to persuade me to follow you."

"What persuade?" Sarah fixed her eyes on his with a look of confusion.

Hassan bit the inside of his lip as he searched for a simpler explanation. "What I am trying to say is that I will follow you regardless of whether you wear a flower or not."

"Aye?" Sarah asked with genuine surprise.

"Aye." He grinned and took the flower from her and placed it behind her left ear before handing the bouquet to her.

Sarah stood and backed away. "I look like bride?" She slowly turned around.

"Um hum." For the first time in his life, Hassan was at a loss for words. Never had he seen anything so beautiful. Though this wasn't the first time that Sarah wore her paru for him, tonight she looked radiant.

For one reason or another, the word "Cattin" stood out to him. Then he realized why. "Come and sit by me. There is something I must tell you."

Sarah approached him with heavy footsteps. "I do wrong?" She asked, resting her hand on her belly.

"Why do you assume that you did something wrong whenever I ask to talk to you?"

"I not know. I no wish hurt you."

"You didn't. Besides, just because I have something important to tell you, does not mean it is bad news." He patted the sand beside him. "Sit here." Hassan reached for her hand and pulled her to the ground. "The reason I wanted to talk to you is that I just realized that I never told you my name. Now that we are about to be married, I thought it was appropriate to do so."

"It Cattin," Sarah insisted. "That what men say."

"Captain is my title, but I will not try to explain titles to you tonight. What you need to know is that my name, my proper name, is Nathanial Shelby." Hassan laughed faintly when Sarah's eyes blinked more than usual. "I shortened my name to Nathan because I never cared for Nathanial - much to my mother's displeasure. Shelby is my family's name. You may address me as 'Nathan.'"

"Natan."

"That's close enough." His grin broadened. "I like hearing you say my name."

Sarah bit the inside of her lip. "I no say 'Cattin'?"

"You may call me 'Cattin' for now, but I would like you to use my Christian name after we return to England." Hassan stood up and offered his hand to his bride. "Shall we?" He led Sarah by the hand to the other side of the fire so that they could enjoy the view of the moon and its reflection dancing on the water. Sarah's face was the only thing he saw that night. "I am afraid that I do not recall the proper wedding vows, so we will have to make up our own." He smiled apologetically.

"It not matter."

"Very well. Let's see." He looked tenderly at his bride and continued, "Will you take me to be your husband?"

"Aye, you take me be you …?

"Wife, and yes, I do." Hassan lifted her hands to his lips and kissed them. "I, Nathanial Shelby, take you Sarah Campbell to be my wife. I promise to love you; to give my life to protect you, and to take care of you in sickness and in health, for as long as I live. Now it is your turn."

Sarah's peach cheeks pinkened ever so slightly as a playful giggle escaped her lips, "I … Sarah."

"Campbell," Hassan added.

"No, that Da's name."

"Campbell is your name too. It is a family name, just like Shelby is mine. Please continue."

"I, Sarah … Campbell, promise …," she sighed. "I no remember what you say."

"I promise to love you."

"Ah, I remember." Her expression brightened. "I promise to love you. I promise to care for you for as long as I live. That right?"

Hassan laughed faintly. "Well done, but there is more. Repeat after me. I promise to obey." *South Seas maidens are incapable of being faithful to only one man.* Hassan's voice trailed off when Peter's warning echoed in his mind. His smile faded and was replaced by a haunted expression.

Sarah gently squeezed Hassan's hand. "Cattin?"

Hassan tore his gaze from the fire. "I want you to promise me that you will never give yourself to anyone but me for the rest of your life."

Sarah looked at Hassan with love in her eyes and said without hesitation, "I promise."

He pressed her again. "You cannot break this promise - ever, Sarah."

"I promise, I no break promise - as long as I live."

"Thank you. Now, we finish with a kiss."

Sarah rolled onto her toes and wrapped her arms around Hassan's neck. Hassan slid his arms around her waist and kissed her slowly and deeply.

She pulled away and looked into his eyes, "We married now?"

"Yes, we are married." Hassan kissed her again.

"What we do now?"

Hassan quirked a lopsided grin, "I do not know. What would you like to do?"

"Show me how be wife?" She eagerly suggested.

Hassan wrapped one arm around her waist and tucked the other behind her knees before carrying her into the tent. He lowered her onto the edge of the feather bed and sat down beside her. "I would like to talk with you before we begin."

Sarah sat with her hands folded in her lap while looking up at him with a childlike trust.

"You will soon learn that English society is laden with rules. There are rules for everything, how to eat, how to greet each other, just to name a few. Many consider these rules burdensome. My grandmother believed that good manners are a way of showing respect to another person. Making love shares the same premise. It's a way to express love to your husband, wife, or lover. Believe me when I say that making love and fornicating are two different things. Fornicating is what animals do. It has nothing to do with love. Making love takes place between two people who already love each other. They teach the other how to please them, including showing how they like to be touched or kissed. I will freely admit that some people prefer to fornicate.

"You forn …?"

"Fornicate. Yes, once or twice," Hassan reluctantly admitted.

"What you prefer?"

"I prefer making love. I like taking my time getting to know a lover. I want her to know me too. I believe this way is far more satisfying than getting the deed over as quickly as possible."

Sarah covered Hassan's hand with hers. "You show me how make love?"

"Oh, I intend to. My first lesson. There are certain places on a man and woman's bodies that are particularly sensitive." He turned her arm over so that her palm faced him. "A person can feel pleasure when their lover touches or kisses them in a certain way, like this."

Sarah cooed when he nibbled on her wrist. "I kiss you?" She offered, reaching for his hand.

"Thank you, but the sensitive places on a man's body are different from a woman's. That is the next lesson; I'm not finished with this one." He nibbled from her ear to her nape, sliding his lips over her soft skin. Hassan's kisses returned to her lips as he guided her to lie on her back. He marveled how she gave herself completely over to his instruction. There was no Christian guilt, just a willingness to learn and an eagerness to please. Sarah moaned when his kisses moved from her lips to her body, slowly and tenderly. Hassan's heart raced when her hands explored his body as she removed his clothes, kissing each place her hands touched.

Overcome with desire, Hassan covered her body with his. "I'm sorry, I cannot wait," he said in a throaty whisper.

"Please," she offered her husband a loving smile, inviting him to enter her.

"Your passage is small. I am afraid it may hurt when I enter you." After lacing his fingers with hers, he whispered, "Squeeze my hand. That will offset the pain." Sarah closed her eyes as she let out a muffled cry. Seeing the pain on her face, Hassan froze as he debated whether he should continue. "Sarah?"

Her face relaxed, and she caressed her husband's cheek with her fingers. "I good," she said, looking at him tenderly.

"Are you certain?"

"Aye," She latched her legs around his waist.

They moved as one. Waves of pleasure rippled through their bodies, building up to one final push. Their energies spent, they laid in each other's arms with their legs intertwined

"Did you enjoy making love?" Hassan whispered as he combed his fingers through her loose curls. Sarah propped her head up on the blanket of hair on his chest. Her faint smile and slow blinking eyes told him everything he wanted to know.

"Aye. You like too?"

"Very much so," Hassan replied in a relaxed voice as he mindlessly wrapped locks of her hair around his finger before letting go. "I see you have had some instruction."

"I...,"she answered, biting her lower lip.

"Go on."

Sarah sighed. "Da say, 'no do'. I no do. I wish learn. My friends teach. I no do." Her lips puckered to one side. "I do a wee bit. I wish be good wife."

"You little vixen."

She studied him. "I do wrong?"

"No, I cannot fault you for being curious, especially since you remained a virgin - at least until a few minutes ago." Hassan mused. "Your friends taught you well. I look forward to discovering what else they taught you. Come here." Hassan shifted Sarah until her back was pressed against his chest. It wasn't long before he heard her soft breaths of sleep, and soon he was asleep too... until his dreams took him to an unexpected place. Hassan sat up sharply when he awoke to his first wife's sobs ringing in his mind.

Sarah rolled over and faced him. "Cattin, you sad?"

The tension drained from his face when he heard his bride's soothing voice. Smiling back at her, he replied, "I am well. I was thinking about my first wedding night."

"It good?"

Hassan laughed faintly. "No, it was quite the contrary." He winced again when he heard Lydia's cries again. "The mother of my first wife ingrained in Lydia that making love was ... torture. My wife was so terrified that she recoiled every time I touched her. She didn't even like holding my hand.

In my country, marriages aren't official until a husband and wife make love," Hassan continued. "Lydia wasn't ready for intimacy on our wedding night. So, I told myself that I could be patient. We were strangers when we married. I only needed to spend one day with her to discover that we had nothing in common. As I told you earlier, the people in my country need a legitimate reason to annul a marriage. Though I had one, I had no wish to humiliate Lydia. So I delayed consummating our marriage until a few nights after our wedding night. We discussed making love earlier that day. She was so nervous about the evening ahead of her." Hassan shook his head. "I felt her terror standing in the doorway when I went to her later that night."

Hassan took a deep breath. He swung his legs over the side of the bed and buried his face in his hands as the sound of the shrill of her voice stabbed him like a dagger. It was the only time Hassan had attempted to consummate their marriage, Lydia just laid beneath him, thrashing her head from side to side, and sobbing.

Sarah knelt in front of her husband, resting her hands on his knees. "You no have to say if not want."

Hassan looked down at his bride with a forced smile. "I am going to tell you something that I have never told a living soul. Lydia and I did not consummate our marriage. No matter how I felt about her, and there was no love between us, I could not bring myself to cause her additional pain by forcing myself on her, even when I had a legal right to do so."

"How Lydia die?"

"I intended to return to the sea several weeks after we were married. Lydia's parents were furious when I told them that I needed to report for duty. They had given us a small cottage on their property. They thought it was proper that I stay and help Lydia set up our new home. I could not wait to leave. At the same time, they saw nothing wrong with leaving me for a few days to visit a family friend - a very prominent viscountess dowager."

Sarah listened with an expressionless face, her eyes, round, and her brow slightly raised. "They not ask you go with them?"

"Lydia and her parents asked me, or I should say, they attempted to shame me into joining them. I declined because I knew I needed to prepare for my upcoming mission. They promised to return home before I departed for Portsmouth. Ironically, that was the last time that I saw Lydia and her parents alive."

"What happen?"

"It rains a lot in England, and it had been raining for days. Many of the roads were washed out, and they were on one of them. Their carriage got too close to the edge of a road. The road gave way, and their carriage plunged into a deep ravine. Lydia, her parents, the driver, and the horses died instantly. The whole community was in shock when they learned of the news. Even I was a little sad … and relieved at the same time. I returned to the sea a week after their funerals. Then I came here."

Sarah kissed Hassan softly. "You good man. Da say, she damn fool if not see it. Lydia big damn fool if no enjoy making love to you."

Hassan tossed his head back and made a loud guffaw. He couldn't remember the last time he had laughed so hard, and it felt good.

"I say wrong?"

"No, on the contrary, I think your word choices were perfect." Hassan looked at her tenderly. "Come here." He lifted his bride onto the bed and laid beside her. Propping himself up on his elbow, he hovered over her and kissed her. "Thank you. I like talking to you; you are a good listener." He kissed her again. "Thank you for making tonight the best night of my life."

"We make love again?"

"Why don't you show me what else your friends taught you?" Hassan and Sarah made love throughout the rest of the night. Exhausted and contented, they fell asleep in each other's arms just before dawn. Hassan had finally drifted to sleep when he heard an unexpected sound the next morning.

Chapter 22

Hassan's eyes snapped open when he heard the bell warning him of danger. He glanced down at Sarah's scarlet hair scattered across his chest. Locking his arms around his bride, Hassan held her tight. It was hard to let go, especially knowing what would follow.

"What wrong?" Sarah bit her bottom lip as she rested her chin on his chest.

"I must leave you here," he said when the bell rang again. This time, Hassan felt his heart pulsing into his throat.

Sarah sat up. "I no understand. Why you frightened?"

When the bell rang the third time, Hassan had finished dressing. They ducked out of the tent, and he led Sarah to the cave behind the beach. "I must leave you here while I go to my ship. You will hear loud noises that may frighten you. I promise that I will come for you when this is over," Hassan said firmly. "Do not leave this cave for any reason." He pressed his bride against him. *Be safe.* Tucking her paru inside his shirt, he handed Sarah her Biblical gown. "Dress yourself after I leave."

Several members of his crew were waiting for Hassan in the jolly. His attention remained focused on his private beach as his crewman rowed him to his ship. All he could see from the water was Sarah's face and her tousled hair, and it was still an intoxicating sight. This morning his bride looked lovelier than ever, perhaps he realized, because he loved her. It comforted him knowing that Sarah could hide in the caves, and he hoped that she would remain undiscovered.

"Captain, it appears that the Frenchies took your bait." The crewman passed Hassan the spyglass. "Do you think Miss Campbell will remain safe?"

"She should be, as long as she stays in the cave," Hassan answered as he watched the Persephone growing larger through his spyglass. "What is the status of the preparations for the battle?" he asked his quartermaster.

"We're ready for them."

"Let's end this," Hassan smiled in spite of the uneasiness growing inside him. He turned the spyglass to the beach for one last look. All he saw was sand and palm trees. "Assemble the crew."

Sarah screamed when she spotted a ship identical to Hassan's firing on the Zafirah. Hassan's ship fired back. Each explosive impact reduced long wooden planks to splinters. The thunderous booms subsided, and one long cry of men's voices followed as Hassan's crew swung over to the invading ship. Even at a distance, she could see men crossing swords, followed by one of them collapsing onto the deck. Sarah was too far away to see which side was winning. Hassan was nowhere in plain sight. She was so engrossed in the fight to notice her former ship sailing into the lagoon, or the jolly-filled with men rowing ashore.

Sarah gasped when she spotted Emile and Gerard running towards her with a small army following behind them. She fled to the cave hoping to find a place to hide. They had swarmed her before she reached the entrance. Sarah squirmed and struggled to free herself, but they were too strong.

Once his crew bound her hands in chains and attached an iron choker around her neck, Gerard stood over Sarah, with narrowed eyes challenging her to give him a reason to punish her. "Savage whore, I would give you to my crew, if I thought I couldn't profit from selling you. Disappoint me, and I will show you how cruel I can be." His thin lips curled into a sneer as he tore her gown from her body and threw it into the water.

"Cattin!" Sarah screamed as Gerard yanked the chain to her choker. She pulled away as Gerard pulled her forward. A few steps later, Sarah tripped and fell, and her captor continued dragging her across the sand.

"Stop," Emile shouted. "It would not be prudent to damage her in transit."

Gerard halted his advance. "Carry her to the boat."

Emile helped Sarah to her feet. "Do not fight me," he whispered with pleading eyes as he scooped her up in his arms.

"Please, I married," Sarah whispered back.

Emile's lips parted when he heard her news. Fearing for her safety, he acted as if he hadn't heard her.

Hassan wandered through the tween deck of the French ship while surveying the damages. Though his mission was a success, it was not without a high cost to both crews. At a glance, he could tell that nearly a quarter of his crew was either wounded or dead, and he imagined that the French lost even more. As Hassan continued surveying the damages, he glanced up and spotted a familiar face.

"Welcome back, Mr. Boyle. Do you need a surgeon?" Hassan asked. His first lieutenant hobbled towards him with the assistance from two of his crewmates. Though Adam's face and body were almost entirely black and blue, he managed to greet his captain with a triumphant grin.

"Thank you, sir, it is good to be back. I imagine I look frightfully worse than I'm feeling. I'm confident that my wounds will mend."

"I trust your crew was taken prisoner again?"

"Yes, Captain, but they knew the risks when they volunteered for this mission."

"We will get them back," Hassan vowed. "Report to Dr. Hyatt, and well done, Mr. Boyle."

Hassan found Claude Fornier tending to some of his wounded in the surgery. A wound on his own shoulder turned his white shirt crimson. His adversary's rounded shoulders and drooping head hinted that Claude had fully surrendered, still Hassan wasn't ready to trust what his eyes were telling him.

Pulling back his shoulders, Claude braced his hand on the table and stood up. "Captain Shelby, may I present my ship, my sword, and my compliments to you for a battle well fought."

Hassan took the bloodied sword from the French captain while resisting the urge to thrust it through his enemy's heart. "Thank you," he said in an icy tone.

"May I ask what will become of us?" Claude enquired.

"I have not decided, but I can assure you that your pirating exploits end today. Know that I have my government's blessing to execute you and your crew."

"Captain Aziz, there is something urgent that you must see," said one of his lieutenants.

Hassan followed his officer to the main deck. His heart sank when he spotted the Trésor sailing away from them. Hassan grabbed the end of a line and swung over to his ship. "Prepare the Zafirah to set sail," he ordered without taking his eye off Sarah's former ship.

"That's not possible, Captain," an able-bodied seaman pointed out.

"What do you mean it's not possible?" Hassan barked.

"Sir, both ships sustained heavy damages during the battle. Neither ship will be seaworthy for a few days. I'm sorry, sir."

Hassan ran down to the hold and found his men pumping out a steady flow of water. He was relieved to see that the damages weren't enough to sink his ship, but his crewman was right, his ship wasn't seaworthy enough to fight another battle. Although he knew Sarah was gone, Hassan returned to the beach with a fool's hope that she remained undiscovered.

He leaped out of the jolly before it reached the beach. "Sarah," he called out in a frantic voice. All he heard was the chatty seagulls flying above him. Hassan only needed to see her gown floating in the shallow water and the footprints in the sand to know what had happened. He could almost see Sarah's struggle and feel her terror. On the outside, Hassan stood motionless; his face void of any emotion. On the inside, he was devastated. "I'm sorry, Sarah," Hassan whispered. By the time he returned to the Persephone, his agony had turned to anger.

Claude was still seated on a table as his surgeon treated his wounds. Hassan grabbed the French captain's arms and pinned him against the wall. "The crew from the Trésor took a woman from the beach. Where are they taking her?"

"They are taking the girl to Naa'il Dhar, just as you should have done after you acquired her." Claude studied Hassan's eyes. "The girl means that much to you?"

"She is my wife," Hassan replied after a pause.

"I did not know."

"Did Rochelle tell you that he and his crew murdered the woman's father so that they could profit from selling her?"

"I swear I did not know, nor do I condone my cousin's actions. How may I assist you?"

"Why should I trust you when none of your actions have been honorable? Need I remind you that you sold my crew and me into slavery, and I have the marks on my back to prove it?"

"You are no different than I am. You, who entered Algiers as Nathan Shelby, and left as Hassan Aziz - the most ruthless pirate on the Barbary Coast," Claude pointed out.

"Only by reputation."

"You are not innocent. You sold my cousin and his crew into slavery not even a week ago."

"I sold the crew of the Trésor to get to you. My government gave me orders to do what was necessary to stop you from selling my countrymen into slavery." Hassan countered with a sneer.

"Say what you will. I know that you are not as innocent as you claim …," Claude paused. "I will help you get your wife back. In exchange, I ask you to spare the lives of my crew."

"You are in no position to make demands."

"Neither are you. My wife lives in Algiers. She can help you find your wife. All that I ask is that you bring her to me."

"How can your wife help?"

"She spent her life in the Palace harem before Naa'il Dhar gave her to me. Janna can also help you slip into the Palace without being noticed," Claude explained.

"Again, why should I trust you?"

"I love my wife, and she carries our first child. I will do anything to keep her safe and prevent her from having to raise our child alone."

The expression on Hassan's face remained hardened in spite of hearing the sincerity in his adversary's tone. "Very well," he said, releasing Claude's arms. "I want to know everything involving Dhar's plans for my wife and me. Know this, if you do anything to deceive or endanger my crew or me, I will kill you myself."

Claude spent the next few hours explaining Naa'il's plan. Hassan was impressed with the level of detail in his explanation. Claude provided enough information for Hassan to formulate a plan – providing that his details were truthful and accurate. Hassan wasn't surprised to hear that Naa'il had ordered Sarah's and his capture. The only thing that wasn't clear was what Naa'il intended to do with Sarah once he acquired her. Claude couldn't provide that answer either. Hassan only hoped that the Dey would decide to keep her for himself. Otherwise, there was little chance of him ever getting Sarah back.

Claude ordered his crew to make both ships seaworthy again. Hassan tasked his men to assist with the repairs. He also gave them permission to execute any of Claude's crew who attempted to cause trouble. To Hassan's surprise, the French pirates were cooperative, and many were skilled carpenters. Not one rebelled. Hassan was sure that the French crew was following their captain's orders.

With repairs underway, Hassan returned to his ship to survey the damages, including the wounded. In his usual professional manner, Peter tended to patients. The orlop deck looked like a hospital ward with bloodied men placed in hammocks near the surgery. Hassan's crewmen were also busy preparing the dead for burial.

"Report?" Hassan asked.

"Twenty are dead, and seventeen are wounded," Peter answered. "It's too soon to know how many of the injured will survive."

Hassan replied with a nod. "Do you need anything?"

"Thank you, no. Did I hear that Sarah's former crew captured her?"

"Yes."

"They won't hurt her, Nathan. She's far too valuable for them to harm her."

"I hope you're right. Sarah must be terrified, though," Hassan grimaced. "Carry on, Doctor."

"Have I ever told you about angels?" Thomas Campbell asked.

"No, what are angels?" Sarah eagerly queried. She was just a small child when that conversation took place. Though it happened a lifetime ago, she remembered every detail of that day. There wasn't a cloud in the sky as they sat by the pool. Sarah could still smell the sweet flowers and hear the melodic birds chirping above them. Her father often brought her to that spot to teach her about his beliefs and traditions. That day, he told her about angels.

"Angels are very important," Thomas continued.

"Why?"

"Because they are God's messengers. Remarkable creatures, angels

are. They surround us and can take any form. You only need to be aware of their presence."

"How do I know when I see one?"

"Oh, that's simple. Angels can be thoughts that tell us what we need to do or say. Sometimes angels are people that say what we need to hear. And sometimes, they are people who are sent to help us when we need them."

Sarah climbed down from her rock and stood directly in front of her father with her tiny hands resting on his knees. She looked up at him with trusting eyes, "Da, are you an angel?"

Thomas laughed. "Well, I hadn't thought about it that way. I suppose God sent me to look after you."

"Will ... will I ever be an angel?"

Thomas lifted his daughter onto his lap. "My sweet child, you give me so much joy. How could you not be one already?"

"How do I know when God wants me to help him?"

"I believe that God is always talking to us. He tells us to be kind to each other. He tells us to help each other, or obey your father's wishes. Sometimes, it means doing the right thing, even if you are afraid to do it. Remember Sarah; you will always be blessed when you do what's right. Now going back to angels, never forget that yours will always be with you. All you have to do is believe, and you will have all the help you need. I promise that your help will come whenever you need it, and in the way you need it. The only time that you can be without them is when you doubt their presence."

"Do you have angels too?"

"Of course; my mother told me about them when I was about your age. I have never forgotten what she said. My angels have seen me through my darkest hours. That is how I know they exist."

Sarah's eyes sparkled. "I'm glad you're my angel," she said as she snuggled against his hairy chest.

Sarah stirred to the stench of her former ship. She was alone with her hands chained to the ship's hull. "Look for the Angels," was the last thing her father said to her before he died. Her eyes narrowed, and her forehead puckered, Sarah pursed her lips as she pondered how she could remember what her father said to her on his deathbed, yet the details about his death completely eluded her.

"Look for the Angels," her father repeated. Sarah bit her bottom lip. She believed her father when she was little but had stopped believing in them until she met Cattin. "Where are my angels now? How can they be with me when these cruel people surround me? I know you've never lied to me. I will believe because you want me to," she mumbled.

Sarah's thoughts drifted from her father to Hassan. She had only known him for a short time, yet she missed him as much as she missed her father. Though she witnessed the battle from a distance, Sarah could only imagine the horror that took place on the ship. The most unnerving part was not knowing if Hassan was alive or dead, or even if she would ever see him again.

The ship was quiet when Emile wriggled out of his hammock. His shipmates were asleep in their cocoons. Emile held his breath when his feet reached the floor, hoping that the creaking deck wouldn't disturb his shipmates when he took a step.

"Sir, don't go down there. The captain is having you watched," said the crewmen guarding the hatch.

"I do not care," Emile maintained.

"The captain is mad. He will kill you if he discovers that you went to the girl."

"You fool, he's already killed us all by bringing us to this region. I at least prefer to choose how I die. If I were you, I would rally the crew to mutiny. That may be the only thing that saves your lives. Now get out of my way." Emile pushed his crewmate aside. He carefully opened the hatch and descended to the hold. Emile used his memory and his touch to find his way to Sarah. When he finally found her, Sarah jerked her face away as he caressed her cheek.

"You have a right to hate me," Emile said in French. "I want you to know that I did not want to kill your father. I'm weak, Sarah, and I am ashamed of the pain that I caused you. It was the only way that I could protect you. I thought that I could spare you from additional pain by not telling you about the poison. If I had my way, you would never know. I would have taken you to France. We would have lived happily together for the rest of our lives. I want you to know that I avenged your father's death, and that I will protect you for as long as I can."

Sarah replied with silence.

Emile offered her some figs, but she refused to open her mouth. Finally, he resigned himself to sit with her in silence. The hatch opened a few minutes later, and Gerard descended the ladder with the aid of a lantern to light his path.

"I warned you about what would happen if you came down here." Gerard hung the lantern from the overhead and pointed his pistol at the surgeon.

Emile stood and grinned at his captain as if he knew a secret. "You don't look well, Captain. Would you not prefer to rest in your cabin?"

"My health is not your concern," Gerard retorted in spite of looking at his shaking hand with concern.

"Oh but it is. You see, the poison that killed Thomas Campbell now runs in your veins. You may not die tonight, but I promise that you will not live long enough to enjoy your profits from selling Sarah." Emile reached for the gun.

Sarah screamed when Gerard fired his pistol. Moments later, the Trésor's surgeon sunk onto the hull. He looked over at Sarah and whispered, "I'm sorry." Emile Dumont died moments later.

The overhead thundered from footsteps running across the deck. They descended the ladder one at a time. The crew stared in consternation at their surgeon's body, and then looked back to their captain for answers.

"Return to your hammocks, and do not come down here until we reach the port. I assure you that you will suffer the same fate as Dr.

Dumont." Gerard pushed past them and pulled himself up the ladder. Some followed their captain. The rest waited long enough to carry Emile's body to the tween deck to prepare him for a proper burial.

Sarah buried her face in her knees and sobbed.

Chapter 23

Excitement filled the harem when Mamnoon issued the Dey's decree: "Whoever provides the information leading to the capture of Cora Bradley's murderer, will win their freedom and passage home."

"Isn't that exciting, Molly?" Tess exclaimed, hugging her daughter. She, Molly, and Abigail sat in their usual corner. "We can finally be reunited with your father. I can't wait for you to meet him. He will love you. Of that, I'm certain."

"You have to find the person responsible for Cora's death first." Abigail nodded to the women lining up to talk to Mamnoon. "Look at them all. It's obvious; isn't it? Ula killed Cora. She was the only one with a motive. She hated my cousin," Abigail said without taking her eyes off Ula. "She even looks guilty."

Ula was the only person who didn't wait in line to talk to Mamnoon or huddle with her friends. Instead, Naa'il's former concubine hid in the corner of the room, trying to look as inconspicuous as possible. Her face remained tilted towards the floor to avoid making eye contact with the women speculating her guilt.

Tess looked back at Abigail. "It also could have been you."

Abigail stared at her friend with a slack jaw. "I would never harm my cousin. Besides, I loved Cora," she insisted with her chin up and her arms crossed.

"You hated your cousin. During the short time that I knew you, I have never heard you say a civil word about Cora, and you were very cruel to her whenever she visited. She had never done anything to deserve your abuse." Tess pointed out as she glared at her friend.

Abigail hung her head. "No, I didn't," Abigail whimpered before looking up at her friend. "But I loved her."

"You can protest all you want. I saw the tears in Cora's eyes the last time she visited us."

Abigail turned her head away and wiped the tear from her eye. "Do you believe there is any truth to what Mamnoon said about Cora? I mean that she allowed men to violate her to protect me?"

"Aye, I do." Tess shuddered as she stared at her red trousers while her fingers mindlessly combed through her daughter's dark chocolate curls. "I heard a woman screaming several times when I went to entertain guests." She answered in a haunted tone. "Cora was also very nervous the day she arrived. We didn't see her for weeks, and she was different the next time we saw her. Cora had a sadness that never left her eyes. It is more than that. His Lordship treated you like an honored guest. Women are never given their own apartment when they first arrive unless he considers them important. Did you ever ask His Lordship what happened to Cora?"

Abigail pressed her lips together in a futile effort to stop her lower lip from quivering. "No," she replied in a voice just above a whisper. "Why would Cora sacrifice herself for me?"

Tess shrugged. "The fool loved you."

"I can't talk about this anymore." Abigail jumped to her feet. "I'm going to take a bath."

"A bath," Tess mumbled as her friend ran away. She looked at her daughter with a bright smile. "That's it. You may get to meet your father after all." Tess waited until there were fewer people in line to talk to Mamnoon. There were enough women ahead of her to hear each one accusing Ula of killing Cora. The bodyguard listened to each one with a smile fixed on his lips, except there were no laugh lines beside his eyes.

As she waited, Tess readjusted Molly on her hip. When it was her turn, she stepped forward.

"Do you have helpful information?" Mamnoon asked in the same polite manner that he offered to the other women.

"It may be something; it may be nothing at all."

"I can see that you feel it is important enough to speak to me. Please speak freely, Tess," Mamnoon insisted.

"Thank you. Before I tell you what I have to say, I want you to know that I am sorry for your loss. I know you and Cora were close; I can see that her death was hard on you. How are you getting along?"

"Thank you for asking. I miss her. It comforts me knowing that Cora is free now. I would like to think that she found peace after the pain she suffered while she was here. What do you have to tell me?"

"As I mentioned before, it may be something, or it may be nothing at all."

"Go on," Mamnoon insisted.

"Well, remember the day when Princess ..." Tess blushed. "I mean Samina attacked Cora."

"Yes."

"Bashira escorted Samina back to the bathing area. They were in there for hours. I remember this because I needed to prepare meself for the evening. I was supposed to dance for His Lordship and his guests, you see. It was late, and the door to the bathing room was still closed, but Bashira reappeared just before the door opened. I complained to her when I noticed her slipping a small green bottle into her pocket. I think …"

Mamnoon pressed his lips together to form a line. "Accusing one of the Dey's wives of murder is a very serious accusation. His Excellency could execute you if you're wrong," he interrupted.

Tess's face burned when she felt his accusing black eyes burrowing into her. "You're right. Please forget what I said." She said, pressing her daughter against her chest.

"I will say nothing. Thank you for coming forward."

Tess replied with a defeated nod. Abigail had just left the bathing room when Tess returned to their corner. She released her daughter, who scampered off to play with her friends and then slumped down on the cushion.

Abigail sat down and studied her friend. "What happened to you?"

"It's nothing."

"No, something is troubling you."

Tess sighed. "I thought I had an idea of who killed Cora. It is nothing."

"I thought we agreed upon Ula?"

Tess's eyes remained fixed on her trousers as though she slipped into a trance. "I thought so too. Then I remembered the day I was brought to the harem. There were but a few women here. Everyone was unnerved. One of them told me that His Lordship's favorite was murdered. She spent weeks and weeks with him. The women in the harem felt threatened when she showed signs of being with child, so someone poisoned her drink. She died instantly. His Lordship was so deeply wroth that he ordered all but a few of the women to be sold at market. He priced them cheaply so that they would be bought by cruel masters. He even sold women with children. The only reason he spared a few was so that they could warn the new arrivals of the price of treachery. The women he kept are still used for cheap whores." Tess tore her gaze from her trousers and looked her friend in the eyes. "Naa'il Dhar can be an unforgiving blighter. Everyone in this room knows the cruelty that His Lordship is capable of."

"So, what are you saying?"

"I'm saying ..." Tess's voice trailed off. "It's nothing."

"Tell me."

"Very well, but you must not repeat what I say to anyone." Tess leaned in and whispered, "I think it was Princess Samina and Bashira. This is why I believe it ...."

"Oh my goodness," Abigail exclaimed. "You should report this to Naa'il."

"I don't know. Mamnoon reminded me that I could be executed for making false accusations against the Dey's wife. Telling His Lordship my theory is not worth risking my life."

"What if you're right? You could be reunited with Molly's father."

Tess winced. "It's a fool's dream. Besides, this is where I belong, and I'm good at what I do. It's best for you to forget what I said."

"His Excellency wants to see you," a guard announced to Abigail.

Abigail glanced up at the guard and nodded. Her whole body trembled when she stood and looked at her friend with worry on her brow.

"Remember what I said," Tess reminded her friend.

Abigail shook uncontrollably on the seemingly never-ending walk to Naa'il's private office. The guards escorting her only added to her dread. She always had one guard to escort her to and from the harem. This morning, there were four, and they surrounded her, making it impossible for her to run away. More than a week had passed since she fell out of Naa'il's favor. She doubted that he summoned her to reconcile. What would she say to him? More importantly, what would Naa'il say to her?

Her heart raced when her escorts stopped in front of an arched doorway. One of the guards knocked on the wooden door. Abigail's hands clutched her elbows when she heard Naa'il calling back, "Enter." A guard opened the door and pushed Abigail inside the room. Shivers spiked up and down her spine when she spotted the Dey standing at the window. She felt his hatred when he turned and stared at her with his black eyes. Still, she had no idea what to say.

"Do you mourn for your cousin," Naa'il asked in a cold tone, "or do you still loathe her? Do not attempt to deceive me. I know when you lie."

Abigail stared at the gilded chair because she couldn't look at him. "I did not hate my cousin, Your Excellency."

"I know better." Naa'il approached her with his fingers laced behind his back. "What I do not know is why."

Abigail bit the inside of her lip as the Dey circled her like a hunter studying his prey. "You're right. I did not like my cousin. Perhaps I even wanted her to die, but I didn't kill her. I swear it," she insisted.

"I have not yet accused you," Naa'il said in a chilling tone. "Do you have any idea what she sacrificed to ensure your protection?"

"That bodyguard said that she was violated," Abigail answered in a timid voice.

"Yes, Cora was violated by many, every night, all in the name of protecting you. She never once thought about herself. Your safety was her only concern. On the day we met, Cora made it plain that she would do anything to protect you, including sacrificing her innocence. Of course, I assumed that you were the pure one at the time. Oh, how she suffered for you. Every morning she asked: 'Are you well? Are you safe? Are you happy?' Not once did you ask what became of Cora. That vexes me more than you will ever know. Now you are going to tell me why you despised the woman who sacrificed everything for you. Know this; there is nothing that can protect you from me." Naa'il leaned in until the ends of their noses nearly touched. "And you *will* answer my questions."

Abigail backed away from Naa'il until she bumped against the door. "I didn't kill my cousin," she insisted in a small voice.

"Why did you despise Cora?" Naa'il repeated in a chillingly calm tone.

"I don't know, sir," she said, staring at the chair.

"You lie!" Naa'il cocked his hand.

Abigail cried when Naa'il's hand struck her cheek. The Dey repeated his question three more times; Abigail was too ashamed to answer. Her refusal was met with one strike after another until she broke her silence. "I hated Cora because everyone loved her instead of me," she shouted as tears streamed down her cheeks. "Cora was a poor relation, a servant that my family took in out of pity. You, Jordan Donnelly, Stephen MacDonald - all of you fell under her spell!"

"Continue," Naa'il raised his hand to strike again.

"No, I can't." Abigail shook her head vigorously.

"Answer!" Naa'il shouted.

Abigail fell to the floor when he backhanded her across the cheek. "I loved Jordan Donnelly since the first time I saw him. I used to watch him at the balls. He was a handsome prince. Every woman in the region loved him. I loved him most of all. One day his eyes fell on me." She sobbed even harder.

"Did you give him your innocence?"

Her lower lip quivering, Abigail snapped her eyes shut. Her whole face puckered from disgust. "He told me that he loved me," she muttered. "Then Jordan cast me aside like a soiled piece of clothing when he transferred his love to Cora. I ceased to exist in his eyes."

"Cora told me about this Jordan. Did you give yourself to Cora's Stephen?"

"No, I swear it."

"Did you pursue him?"

"Yes," Abigail whimpered.

"Why did you pursue this Stephen?"

"Because he and Cora were in love. I wanted my cousin to know how it felt to have the man you loved stolen from you," Abigail sneered.

"And were you successful?" Naa'il demanded as he hovered over her.

"No," Abigail quietly replied. "Why doesn't anyone love me?"

"Cora did. She loved you enough to give her life for you, and you treated her with contempt. Yes, I received reports on your activity in the harem. You should be ashamed."

"I still didn't kill my cousin."

"Perhaps, perhaps not. I am certain that you would have poisoned her if you were given the opportunity."

"Is that what you think of me? I am not a murderer," Abigail shouted. "I may have hated Cora, but I did not spread filth on her back on the night we arrived."

Naa'il's lips parted. "Who did?"

"It was Ula. You should ask her if she killed my cousin, or …" Abigail's voice trailed off.

"What?" Naa'il sneered. "Speak now, or I will beat it out of you."

Abigail bit her lip. "It's just …"

Naa'il pinched her cheeks between his fingers. "I said, speak."

Abigail swallowed hard. "My friend offered another theory. A few days ago, your second wife, Samina attacked Cora when she entered the harem."

"Yes, I heard." Naa'il released her cheeks. "What else?"

Abigail told Naa'il the rest of Tess's theory. The Dey remained stone-faced as he listened. Not knowing what he was thinking made her voice quiver all the more as she continued. "Was I wrong to tell you?" She timidly asked at the conclusion of her theory.

"No. I want to bring Cora's murderer to justice. Every lead is important." Naa'il pursed his lips.

"Tess said that I could be executed for making such accusations."

"Yes. I will make an exception this one time."

"Is it true that you will grant freedom to the person who provides the information leading to Cora's killer?"

"Yes. That is true." Naa'il paused. "Do you have anything else to tell me?"

"No." Abigail looked into Naa'il's eyes for the first time since she entered his office. "Your Excellency, may I ask what is to become of me?"

"You still think about yourself. If I had my way, you would be sold at market. But because of Cora's sacrifices, you will live in the harem under my protection."

"Then I will never leave Algiers."

"Be grateful for what your cousin did for you. That will be all."

Mamnoon passed Abigail just as she slunk out of Naa'il's office. After offering her a curious look, he marched into the room and bowed to his master after closing the door behind him.

"Report," Naa'il said, standing in front of his bodyguard with his hands still clasped behind his back.

"I interviewed women all day, Your Excellency," Mamnoon replied.

"What did you learn?"

Mamnoon's jaw tightened. "Cora had many enemies."

"Yes, you told me. What else did you learn?"

"Most of the women believe that Ula murdered Cora." Mamnoon hesitated. "Ula blamed Cora for replacing her."

"Is it true that Ula spread filth on Cora's back on the night she arrived?"

Mamnoon straightened his back and looked away. "As you may recall, I was not present in the harem during the first night of Cora's captivity, but I did witness Ula making the same mischief to another woman."

Naa'il's eyes narrowed to slits. "Why did you keep this information from me?"

"Cora pleaded with me not to say anything."

"Cora pleaded with you not to say anything," Naa'il repeated. "I am your master, not Cora. You seem to have forgotten that ever since you met her. You knew that Ula's mischief was the primary reason why Cora was tortured."

"Your Excellency, I didn't discover Ula's treachery until after you returned Cora to the harem," Mamnoon swore.

Naa'il glowered at Cora's bodyguard. "You should have come to me with this information the moment you discovered it," he shouted with nostrils flaring. Naa'il closed his eyes and turned away from Mamnoon when he heard Cora pleading with him. *Please don't punish my cousin. This wasn't my fault.* Naa'il covered his mouth with his hand. "Damn that woman. Cora told me that she was not responsible for spreading the filth on her back, yet she refused to tell me who did. Why would she protect Ula?"

"As you may recall, Your Excellency, Cora did not return to the harem until after you ended the attacks. I doubt she discovered Ula's name until then."

Naa'il turned and studied his servant. "What was Cora's excuse after she returned to the harem? She must have said something to you."

"I was prepared to bring Ula to your attention, but Cora pleaded with me not to involve you."

Naa'il stared at his servant with a gaping jaw. "Why?"

"Cora insisted on fighting her own battles involving the women in the harem," Mamnoon paused. "She also believed that forcing Ula to spend the rest of her life as a slave was sufficient punishment."

"I hardly believe that living in the Palace Harem is a hardship," Naa'il said bitterly.

"I understand and agree with you, Your Excellency. It is a harsh world beyond the Palace gates. You must remember that Cora came from a place where she was free to choose the life that she wanted. From what she told me, she had a good life in America. More importantly, she was happy there. Living in our culture where she was not free to come and go as she pleased was a prison to her."

Naa'il's hand locked around the edge of his maroon robe. His wide eyes and gaping mouth mirrored his shock. "Did Cora tell you that?"

"No, Cora never complained, even to me. I knew that living in the harem was difficult for her."

Naa'il pursed his lips. "Do you believe Ula poisoned Cora?"

"It is too soon to say, Your Excellency."

"I am certain that Ula hated Cora. I doubt that she was foolish enough to kill her. Tell me about Cora's relationship with Bashira."

"Bashira?" Mamnoon's tone rose with genuine surprise.

"Yes, Bashira. I understand that she and Cora quarreled on the day Cora was assassinated."

"Yes, that is true."

"Abigail said that some of the concubines witnessed Bashira slipping a vial into her pocket. I want you to search Bashira's chamber and bring Ula to me."

"Yes, Your Excellency." Mamnoon bowed.

"Mamnoon, if I learn that you are keeping information from me again, I will execute you for treason."

Mamnoon bowed again. "My life is still yours to take, Your Excellency."

Ula fell to her knees when she entered Naa'il's office. "Please, have mercy upon me, Master," she pleaded as she pressed her forehead against the floor.

A faint smile formed on his lips when he spotted the bruise on her face. His delight turned to a scowl. "Why should I show you mercy? Do you know what you did?" he shouted. "I tortured Cora Bradley because of your mischief!"

She sat up with her face still tilted towards the floor. "Master, I did not know you would punish her so severely." Ula cried when Naa'il backhanded her across the cheek.

"You lie," Naa'il hit her again. "You of all people know what I am capable of doing. If I had my way, you would experience the same torture that I had inflicted on Cora before I sell you at market."

"Please, I beg you; have mercy on me, Your Excellency." Ula pleaded with tears streaming down her cheeks.

"You are very fortunate that Cora would not want me to punish you for your treachery. I love her too much to go against her wishes," Naa'il said in a calmer tone.

Ula looked up at him with a slack jaw. "What is to become of me, Master?"

"You will remain in the harem for now." He pinched her jaw between his fingers. "Know this; I will have you watched carefully from this time forth, and I will receive daily reports of your behavior. If you do anything to displease me, I will sell you at the slave market myself. Now leave me."

"Thank you, Master." Ula crouched down and kissed his leather slipper.

"(Mercy) It is twice blest: It blesseth him that gives and him that

takes," Cora reminded him as Ula left his office. Naa'il looked up at the intricately carved ceiling and said to Cora. "I do not feel blessed showing mercy to this slave. She deserved to be punished." Naa'il stifled a laugh as he envisioned Cora smiling down at him. He could almost hear her intoxicating laugh. His smile faded. "How could you leave me?"

Bashira was busy getting women ready for the nightly entertainment. Though no one would be dancing for the Dey that night, concubines were still needed to entertain distinguished residents and guests. The valide looked up after adjusting a concubine's vest and frowned when she spotted two palace guards standing behind Mamnoon. "I thought you left for the day," she said in a casual tone while pretending not to notice the grave expression on Mamnoon's face.

"I came here on the Dey's business. Can we talk in private?"

"Of course." Bashira followed Mamnoon to a corner of the room. "What does this concern?" she whispered once they were alone.

"His Excellency has reason to believe that you were involved with Cora's murder. He ordered these guards to search your quarters," Mamnoon said in a voice loud enough for the guards to overhear.

Bashira closed her eyes and hung her head. "Of course. You have my full cooperation."

Once she was dressed and ready for her evening, Tess scampered back to Molly and Abigail. "What did His Lordship want with you?"

"I don't want to talk about it," Abigail wiped the tear from her cheek.

"Did you tell His Lordship what I said to you earlier today?"

Abigail threw her shoulders back. "Yes, Naa'il forced me to tell him, but I didn't say that it was your theory."

"I'm surprised that he didn't cut you down where you stood," Tess hissed.

"Naa'il is very distraught about Cora's death, and he is determined to bring her murderer to justice. Please don't be angry with …" Abigail's voice trailed off when she spotted Mamnoon and the guards leading Bashira out of the harem like a prisoner. "My God, you're right."

The crimson sun had just begun to dip below the horizon when Mamnoon escorted Bashira into Naa'il's office. "Your assumptions were correct, Your Excellency," Mamnoon said, releasing the valide's arm. "We found this in her chamber." He handed Naa'il a small green vial, capped with a cork. "There is still a little poison left."

Naa'il uncorked the bottle and sniffed the clear liquid. "Are you certain that this is poison?"

"Yes, Your Excellency. I poured a little into the mouth of a mouse we caught. It died instantly, like Cora," Mamnoon confirmed.

"Leave us," Naa'il said to Mamnoon. He waited to speak until they were alone. "What do you have to say for yourself?"

Bashira looked the Dey in the eyes and said without hesitation, "I am guilty of the charges of which I have been accused."

Naa'il backhanded her across the face. "Where did you get this poison?"

Bashira toppled to the floor. Though her face stung, she propped herself up enough to answer. "The poison was in my possession."

"Who helped you?" Naa'il hit her again.

"I acted alone," she said, without taking her eyes off her master.

Naa'il struck her over and over again, always asking the same question. Each time Bashira looked him in the eyes and offered him the same reply. Exasperated, Naa'il shouted. "Why, why did you kill Cora?

She did nothing to you."

"The American was a dangerous influence in the harem. She preached the teachings of Jesus. Many listened to her. She needed to be silenced."

"You had no right to assassinate this woman," Naa'il shouted.

"I will not apologize for my actions. I acted to keep our ways pure, and I will accept the punishment awaiting me," Bashira said defiantly.

"Very well." Naa'il pulled a small knife from his belt and slit her throat. Bashira fell backward and gasped for breath before she drew her last.

CHAPTER 24

Naa'il dabbed the perspiration from his forehead with his white handkerchief. Though the purple canapé shielded him from the scorching sun, the cover couldn't eliminate the still air or the oppressive humidity. He had only been in the slave yard for an hour, and his silk bürümcük was already sticking to his back. Surveying the sea of slaves reminded Naa'il that he hadn't worked a full day in several weeks, and unprocessed slaves occupied nearly every inch of the spacious courtyard.

"Never look at the slave's faces," Naa'il's mentor instructed. "You will pity them if you do."

Naa'il broke his rule for the first time by allowing his eyes to drift from the boy's flaxen curls to the beads of sweat dripping from his forehead. It didn't take much effort for Naa'il's gaze to drop even further. If he had to guess, the boy couldn't have been more than sixteen.

We may be your property, but we are all God's children, and therefore, we are precious to Him. We laugh, we cry, we love, and want to be loved. Cora reminded him in her usual passionate tone.

Naa'il understood his mentor's warning because his heart raced when he spotted the fear in the boy's hazel eyes. The Dey motioned to the guard to bring the prisoner to the front of the group. The shackles attached to the prisoner's ankles clanked as he moved. The ends of the Dey's lips formed a lopsided grin when the prisoner looked him in the eye in defiance. "Where are you from?" Naa'il asked in English.

"I'm from Georgia, sir," the prisoner answered.

"Is it true that Georgians own slaves?" Naa'il challenged.

"Yes, sir."

"Does your family own slaves?"

"No, sir. My family can't afford 'em," the boy explained. "Only a few rich landowners own slaves, sir."

"If you were wealthy enough, would you own slaves?"

The irons on the boy's wrists clanked when he scratched his cheek. "That's a hard question to answer, sir."

"Explain," Naa'il demanded.

"Well, sir, I know the landowners can't survive without the slave labor to plant and harvest their crops. I can't say that I share their beliefs, now that I'm about to become one of 'em." The boy shrugged. "It just don't seem right anymore."

Naa'il tilted his head to the side. "Would you embrace an American slave as your brother if you returned to your country?"

"I certainly have more sympathy for 'em now," the boy replied. "I suppose you can't find it in your heart to release us."

Naa'il answered with a snicker. He scanned the faces of the other prisoners. It didn't matter whether they were a man, woman, or child. It didn't matter if the color of their skin was black, brown, or white; nor did it matter which nationality they were. Every face wore an expression of hopelessness; the same hopelessness that Cora's face expressed on the last night that she was attacked. The Dey pulled himself up from his pillow and walked to the exit.

Jamal chased after Naa'il. "Are you ill, Your Excellency?" he asked when they reached the hallway.

"Your Excellency," a man called out as he approached Naa'il from the opposite end of the corridor.

Naa'il closed his eyes when he recognized the English regal voice. Nodding to the soldiers, the guards stopped the gentleman before he could reach the Dey.

"His Royal Highness, the Prince Regent of England, instructed me to deliver his message. I will convey it whether you want to hear it or not," the gentleman called out as Naa'il walked away. "England will not tolerate your enslaving our people. We are prepared to go to war if you continue to capture our ships and enslave the subjects of the British crown, and you *will* lose."

Naa'il turned and faced the intruder. Dressed in fashionable European clothes, Ambassador Browning looked as regal as he sounded. His neatly trimmed beard and the lines on his face had aged enough to command respect. Naa'il looked into the Ambassador's gray eyes and said, "Do what you wish. I do not care what your country does." Naa'il offered Jamal a downtrodden look. "Process the slaves; I cannot do this right now."

"Your Excellency!" Jamal called out in a panicked voice.

Naa'il didn't turn around, even when he heard Jamal apologizing to the Ambassador. Mentally exhausted, Naa'il stole away to his apartment. After retrieving Cora's Bible, he turned the knob at the base of the fountain, sending water spilling from the top tier to the ones below it. Naa'il made himself comfortable on his lounge chair. It was hard not to think about Cora when he felt the sun's rays caressing his face. "Hello, my love," Naa'il said, looking up to Heaven with a rueful smile. "I hope that you can feel the sun's warmth where you are. I hope that you are happy. I hope that you miss me, even if it is only a little. I miss you … I miss our talks …. I wish …." Naa'il looked down and opened Cora's Bible to a random page filled with notes about loving people as themselves.

Jamal barged into Naa'il's apartment. "Your Excellency," he said in an insistent tone.

Naa'il kept reading. It was only when Jamal entreated him for the fourth time that Naa'il acknowledged his presence. The Dey casually closed Cora's Bible and looked up at his advisor.

"Are you …?" Jamal's voice trailed off when he read the book's title that Naa'il's hand attempted to conceal. "Are you reading a Bible?" the advisor sneered.

Naa'il glowered at the Vizier. "What do you want?"

Jamal couldn't tear his gaze from the cover. "Are you reading a Bible?"

"What do you want, Jamal?" Naa'il snapped.

The Vizier gave Naa'il a frosty look. "You left the slave yard without offering an explanation; then you gave Ambassador Browning your blessing to start a war with our country." Jamal summarized with dismay. "I know you are mourning the loss of your American, but she is not worth sacrificing your noble heritage."

"Are we noble when we enslave thousands of people each day?" Naa'il challenged. "Have you ever been to the quarries? I went to one yesterday. The men work from early morning to late at night. They slave under the hot sun moving heavy rocks. They will die there only a few short months after they arrive. Some will die sooner."

"What do you suggest? Free the slaves? Our empire has employed slaves since the beginning of civilization. We are no different from the Americans, the Europeans, and all the other countries that enslave people," Jamal shouted.

"Just because slavery is an ancient tradition does not mean it is right."

"Again, what do you propose, freeing all the slaves in the Ottoman Empire? Doing so will destroy our economy and the lives of our people."

"I understand the costs, Jamal." Naa'il gritted his teeth. "I voiced my disagreement with slavery; I did not say that I would end it." He took a deep breath. "The American's murder haunts me. I wish I had treated her with kindness. She was worthy of being spoiled. I should have never ordered the attacks against her. She is gone, and I will never have the opportunity to tell her that I am sorry for the pain she suffered at my command. That is the sadness you are hearing." Naa'il sighed and held up the book. "I read her book because it is all I have left of my Cora. Her notes, the passages she underlined, they comfort me more than I can say."

"Your Excellency, Naa'il, you are my brother. I am sorry for the pain you have suffered from the American's death. Your wives and your children love you. They *need* you, and so does your country. You must be strong for them. Take the time you need to mourn for your American, but do not stay away too long. It would be dangerous for you to become unnecessary. I will leave you to your thoughts."

Naa'il jumped to his feet. "Is that a threat?" he called out as Jamal headed to the reception room.

Jamal stopped under the courtyard doorway and turned back to the Dey. "Not from me. You appointed me to be your Vizier. I am merely performing my duty by warning you of possible dangers. I should not need to remind you that you have made enemies in Algiers and the Ottoman Empire. Every one of them would gladly assassinate you and take your place as the Dey of Algiers. Do not give them a reason to act."

Naa'il laid Cora's Bible on the lounge chair. "Of course you are right. I am being foolish. Thank you for your counsel."

CHAPTER 25

Time had stopped for Sarah after she was taken captive. There was no day sitting in the hold, only darkness.

The ship's rocking had finally subsided and was followed by the sound of thundering footsteps above her head. The hatch opened, and three men climbed down the ladder. Sarah closed her eyes to offset the lantern's glare. Her eyes snapped open when she heard Gerard's voice. Having sat in the same position for hours, if not days, Sarah was too sore to fight or to run away when Gerard unlocked the chains binding her hands and ankles to the hull. The only fight she had in her was to bite Gerard's arm when he reached across her. The captain shouted and kicked her in the ribs when her teeth locked onto his arm. Clutching his arm, Gerard stepped aside to allow the largest of the three to pull her to her feet while another shackled her hands behind her back. Her captor hoisted Sarah over his shoulders and carried her up to the main deck.

For the first time in her life, Sarah felt conscious of her naked body. Cattin and her father had conditioned her to cover herself during the past year. In her defense, Sarah had always worn a paru tied around her waist, and her hair sufficiently covered her chest. The only time that she went naked was when she bathed. Not one person among this crew offered her clothing to replace the dress they had stripped from her body. Even Emile, her friend who claimed to love her, gave her nothing to cover herself. Now, her waist-length hair betrayed her while her captor draped her over his shoulder.

Sarah raised her head when she heard Gerard and another crew member shouting at each other. She had no idea what they said, or why they were yelling. Her thick hair, dangling over her eyes, prevented her from seeing anything but the weathered deck. The next thing she knew, she was being lowered to the jolly floating in the water. Gerard and one other sailor were already seated. Sarah grunted when her captor dropped her onto the seat beside the captain. She attempted to dive out of the boat, but Gerard halted her escape when he yanked the chain to her choker. Gerard scolded her in French. Sarah looked away as she watched the sailor who carried her to the jolly, ascend the line to join his crewmates. Everyone aboard was busy getting the ship ready to set sail. The scowl on the captain's lips and the glares he exchanged with his men hinted that Gerard's crew intended to leave them behind. She concluded that was the reason they shouted at each other.

The South Seas maiden adjusted her hair to cover her chest. Then she tilted her face to the sky and welcomed the sun's warmth on her face, but the scene unfolding before her commanded her attention. Ships filled the azure harbor. The French cutter was the only one that resembled the Zafirah. The rest of the vessels had long narrow hulls with three masts. Instead of having several columns of smaller sails, each mast had one sail extending the full length of the pole. Many of the men on the other ships looked and dressed like Hassan's crew. They were busy either loading or unloading cargo from or into smaller vessels. Sarah gasped when she spotted people linked together by chains filing into the jollies. Unlike the crews who had dark hair and dark skin, most of the prisoners had fair skin and light hair. They also wore the same style of clothing as Gerard's crew, and every prisoner's face mirrored her terror.

Sarah's attention drifted to the land when she heard the call to prayer ringing out from the shore. The strangest mountain she had ever seen sat at the edge of the shoreline. It was tall and formidable at a distance, with one smooth, straight cliff expanding the length of the harbor. The mountain top was long and flat with two matching mountain peaks at each end. Sarah stared at the Algerian flag waving proudly over one of the towers. Her jaw dropped when an arched door at the base opened, allowing people to enter the cave, except there was light on the other side of the entrance. Then it occurred to her that the mountain wasn't a mountain at all. It was a man-made structure like Hassan's ship, except this was built with small gray blocks. All the jollies, including hers, were headed to the dock at the base of the wall.

A line of black skinned men stood on the pier. They were all dressed like Hassan. One with a muscular chest grabbed the dinghy's rope. He took one look at Sarah and began shouting at Gerard in a strange language. The French captain climbed onto the dock and yelled back in French as he yanked the chain to Sarah's choker. She grabbed hold of the chain and scrambled onto the dock. Mumbling in his language, the Algerine walked over to a small structure and returned with a bundle of gray cloth. Sarah smirked when he unfolded the garment and threw it over her head. She wiggled a few times to adjust to the scratchy fabric and gasped when the Algerine covered her head and her face with a matching veil. Though the fabric wasn't heavy or uncomfortable, she didn't like the way it obstructed her view.

While Gerard continued talking to the guard, Sarah observed that the captain didn't look well. His bronze face was pale, and his sandy hair was noticeably thinner since the last time she saw him. The two men finished their conversation, and Gerard turned towards the city. Sarah eagerly walked through the arched doors without Gerard needing to tug on her chain. Her jaw dropped, and her eyes widened when she spotted the buildings towering over the people. They looked like perfectly formed stones that were neatly assembled into rows. At first, Sarah wasn't sure of their purpose other than to create narrow passageways. Then she spotted people standing in the doorways and windows, and she realized that the blocks were their homes. The only buildings they had on her island were small huts consisting of a roof woven out of palm leaves and tied to four poles. She and the other people in her village also made walls out of woven palm leaves to shield them from the rain, but they invariably blew away during the storms. On the warm clear nights, Sarah and the other families removed the walls so that they could enjoy the fresh breeze the nights usually provided.

Sarah yelped when Gerard pulled her through the sea of people. She had never seen so many at one time. All of them dressed in clothes like Hassan's, and each one went about his daily business. They passed through a narrow alley that opened up to a large square. Food stands were set up on one side of the plaza. Men and women stood in front of the stands carefully examining the food before stuffing their choices into the bags draped over their shoulder. Sarah bobbed her head to a tune a musician played on one of the corners. A few steps later, she gasped in horror at the other end of the square when she spotted a young boy and two men standing on a platform. The crowd cheered as one man pinned the boy's hand to a box while the other sliced off his hand with a saber. Sarah's eyes snapped shut to block the images of blood spewing from the boy's hand, but nothing could shield her ears from his piercing screams. Her thoughts drifted back to the day she met Hassan, when he pinned her hand to the table, threatening to slice off her hand for taking something that didn't belong to her. It wasn't until that moment that Sarah understood why Hassan threatened to cut off her hand. She was grateful that he cared enough to warn her of the penalty for stealing.

The guard escorted Sarah and Gerard down another alley leading to a smaller square filled with people, including another cheering crowd. Sarah cried again when she caught a glimpse of a woman buried up to her chin while people hurled rocks at her head. Sarah's knees buckled when she heard the woman's screams. Gerard attempted to force her to her feet. Having little to eat since her captivity, Sarah was too weak to walk any further. The cobblestone also burned the bottom of her feet, making it impossible to take another step. The ebony guard pushed Gerard aside, scooped up Sarah into his arms and carried her the rest of the way.

Naa'il left the slave yard when he received a message from Mamnoon. All the note said was that his servant had requested an audience with him in the Palace garden. The Dey sighed after surveying the yard packed with new slaves.

"Are you leaving, Your Excellency?" Jamal asked as an etched line formed on his brow.

"I just received an urgent message from Mamnoon. I will return as soon as I can. Please continue without me," Naa'il answered, looking over his brother-in-law's head.

"Of course," Jamal replied with a clenched jaw.

Naa'il's lips formed a faint smile as he stepped outside the yard and strolled down the corridor. He made several turns and found Cora's bodyguard standing on the edge of the garden. "You wanted to see me?" Naa'il asked, silently observing the pleased expression on Mamnoon's face as he bowed to his master.

"Thank you for granting me an audience, Your Excellency. I wanted to show you something." Stepping onto the lawn, Mamnoon led Naa'il past the rows of flowering bushes.

The Dey rubbed his chin when he spotted a patch of fresh dirt at the far end of the garden. The length and width looked as if it could fit a person's body. Someone had also placed a stone bench at the foot of the grave. Stopping next to the edge of the dirt, the Dey cocked his head and asked, "Is that …?"

"It is. I thought it would please you to be close enough to visit Cora whenever you wished. I will move her if you would prefer."

"No, it is perfect," Naa'il said. "The grave is not pointed towards Mecca."

"That was intentional. I thought that Cora would prefer to face her homeland."

"That is very thoughtful. Thank you for doing this for me."

"I want to apologize for my recent behavior. I took liberties with Cora in direct opposition to your wishes. I submit myself for any disciplinary action that you deem necessary."

Naa'il studied his servant. He knew by the way Mamnoon avoided his gaze that he felt remorse for his recent behavior. The Dey rested his hand on Mamnoon's shoulder and offered him a sympathetic smile, "Yes, you did, but you are a man of conscience. I am grateful for all you did for Cora. Consider this matter closed." Skirting her grave, Naa'il lowered himself onto the bench and studied his friend. "Were you in love with Cora?" he asked, even though he already knew the answer. Mamnoon hung his head. "It is alright; I know that you were. Why else would you offer to pay me all you had to acquire her?"

Naa'il's servant still didn't answer right away. When he was ready, Mamnoon looked his master in the eyes and replied, "Yes, I loved her. Cora and I had bonded through a painful ordeal."

"I did not think that eunuchs were capable of loving women."

"I may not be able to act on my love, but that does not mean that I am incapable of loving another."

"Did Cora love you?"

"Cora cared for me in her own way. The attacks wounded her deeply. Her scars made it difficult for her to love anyone, including me. Perhaps it might have been different had she lived. I hope that she found peace after she left us."

"I appreciate your candor," Naa'il said.

"If it helps, I know she cared for you. Your morning visits meant a great deal to her."

"That is kind of you to say, but we both know that I hurt Cora. She would not have been harmed had I not ordered my men to ravage her body."

"Cora hurt you too. You were only reacting to her obstinacy," Mamnoon paused. "Your Excellency, Cora wouldn't have forgiven you had she not been fond of you."

"Thank you for that." Naa'il glanced at the guard approaching them. "What is it?"

The guard bowed. "Your Excellency, the ship carrying the South Seas woman dropped anchor in the harbor early this morning. The person who received her reported that she arrived at the dock naked with chains binding her hands. He provided proper cover to her. What are your orders?"

With narrowed eyes, Naa'il pursed his lips. "Is the French captain with her?"

"Yes, Your Excellency. He was her only escort. It appears that his crew mutinied."

The end of Naa'il's tongue made a tiking sound as he subtly shook his head. "Did they?" he said as a faint smile curled on his lips. "This is what I want you to do …."

"I will not fail you." Mamnoon bowed and walked away with the other guard.

Naa'il stood and carefully picked a red rose. He squatted and laid the flower on Cora's grave. "I miss you; I miss waking up to your prayers. You will be pleased; I have been reading your Bible, and I am comforted from what it teaches me. Your notes are also helpful. I must go, my beloved; I promise I will return when I can."

The guard lowered Sarah onto the cobblestones in front of the Palace. She was still trembling as she reflected on her fate. Seeing the Palace's front entrance made her all the more nervous. The two-story building, lined with arches, stared down at her like a god passing judgment. Each arch contained a soldier; all of them stared at Sarah.

Another man met them at the Palace entrance. His skin was much darker than that of the man who carried her through the city. This man was also taller than Hassan, and his muscular chest filled his tan shirt and brown robe. His head was smooth, and void of hair, at least the parts peeking out from under his cream pointed hat. He gave her a reassuring smile as if to say that she didn't need to worry. Gerard's luck didn't improve. Sarah's new protector forced him to unlock her shackles.

Other guards surrounded the French captain and escorted him inside the Palace. That was the last time that Sarah saw Gerard Rochelle.

Her escort spoke in an unfamiliar language. The only answers that she could provide was shaking her head and shrugging her shoulders. He tugged on her arm and motioned her to walk with him. He led her through a courtyard surrounded by three–two story walls, each floor lined with a row of arches. Clusters of men dressed like her escort dotted the square patio. A hush fell on their conversations as they watched Sarah pass by them.

Her companion led her through a set of archways. They stopped in the center of the great room. Sarah was too busy admiring the blue and white tiles covering the base of the walls and the roped pillars to question why they had stopped. She frowned when her escort bowed and moved directly in back of her. Something small caught her eye when it sparkled back at her. It was embedded in the base of a pointed hat worn by a dark man lurking in the shadows. With a nod from the mysterious stranger, her escort removed her head cover so that he could inspect his prize. The man standing on the second floor, motioned with his hand for Sarah and her companion to continue. As they passed through a series of corridors, Sarah welcomed the cold marble under her feet. Then their journey came to an abrupt end when they stopped in front of another arched door.

Sarah shuttered at the thought of who was on the other side. She was sure that it was the man dressed in black. Her lips curled into a beaming smile when a young woman answered the door.

Mamnoon's jaw dropped when Tess stepped out to greet them. "His Excellency appointed you to oversee the harem?" he exclaimed with a broad grin.

Tess tilted her head back, and thrust her jaw forward. "No, I appointed meself. The bloody harem has been in chaos ever since

Bashira's execution. We had guests to entertain. No one knew what to do. So I stepped in to organize the lasses," Tess said with a proud grin. "So far no one has complained. We'll see how long it takes for His Lordship to replace me."

"I cannot think of a better-suited person to perform this important duty."

Tess turned her attention to Sarah as she scanned the new arrival from head to toe. The interim valide glanced back at her friend and asked, "What do we have here?"

"She is from the South Seas," Mamnoon explained.

"Indeed?" Tess held up a lock of Sarah's hair then released it when Sarah pulled away. "She looks like an Irish lass to me."

"Be that as it may, she needs to be inspected and prepared for His Excellency," Mamnoon insisted.

Tess grimaced. "I'll see what I can do."

"I will wait for your findings."

"Very well. Come with me," she said in English to Sarah.

"You speak English?" Sarah gasped with widened eyes.

"Aye, and so do you," Tess answered in a condescending tone. "Come with me." The interim valide tugged on her arm.

Sarah paused and said something in Polynesian to Mamnoon, who nodded before Tess pulled her into the harem. The valide laughed to herself as she observed Sarah's reaction to her new home. Like all newcomers, Sarah stood motionless in the doorway with a gaping jaw as she took in every detail of this opulent room. Tess was sure that her reaction was no different when she arrived at the Algerian Palace, but seeing Sarah's wonderment still brought a smile to her lips.

Mamnoon groaned when Sarah ran her hand across the marble columns. "Tess, His Excellency is waiting."

"Alright, I'll get her," Tess promised when she caught Mamnoon rolling his eyes. "Come on." She hooked her hand around Sarah's arm just as Sarah squatted in front of a girl around Molly's age. "You can meet the lasses later. I must perform your examination first." Tess and Mamnoon escorted Sarah to the bathing room. "Stay here," She said. No sooner had Tess turned to walk away when Sarah stripped off her garment and made a beeline to the pool. "Wait!" Tess's hand had latched onto Sarah's arm before her toes touched the water. "Lord Almighty, you're worse than me daughter, and I can't let Molly out of me sight for even a moment."

Sarah sighed with pouty lips when her new friend led her away from the pool. "Please, I have." Sarah pointed to a white cloth that lay folded on the bench and then to her waist.

"Oh, here," Tess said in a flustered voice as she handed the cloth to Sarah. Cocking her head to the side, she frowned when Sarah tied the cloth around her waist. "Are you really from the South Seas?"

"What is South Seas?"

Tess opened and closed her mouth without answering. "Well, it's … I honestly don't know where the South Seas is, other than it's a place far from here. All I know is that the women are willing lovers and run around naked," she paused. "You are not from Ireland are you?"

"What is Ireland?"

"It's …," Tess sighed, "an island far from here."

Sarah giggled. "I live with Da on island far from here."

"Is that how you dress on your island?"

Sarah held up the edge of her white cloth. "Aye, we say this paru."

"I see."

"Tess, His Excellency is waiting," Mamnoon interrupted.

"Very well," Tess said, unable to tear her eyes from Sarah's paru. She just stood there with her thumbnail pressed between her teeth.

"What is wrong?" Mamnoon demanded when Tess made no effort to examine the new concubine.

"I have never examined a woman before. That was always Bashira's responsibility. I wouldn't know what to look for even if I inspected her," Tess replied in Algerian. "Sarah, are you a virgin?" she asked in English.

"What is virgin?"

"Have you ever made love to a man?"

"Aye. I married," Sarah said proudly.

"You're married," Tess clarified.

"Aye."

"I'll take your word for it," Tess mumbled. "She said that she is not a virgin. That should please His Lordship."

"Are you certain?" Mamnoon raised his brows.

"Aye, she told me. That is good enough for me."

"I know you two are conversing in English, but I cannot understand you two," Mamnoon complained.

"I have more practice with this language than you do. Now, off with you. I'll prepare her for His Lordship."

"Thank you, Tess. I will return for her in a few hours." Mamnoon turned and left.

"I, Sarah," she pointed to herself.

"I'm Tess. I imagine you would like to take a bath?"

"Oh, aye," Sarah replied with an energetic nod.

"Follow me," Tess laughed.

Gerard waited outside the doors of the great room. His anticipation of his meeting with the Dey was enough to subdue his body's complaints. He was anxious to learn what the Dey thought about his Tahitian prize, and more importantly, what kind of compensation he would receive for her. Finally, Jamal appeared an hour later, announcing that Naa'il Dhar was ready to see him.

In a small way, Gerard wished that his cousin were there to guide him through the meeting. Still, he was confident enough to believe that the Dey would be pleased with Sarah, and would pay handsomely for her. Tonight he would feast and pass the evening as the Dey's honored guest.

Gerard expected Naa'il to be smiling and parading his newest acquisition in front of everyone. His face, however, was stern, and Sarah was nowhere in plain sight. Gerard's heart throbbed as he made his way to the center of the room. He didn't need to be reminded to crouch before the Dey.

"How dare you arrive in our port with a naked woman?" Naa'il shouted as soon as Gerard was settled.

"Forgive me, Your Excellency. I did not have any clothes to give her. Besides, it is her custom to wear nothing at all," Gerard explained in the most obsequious tone he could muster.

"You should have given her yours," Naa'il countered and paused. "Where is Captain Fornier?"

"I thought he had returned, Your Excellency," Gerard lied. He hadn't the courage to admit that he left his cousin in battle. Moreover, this was the first time that he had even thought about Claude. It hadn't occurred to him that his cousin may not have survived the battle. Gerard swallowed hard when he spotted the Dey's frown and his narrowed eyes.

"Your prize has been examined," Naa'il continued. "She is worthless."

"That cannot be. She was a virgin, I swear it."

"She is no longer pure. I warned you, Captain Rochelle. You and your men will spend the rest of your days working in the quarry as payment for your quest. Your crew has been apprehended and are being taken to the quarry, even as we speak. Know that not even abandoning your faith for ours will spare you from this labor. If I were you, I would pray for a quick death." Naa'il motioned to his guards to apprehend the French captain. Gerard screamed as the Dey's guards dragged him out of the room. He screamed all the way to the quarries, and not once did he reflect on his cousin's fate.

CHAPTER 26

"Here, tie this around your waist," Tess handed Sarah a green silk cloth with a golden thread woven throughout the fabric.

"Thank you," Sarah replied in Polynesian. She took the cloth from Tess and tied it around her waist.

Tess stood back with her thumbnail clinched between her teeth. "My, how exotic you look." Her eyes narrowed as she surveyed Sarah from the top of her head to her toes and back again. "I imagine His Lordship will be very pleased with you."

Sarah shot her new friend a quizzical glance. "Who is?"

"His Lordship is your new master."

"What is master?"

Tess opened and closed her mouth when she couldn't think of a simple answer. "You'll figure it out when you meet him," she said, still flustered by the question.

"Who is?"

"Naa'il Dhar," Tess's voice trailed off. "May I give you some advice?"

"What is advice?"

"Your English is not very good, is it?" Tess chuckled. "What I am trying to tell you is, say nothing about your husband. That is for your protection."

"He come for me," Sarah insisted.

'You'd better pray that he doesn't. I know you will not understand this, but you must forget about your husband. You belong to Naa'il Dhar now. It is important that you do everything you can to please him."

"I no see Cattin?"

Tess offered Sarah a sympathetic smile. "I am sorry. Your life is here now. It will be alright; you'll see."

Mamnoon appeared a moment later. "Is she ready?" he asked, surveying his master's newest acquisition.

"Aye." Tess threw a white cloth over Sarah's shoulders. "I think she will please His Lordship." She leaned in and whispered to Sarah. "Go with Mamnoon. It will be alright."

Sarah's hand clutched her other arm. "I not stay here?" she asked in a timid voice.

"No, but you will return. Go with Mamnoon."

"I see you again?"

"You will. I am not going anywhere," Tess sighed.

Abigail led the charge towards Tess after Sarah and Mamnoon exited the harem. "Who was that?" she asked as women gathered around the valide.

Tess smirked at their curious stares and shrugged her shoulders. "That is His Lordship's newest amusement."

"Why does she only wear a cloth tied around her waist?" Abigail queried.

"That is because she was raised in the South Seas."

"Oh, I hate her already," Abigail cringed.

"Of course you do. You hate anyone who threatens to take your place as the center of the world."

"That is not true."

"Of course it is. I witnessed the way you treated your cousin when she took your place, remember?"

Tears flooded Abigail's eyes. "You weren't exactly kind to Cora either." She turned on her heels and ran away.

"Get back to work." Tess barked before walking away in the opposite direction.

Mamnoon stopped in front of a door halfway down the hall from the harem. His hand turned the brass doorknob and flung the door open; Sarah froze for a moment. Once she saw that the room was vacant, she eagerly wandered inside to take a closer look. This chamber was much smaller than the harem, yet it was every bit as beautiful. Like the harem, blue and white mosaic tiles covered the lower half of the walls. There were also long pillows lining the base of three out of the four walls, but Sarah was drawn to the intricate wall carvings that began above the tile and covered the whole ceiling. The design reminded her of a small piece of lace that belonged to her mother, except the flowers in the carvings were the size of the palm of her hand. Ever a prisoner to her curiosity, she couldn't resist tracing one of the squiggly lines. Her lips parted when she discovered the tan carvings were made of smooth stone and were cool to the touch.

A delicious fragrance lofting into the room was the next curious thing to command Sarah's attention. She followed the sweet scent to a window. It was positioned near the ceiling, making it impossible for Sarah to see what grew in this strange land. Though she had grown accustomed to seeing windows during her journey, Sarah had never seen one made with colored glass.

Mamnoon interrupted her inspection when he spoke to her in his language. Sarah gasped when she spotted him standing at the door with his hand on the doorknob. Fearing he would leave her, Sarah raced across the room before he opened the door. "I am frightened. May I return to the other room, please?" Mamnoon shook his head as if he understood her. She grabbed his arm just before he stepped out of the chamber; his brow furrowed as she searched for a way to communicate with him.

"Sarah," she pointed to herself and then pointed to him. She repeated her name several times.

"Mamnoon," he pointed to himself.

"Thank you, Mamnoon," she said in Polynesian before releasing his arm as he replied in his own language. Though she didn't understand what he said, a part of her knew that he told her not to worry. Leaving her alone in this small room was anything but comforting, especially after hearing the lock click. Sarah knew her effort was futile; still, she attempted to open the locked door just the same. "Cattin." She leaned against the door and slid down to the marble floor.

Naa'il waved off another prisoner when he spotted Mamnoon standing in the doorway. He knew his servant came to tell him that his Polynesian prize was ready for him. Naa'il acted as though Mamnoon wasn't there. For as excited as he was to have the rarest woman in the world in his possession, Naa'il couldn't bring himself to go to Sarah. Cora cried when he told her about his South Seas maiden on the morning she agreed to marry him, the same morning that she was assassinated. He wanted to tell Cora that no one could take her place in his heart. His conscience admonished him to prove his love by selling his South Seas prize, yet his curiosity forbade him to give Sarah up. Naa'il rose from his pillow after finishing for the day.

"What news of the South Seas maiden?" Naa'il casually asked.

"She is waiting for you, Your Excellency." Mamnoon bowed to his master.

"What are your observations?" Naa'il asked as they strolled down the corridor.

"She is very sweet and frightened. I also sense that she has a heavy heart."

"As do I. I do not think I will see her tonight."

"Shall I return her to the harem?"

"No, have food and water brought to her. Stand guard outside her door."

"As you wish, Your Excellency. If it pleases you, I will show you where I placed her in case you change your mind."

"Very well."

Naa'il woke early the next morning. His first thought was always about Cora. This morning, his thoughts fell on his newest acquisition. He had only seen her face for a few brief moments. At a glance, she was the most exotic creature he had ever seen. Naa'il bounded out of bed and dressed. A moment later, he sank onto his bed when he spotted the cover of Cora's Bible staring back at him as if it were passing judgment. *The South Seas woman is your concubine, not your wife. You can have her as often as you wish*, his traditional side argued. Picking up the book, Naa'il pressed it against his chest and laid back on his bed with his feet touching the floor. "I have not been with anyone since Samina," he said defensively to Cora as if she were sitting beside him. He could see her disappointment. "Why should I not have my prize? I would not have this dilemma had you not left me." Tossing her book aside, Naa'il rose from his bed and headed to the room holding the South Seas maiden.

Sarah lay on the cold floor with her head resting on a pillow that was meant for her whole body. His heart tugged when he spotted the tears streaming down her cheeks. She sat up as Naa'il approached her with her attentive eyes studying his every movement. Cupping her chin between his fingers, he leaned down to inspect her.

"I understand why Aziz did not want me to know about you. I would not share you either," he said in his own language, even though he knew she wouldn't understand a word he said. He rolled his hand into a fist to diffuse the anger building inside him, as he envisioned this woman and Hassan together. "You should have been mine," Naa'il paused. "I suppose Aziz made it possible for me to keep you. I would be required to send you to the Sultan's Palace had Aziz not taken your innocence." He tilted his head to the side and squinted, "but do you love him?"

She answered him in her own language.

"You are mine now. I am the Dey of Algiers and your master. My name is Naa'il Dhar. You will live well if you please me; and if you resist, well," he said, hovering over her. Locking his hand around her arms, Naa'il pulled his prize to her feet. Sarah backed away as he attempted to take her into his arms. Naa'il advanced towards her for every step she took backward.

Sarah yelped when her back bumped into the corner. Naa'il blocked her in a way, making it impossible for her to escape. He grabbed a fist full of hair as his lips came down hard on hers. His kisses demanded her to answer him, but Sarah froze just as Cora did during their initial meeting. Unlike his first encounter with Cora, there was no interruption. Naa'il's tongue pried Sarah's lips apart. He screamed a moment later when her teeth clamped down on his tongue. Naa'il retreated and cocked his hand back. "Whore," he shouted, backhanding her across the cheek. His eyes widened when he spotted Sarah pressing his knife against her belly. "Give that to me," he gently demanded, holding his hand in front of her.

Sarah sneered and muttered something in her own language. This time, she pressed the knife hard enough to draw blood.

Naa'il's eyes, round and dilated, were wide enough to see the white surrounding his black irises. Holding his hands up, the Dey backed away. "I will not hurt you," he said in a soothing voice; Sarah didn't budge. Naa'il fled the room when his thoughts drifted back to his first meeting with Cora. He came to a screeching halt when he almost collided with Mamnoon.

Mamnoon feverishly scanned his master from head to toe. "Are you hurt, Your Excellency?"

"Take her to the market and sell her," Naa'il said, gasping for breath. "Spread the word that she is from the South Seas. She should command a handsome price. She also took my knife. Confiscate it from her," he commanded before brushing past his servant.

"Yes, Your Excellency," Mamnoon answered with a doleful expression before charging into the room. Sarah cowered in the corner with the knife still pressed against her bloodied stomach. From what

Mamnoon could see, there was not enough blood to cause concern.

The bodyguard raised his hands in front of him and said in English with a soothing voice, "I will not hurt you." He moved slowly so as not to give Sarah a reason to kill herself. She didn't move. When he finally reached her, Mamnoon held out his hand and said, "Please give the knife to me. I give you my word; I will not harm you." Sarah turned away from him like a person who had been betrayed one too many times. "I will not hurt you," Mamnoon whispered.

Sarah's trembling hand laid the knife in the palm of Mamnoon's. "Did he harm you?" He asked as he carefully tucked the poniard under his burgundy belt.

Sarah slowly shook her head. Her chest rose and fell as tears spilled onto her cheeks.

"Shhh, it is alright," Mamnoon said, wrapping his arms around her while she wept. Once she was calm, he escorted her back to the harem.

Tess was there to greet them. "What happened?" she gasped when she spotted the blood on Sarah's stomach. "Please don't tell me that His Lordship violated her."

He signaled with his eyes that they needed to speak in private. "Sarah was spared. I believe she would appreciate a bath."

"Of course," Tess said. "Sarah, come with me. You look like you could use a bath."

The tension on Sarah's face eased as she nodded.

Tess escorted Sarah and Mamnoon to the bathing area where she turned Sarah over to several servants. Once Sarah was in the pool, Tess led Mamnoon to a small alcove off to the side of the bathing room. "What happened?"

"It is very serious. His Excellency commanded me to sell her at the market." Mamnoon told Tess what he knew of Naa'il's meeting with Sarah.

Tess's hand cupped her mouth. "My God," she mumbled before crossing her arms. "After what His Lordship did to Cora, I thought he would be different with Sarah. The fool should not have resisted him."

"I believe His Excellency is selling Sarah because he *is* drawn to her.

During the years I have served His Excellency, he attacked only one other woman several weeks ago. His Excellency was drawn to her too."

"Cora," Tess mumbled.

"Cora. The similarities between the two women and the meetings unnerved even me."

"Why do men always want the women they can't have," Tess sighed. "It is a pity His Lordship decided to sell Sarah."

"I think His Excellency is selling Sarah for her protection."

"From whom?" Tess scoffed. "We both know the masters outside the Palace walls can be cruel and domineering. I would much rather take me chances with His Lordship than with another Ottoman black heart." Tess chuckled to herself and winked at her friend. "Present company accepted, of course. You could be my master any day."

Mamnoon thanked her with a subtle nod. "I believe he fears being alone with her. I saw it in his eyes as he fled Sarah's room."

"That is still a bloody shame." Leaning against the wall, Tess crossed her arms and shook her head. "How long does she have?"

"I will come for Sarah tomorrow morning. His Excellency wants to spread the word of his intention to sell a South Seas maiden."

"Molly and I will watch over Sarah until you come for her." Tess rested her hand on Mamnoon's crossed arm. "You are a good man, perhaps the most honorable man I have ever known."

"And you are a good woman."

Naa'il marched past the soldiers guarding his apartment. Closing the door behind him, the Dey pressed his back against the door and slid to the floor, burying his face in his knees. His whole body shook as he reflected on his meeting with Sarah. "You still haunt me," he complained to Cora. Had he known better, he would have believed that Cora's spirit had entered Sarah. There were too many similarities between these two women to count. They were both beautiful. They shared the same sweet disposition, the same spirit. Perhaps there was truth to Cora's theory that people live on borrowed light.

His meeting with Sarah unnerved him. Naa'il was sure he had learned his lesson from his experience with Cora, yet he just repeated making the same mistake for virtually the same reasons. Naa'il was drawn to this exotic beauty. Though they had just met, he resented Sarah giving herself to someone other than him. He attempted to take Sarah by force - just like Cora. The only difference between their first meetings was that Sarah threatened to take her life. Naa'il couldn't help wondering if Cora would have done the same had she arrived in Algiers alone. Tension billowed inside him as his thoughts returned to Sarah's fate. He hated to give her up, but he didn't want to betray his love for Cora either.

The morning turned to afternoon, and the late afternoon sunlight faded to dusk. Naa'il pulled himself off the marble floor and tottered into his bed chamber. Tossing his headpiece to the floor, he climbed onto his bed and retrieved Cora's Bible. Naa'il didn't bother opening the book because he doubted that it could solve his dilemma. Pressing it against his chest, Naa'il closed his eyes and whispered to Cora, "What do you want me to do?"

Sarah closed her eyes and slowly turned around with one arm extended in front of her and the other out to her side. The little girls surrounding her, giggled as they darted up to and from her. Sarah's arms moved as she attempted to capture one of them just from hearing their voices. She frowned and opened her eyes when her hand landed on a person who was about her height. The girls she sought were only waist high. Sarah lowered her hands when she realized that she had caught Tess. Her smile faded after spotting the grave expression on her friend's face. Mamnoon stood beside her with a look that matched Tess's. Some of the other women watching them shared Tess's worry while others snickered with the women standing beside them.

"You must go with Mamnoon," Tess said somberly. She held up a gray gown. "Here, put this on."

"Why?" Sarah demanded in her usual childlike way.

"Because you must," Tess snapped as she slid the robe over Sarah's head. Once the robe was in place, Tess covered Sarah's face with the same veil she wore when she set foot on the dock.

Sarah wriggled to adjust to the scratchy fabric. "I come back?" she asked timidly.

"I'm sorry, but you won't return to the harem. I know that you will be alright, though," Tess explained.

"I not see you again?"

"No, we will not meet again. Go with Mamnoon."

"Come." The bodyguard held out his hand.

Sarah bit her lip when several more guards surrounded her. Knowing she didn't have a choice, Sarah left with Mamnoon and her escorts. After exiting the Palace, they turned down an alley. Sarah heard shouting in the distance. The noise grew louder as they moved deeper into the city. Sarah spotted the crowd in front of her and attempted to pull away, but she couldn't break free of Mamnoon's iron grip. Her struggle halted long enough to watch an older man leading a young girl bound in chains. "Please, I am frightened," Sarah pleaded as she pulled away even harder.

"I am sorry," Mamnoon said with a sullen expression. He hoisted her over his shoulder like a sack of flour and ducked down another alley. Two turns later, they arrived on the other side of the square. Mamnoon set her down behind a stage. Sarah was one of many girls and young women. Each was bound in chains and looked as terrified as she felt. Sarah's heart ached when she spotted a girl who was no more than fourteen years old standing on the platform. The gentleman standing beside her called out to the audience who shouted back to him. A hush settled over the mob. One of the spectators stepped forward and led the girl away, and another took her place.

"*Cora!*" Naa'il said when he spotted her standing beside his bed.

He was conscious enough to recognize that he was dreaming. It was the only logical explanation for seeing her again. Still, he was glad to be reunited with the great love of his life. Dressed in a simple white gown, she was more beautiful than he remembered. Her waist length hair was neatly combed and hanging loosely down her back. The injuries she sustained during her stay at the Palace were gone, and only perfection remained.

She looked at him tenderly and held out her hand. Not caring where Cora would lead him, Naa'il slid off his bed and placed his hand on hers. His bedchamber and its furnishings faded from sight. They appeared in Cora's apartment a moment later. Naa'il gasped when he spotted Sarah talking with four small boys; each was a perfect likeness of him. A knock on the door followed, and the door opened. Naa'il's lips parted when he discovered a happier version of himself standing in the entrance.

"Babba," one of the boys called out. He ran to the man just as he stepped into the room. His father picked up his son and carried him to the rest of his family. They were laughing and talking together. Naa'il's heart tugged when he saw the love between Sarah and his second self. He looked over at Cora and asked, "Are you certain that this is what you want for me?" She smiled and nodded.

Naa'il opened his eyes when he heard Cora say, "Start anew." He was back in his room, lying on his bed in the same position from the previous night. The shadows outside the window hinted that it was late morning. Rolling onto his back, Naa'il's grip tightened around Cora's Bible. "I thank you for the beautiful vision, beloved. It is too late for that." He sat up sharply when he heard the second call to prayer. He knew that Mamnoon had already brought Sarah to the slave market. Still, he could almost hear Cora admonishing him to find a way to save her. Tossing her book aside, Naa'il swung his legs over the side of his bed. He stood up, slid his feet into his slippers and started running.

Sarah remained close to Mamnoon during the entire auction. One girl after another was ushered onto the auction block and were taken away by strangers. She felt their terror and their desperation, and she felt helpless to save them. When the new owner led the second to the last girl away, it was Sarah's turn to ascend to the block. The man standing on the stage spoke for a few minutes and was followed by riotous cheering.

"I am sorry," Mamnoon's voice cracked as his gaze darted from Sarah.

Sarah knew by Mamnoon's somber expression that he hated bringing her here. She removed her head cover and gown. "It is alright." She consoled her protector with a reassuring smile. The South Seas maiden squared her shoulders and climbed onto the block while glaring at the mob. For all the women that had been sold, anxious men still filled the square, leering at her as if she were their next meal. Mamnoon followed Sarah onto the block and remained by her side, sneering at anyone threatening to harm her.

Naa'il heard the cheers from the slave market from the opposite end of the alley. For as exhausted as he felt, he kept running as several of his guards struggled to keep up with him. A girl standing on the auction block and the mob cheering in front of him made it impossible for him to see Sarah. Naa'il stopped when his gaze returned to the girl standing on the block. He had visited many slave markets throughout his life. This was the first time he felt a girl's terror. Had he been closer, he would have bought her if only to spare her from a lifetime of misery. Naa'il pressed his lips together when a gray-haired man led the girl away from the market. His heart raced when Sarah stepped onto the block. His frown curled into a subtle grin when he spotted her fearlessness as she stared defiantly at the crowd. The spectator's cheers reminded him that he had to move quickly if he wanted to save her.

CHAPTER 27

The auctioneer started the bidding low; the people in the crowd eagerly met his opening price. Soon a bidding war began for this exotic prize. For all the times that Naa'il had visited the slave market, he had never witnessed the bids rise so quickly that the auctioneer had trouble keeping up. The Dey kept his eyes focused on Sarah as he and his bodyguards pushed through the crowd.

"Two hundred in gold," the portly auctioneer announced with a pleased look on his face.

To Naa'il's knowledge, that was the most anyone had offered for a concubine. For a brief moment, the Dey considered allowing the sale to go through. Seeing Sarah's defiant demeanor only heightened Naa'il's resolve to hold on to his prize.

"Sold." The auctioneer's voice trailed off when Naa'il and his guards ascended the stairs. He and everyone else in the square immediately bowed to the Dey of Algiers.

"Forgive my intrusion," Naa'il said coolly as he approached the auctioneer like a king.

"You are welcome at any time, Your Excellency," the auctioneer replied as his tan cheeks turned a few shades lighter.

"You may not thank me after you hear what I have to say. This woman was stolen from me and was sold against my wishes," he glanced over at

Mamnoon, who bowed his head to his master. "Therefore, I cannot allow this sale to go through. Return her to me, and I will say nothing more about this matter. If not, I will punish you for stealing."

"My apologies, the mistake was mine. Please forgive me for any offense I have caused you," the auctioneer said, bowing his head again.

"Thank you." Naa'il nodded.

Dressed in various shades of gray silks, a portly gentleman stepped forward with his long robe flowing behind him. "I bought her!" he protested.

Naa'il recognized him from the court in the Sultan's Palace. His name was Burhaan Hakim, who was a wealthy patron and a close friend of the Sultan. Undaunted by the threat, Naa'il's eyes narrowed as he stood nose to nose with Burhaan with his guards standing behind him. "You bid for her, but you did not pay for her."

"Do you know who I am?" Burhaan growled.

"Yes, and I am the Dey of Algiers," Naa'il growled back, mirroring Burhaan's threatening demeanor.

"I can have you removed."

"And I will kill you if you try. This woman is my property; I am returning her to the Palace."

"For now," Burhaan stepped aside. "Enjoy her while you can."

Naa'il gave his nemesis a menacing grin and brushed past him. He motioned with his eyes for Mamnoon to escort Sarah off the block.

Glaring at Naa'il, Sarah turned her nose in the air and trotted down the stairs with Mamnoon chasing after her.

Mamnoon and Naa'il waited for Sarah to cover her head and scantily-clad body with the clothes Tess gave her; then Mamnoon led Naa'il and the others through the back alleys leading to the Palace. Sarah went with them willingly, yet she kept her distance from Naa'il. Once they reached the Palace, her escorts delivered her to her room and left without saying a word to her.

"I apologize, Your Excellency. I thought you commanded me to sell Sarah. I submit myself for disciplinary actions," Mamnoon said as soon as the Dey closed the door to Sarah's temporary quarters.

"I did; I changed my mind this morning. I hope the wench doesn't make me regret my decision," Naa'il said with an impish grin.

"What are your orders, Your Excellency?"

"This is what I would like you to do ..." Naa'il explained his wishes for Sarah.

"You are a wise Dey, Your Excellency. I think you will like Sarah," Mamnoon said. "I will inform you once the task is complete."

Naa'il nodded back.

Mamnoon took a step in the opposite direction, paused, and turned and faced Naa'il again. "Your Excellency, Sarah speaks a little English. She may understand you as long as you speak slowly."

Naa'il looked back at his servant. "Thank you. That is helpful." He returned to Sarah's room after bathing and changing his clothes. Sarah paced the room and stopped suddenly when Naa'il entered. The Dey bit his lip to stifle a laugh when he spotted her outer-garments piled in the middle of the floor. Moreover, she seemed to be oblivious of her partial nudity. Naa'il raised his hands in front of him and said in English, "I will not hurt you."

Glaring at her captor, Sarah backed away from him.

"I give you my word that I will not hurt you," Naa'il repeated. This time he kept his distance from her. Servants arrived carrying plates and bowls filled with food. "Place the food here," Naa'il pointed to the floor in front of the pillow in the center of the room. Once the servants delivered their meal and left them alone, Naa'il approached Sarah. He knew by the way she stared at his gray sash that she was searching for his knife. "I am unarmed this time." Naa'il held his hands in front of him and continued, "My Cora was a very wise woman. I think she would want me to find a way to begin anew with you. She believed that the most meaningful kind of love starts with friendship. That is how we will begin." Naa'il pointed to himself. "I am Naa'il Dhar." He pointed to her and continued, "You are Sarah."

Sarah answered with a timid nod.

Naa'il laughed to himself and said, "Sarah is a pretty name. I would like to call you Jamilla. The name suits you; it means beautiful. I fear you are too obstinate to answer to it, so I will yield this time and call you by your name. Are you hungry?" Naa'il spotted her vacant expression and retrieved the bowl of dates when he realized that she didn't understand him. "This is a date." He picked one up and took a bite. "Try it; they are very sweet." He extended the bowl to Sarah.

Biting her lip, she delicately plucked the plump fruit from the bowl and nibbled tentatively. Her eyes widened with delight before devouring the rest of the date.

"It is good – yes?"

Sarah nodded and reached for another.

Naa'il laughed at her enthusiasm towards the fruit. "Come. Let us eat." He extended his arm, inviting Sarah to sit on the cushion in front of the food. Sarah sat with her feet tucked beneath her. Naa'il placed another pillow across from her. Sitting down, he picked a grape from the cluster and said in his language, "This is a grape. Grape." He held the fruit in front of her face.

Sarah repeated the word.

"Yes." Naa'il offered her the fruit, then plucked one for himself. He spent the rest of their meal teaching Sarah the names of the foods they ate. To his surprise and delight, she learned their names quickly.

Sarah's shoulders relaxed, and her apprehension turned to curiosity. She couldn't take her eyes off his pointed headpiece. Her hand darted to and from the stone embedded at the base. Wondering what she would do, Naa'il removed his hat and held it in front of her. Sarah's eyes twinkled as she rubbed her finger across the fig-size diamond broach.

"I imagine that you do not have diamonds in the South Seas. Or if you do, you do not have a means of turning them into gems like this one," Naa'il mused out loud as he placed the velvet headdress on the floor beside him. He removed a small diamond and ruby ring from his finger and slid it onto her middle finger.

Sarah's lips parted as she traced the stones. She looked at Naa'il as if to ask if the ring was hers to keep.

Naa'il grinned, "Yes, you may keep this ring." His gift was a little thing, and yet she looked at it as though it were a priceless treasure. For Naa'il, this gift was a means for putting their first meeting behind them so that they could start anew.

Sarah turned her attention from her ring to his head. Like before, her tentative fingers darted to and from his bald crown.

Naa'il's brows drew together as he wondered what intrigued her. Then it occurred to him that she had never seen a shaved head before. "I suppose you are unaccustomed to seeing men without hair on their head. I cannot give you the reason why we shave our heads other than that is our custom. I do it because I hate combing out the tangles in my hair every morning." Naa'il grinned as Sarah continued looking intently at the top of his head. Curious what she would do next, the Dey leaned forward.

Once again, Sarah's hand darted to and from his head until she mustered the courage to rub her fingers across its smooth surface. Her demeanor was childlike and innocent, just like his young daughters. Sarah's touch also matched her gentle nature. When she finished inspecting his head, Naa'il guided her hand to rub across his arm. "We also remove hair from our bodies."

With a gleam in her eyes, Sarah took his hand and bid him to rub across her arm. It surprised Naa'il to discover that Sarah also shaved the hair from her body. His loins tightened when he spotted her perfect breasts peeking out between the long curly locks of her exotic hair. Naa'il moved his hand away from her before succumbing to temptation and doing something that he would later regret. In a desperate attempt to distract the unbidden images flooding his mind, Naa'il tore his eyes from her breasts and asked, "Tell me about your home." When Sarah answered him with a puzzled look, he pointed to her and said, "Your home."

"Home," Sarah repeated.

"Do you understand 'home'?"

"Aye," Sarah bit her lip. She stared at the carved ceiling for a few minutes. Then her finger drew an L-shaped island with a mountain centered on each wing on the marble floor. "Tikutoa, my home," she said when she finished her outline.

"I see." Naa'il stared at her picture with a lopsided grin when he realized that she had shown him a way to communicate with him. He caressed her round cheek with the back of his fingers and said, "Thank you for telling me about your island. I must leave you." He stood and headed for the door. This time Sarah followed him.

"You come back?" She asked with a hopeful look.

"Yes, I promise that I will return soon," he said with a wink. Naa'il laughed to himself as he closed the door behind him. He glanced up and noticed Mamnoon approaching him.

The servant bowed and said, "I trust that your meeting with Sarah went better, Your Excellency."

"Yes," Naa'il replied with a wide grin. "Sarah did not want me to leave her. You are right; she is very sweet. I am glad that I changed my mind."

"I am pleased to hear it." The two turned and strolled down the corridor. "Everything is arranged. Are you certain that you want Sarah to reside in Cora's apartment?"

Naa'il laced his fingers behind his back, "Yes, I am certain. It is an apartment, not Cora's mausoleum." He paused. "I like Sarah; she reminds me of my Cora. She even looks like my Cora," Naa'il said with an affectionate smile, "and they both have crimson hair. Perhaps this is a second chance to find happiness. I also do not want to make the same mistakes that I made with my Cora. More importantly, I do not trust the women in the harem, especially after they poisoned her." He looked thoughtfully at his servant. "I am curious how you discovered that Sarah speaks English."

"Tess O'Shea discovered it. She assisted Sarah in the harem. The two women got along very well."

Naa'il bit his lip. "Hmm. That gives me an idea. Bring Tess to Sarah's new apartment within an hour."

"Of course, Your Excellency. May I assist you with anything else?"

"Yes. Watch over Sarah while she is outside her apartment."

"I will guard her with my life."

"You are a good servant," Naa'il said. After spending an hour collecting things for Sarah, he headed to her new apartment. He arrived in time to look over the room. Everything was perfect, yet Naa'il's heart ached as it reminded him of all the kind things that he should have done for Cora. Even though he gave the apartment to her in the end, his efforts proved to be too late. "Start anew," he mumbled as he inspected the baskets filled with gifts for Sarah.

"Enter," Naa'il called out when he heard a knock at the door.

Mamnoon ushered Tess inside.

The odalisque fell to her knees. She stretched her arms over her head and bowed until her forehead touched the floor. "Your Lord ... I mean, Your Excellency." She blushed.

"Rise," Naa'il commanded. As Tess scrambled to her feet, Naa'il nodded to Mamnoon to close the door. "I understand that you befriended the South Seas woman," he said, pacing in front of her.

"Yes, Your Excellency." She stood before him with her hands at her side and her head tilted towards the floor.

"You were able to communicate with her in English."

"I was."

"I want you to be Sarah's companion. I also want you to report everything she tells you in confidence. You will sleep in the room next to this one as payment for your service."

Tess stared at Naa'il with a furrowed brow. "But Your Excellency, Sarah was sold at market this morning."

"I decided to keep her."

Tess offered him a confident smile. "I will be honored to do this for you ...," her voice trailed off.

"What is wrong?" Naa'il demanded when she made a sour face.

"I have a daughter," Tess explained. "Please, I do not want to be separated from her. If it helps, Molly and Sarah became instant friends."

"Your daughter may join you, providing she is no trouble."

"I promise Molly will not be. She is a little angel."

"Very well then. You may return to the harem."

"Thank you, Your Excellency." Tess bowed and backed out of the room.

Mamnoon poked his head through the door opening and asked, "What is your command, Your Excellency?"

"Bring Sarah to the apartment," Naa'il paused. "Never mind, I will bring her here myself." The two men meandered down the corridors leading to the room where Sarah was being kept. Naa'il studied his friend. "You look as if you want to ask me a question, but are afraid to ask."

"You are correct."

"Ask," Naa'il prodded.

"I was curious what you intend to do with Hassan Aziz. I understand that he served you well …," Mamnoon's voice trailed off.

"He betrayed me by keeping Sarah for himself – not that I blame him. She is an exquisite creature," Naa'il said. "I think it is logical that Aziz will come for her. That is what I would do. Set a watch at the gate. I want him captured and brought here the moment he arrives."

"I will make the arrangements."

They stopped in front of Sarah's door. "Return to the apartment in a few hours with Tess and her daughter."

"I will, Your Excellency." Mamnoon bowed.

Naa'il opened the door and gasped when he found her climbing onto a stack of pillows under the window. He ran over to Sarah in time to catch her just as she toppled into his arms. "What are you doing?"

Sarah wriggled out of his arms and pointed to the window. "I wish to see."

Naa'il took her hand and led her to a courtyard garden. Sarah's eyes lit up when she saw the flowers lining the walls. She went over to the roses planted under her window and sniffed the flowers on each bush. Naa'il couldn't help smiling when he spotted her joy as she inspected the garden. He carefully picked a yellow rose and plucked the thorns off before giving it to her.

She said something in her native language and tucked the flower behind her left ear.

Crinkles formed in the corners of Naa'il's smiling eyes as he admired the way the yellow complemented her burgundy hair. "You are beautiful," he said in a hushed voice.

Once she finished inspecting the flowers, Naa'il continued, "Come, I have something else to show you."

Sarah replied with a hesitant look.

"I know I have not given you a reason to trust me. I promise you that you will like what I have to show you," Naa'il said, extending his hand to her. He knew she didn't want to go with him by her heavy footsteps, yet she walked with him willingly. "This is your new home." He winked and opened the door.

Sarah froze outside the room.

"You need not fear me." Naa'il entered the apartment. "I will not hurt you." Sarah followed Naa'il inside. He grinned when she looked at every detail with astonishment. It didn't surprise Naa'il when she wandered into the courtyard and admired the flowers planted in the raised beds. Her eyes lit up after Naa'il turned the knob at the base of the fountain, causing the water to trickle from the fountain's top tier to the ones below it.

Naa'il's brow snapped together when he spotted a black and white kitten playing with an orange under a stone bench, all the while wondering how it got into the room without his notice. The intruder mewed when Sarah picked it up and held it in the palm if her hand. The kitten's mewing turned into purring when Sarah rubbed behind its ears. Naa'il gave a reluctant nod when Sarah silently asked for his permission to keep it.

Sarah cooed, conveying her delight.

"I am pleased that you are happy with your new home," Naa'il answered in his own language. "Come, I have more to show you." He pointed to a basket sitting beside a stone bench.

Sarah's eyes sparkled when she spotted a royal blue and gold cloth folded in the basket. Kneeling beside the bench, Sarah lowered her kitten to the floor and unfolded each cloth stacked under the blue one. Naa'il took a seat on the bench and watched her examine her gifts. The cloths were the same dimensions as the one she wore. Each was made of silk and embroidered with gold thread. Lined up together, they formed a brightly colored rainbow.

While Sarah examined her cloths, Naa'il retrieved a full-length mirror and leaned it against the wall. Sarah blinked rapidly as her gaze darted back and forth between his reflection and him. She rose from the bench and stood beside him with a crinkle on her brow. Sarah stared intently at her image. She lifted her arms, stuck out her tongue, and spun around slowly, never taking her eyes off her reflection. Naa'il rubbed his chin with the back of his hand and shifted to the side of Sarah. Then it occurred to him that this was the first time she had ever seen her image. Naa'il moved in back of her and rested his hands on her shoulders. "You are beautiful," he said in English.

Tess skipped from Sarah's new apartment to the harem. She scooped up Molly in her arms and twirled her around and around and exclaimed, "Mama just made our lives better."

Abigail approached Tess with her arms crossed. "Why are you so happy?"

Still holding Molly in her arms, Tess stopped spinning and looked at her friend. "His Lordship just gave me a special assignment. In exchange for my service, Molly and I will get to live in a room of our own."

Abigail's jaw dropped. "What exactly do you have to do?"

"I just have to be Sarah's friend."

"I thought that the harlot was sold at the market this morning," Abigail frowned.

"His Lordship changed his mind and gave her a very nice chamber. Molly and I will sleep in the room next to hers."

"Does this room have a small courtyard with a fountain?"

"Yes."

Tears flooding her eyes, Abigail wiped them away before they spilled onto her cheek. "That was my bedchamber."

"It is not yours anymore," Tess pointed out.

"I hate her," Abigail whimpered.

"That is your choice," Tess shrugged. "I am just happy that Molly and I won't have to sleep here anymore. No more having to fight for a place to sleep. No more fighting for food. We will no longer have to watch out for wenches looking to have fun at our expense."

"Tess, His Excellency sent for you," Mamnoon interrupted.

Tess nodded to Mamnoon and said to Abigail, "Enjoy the harem." She quickly gathered a few of her belongings and handed them to Mamnoon. "Could you be a love and carry these for me?"

"Of course," Mamnoon said, taking the stack of folded clothes. "Do you have anything else?"

"No, that is all I have," Tess replied, grabbing Molly's hand.

The three walked back to Sarah's new apartment. They stopped at the room long enough to drop off her belongings.

Sarah and Naa'il were sitting on a bench facing each other. While Naa'il held up brightly colored cloths next to her face, Sarah held a sleeping kitten in her arms. The Dey stood and said, "Ah, there you are."

"Your Excellency," Tess and Mamnoon bowed to the Dey as Tess carefully balanced her daughter on her hip.

Sarah jumped up and ran over to her friends.

"These are your attendants. They will be with you when I am away. Now that they are here, I must leave you. Enjoy your afternoon. I will come to you tonight," Naa'il said to Sarah. He offered Tess a subtle nod and headed to the door with Mamnoon.

Chapter 28

"I feared that you had been sold," Tess exclaimed once they were alone.

"Naa'il help me," Sarah replied.

"Where did you get that kitten?" Tess said as Molly stared intently at Sarah's pet.

"It here. Naa'il say I keep."

"His Lordship must really like you enough to allow you to keep a pet. This is a kitten, Molly. Would you like to pet it?"

Sarah held her kitten close enough so that Molly's little hand could reach her.

"Be very gentle." Tess demonstrated how to stroke the kitten's silky fur before allowing her daughter to touch it.

Molly carefully slid her hand down the whole length of the kitten's back.

"Very good, Molly," Tess said. "Does it have a name?"

"Hmm. I call it … Poe'. It means …," Sarah shook her head when she couldn't remember the English word for pearl. Poe' woke up and mewed loudly; Sarah lowered her kitten to the floor.

Molly squealed when Poe' scampered away.

"Go," Tess said, lowering her daughter to the floor. "Be gentle with the kitten."

Sarah sat down on the bench as she watched Tess drag a small branch in front of Poe'. Molly giggled when the cat pounced on the leaves before Tess wriggled it out of its claws. Sarah couldn't take her eyes off Molly. She was a beautiful little girl, but she wasn't a perfect likeness of her mother. Sarah couldn't help wondering who her father was, and more importantly, why they weren't with him. Her skin was light like her mother's, and Sarah doubted that the tan-skinned men in this region could be Molly's father. Her train of thought was interrupted when Molly rubbed her eyes and announced to her mother. "I'm tired, Mama."

"Then sleep." Tess looked up at Sarah and asked, "Would you mind if Molly slept on your pillow?"

"No, please," Sarah replied.

Molly didn't move, and Tess made no effort to carry her daughter over to the bed.

"I take her?" Sarah offered.

Tess shrugged. "If you wish."

Molly rubbed her eyes with her fists and began to cry.

"That's enough," Tess snapped.

Sarah squatted in front of the child and held out her arms. Molly didn't move. She just looked up at her mother for guidance.

"I will take her." Tess jumped to her feet and snatched up Molly just as Sarah reached for her daughter's waist. Sarah fell backward when she spotted Tess's sneer. Tess carried her daughter to Sarah's bed. She laid her in the middle of the pillow and said, "Sleep."

Sarah retreated to her courtyard and sat on the bench. Tess joined her a few minutes later.

"I sorry. I no wish ...." Sarah didn't know what to say. It was hard enough summoning the right Polynesian words, let alone the English ones. Her breath hitched when she spotted Tess wiping a tear from the corner of her eye.

"I love me daughter," Tess said, crossing her arms.

"I know."

"Me mother wasn't a very good one. She never showed me much affection. I imagine your mother was perfect."

"My ..." Sarah paused when she couldn't remember the right words. "My mother died? Right word?"

"Well, 'die' is a word, although, I don't know if it's the one you meant."

Sarah stared at the fountain. "I not remember. I same as Molly."

Tess bit her bottom lip. "Are you trying to tell me that your mother died when you were Molly's age?"

"Aye."

Tess sat beside Sarah. "Well, if you ask me, it's better to have no mother than to have a bad one."

"You not bad mother."

"Thank you, but I think Molly would disagree with you. I didn't want Molly after I learned that I was carrying her. She made me love her, though. Then I discovered how difficult it was to raise a child. Molly is so demanding. I didn't know what I was doing. So I did the easiest thing. I passed her to the women who could give her the mothering I could not."

"It same on my island, women ... are mother ... to all children."

Tess laughed faintly. "You and Molly will get along well."

Sarah looked thoughtfully at her friend and asked. "Where is Molly Da?"

"Oh that," Tess blushed. "I would imagine that he is on his ship somewhere."

"You see him?"

"Aye - from time to time. It's been a long while since I last saw him," Tess said with dreamy eyes. "Molly's father was a frequent Palace guest in the beginning. I was chosen to serve him because we are both from the same part of the world. He is an Englishman who became a bloody pirate. We fell in love, and he gave me Molly."

"Why you not with him?"

Tess lowered her gaze to her lap, "He cannot offer me and Molly a proper life right now. Perhaps one day we'll be together. Tell me about your husband."

"Um, Cattin help me ... Um, he keep me ... safe." Sarah sighed as she struggled to find the right words. She wanted to tell Tess that Hassan was the bravest and noblest man that she had ever known. She wanted to tell her friend how he saved her from cruel men, and how they fell in love. That explanation was beyond her command of the English language.

Tess covered Sarah's hand with her own. "It's alright; I know English is hard for you."

"You help me speak English?"

"I don't think I'm the best person to teach you, but I'll try."

"You miss home?" Sarah asked thoughtfully.

"No, not at all. Me life in Ireland was difficult." Tess grimaced and stared at the fountain. "I always say that I was reborn when I arrived here. Living in the Palace gave me an opportunity to start over. Oh, I complain about the harem, but it's not so bad. The harem provides for all me needs. I have clothes; I have an endless supply of food; I have a place to rest me head. I have women to watch over Molly. The demands are not so terrible. Not all the men I serve are cruel blackhearts."

"If you choose life; what you choose?"

"Oh, that's simple." Tess glanced back at Sarah and said with a blissful grin, "I would start a new life with Molly's father. Nathan is a good man, a kind man. I believe that we would be happy together."

Sarah's forehead puckered when Tess said Nathan. She had heard that name before, but for the life of her, she couldn't remember where she had heard it. Sarah reached over and gently squeezed her friend's hand, "I hope you be with Natan."

"So do I. Nathan was the only man that was ever kind to me. Now, I have a question for you. Do you dance where you come from?"

Sarah bit the inside of her lip. Hassan forbade her from dancing in front of others. However, she didn't know if Hassan meant that he didn't want her dancing in front of men or anyone. Sarah couldn't deny that she missed the camaraderie that dancing with her friends afforded her, yet she yielded to caution and asked. "You dance too?"

"I do."

"You show?"

Tess's eyes narrowed. "I'll dance for you if you dance for me." She rose from the bench and stood in front of Sarah. Holding her arms out to her sides, Tess closed her eyes, and her hips began to sway.

Sarah couldn't believe how similar Tess's dance was to her own, and yet it was different. Her whole body moved, twisting, ebbing and flowing, slowly and unhurried. Sarah jumped up and began to dance alongside her new friend.

Tess stopped in the middle of her dance and watched Sarah gyrating her hips rapidly in a sensual dance that had never been seen in this part of the world. "You're going to have to show me how you do that. How can you move your hips so quickly?" she asked when Sarah finished.

"You show me?"

"Aye," Tess agreed. A knock on the door cut their dancing exchange short.

"Tess, His Excellency will be spending the evening with Sarah. I was sent to escort all of you to the harem," Mamnoon said, poking his head through the door's opening.

Tess groaned when she heard her daughter's muffled cry. She went over to Molly. "Stop your crying. I'm taking you back to the harem so that you can play with your friends," she said, hoisting her daughter onto her hip.

Sarah knew by Tess's pursed lips that she didn't want to return to the harem, but Sarah didn't mind. Of all the things she missed on her island, Sarah missed being with her friends the most, and she looked forward to making new ones. Her excitement was cut short when she felt a tidal wave of hatred emanating from the women in the harem the moment she stepped through the entrance.

"Don't mind them," Tess marched into the harem as if it belonged to her.

Sarah followed closely behind her friend. She recognized the children who played with her earlier that morning, but this time they stayed away. Tess delivered her daughter to a group of mothers watching their daughters.

"Come on; we need to get you ready for tonight." Tess hooked her hand around Sarah's arm and led her through a door in the back of the main room.

They passed the bathing room and continued down the hallway to the last room on the right. Sarah and Tess undressed and entered a room filled with steam. This was the first steam bath Sarah had ever had. It was hard to breathe at first, but then she followed her friend's example and laid down on the bench. Soon her muscles relaxed as the steam soaked into her skin.

"Tess." Sarah sat up and looked at her friend.

"Um," Tess answered without opening her eyes.

"Why they hate me?"

"That's simple; they're not you."

"I not understand."

Tess sat up, resting her elbows on her thighs. "The women hate newcomers because they feel threatened by them."

"Why?"

"They want the attention that Naa'il Dhar is giving you."

"They can have; I go with Cattin."

Tess grabbed Sarah's arms and shook her. "You listen to me; your Cattin is not coming for you. Your life is here now. His Lordship will treat you like a queen so long as you please him."

"I married."

"Not anymore, you're not. I don't know why His Lordship spared you from the slave market today, but you're damn lucky that he did. If you want to keep his favor, you will do everything you can to please him. Believe me when I say that every woman in this room would give anything to take your place."

"They can have; I made promise to Cattin," Sarah said, fighting back her tears.

"If you do that, you're going to end up back at the slave market," she shuddered, "or even worse. His Lordship is a proud man. He does not handle rejection well. A woman who died recently learned that the hard way," Tess warned. Releasing Sarah's arms, she stood and left the steam room. "Come, it's time for our massages."

Sarah followed her friend into the bathing room. Tess went over to two empty stone benches. "Lie down on your stomach," Tess said to Sarah, before lying down on her own. Sarah obeyed. Moments later they were approached by two women who began rubbing Sarah's and Tess's backs. Tess closed her eyes and moaned with a blissful smile on her face. Sarah didn't know what to think about the woman's fingers pressing hard on her back in a slow, methodical motion. At first, the pressure was uncomfortable, but like the steam bath, Sarah began to relax.

"Did you like the massage?" Tess asked.

"Aye," Sarah said with eyes still closed and a lazy smile on her lips.

Tess got up from her bench. "Come, it's time for our bath."

Sarah didn't move.

"Sarah, you're the one spending the evening with His Lordship, not me. You must keep moving." Tess grabbed Sarah's arm and tugged.

Sarah still didn't want to move. More importantly, she dreaded spending the evening with Naa'il.

"Sarah, get up, or I will force you to move," Tess snapped.

Sarah spotted a woman in the corner of her eye. She was very beautiful with hair as light as the sun. Sarah jumped up from her bench when a small group of women approached the woman from behind. Every one of them wore a sneer on their lips and mischief in their eyes. The women cackled when their leader pushed the straw hair girl to the hard floor. Sarah ran over to the women and stood with her legs splayed apart and her fists at her side. The women were about to attack when Tess ran up from behind.

"I wouldn't do that if I were you," Tess warned in spite of her black eyes daring them to defy her. "You're about to attack His Lordship's new favorite. He won't like it if you harm her. I hate to think what he will do to you if you do."

The women's fists loosened, and they slunk away without saying another word. Sarah crouched down to the woman lying on the floor and helped her sit up.

"You are very kind," the woman cried.

"You ill?" Sarah asked.

"I am unharmed," she whimpered as tears streamed down her cheeks.

Sarah stood and helped her up. "We go there." She pointed to the pool. "You come?"

"Yes, I would like that," the woman said as she wiped a tear from her cheek.

Sarah pointed to herself. "Sarah."

"I am Abigail."

Tess rolled her eyes. "Come on." She led the group to the pool. Women occupied nearly every space on the edge of the basin. Tess nudged several of them to make room for herself and her two companions.

"I understand that you are from the South Seas," Abigail said, after sinking into the warm water.

In her broken English, Sarah told them about her life on her island and her journey to the Barbary Coast.

"Weren't you ever afraid of sailors attacking you?" Abigail asked.

"One man tried to hurt me. My friend made him stop. Cattin Gerard killed man. He say they will die if they hurt me again. They stop."

"You're very fortunate. I had traveled with my cousin, and I still didn't feel safe being around them," Abigail said.

"It's not all that bad," Tess interjected.

"I doubt that you were on the ship for as long as I was," Abigail hissed.

Tess rolled her eyes again. "Come, Sarah, we must keep moving." She climbed out of the water and offered her hand to Sarah.

Sarah got out of the pool without needing her friend's assistance. Servants bustled over to them and gave a cloth to each woman to dry off and a bottle of oil to cover their bodies. Sarah closed her eyes and smiled as she sniffed the oil's delicious fragrance. The scent reminded Sarah of her home. She had spent many hours making monoi oils from coconuts with her friends. Though this oil was different from the ones that she made on her island, she was grateful to have something to keep her skin soft.

After the women had dressed, they returned to the main hall to collect Molly, who cried when it was time to leave her friends. "That's enough," Tess snapped after picking up her daughter. "It's time to go, and that's all there is to it."

"You come too?" Sarah asked Abigail.

"I would love to join you," Abigail replied with a beaming smile.

"You know you can't come with us. His Lordship would not approve, and you don't want to anger him any more than you already have."

Abigail's lower lip quivered. "You're right," she said as her shoulders slumped.

"Why you not come?" Sarah frowned.

Abigail took Sarah's hands in her own and said, "Because I must stay here. We will see each other tomorrow – I promise. Thank you for what you did for me today."

Tess seemed to be the only one who was happy about leaving the harem. Molly cried the whole way back; Sarah walked with heavy footsteps too. With Poe's help, Tess was able to turn her daughter's tears into laughter. Sarah just sat on the bench, dreading her evening with Naa'il.

The sun was just starting to set when Jamal finished a very long day at the slave yard. He stood up to leave when the guards escorted the last of the slaves out of the yard. No sooner had Jamal stepped into the corridor when he heard someone calling his name, and his voice wasn't Naa'il's. He turned and spotted a young man approaching him. He looked like most Algerine twenty-year-old men, except he was dressed in fine muslin.

"Yes?" Jamal said curtly.

The man bowed and said with his black eyes focused on the marble floor. "Forgive my intrusion, Vizier. Please accept my master's message." He handed Jamal a folded parchment. "He said he would pay you handsomely for your discretion."

Jamal nodded and unfolded the note. His breath hitched as he read the message.

"What is your answer, Vizier?"

"Tell your master that I will meet with him tonight."

"Very good, Vizier."

Jamal's Adam's apple bobbed up and down as he watched the servant walk away. Covering his mouth with his hand, he turned and headed to Naa'il's quarters. "I need to see the Dey at once." Jamal barked at the soldiers guarding the door to the apartment.

"His Excellency is not here, Vizier" one of them replied.

"Where is he?" Jamal demanded.

"We have not seen him since we escorted him and the South Seas infidel from the slave market."

Jamal's brow furrowed, "What happened?"

The guard recounted the events from that morning. The Vizier purposely kept his hands by his side and his expression placid to conceal the consternation growing inside him. One hand, however, crumpled the parchment when the guard mentioned Burhaan's name. "Inform the Dey that it is urgent that I speak with him tomorrow morning."

For as exhausted as he felt, Jamal would have liked nothing more than to relax in his apartment with a concubine. He still needed answers, and he hoped Mariam could provide them. He found her sitting in her garden.

"There you are," Mariam said when she saw him standing in her doorway. "What is the matter?"

Jamal closed the door and approached his sister. "I was hoping that you heard from your husband today."

"I have not seen him since the American's death. You have also been absent," Mariam gently scolded her brother.

"I apologize, Mari," Jamal said, taking a seat beside her. "My work has been demanding as of late. I fear that the infidel's death hurt Naa'il deeply. His attendance in the slave yard has been sporadic. He also leaves without warning and does not return. I ask him what is troubling him, but he refuses to confide in me."

"I know. I also received some troubling news in the harem today. Apparently, another infidel caught his eye. This one is a savage from the South Seas. I cannot imagine what God she worships. I was encouraged when I heard that my husband had the sense to sell her."

"Yes, I heard. Naa'il insulted Burhaan Hakim in front of everyone at the slave market." Jamal's voice trailed off.

"What?" Mariam gasped.

"One of Naa'il's guards informed me that your husband changed his mind about the South Seas savage. I just received a note from Hakim, requesting me to meet with him tonight."

Mariam's lips parted. "Are you going?"

"Yes."

"Jamal, that is madness. Burhaan Hakim is a powerful and dangerous man. So is my husband," Mariam warned.

"I know who they are," Jamal snapped. Taking a deep breath, he covered her hand with his. "Forgive me; I do not mean to take my frustrations out on you. I need to know what I am facing. You have my word that I will protect and provide for you as long as I am alive."

"Please be careful. Naa'il and Burhaan have always hated each other. My husband will consider your meeting with Burhaan a betrayal."

"I will." Jamal wrapped his arm around his sister's shoulder and kissed her temple.

Chapter 29

Jamal slipped out of the Palace early that evening, making his excuse to the palace guards that he intended to say his prayers in the city. He went to the city mosque often, mostly because he liked the architecture. It also afforded him an opportunity to escape the ever-watchful eyes in the Palace. No one questioned him when he left. He wasn't lying; the mosque was his first stop. He just neglected to tell them that he hadn't planned to return immediately.

Jamal exited the mosque, covered his head with a cloak and ducked down an alley. Like Naa'il, Jamal had known Burhaan ever since he was a boy, except Burhaan was his father's friend, not his. What little he knew of him, Burhaan never held private meetings in familiar places. Jamal turned down another narrow alley. He was sure that he was on the right street. However, the location in Burhaan's message was vague. His pace slowed as the Vizier casually glanced into every window he passed. When Jamal reached the midpoint in the street, he spotted Burhaan's servant stepping out of a shop. Jamal nodded and followed him inside. The servant led him into a small store that smelled like spices and a hint of sweet smoke. Six or seven stained-glass lanterns hung from the ceiling. Together, they emitted enough light to see the bolts of brightly colored fabrics displayed on the shelves, and bowls of spices lined up on a long table.

The servant moved to the far corner of the room and stood beside a door covered with a black cloth hanging from the top of the doorway. The servant pulled the curtain aside. "My master is in here."

Jamal replied with a subtle nod and headed towards the back room. He remained standing in the doorway until he could see past the cloud of smoke. Once the air cleared, Jamal spotted Burhaan Hakim sitting in a winged-back chair. Dressed in black and gray silks, Burhaan's body filled his seat with his belly spilling over in front of him.

Burhaan inhaled from a sterling silver shisha sitting on an ornately carved table in front of him. Leaning his head against the back of the chair, Burhaan closed his eyes and slowly exhaled the smoke. He looked at Jamal and said, "Blessings be upon you, Jamal Rahmani. Please sit beside me." The Vizier took a seat in a matching chair; Burhaan handed him the extra shisha pipe. "Try this. It is the best tobacco that money can buy."

Jamal lifted the ivory mouthpiece to his lips and inhaled slowly to savor the taste of the elixir. He exhaled and said, "You are right; it is good." He tilted his head to the side and asked, "Did I taste apple?"

"You have a keen palate. Would you care for some tea and refreshments?"

"Yes, please. I have not eaten since the noon meal," Jamal smiled politely.

Burhaan clapped his hands. Three girls rushed into the room from another door carrying a silver teapot, cups, and a tray filled with food. The girls couldn't have been more than fourteen years old. Each was a Persian beauty and dressed in silk-translucent Ottoman trousers and a matching silk vest that was open enough to expose their girlish chests. They left the room and returned with two more trays of food.

After setting the last of the refreshments on the table, Burhaan grabbed the arm of one of the girls. She let out a faint cry as he ripped the vest from her chest. "She's a pretty thing. Notice her firm breasts. They are almost perfect, are they not? She is still pure. I bought her at the market this morning."

She was *very* pretty, Jamal silently noted, and she was terrified of her new master. "Yes. She is lovely. Why don't you tell me why you wished to see me?"

Releasing the girl's arm, Burhaan threw her to the floor and shouted, "Join the others."

The girl scrambled to her feet and ran out of the room, sobbing.

Burhaan chuckled. "I understand that your master demands much of you at the Palace. I offered you the girl because I feared that you do not have time to enjoy pleasure."

"You are most generous. His Excellency allows me the pleasure of the Palace concubines," Jamal replied. "Besides, I have two wives of my own."

"They are all dirty. The one I offered you is pure." Burhaan pulled a leg from a roasted pheasant and bit into it as if he hadn't eaten for days.

Jamal stared at the bowl of figs to conceal his disgust for his host's insatiable appetite. The Vizier grabbed a fig and held it in his hand. He looked thoughtfully at Burhaan and said, "I heard what happened at the slave market today."

Burhaan finished eating the meat on the leg and threw the bone on the table. "Dhar made a fool of me today. I bought the South Seas whore, and Dhar stole her from me," he said bitterly.

"I am curious. You, like all men of our faith, prefer pure women. The South Seas maidens have a reputation for being willing lovers," Jamal pointed out.

"Yes, I am familiar with their reputation."

"Then why did you offer to pay two hundred in gold for her?"

"She is very beautiful. Even I would have made an exception for enjoying her pleasure, but that is not the reason that I bought her."

"Oh?" he casually asked.

"I am a businessman, Jamal. I believed that I would have made a handsome profit from selling her services. The slaves in my brothels are pretty, but they are common. At least this whore looks exotic," Burhaan explained.

"Naa'il Dhar saved you money," Jamal chuckled. "It is whispered that the South Seas infidel attempted to take her life after Dhar attacked her. Though I have not met her, I have no reason to believe that she would not hesitate to take her life if she were attacked again," Jamal said, before popping the fig into his mouth.

Burhaan studied his guest. "You are very loyal to Dhar."

"I am loyal to my faith and my family," Jamal amended.

Burhaan smirked. "That is very noble of you." He ripped off the other pheasant leg. "You are also young and naïve. I can give you so much more."

Jamal bit the inside of his mouth. "Indeed," he replied after a few uncomfortable moments of silence had passed. "What do you have to offer me?"

"I could make you the Dey of Algiers. Think of it; you can be the most powerful man in our country. The king's treasure will be yours. You will only answer to the Sultan … and to me from time to time."

Jamal readjusted his position in his chair. "I see. What would happen to Naa'il Dhar?"

"You should know by now that the Deys come and go as quickly as a person changes his shirt. They are slain at night and replaced in the morning. People hardly notice the change of leadership. However, with my support behind you, I can ensure that you will reign a while longer."

Jamal crossed his legs and rested his chin between his thumb and forefinger. "Just to be clear, are you saying that you would make me the Dey of Algiers if I assassinate Naa'il Dhar?"

"Yes."

"What do I tell my sister after I murder her husband and the father of her children?"

"Make Dhar's death look like an accident. You do not need to be present when it happens."

"That is very tempting. I will take your offer under advisement."

"Take all the time you need to consider our arrangement. I promise you that Dhar will die – one way or another." Burhaan clapped his hands. The girls scampered into the room moments later. "Choose one. She is my gift to you, or take all of them. I can always get more."

Jamal shuddered when he heard the malice in their master's tone. He glanced over at the girls who still looked terrified. Jamal looked back at Burhaan and said casually, "Thank you. That is a most generous offer. You know I cannot introduce new concubines into the harem without the Dey's permission. If I may, save them for me and present them to me should I decide to accept your offer. They will be my first additions to the harem. If you will excuse me, I must return to the Palace before I am missed." He stood and left the shop.

Sarah jumped when she spotted Naa'il standing in her doorway. Tess grabbed Molly's arm and forced her daughter to kneel beside her as Sarah scrambled to follow her friends' lead. With their arms stretched above their heads, Molly and the two women leaned over and pressed their foreheads against the floor as Naa'il ambled into the apartment.

"Rise and leave us," Naa'il barked.

Unsure who Naa'il was speaking to, Sarah followed Tess and Molly until Naa'il's hand latched around her arm.

"Not you," Naa'il crooned. He waited for Tess and Molly to exit the room before continuing. "You are spending the evening with me." He took her hand and led her to the bench. "Please sit. I have more gifts for you." Naa'il waited for Sarah to sit before sitting beside her. He removed a brocade bag draped over his shoulder and rested it in his lap. With a playful gleam in his eye, Naa'il unbuttoned the flap and flicked the cover to the back. He held the bag close to his chest when Sarah attempted to peek inside. "No, it is a surprise." Naa'il winked and pulled out a string.

Sarah couldn't take her eyes off the alternating green and white sparkling stones. Naa'il laid the string across his hands so that Sarah could trace each gem with her finger.

Naa'il pointed to the green stone and said, "This is an emerald." He pointed to a white stone that looked identical to the one attached to his headpiece, except they were much smaller. "These are diamonds."

It took a moment for Sarah to realize what he was telling her. She pointed to the green stone and said, "Emerald."

"Yes," Naa'il replied.

Sarah pointed to a white stone and said, "Diamond."

"Yes, very good." Naa'il's smile broadened.

Then Sarah pointed to the yellow metal that held the stones together. "What is?"

"That is gold."

Sarah glanced down at the yellow thread in her paru. It shined like the gold holding the stones together. She wondered if they were related. Sarah pointed to the gold in the necklace and then to the yellow in her paru. She looked up at Naa'il and asked, "This same?"

"Yes. You are very clever," Naa'il said, looking at Sarah with a gaping jaw.

Sarah crinkled her brows together when she heard another word that she didn't recognize. "What is 'clever'?"

"Clever means smart."

"Smart" was a word she recognized. Sarah's puzzled expression turned into a frown. "Why you not think I smart?" she blurted out.

Naa'il raised his hand to strike her.

Sarah jumped up from the bench and backed away until she was at a safe distance when she spotted his sneer and threatening eyes. Her father taught her to use humor to ease tense situations. Sarah bit her lip and said, "I sorry. I no understand … I no wish hurt you." Those were the only words that came to her thought. She hoped that they were enough to weaken his anger.

Naa'il lowered his arm. "You are right; you are new here. We do not know each other. I should not punish you for your ignorance." He studied her. "Do you understand me?"

Sarah shook her head.

Naa'il laughed and patted the bench. "Sit, I will not hurt you. You understand me now?"

"Aye," but Sarah was still hesitant to move.

Naa'il laid her necklace on the bench and approached her. Looking into her eyes, he repeated, "I will not hurt you."

"My English bad." She whispered.

Naa'il cupped her cheeks with his hands and kissed her forehead. "Yes, English is a complicated language. It took me years to learn to speak it properly."

"You help me with English?"

"No, I will teach you my language and our ways." Naa'il retrieved Sarah's necklace and said, "May I?"

Sarah answered with a reluctant nod.

Naa'il locked the jeweled choker around her neck and stepped back to admire his prize. "I thought this necklace would suit you." He asked, "Do you understand me?"

Sarah shook her head.

"You are beautiful," he sighed.

"Thank you," she said in Polynesian. Naa'il's blank stare hinted that he didn't understand her. Sarah wanted him to know that she was grateful for his kindness. "Thank you," she said in English before kissing the back of his hand.

"It is my great pleasure, my sweet Sarah." Naa'il caressed her cheek again. "Come, I have more to show you." He led her back to the bench and waited for her to sit before sitting beside her. "This is for you," he laid the bag on her lap.

Sarah's eyes twinkled as her fingers traced the embroidered flowers on the silk fabric. The bag's color reminded her of the turquoise water in her island's lagoon.

"Open it," Naa'il said.

Sarah peeked inside the bag. Her eyes gleamed when she spotted an inch-thick stack of blank parchment paper.

"May I?" Naa'il took the bag from her and removed a small canvas pouch. He winked and peeled back the edges of the bundle.

Sarah gasped when she spotted a rainbow of sticks. She picked up the green one and asked, "What is?"

Naa'il winked at her and drew a line with a blue pastel. Sarah stared at the line as if he had performed a magical feat. She then drew a line with her green one and proceeded to draw lines with the rest of the colors.

"This is how we will communicate," Naa'il said after Sarah finished testing her entire collection.

At first, Sarah didn't understand what Naa'il was saying. Soon she realized that he offered her a way to communicate with him when he pointed to her and then to the piece of paper and said, "Your home."

Sarah turned the parchment over and drew a picture of her island using almost every color in her collection. "Tikutoa, my home," she said after completing her drawing.

Naa'il didn't acknowledge her explanation. He just stared at her picture with astonishment. "Who taught you how to draw?"

Sarah bit her lip. "Um, Me," Sarah pointed to herself, "Da."

"I do not understand." Naa'il frowned.

Sarah pulled out a clean parchment from the stack and drew a little girl with her parents, each dressed in true Polynesian fashion. The man wore only a sackcloth over his man parts; the woman a paru, and the little girl wore nothing at all. Sarah pointed to the man and said, "Me Da."

Naa'il stared disapprovingly at Sarah's family and said, "Your father."

"Aye," Sarah nodded. "You family?"

"Yes." Naa'il pointed to the woman and held up two fingers. "I have two wives." He pointed to the girl and held up four fingers. "I have four daughters."

Sarah bit her bottom lip and said, "You two wifes?"

"Yes, my faith allows men to have as many as four." Naa'il pointed to the woman again and held up four fingers.

Sarah pointed to the man and held up two fingers. "My island, woman can have."

"Women on your island can have two husbands?" Naa'il clarified.

"Aye."

"Did you have a husband?" Naa'il asked.

A knock on the door interrupted Sarah's reply.

Naa'il left her sitting on the bench to answer the door. Two servants stood in the hall holding trays of food. Naa'il barked instructions; they bustled into the room and set up their dinner by the cushions near the windows. The servants left and returned carrying a stained-glass lantern in each hand. One hung two from the ceiling while the other placed the remaining lamps on the floor near the food. The servants bowed to Naa'il and backed out of the room.

Just then, Poe' trotted into the chamber as though Naa'il called her to dinner. The kitten sniffed the cushions and the food. Sarah took an empty bowl and retrieved some water for Poe'. She returned just in time to watch Naa'il taunting her kitten. Poe's eyes followed Naa'il's hand as it moved a small fish all around her head before tossing her dinner across the room. The Dey threw his head back and laughed when Poe' skidded across the smooth floor. And wham! She collided with the opposite wall. His laughter stopped when he caught Sarah smiling at him as she carried a bowl of water.

She placed the bowl next to the cushion and sat down beside Naa'il. She pinched off a grape from the cluster and said, "Grape," in Arabic before handing it to Naa'il.

"Very good," Naa'il arched his brow.

That night Naa'il introduced Sarah to couscous. She liked the dish's savory smell before she had even tasted it. Naa'il dipped his thumb, pointer, and middle finger into the bowl and lifted the bite to his mouth. She could almost see Hassan's disapproval of her eating this meal with her fingers, and yet she was relieved not being required to use a fork or spoon.

"Try it," Naa'il gently encouraged her.

She dipped her fingers into the bowl and lifted a bite to her mouth. She closed her eyes and savored the food's unexpected flavors. Her people only used sea water to season their meals. This dish was a blend of sweet, savory, and spice.

"Do you like it?"

Sarah replied with an energetic nod and took a few more bites. She would have gladly finished the dish had she not been sharing it with Naa'il. Sarah moved on to the meats and the vegetables. Each was as tasty as the other. Naa'il broke off a piece from a brown mound and handed it to Sarah.

"This is bread," Naa'il said after she gave him a quizzical look. He broke off a piece for himself and popped it into his mouth.

Giving into her curiosity, Sarah took a bite and was surprised by its sweet flavor. She eagerly broke off another piece and took another bite and another. Once they finished their dinner, Naa'il handed her a bowl of water with a white flower floating on the top. She lifted the bowl to her nose to smell the flower's sweet scent. Sarah was about to take a sip when Naa'il set his dish in front of him and dunked his fingers into the water before wiping his hands with a cloth. Sarah grinned when she realized that Naa'il valued cleanliness as much as she did.

"Now for dessert." Naa'il set aside the dishes from their main course and moved a smaller bowl filled with grapes and other colorful foods in front of them. He picked up a small red ball and said, "Melon. Be careful of the seeds." After picking out the black seeds, he took a bite before encouraging Sarah to sample it.

Sarah took a piece of melon and plucked out the seeds before taking a bite. Her eyes closed and a faint smile graced her lips when its sweet juices filled her mouth. Sarah sampled the other fruits in the bowl. Each was as sweet as the other. Though she didn't know what she was eating, the only thing she knew was that she could be contented eating this food for the rest of her life. After they finished their dessert, they cleaned their hands again. For the first time since she left her island, she ended her meal with a full belly.

Naa'il went over to the door and invited the same men into the room. He barked an order, and they began removing the empty plates of food. Once the servants had left them, Naa'il attempted to teach Sarah other phrases in his language. She had no idea of the words' meaning. She knew that he was frustrated by the way he groaned and massaged his temples with his fingers. Still wanting to communicate with him, Sarah retrieved her pastels and parchment paper. By that time, Poe' had curled up beside Naa'il. While he mindlessly petted the sleeping kitten, Sarah drew pictures of her island, the life she left behind, and her journey to this part of the world.

Naa'il's eyes grew heavy as the evening wore on. Sarah laid her drawings aside and retrieved a blanket.

"No, I must go." Naa'il stood up and walked to the door.

Sarah answered with a sad nod.

He caressed her cheek with the back of his fingers. "I will see you tomorrow morning. Pleasant dreams, my sweet Sarah." Naa'il kissed her cheek and left her apartment.

Still wide awake, Sarah continued drawing as she reflected on her day. For as terrifying as it began, it blossomed into one of the happiest days since her wedding night. She still missed Hassan and desperately wanted to be with him. As thoughts of him filled her mind, her hand mindlessly picked up a brown pastel and began drawing his face. She still had no idea if he was alive or dead – or even if she would ever see him again. Still, she refused to give up hope that they would be reunited. When Sarah finally closed her eyes, her last thought was how similar Naa'il was to her father.

Hassan worked tirelessly alongside his crew to repair the damages to the ships. Working was the only thing that took his mind off his concern for Sarah. The repairs to both vessels were progressing, but not nearly fast enough. Both ships would be ready to sail in a day or two. At his crew's insistence, Hassan gave in to his body's exhaustion and retired to his quarters. A faint grin formed on his lips when he spotted the plate of food waiting for him on his dining table. He approached it as if it were a homing device, yet all he could do was nibble and stare out the window at the stars sparkling against the velvet black sky.

Peter knocked, cracked the door ajar and poked his head through the opening. "May I speak to you?"

The captain motioned to his doctor to enter. "Please. How are the wounded?"

Peter stepped into Hassan's quarters and closed the door behind him. He sat beside his captain and said, "They are resting, and you have already taken care of the dead. Are you still concerned about Sarah?"

"I can't imagine what she is feeling right now. I feel so damn helpless."

"I recognize that now may not be the best time to discuss this with you, but I'm curious what you intend to do with Sarah should you find her?"

Hassan cocked his head and gave his friend a quizzical glance. "I plan to take her to England. Why do you ask?"

Peter hesitated, "I would like you to consider leaving Sarah in Algiers."

"Are you mad? I have no intention of allowing her to spend the rest of her life as a slave."

"Please, hear what I have to say. I do not make this suggestion to be cruel. I believe that Sarah will be happier in Algiers. The customs on her island are closer to the Ottoman's than they are to the Anglo-Saxon's. Sarah is a very sweet and beautiful young woman. Although she is a slave, I am certain that her master will treasure her as much as you do."

"This part of the world also values a woman's virginity …. Sarah is no longer a virgin," Hassan grimaced. "That is my doing." He looked down at his lap and paused. "I wouldn't have compromised her had I not intended to keep her."

"Then you intend to marry her."

"Yes, she makes me happy," Hassan said emphatically.

"Nathan, please …."

"No!" Hassan shouted. "Sarah's mine and I will not give her up. Return to your duties and never raise this subject again."

Peter rose from the table and headed to the exit. Resting his hand on the latch, he looked back at Hassan and said, "Sarah's not worth risking your crew's freedom or their lives, especially after she betrayed you."

Hassan's lips parted. "What are you saying?"

"Sarah kissed me on the night that you fell ill. I had to push her away to remind her of her allegiance to you. She behaved as if she didn't care if you lived or died."

Hassan shivered when a sudden cold hit the core of his body. "We must finish our mission, Doctor."

Peter hung his head. "Very well; I will leave you with this final thought. There is a reason why botanists do not transplant tropical plants to cold climates like England. They understand that these plants cannot survive the harsh environment. British customs are opposite to hers. Sarah may find the British society too harsh for her, and it *will* be harsh by her standards. I doubt that she is strong enough to endure it."

"So be it. Will you excuse me, please?" Hassan said tersely. He threw his plate against the bulkhead as soon as Peter closed the door.

CHAPTER 30

"You are not feeling better, Da?" Sarah frowned when her father pulled out another clump of hair from his head. Bracing his hand on her arm, he attempted to pull himself up before collapsing onto his berth. He had been sick for months; it wasn't until they reached the coasts of Africa that his condition grew worse.

"How can I not be well when you are here to keep me company? Here, help me up, lass," Thomas said cheerfully as he reached for Sarah's hand.

"You do not look good. You should rest, and I will ask for more medicine." She kissed her father's forehead. "I will return soon." Removing her paru, Sarah dressed in a pair of breeches and a peasant shirt and scampered out of their quarters. The ocean was particularly rough that day. Teetering back and forth, Sarah grabbed hold of anything that was within an arm's reach to steady herself as she made her way to the quarterdeck. Emile stood beside his captain.

"What are you doing here? You should stay below deck with your father," Emile exclaimed as the rain pelted them.

"Da ill. Help, please," Sarah pleaded.

Emile and Gerard looked at each other as if they shared a secret. With a nod from the French captain, Emile said, "Come with me; I will give him some more medicine." The doctor retrieved a little red wine and added a drop of clear liquid. "Red wine always makes medicine taste better." He stared at the liquid with his lips pressed together. *"Your father is very ill. I am not confident that I can save him, but this should ease his pain."*

Sarah was too concerned about her father to notice that Emile couldn't look her in the eyes. "Thank you," *she said with a broad grin before scampering back to her father.*

Emile held up the same pewter mug and shouted. "This killed your father!"

"No," Sarah whimpered, her head thrashing from side to side.

"I cannot help your father. You killed him with the poison you fed him," said Peter Hyatt.

"Te pe'ape'a nei au," Sarah cried and opened her eyes when she felt someone shaking her. She sat up and realized that she was in her beautiful apartment. Naa'il was sitting beside her, speaking to her in a soothing voice. He looked at her tenderly as he caressed her cheeks. Fighting back her tears, she flung her arms around his neck and whispered, "Da!"

"Shhh, it's alright," Naa'il said, enveloping her in his arms.

"I dreamt that I killed you," Sarah whimpered in her own language.

Naa'il pulled her away and gave her a puzzled look. "What did you say?"

Sarah bit her lip when Naa'il didn't understand her. She took a deep breath and said in English. "It … bad dream. I … sorry."

"All is well. You are safe." Naa'il kicked off his slippers and moved to the other side of the pillow. "Come here," he said, laying down beside her. Sarah entered his arms willingly.

She felt more like herself when their breakfast arrived. They ate in the same place where they had their dinner. The food, of course, was different. This morning, Naa'il introduced Sarah to M'shewsha; Poe' contently ate another fish. Not knowing if Tess and Molly had eaten, Sarah set aside two slices of M'shewsha and several helpings of fruit.

Naa'il sipped the last of his tea and wiped the corner of his mouth with his muslin napkin. "I must leave you." He went to the door and instructed the servants to remove their breakfast dishes. One of the men picked up the tray of food.

Sarah touched Naa'il's arm and said, "I keep food."

"Of course," Naa'il barked out a command to the one holding the tray. The servant bowed and returned the food to the floor.

Sarah followed Naa'il and the servants to the door. "I see you again?" she asked after the servants exited the apartment.

"Yes, of course." Naa'il kissed her cheek. He stepped out of the room and returned with Tess and Molly. "Enjoy your day."

"Beautiful necklace," Tess said in a casual tone as she scanned Sarah from head to toe. Balancing Molly on her hip, Tess strolled into Sarah's apartment as if it belonged to her. She lowered her daughter to the floor, and Molly immediately began chasing Poe'. Tess scanned the room until her eyes fell upon Sarah's drawings lying on the bench beside the basket of parus. She sat down on the bench and shifted the stack to her lap.

"Did you draw these?" Tess gave Sarah a casual glance after examining the drawing of Sarah's island.

"Aye."

Tess continued sifting through the stack. She examined each drawing one at a time before moving on to the next. "You are very talented." She said before examining the next one in the stack. Her breath hitched, and her lips parted when her eyes fell on the portrait of Hassan. She held up the picture and asked with a casual interest, "Do you know him?"

"Aye, he Cattin – my husband." Sarah's cheeks burned when Tess gave her a murderous glare. "You … know him?"

"He's Molly's father."

Shivers spiked up and down her spine when she remembered hearing the name – Nathan. "No," Sarah gasped. "He say his wife die. He say he not have wife."

"We're *not* married," Tess retorted, "but we were in love. He promised to take Molly and me away from here."

Sarah rested her hand on her stomach, and her whole body felt numb. "No, it not true."

Tess held out her hand and said in a firm voice. "Come here, Molly."

"Yes, Mama," Molly said as she triumphantly held the kitten in her arms while Poe' mewed to protest her capture.

Tess held her daughter in front of her and said, "I understand that you have only been here for a few days. You've been here long enough to notice that His Lordship and the other men in this region have dark skin. As you can see, Molly's skin is white. The people from the British Isles are the only ones with white skin." Tess glanced down at her daughter before looking back at Sarah. "Men with light skin are few and far between in this Palace. Nathan Shelby was a frequent visitor. I know this because I entertained him every time that he came."

"No," Sarah shook her head again. She couldn't deny that Molly's skin was lighter than the other men that she had met. Her hair was also a similar color to Hassan's. Otherwise, they looked nothing alike. Still, Sarah couldn't explain the similarities between the two – other than Hassan was her father.

"Go play in the garden." Tess released Molly's arm and waited until they were alone. "Why is that so hard for you to believe that your husband and I were in love? Seeing you wear His Lordship's necklace makes me wonder if you loved Nathan at all."

"No, I love Cattin; I wait for him," Sarah insisted.

Tess jumped to her feet and squared her shoulders. "I'll bet you do." Tess leaned into Sarah. "I think you will love any man who will take care of you. If you had to choose between Nathan and His Lordship, you would choose His Lordship because he treats you like a bloody princess. Your fancy necklace and your fancy apartment are proofs of them, aren't they? You must be a bloody good lover for him to give you all this."

For the first time in her limited comprehension of the English language, Sarah knew exactly what she wanted to say. She squared her shoulders with her legs splayed apart and her fists by her side. "Leave," she shouted.

Mamnoon rushed into the room without knocking. His eyes darted between the two women with worry lines etched on his brow. "Is there a problem?"

"You leave. No come back," Sarah shouted.

Mamnoon's hand hooked around Tess's arm. "Come, Tess, and bring your daughter. I will return you to the harem," Mamnoon said calmly.

Tess sneered. "Fine. I don't want to spend another minute with this whore." Tucking Hassan's portrait under her arm, she picked up Molly and headed to the door. Tess had almost reached the exit before looking back at Sarah. "Don't get too comfortable in this room. The last two people who stayed here only lasted a few days before His Lordship tired of their company."

"Come, Tess." Mamnoon tugged on her arm before she could say anything else.

Tears streaming down her cheeks, Sarah glanced at her reflection in the mirror. She hadn't done anything wrong, she told herself. Her heart still belonged to Hassan. She would leave with him if he came for her. Seeing the gems sparkling back at her made Sarah feel like she had betrayed her husband. She tugged and tugged on her necklace until it drew blood, but her sparkling shackle refused to budge.

Naa'il ambled down the corridor with a spring in his step. The heaviness in his heart over Cora's death had started to fade, and the hope for a happy future was dawning. The position of the sun's rays reminded him that he should have reported to the slave yard over an hour ago. Thinking about his family, he mindlessly turned down the corridor leading to his wives' apartments. Samina, he was told, was already in the harem. She wouldn't return for hours. Naa'il continued on his path until he reached Mariam's apartment.

The Dey leaned against the arched doorway with a broad grin on his lips as he watched Mariam hold court with his daughters. Their youngest,

Zeba, sat on her lap. She looked up at her mother as if she were an angel while her sisters stood around them. For as plain as she was, Mariam's face was radiant when she spoke to her daughters in her usual loving tone. She listened to their every word with her undivided attention. For as little or as much as she was to him, Naa'il couldn't deny that Mariam was a good mother to his children, perhaps even the best.

"Babba," his second oldest daughter called out. Laila was the most outgoing of her sisters.

Naa'il squatted on the floor and held out his arms to his daughters. "Come here, my darlings." Laila was the only one to run into her father's arms.

"Go to your father," Mariam said sternly when Laila's sisters didn't budge.

The oldest, Yasmine, took her sister, Nahla's hand and pulled her towards their father. Naa'il pursed his lips when he spotted his daughters' reluctance.

"Forgive them, my Lord. It has been a long while since the last time they saw you," Mariam explained.

"They are right; I have been neglecting my children. I promise to change my ways." Naa'il stood aside as Mariam's attendants filed out of the room.

"We missed you, Babba," said Yasmine.

"And I missed you, my darling." Naa'il kissed his eldest daughter's forehead. He wrapped his arms around his children and pressed them against his chest. The girls squealed with glee as they tumbled onto their father.

"Now, children, let your father stand," Mariam said in her matronly voice.

Propping himself up on his elbow, Naa'il studied his wife as she gently pulled his daughters off him. He had forgotten how beautiful Mariam's smile could be. When she smiled, she smiled with her whole face. Taking her slender hand, he pulled himself to his feet and wondered if he could be contented having only Mariam and their daughters for his family. This morning, his answer was yes.

"Let me have a look at you," Naa'il continued. Mariam had already lined his daughters up in a row in front of her, ranging from the eldest to the second youngest. Yasmine was nine and was quickly growing into an Arabian beauty. His eight-year old, Laila, was still a little girl, and yet it wasn't hard to imagine her growing into a beautiful woman. Nahla, his second youngest was five. She also had a sweet face and her mother's reserve. Finally, his three-year-old Zeba's playful demeanor always made him laugh. At that moment, little Zeba hid behind her mother's green and gold hirka. Ignoring his youngest, Naa'il continued his inspection. "You all have grown since the last time I saw you. It will not be long before I need to find husbands for you."

"Not yet, Babba," Laila insisted. "I want to be with you a while longer."

"That pleases me more than I can say." Naa'il caressed his daughter's soft cheek. The Dey straightened his back and pretended not to notice his youngest peeking up at him from behind her blue blanket with her thumb in her mouth. "Now, where is my little Zeba?"

"She is still a little shy," Mariam smiled apologetically.

Undaunted, Naa'il strolled behind Mariam, looking everywhere in the room but at his daughter. "Where oh where is my little Zeba. My heart is so saddened that I cannot see her."

She tugged on her father's maroon pant leg and looked up at him with a playful grin. "Here I am."

Naa'il's face lit up with a bright smile when he looked down at his daughter. "There is my precious, Zeba." Naa'il scooped up his youngest into his arms and hugged her. "How pleased I am to see you."

Zeba giggled and hugged her father back.

"Let us adjourn to the garden," Naa'il suggested as he looked to Mariam for her approval.

"Of course," Mariam said. "I will send for refreshments."

Molly cried in her mother's arms as Mamnoon escorted them back to the harem. He glanced over at Tess who seemed too distraught to hold a conversation. She just stared ahead with her lips slightly parted as she trudged down the corridor. Molly's tears dried up when she spotted her friends playing together. Tess lowered her daughter to the floor; Molly broke away from her mother and scampered over to her friends.

Mamnoon followed Molly over to the group and said to the women watching their children, "Please watch Molly until Tess and I return to the harem." Tess remained motionless by the exit. "Come, let us talk in private." He grabbed her arm and took her to a private room adjacent to the harem.

Tess still remained motionless after Mamnoon ushered her inside and closed the door behind them. "Come, let us sit." Mamnoon extended his hand to the cushions beneath the window. Tess answered with a faint nod and followed her friend to the seating area. Mamnoon waited for Tess to sit before taking a seat beside her. "What happened between you and Sarah?"

Tess unfolded Hassan's portrait. Her eyes glistened with tears spilling onto her cheek as she stared at the picture with a quivering lip. "This is Molly's father," she mumbled.

He took the portrait and studied it as doubts flooded his mind. "So this is Molly's father. You speak of him often. However, you have never uttered his name until now."

"He is Molly's father. I swear it," she said defensively.

"We have always been honest with each other. It is prudent that we be honest now. If I recall, your child was already growing inside you when you arrived at the Palace. I know you tried hard to conceal Molly. It wasn't until after your child was born that you were called on to entertain the European and English-speaking guests."

Anger flashed in Tess's brown eyes. "Nathan promised that he would take Molly and me away from here."

"Did he tell you that?"

"Yes, of course he did. He loved me," Tess insisted.

His face, wrenching in pain, Mamnoon jumped to his feet and stood with his back to her. He covered his mouth with his hand.

"You know something."

Mamnoon turned and faced his friend, but he couldn't bring himself to look her in the eyes.

Tess stood up and approached Mamnoon. "I can tell that you are keeping something from me. I have a right to know what it is."

Mamnoon swallowed hard and said, "His Excellency knew you entertained Nathan Shelby exclusively. One night, His Excellency commanded me to inquire about offering you as a gift. Shelby declined."

A gasp escaped from Tess's lips. "Did he say why?"

"No."

Tess straightened her shoulders and held her head high. "That doesn't mean anything. You know corsairs' lives are fraught with danger. Nathan declined because he believed that Molly and I would be safer living in the Palace."

Mamnoon looked away. "Perhaps."

"What?" Tess bit her quivering lip. "What did Nathan tell you?"

"Captain Shelby did not say anything, other than he felt that it was best for you to remain here." Mamnoon didn't have the heart to tell his friend that Hassan showed no signs of being in love with her when he presented Naa'il's offer. His mannerisms were just the opposite, cold and unattached. Mamnoon was sure that Hassan knew that he was one of Tess's many lovers.

Tess hugged herself and said. "Nathan didn't love me, did he?"

"Captain Shelby did not say one way or another." Mamnoon paused and thought back to Tess's confrontation from earlier that morning. "Why were you so angry with Sarah?"

"She had the audacity to tell me that she and Nathan were married. Can you believe that? Why would she say such a thing?"

"Why would Sarah lie? She could not have known about your history with Captain Shelby," Mamnoon pointed out.

"Why would Nathan do such a thing when he loved me?"

"You know that I cannot answer your question. I am curious about why you chose to set your affections on him?"

Tess looked at her friend with love in her eyes. "Because Nathan was a gentleman, a real gentleman. I liked the way that he treated me. He made love to me with a tenderness that I have never known before." Tess said as tears filled her eyes. "Why doesn't he love me?"

"I can't answer that. Molly loves you; I care for you. In my humble opinion, Captain Shelby is unworthy of you." Mamnoon wrapped his arms around his friend's shoulders and pressed her against him. He kissed her forehead and said, "Do not blame Sarah for Shelby's treachery. She is not a cruel person."

Tess pulled away and looked at Mamnoon. "Isn't she? Sarah professes to love Nathan, yet she betrayed him by giving herself to His Lordship."

"As you know, Sarah tried to kill herself when His Excellency forced himself on her."

Tess pulled away and crossed her arms. "Aye, I know. Now they behave like they are bloody in love. I am certain that they are lovers."

"I have not seen evidence to confirm your suspicion. Even if she and His Excellency were lovers, Sarah may live in an apartment. She may wear beautiful jewels, but she is *still* an odalisque – like you. I am certain that she is doing what is necessary to survive. You are no different. You profess to love Captain Shelby, and yet you have shared a bed with many men."

"I have no choice." Tess insisted. "I am just a slave."

"So is Sarah. Even His Excellency's wives are slaves of sorts."

"His Lordship fancies Sarah," Tess pointed out.

"As you know; His Excellency is fickle."

Tess glanced up at the sunlight streaking through the window. "Did His Lordship love Cora?"

"Yes, I believe that he did. Cora's death was very difficult for him to bear. It is remarkable that he wanted to marry her after ordering men to violate her."

"Did Cora love him?"

"I believe that she cared for him. But I am uncertain that she loved him."

"I wish I had been kinder to Cora. I think that we would have been friends."

"Yes, I think that you would have been. Come, I should return to the harem before Molly discovers that you are missing." Mamnoon extended his hand to her.

She took his hand and said, "Thank you for being a good friend."

"I am sorry if I hurt you."

"No, once again, you made me come to my senses. I suppose that I should apologize to Sarah."

"Yes, you should. I must tell His Excellency about what transpired between you two. He will decide if you will continue as one of Sarah's attendants."

"I think that we both know His Lordship's answer. It's a pity. I enjoyed sleeping on me own pillow," Tess sighed.

"His Excellency may decide to allow you to remain as Sarah's companion," Mamnoon said as they walked back to the harem.

"I doubt it. Thank you again for listening to me," Tess rolled up on her toes and kissed Mamnoon's cheek before rejoining her daughter.

Mamnoon turned to leave when he heard the voice of the last person that he wanted to see calling his name. He rolled his hand into a fist and turned around slowly. "Yes," he said through gritted teeth. His lips parted when he spotted her blood-shot eyes. Mamnoon had spent little time in the harem ever since Cora's death. Abigail was usually in a corner, weeping during the few times that he saw her. It was difficult to pity her after seeing the way that she treated her cousin. Even now, he still wanted to strangle her. Out of love for Cora, he suppressed his rage.

Abigail approached Mamnoon with the same caution as a person approaching a wild animal. "I know that you hate me. May I speak to you in private - please?" She lowered her eyes to the floor, "I promise to be civil."

Mamnoon nodded. "Come with me." He escorted Abigail to the

same room where he and Tess talked.

Abigail crept into the center of the room. She held her hands tight around her middle with her hands clutching her elbows.

Mamnoon closed the door and remained standing at the exit.

She turned and faced him with a tortured look on her face. "I am sure that you are wondering why I wanted to speak to you," she said after an awkward silence.

"Yes," Mamnoon replied in a quiet voice.

"Naa'il … I mean His Excellency told me that Cora was … you know. She sacrificed herself to protect me."

"You are correct."

Tears filled her blue eyes; her bottom lip quivered. "I know that you cared for my cousin; why didn't you help her escape?"

"I tried on several occasions. I could have gotten Cora safely out of the Palace; I was even prepared to flee with her."

"Cora wouldn't leave without me," Abigail surmised.

"Yes, Cora feared that you would suffer the same fate that she did had His Excellency discovered the truth. Even if he did not, I could not get you both out."

"So, she suffered because of me." Abigail's whimpers turned into sobs as she hugged herself. "I know you won't believe me, but I *am* sorry about what happened. I'm sorry I was cruel to her. Cora didn't deserve it."

"No, she did not," Mamnoon said in a softened tone.

"What do I do now?"

"For the moment, you are under His Excellency's protection."

"Yes, His Excellency told me. He also told me that I will never leave the harem," Abigail reasoned.

"It is not likely. Be grateful for Cora's sacrifice. She is the reason that you will never be used as a concubine."

Abigail shuddered as she continued hugging herself. "I am," she said in a small voice.

"If I were you, I would find a way to repay your debt to your cousin."

"How? How do you repay a debt like that?"

"I would devote every day of the rest of my life proving myself worthy of her sacrifice. You will accomplish this not by a single good deed, but a lifetime of them."

Abigail wiped a tear from her eye and nodded, "I understand why my cousin cared for you. I *am* sorry for the way that I treated you."

Mamnoon swallowed hard. Though he still wasn't ready to forgive Abigail, he knew Cora would want him to set aside his anger and offer her his friendship. "I forgive you. I should return you to the harem."

Abigail nodded. "Thank you for talking with me. Perhaps we can talk again?" she asked as they walked back to the harem.

"Perhaps," Mamnoon said even though he doubted they would ever speak again.

Naa'il spent the whole day with Mariam and his children. They talked; they told stories; they ate; they laughed. Naa'il couldn't help thinking that Cora would be pleased to see him passing a perfect day with his wife and children. Then it ended when the governesses came to collect his daughters.

"Thank you for taking time away from your work to be with our children. It meant the world to them. I am certain that they will remember this day fondly for the rest of their lives," Mariam said once they were alone.

"So will I. It has been too long since I passed a morning or a day with our children. I apologize for being away." Naa'il squeezed his wife's hand.

"You have had much on your mind during these past few weeks."

"There is no excuse for ignoring my children. I shall not do it again." Naa'il slid his arms around Mariam's waist. "I know we have not always agreed on matters."

"No." Mariam laughed faintly.

Naa'il looked thoughtfully at his wife. "You understand me. I think we should try to make another son. I still need an heir, and I want you to give him to me."

"What about Samina?"

"I care for Samina, but you are a better mother." Naa'il kissed her.

Naa'il and Mariam had finished dressing each other when the governesses returned with his children the following morning.

"Babba," his daughters said in unison as they swarmed their father.

"Good morning, my darlings." Naa'il squatted and hugged each one. Only Zeba insisted that her father carry her.

"Did you stay with Mama the entire night?" Yasmine asked.

"Yes, I did," Naa'il replied.

"Are we going to have another sister?" Laila probed.

"Laila!" Mariam snapped.

Lowering Zeba to the floor, Naa'il squatted in front of his second daughter. He rested his hand on Laila's waist and said, "It is too early to know if your mother is with child. You are right; I would like to give you a brother."

"Not a brother!" Nahla groaned.

"Your father is right, it is too soon to say if I am with child," Mariam said, resting her hand on her belly.

Servants delivered their breakfast; the family continued their visit while feasting in the courtyard. They were all too deeply engaged in their conversation to notice Zeba wandering into her mother's room or opening a small chest and pulling out a green vial.

"Zeba, put that down!" Mariam jumped to her feet and ran over to her daughter. Zeba had already uncorked the bottle by the time her mother snatched it from her. Mariam recorked the vial and returned it to the small jeweled chest.

"There, there," Naa'il said, picking up his crying child. "What the devil just happened?" he demanded as Mariam placed the chest out of her daughters' reach.

"It is nothing," Mariam blushed.

Cuddling against her father's chest, Zeba put her thumb in her mouth. Immediately, she began gasping for breath.

"Zeba!" Naa'il shouted, shaking her vigorously.

"Mama," she said in a weak voice before closing her eyes forever.

"No," Mariam cried in a blood-curdling scream.

Guards rushed in when they heard the first wife scream.

"Send for the healer," Naa'il shouted after laying the child on the pillow bed. "Take my daughters out of here. Now!" He barked to the governesses.

"Come, children," the nurses said, tugging on the girl's hands.

Mariam crouched beside her daughter. She took Zeba in her arms and pressed the child against her chest.

During the brief moment when they were alone, Naa'il shouted, "What have you done?"

Mariam couldn't answer.

Naa'il retrieved the chest and discovered five bottles identical to the one found in Bashira's chamber inside the chest.

The healer arrived moments later. She knelt beside Mariam and examined the child and said, "I am sorry. Your daughter is gone, and there is nothing that I can do for her."

"Take this." He handed the box to the healer. "The bottles are filled with poison. Dispose of the contents and return the box and vials to me."

The healer bowed. "Of course, Your Excellency. I am very sorry."

CHAPTER 31

Jamal was still in his apartment when he received the news about Zeba's death. His knees buckled as he fell onto this burnt-orange Persian rug. "No!" he cried out, holding his stomach as if someone had punched him. Jamal loved his youngest niece and her older sisters as if they were his own children. His eyes fell on the message lying beside him. He read it again and frowned. The note only informed him that his niece was dead. However, it didn't provide any details about how she died. Returning his thoughts to his sister, he pulled himself off the floor and raced to Mariam's apartment. Jamal's heart ached when he found his sister sitting alone on the bench in her garden, clutching Zeba's blue blanket.

Jamal touched her shoulder. "Mari," he said tenderly.

Mariam just stared at the fountain as if she hadn't heard him.

"I am so sorry."

Mariam looked at him with a tortured expression. "It was my fault," she whispered.

"What happened?"

"It began as a happy day. We were all together. Even Naa'il was here." Mariam told her brother about the events leading up to her daughter's death.

Jamal jumped up from the bench and went over to the fountain. With his back to his sister, he covered his eyes with his hand. There were so many questions that he wanted to ask her, including why she kept bottles of poison in her apartment. He knew there was nothing he could say that she wasn't already thinking. Jamal was equally sure that his beloved sister would have drunk the same poison had it not been confiscated.

Mariam looked up at her brother. "What am I going to do?"

Jamal returned to his sister's side. He sat beside her and held her hand. "I will not deny that this tragedy will haunt you for the rest of your life, but you are going to live through this. You must. Your daughters need you. In time, the pain will subside."

"What am I to do about Naa'il? He will never forgive me."

Jamal gently squeezed his sister's hand. "No, it is unlikely that he will. You will survive this too."

"How do you know that he won't have me stoned to death?"

"I won't let that happen. You should know by now that I will fight to the death for you. We will survive this. I promise."

The official Palace activities were suspended for three days of mourning out of respect for the Dey's family. All the women in Mariam's family gathered in a small room to clean Zeba's body. The only person who wasn't present was Mariam.

Naa'il arrived just after the women said their goodbyes. "Leave us," he barked.

"Take as long as you like. We will wait outside the room," said one of the women.

Naa'il nodded. Standing beside the table where his daughter laid, his fingers combed through her chocolate curls. Her body looked so small compared to the table that was sized to hold an adult. Naa'il leaned down and kissed his daughter's forehead, marveling how someone so small could bring him so much joy.

"Oh, my sweet child, how I will miss you. I will miss your smile and your little finger tracing the outline of my face. Above all, I will miss your sweet laugh." Naa'il paused and caressed her cheek. "I am sorry that I was not a good father to you. I should have spent more time with you and your sisters. I wish I had a good reason for staying away, but I was selfish." He whispered, "Be happy, my little Zeba." He looked up at the ceiling and said, "Please take care of her and send Cora to watch over her." Looking down at his child, Naa'il smiled tenderly and said, "I love you, Zeba. I look forward to the day when we can see each other again." He kissed her forehead and left the room. "You may continue," he said to the women standing in the corridor.

They wrapped Zeba's body in white muslin. That afternoon, family and friends gathered for the Salāt al-Janāzah funeral prayer. By the evening, Zeba was buried with her head facing the homeland.

Naa'il lingered by his daughter's grave while his family and friends departed.

Samina approached him and rested her hand on his shoulder. "I am so sorry, Naa'il. What can I do to help you?"

Naa'il didn't stir to his wife's entreating. He tore his gaze from Zeba's grave when Samina pressed him again. "You can help me by being a dutiful wife. Return to your apartment," he said tersely.

The last of the guests left, or so Naa'il thought. He hadn't noticed Mamnoon's approach.

"Your Excellency," the servant bowed his head. "I am so sorry for your loss. Please let me know if there is anything I can do for you."

Naa'il jumped when he heard Mamnoon's baritone voice. Still, his servant's soothing tone was comforting. He looked up at Mamnoon with a thoughtful expression. "Thank you. You can assist me by doing your duty."

"Of course."

"Wait," Naa'il called out just as Mamnoon turned away. "Bring John Montgomery to my apartment."

"Consider it done, Your Excellency." He nodded and walked away.

Naa'il returned his attention to his daughter. He wiped a tear from the corner of his eye and said, "Be happy, my darling, Zeba." Naa'il returned to his apartment and found a fire blazing in the hearth. Someone had placed a bowl of fruit on the table in front of the couch. He went into his bedroom and retrieved Cora's Bible. After sitting down on his couch, Naa'il opened the book even though he doubted that it would help him, let alone explain why his innocent child was taken from him. Still, he flipped through the pages in a desperate search for an answer. A knock at the door followed moments later. Tearing his gaze away from his book, Naa'il called out, "Enter."

The door opened, and Mamnoon and John entered his apartment. John bowed. Mamnoon's bow was delayed after spotting Cora's Bible lying open across the Dey's lap.

Naa'il bit the inside of his mouth when he spotted the disapproval on Mamnoon's pursed lips. He was sure that his servant had recognized the Christian book and understood the law forbidding people of his faith from reading religious books outside of his own. "Leave us." Naa'il calmly barked.

Mamnoon backed out of the apartment, closing the door behind him. John remained frozen with his torso bent at an angle at the hip.

"Sit," Naa'il commanded.

The servant straightened himself and took a seat in a red wing-back chair. "I am sorry to hear about your daughter, Your Excellency."

Naa'il winced. He glanced down at his Bible then back to John. "Is your god punishing me for persecuting one of his own?"

"Well, uh," John was taken back by the question. "Some in my faith would hold that opinion."

"But not you."

"Honestly, I cannot say, Your Excellency. Although I do believe that God sends challenges to chasten us to become better people. I have difficulty believing that God is cruel enough to take our children away from us." John said.

Naa'il looked down at his book. "I think that your God is punishing me." He knew by the way that John opened and closed his mouth that he wanted to ask why but was too afraid to pry. Still needing answers, Naa'il told Cora's story to his servant. "I acquired two American women over a month ago. One was a Christian of an unwavering faith; the other was a whore. I ... mistakenly concluded that the whore was the pure one ...." Like a sinner confessing his sins to a priest, Naa'il told John everything. The servant silently listened to the Dey's tale with a slack jaw. Naa'il's face burned with every detail that he provided. Seeing the shock on his servant's face made him want to stop, yet he pressed on to the end. "Cora was strong; she never once allowed me to see her defeated. I know her pain was great, but she never turned from her faith. I loved her for that reason. I wanted to marry her, and that is extraordinary because men of my faith do not marry impure women. It is simply not done, especially for a man of my importance. My first wife was bitterly opposed to my marriage to Cora. I did not care. Cora deserved better than to remain a lowly concubine." Naa'il stared at the flames dancing in the hearth as if he were in a trance. "I could have sent her home, but I loved her too much to part with her. Ironically, Cora was slain because of my selfishness." Naa'il paused as his lips curled into a faint smile. Tearing his gaze from the flames, he glanced over at his servant. "After all that she suffered at my command, Cora forgave me just before she died. My beloved daughter died from the same poison that killed my Cora. My heart is overcome with inconsolable grief, and all I can do now is ask, 'Why?'"

"I'm sorry, Your Excellency. I don't have an answer for you. I believe that God will watch over Cora and your daughter."

"Do you believe that your god would send Cora to watch over my Zeba?"

"I don't know. I believe that your daughter will be cared for."

"Thank you. Your comments are comforting. We will talk more tomorrow. That will be all, John." Naa'il leaned back in his seat as he watched his servant exit his apartment.

John stopped just before reaching the door. He turned and faced the Dey and said. "Cora sounds like she was a remarkable woman. If she cared enough to forgive you, I would think that she also would want you to forgive yourself, and in time, find peace."

Naa'il nodded. Leaning his head against the back of the couch, he closed his eyes as his mind drifted from Cora to Zeba, and then to his other daughters. He grimaced as the tension inside him began to churn when his thought rested on Mariam's fate. Deep down, he knew that Zeba's death was an accident, but Cora's death wasn't.

Naa'il pulled himself off his couch. With heavy footsteps, he wandered through the corridors like a spirit haunted from a previous life. His journey took him to the last place that he wanted to go. For as much as he wanted to pass by it, he couldn't resist entering Cora's torture chamber. It didn't surprise him to discover that someone had erased all traces of Cora's captivity. They removed the chains and the bolts from the wall and covered the holes with matching tiles. They had also replaced the soiled cushions with fresh ones, and cleaned and polished the blood-stained tiles. Anyone entering this room for the first time would never suspect the atrocities that had taken place in there. Even though the room was spotless, Naa'il couldn't prevent the shivers from spiking up and down his spine as Cora's pleas with Mamnoon to end her suffering echoed in his mind. He moved the cushion to the place where they ate their breakfast. He sat down, and a faint smile graced his lips as he remembered his conversations with the only woman that he had ever loved. "I wish I could talk to you. I need your wisdom now more than ever," Naa'il said as if she were sitting across from him. He could almost see her angelic face smiling back at him. Naa'il laughed to himself. "I know what you would say. You would encourage me to forgive Mariam. How can I forgive a person who took you and my little daughter from me?"

Jamal paced across Mariam's apartment. He was anxious to talk to Naa'il about his intentions towards his sister. Fearing that Mariam would take her life out of guilt over her part in her daughter's death, Jamal refused to leave her side.

Mariam sent her family and friends away after Zeba's burial. All she could do was sit on the bench in the garden and hug her daughter's blanket. The only reason she allowed Jamal to stay with her was because he refused to leave her. He glanced over at the plate of food sitting beside her and sighed, silently noting that not even a grape was missing from her plate.

Jamal sat beside his sister. He picked up the plate and held it in front of her. "Please eat something, Mari."

Mariam looked away. "I am not hungry."

"You have not eaten anything since yesterday. Take something from this plate. It is not beneath me to pin you down and force you to eat."

Mariam cracked a smile and plucked a grape from the cluster.

"Now, put it in your mouth," Jamal said when his sister hid the fruit in her hand.

"You never miss anything, do you?" She popped the grape into her mouth.

"Now chew, swallow, and repeat," Jamal gently ordered.

"You do not need to stay," she said, reaching for a piece of cheese.

"I am not leaving you, Mari."

Mariam took the plate and lowered it to her lap. "I will be alright – I promise."

"I know you will. I am going to make certain of that."

"Taskmaster," Mariam studied her brother and frowned. "Are you worried about my meeting with Naa'il?"

Jamal knitted his brows together. "What meeting?"

"The one where he decides my fate," she said, staring at her lap.

"Look at me. No harm will come to you. I will not allow it."

"You are too good to me, but I am not worthy of your protection."

"Yes, you are; now finish your dinner, and try to sleep."

Mariam surrendered to her exhaustion later that night. Jamal, on the other hand, was too worried about his sister's fate to sleep. He and Naa'il had known each other for years. During their long friendship, not once had he known Naa'il to show compassion to an enemy, and he was sure that Naa'il now regarded Mariam as one of them. A messenger arrived at her door the following morning.

"What is it," Mariam asked before Jamal closed the door.

"Naa'il wants to see you," he said with a grave expression.

"Very well," she said, heading to the door.

Jamal scanned Mariam's brown hirka for stains. "Mari, why not change your clothes first? You are still wearing the ones from yesterday."

Mariam shrugged. "Does it really matter? Besides, I should not keep Naa'il waiting. I will inform you of his decision when I return," she said as she attempted to brush past her brother.

Jamal blocked Mariam's path to the door. "I am going with you."

"You know that Naa'il will not permit you to be present at our meeting."

"Then I will stand outside the door until you leave the room."

"You still do not trust Naa'il, do you?"

"I understand him. Now change your clothes; I will wait for you in the hall." Jamal pressed a kiss to his sister's forehead. He stepped outside his sister's apartment and closed the door. Mariam appeared a few minutes later wearing various shades of maroon with black slippers. There was not a single jewel on her body, and Mariam loved gold and other jewels. Jamal couldn't remember the last time when she didn't wear a jeweled necklace, sparkling rings on her fingers, and gold bangles around her wrists. "Are you ready?"

"Yes," she answered.

"Naa'il's message instructed you to meet him in his private study," Jamal replied.

Naa'il spent the rest of the night walking through the corridors as he pondered Mariam's fate. It wasn't until he reached his office that he knew what he wanted to say. When he saw his wife, he couldn't decide whether to kill her or pity her. At age thirty, Mariam looked and moved like an old woman.

"So you were the one who provided the poison that killed my Cora." Standing by his desk, Naa'il held up the bottle that was confiscated from Bashira's chambers. "Can I assume that you are also responsible for poisoning my other American concubine?"

"Take my life if you wish; I do not want to discuss this."

Naa'il circled his prey, his movements slow and still. "Our daughter died from the same poison that you gave to my concubines," he said, his eyes never leaving his wife. "And now you are going to tell me why."

Mariam looked him in the eyes and hissed. "Because you drove me to it."

"I drove you to it," Naa'il repeated with disdain. "I gave you *everything*," he shouted.

Mariam stifled a laugh. "You are so innocent. You could not possibly do any wrong."

Naa'il gave his wife an incredulous stare. "Are you bitter because I invite concubines into my bed?"

"I could care less if you lie with every woman in the Ottoman Empire. The women of our faith bore you, don't we? Perhaps we are too compliant and too meek for you. Is that not why you are drawn to infidels like Cora Bradley. They are clever; they are educated, and they can think for themselves. You like the challenge that comes from wooing such a woman," Mariam shouted back.

"What if I do? You are my wife - my *first* wife, and I have never neglected my duty to you. Our four daughters are proof of that."

"I do not care if you never touch me again! I cringe at the way these infidels affect you!"

"I have not changed!" Naa'il shouted.

Mariam lifted her chin and met his accusing eyes without flinching. "Yes, you have. This Cora turned you away from your beliefs, and you are too blind to see it. I have devoted my life to our faith and protecting our family's honor and our way of life. You were going to destroy our good name by marrying this Christian," Mariam shouted back.

"Yes, I loved Cora. She was the best thing that had ever happened to me. She made me want to be a better husband, a better father, and a better man. Yes, she taught me the virtue of compassion, but that does not make me an apostate," he said, pinching her cheeks between his fingers. "I should make you drink the same poison that killed my beloved Cora and my little Zeba. I know that you would gladly take your life out of guilt for slaying our daughter, but I will not grant you that reward. Instead, you will pass many weary years in a small prison cell. You will never see or hear from your children again. Your thoughts will be your only company. After this meeting, I shall not think of you again. I divorce you; I divorce you; I divorce you."

Mariam closed her eyes when he pronounced his last divorce decree. Her nails digging into her arm was her only display of emotion. Mariam moved with heaviness when his guards led her away. Still, not a single tear fell from her eyes. Naa'il collapsed onto his chair, burying his face in his hand.

"What are you doing?" Jamal shouted. "Release her at once!"

Naa'il jumped up from his chair when he heard his brother-in-law's voice. Mariam was surrounded by four guards. Jamal blocked their path by waving his saber at them. Naa'il's soldiers stood at least a half head taller than Jamal. Each was an expert swordsman, but none of them wanted to take action against their revered Vizier.

"Your sister is under arrest. Do not interfere, Jamal," Naa'il said calmly.

"We shall see about that," Jamal said, glaring at the guards. He glanced at Naa'il and asked, "May we speak in private?"

Naa'il nodded and silently motioned instructions to his guard. The two tallest of the soldiers stepped away from Mariam and escorted Jamal to the door. "Leave your weapons with my guards," Naa'il commanded.

Jamal lowered his saber but was reluctant to surrender it.

"I will not grant you an audience unless you are unarmed." Naa'il maintained.

"Please, hand me your saber, Vizier," said one of the guards.

Jamal glanced at Mariam and Naa'il. He reluctantly lowered his weapon and gave it to the guard.

"All of them." Naa'il reminded his brother-in-law.

Rolling his eyes, Jamal retrieved several knives concealed in his brown cloak and surrendered them to the other guard. "Any other requests?"

Naa'il stepped aside and extended his arm towards his office. Jamal passed by him; the Dey closed the door. "You are not going to persuade me to change my mind, Jamal."

The Vizier turned and faced Naa'il. "I am not condoning my sister's actions. Please show Mariam mercy in this instance. Release her. Her guilt over Zeba's death is punishment enough."

His back straightened and his head held high, Naa'il glared at his brother-in-law with narrowed eyes. "No, my daughter died from the poison in Mariam's apartment."

Jamal mirrored Naa'il's stance. "You know that Zeba's death was an accident, a *tragic* accident."

"Perhaps, but my daughter was not the first person that Mariam slew."

Squaring his shoulders, Jamal crossed his arms. "Just who exactly did my sister slay when she is under constant guard?"

"Mariam poisoned Cora Bradley and another concubine,"

"What proof do you have that Mariam murdered these women?"

Naa'il retrieved the box that was confiscated from Mariam's apartment. Standing in front of his Vizier, he opened the lid. The inside was divided into six compartments. All but one section contained identical green bottles. "This was taken from Mariam's apartment. Each of these bottles was filled with the same poison." Setting the box on his desk, Naa'il retrieved the missing vial from his desk drawer. He held the bottle in front of his brother-in-law's face. "This was found in Bashira's apartment." Naa'il picked up one of the bottles from the box and held up the two side by side. "As you can see, this bottle is identical to the ones in the box," the Dey snarled. "Mariam had plenty of opportunities to give this to Bashira. I will never understand why she needed so many bottles of poison."

"That infidel was a slave! Her life does not matter," Jamal shouted.

"Cora mattered to me! She was stolen from me, just like my daughter. I cannot forgive Mariam for her treachery," Naa'il shouted over his brother-in-law.

Jamal edged in until their noses were almost touching. "Let this matter pass, or you will regret your actions," the Vizier said, emphasizing each word.

Naa'il stood back and squared his shoulders. "Are you threatening me?"

"You may interpret my actions any way you wish. I have heard many whispers as of late that you are turning from our faith. What do you think the Sultan will do after he discovers that you became an apostate? I can silence those whispers in exchange for showing mercy to my sister."

Naa'il stared down his nose at his brother-in-law. "You have no proof."

"I do not need proof. You were careless, Naa'il. At least a dozen people witnessed you reading the infidel's Bible. They may be loyal to you, but I assure you that they will place their loyalties to our faith above their loyalties to you. This is your only opportunity to let this matter pass."

"Yes, I read Cora's Bible. I assure you that my loyalties have not changed. To prove my devotion to our faith, I will not show you or your sister mercy. 'An eye for an eye' is our way after all." Naa'il opened the door. By this time, two guards multiplied to four. "Take this man and execute him. He is guilty of treason."

"You will regret this," Jamal vowed as the guards escorted him out of the room.

"I regret many things. Executing you and divorcing your sister are not among them. Take him away." Naa'il braced his hand on the desk to prevent him from collapsing to the marble floor after Jamal was led away.

Sadness had given way to rage; rage had surrendered to despair. "Begin anew," Cora reminded him. Naa'il knew that Cora was right; he had to start over. Straightening himself, Naa'il walked with a renewed purpose.

Chapter 32

Sarah paced across the floor of her apartment. She glanced at the door every few minutes while hoping for a visitor. Mamnoon was the only person who came to her to see her, except he only stayed long enough to deliver food and water. For as much as Sarah hated being alone, she was grateful to have time to think through Tess's revelation. It didn't surprise her that Hassan had lovers before they met. Even she had a sweetheart when she lived on her island. What she couldn't understand was why Hassan hadn't told her about his daughter, and more importantly, why he had abandoned her. Molly was a beautiful little girl. She was so sweet and so easy to love. Sarah wouldn't part with this child if Molly were hers.

Sarah sat down and picked up her portrait of her father stroking Poe's fur. *Of course, she loved him.* She smiled tenderly at his portrait. Her father wanted her to be with Hassan - at least, that was what he told her. Sarah couldn't understand why Tess believed that Sarah's bond with her father was anything but a loving father-daughter relationship.

Sarah jumped when she heard the lock turn. She knew by the position of the morning sun that it was too early for her noon meal. "Da," she exclaimed with a radiant smile when she saw her father standing in her doorway. Jumping up from her bench, she bounded across the room and stopped halfway when she spotted the change in Naa'il's demeanor. He usually stood erect, with his head held high. Today, his posture was slightly hunched over and his eyes bloodshot.

Naa'il met her halfway across the room. "Hello," he said with a quivering lip.

Sarah hugged him and then looked at him with concern. "Da, why are you sad?" she asked in Polynesian. Holding his hand, she led him over to the cushions where they ate their supper.

Naa'il spoke in his own language.

Sarah held his hand as she listened to his story. Though she didn't understand what he said, Naa'il's demeanor told her that he recently suffered a heart-breaking tragedy. "I am sorry," she said after he finished his story. Naa'il leaned over and kissed her tenderly. Sarah pulled away and stared at him with dismay. Her father had spent many hours teaching her about proper relationships. There was nothing he considered more offensive than when parents made love to their children. It only happened once on her island. Sarah had never seen her father so angry. What she couldn't understand was why he kissed her now.

Naa'il pulled away and said. "You are not ready."

"I sorry," was all she could mutter.

"I can be patient." Naa'il frowned as he stared at her necklace. After standing up, he pulled her to her feet and led her over to her basket of parus. He sat down on the bench and began rummaging through her parus until he found the one that he was searching for. "Wear this one." He handed her a purple and gold one.

Sarah turned away from him and changed into the one that Naa'il had selected for her. She jumped when she felt him twisting her white and green choker around her neck. His fingers fidgeted with the clasp; moments later her necklace fell into his hands. Covering the front of her neck with her hand, she breathed a sigh of relief to be free of her sparkling shackles. Her elation was short-lived when Naa'il attached another one around her neck. This choker was frightening and beautiful at the same time. A tear-drop blue stone surrounded by diamonds were centered between two strings of diamonds. The center stones were large enough to fit in the palm of her hand. It was heavy too. Sarah glanced over at Naa'il, who stood back and admired her as if she were his prized possession.

Shifting her in front of the mirror, Naa'il stood behind her with his hand resting on her arms. "What a wife you will make. I will be the envy of the Ottoman Empire."

Sarah just stared at the necklace, wondering how to remove it. Her thought was interrupted by a knock at the door.

Naa'il's hands fell away from her arms, and he walked over and answered the door. He glared at the guard standing in the doorway who ogled at Sarah. Naa'il shouted when the guard failed to state his purpose for the interruption.

The guard shook himself from his trance and delivered his message.

Naa'il groaned and said to Sarah, "I must leave you. I promise to return."

Sarah nodded.

"I will send for Tess to keep you company."

Sarah wasn't sure what upset her father, but it was enough to transform Naa'il back to the confident man that she admired.

Slamming the door behind him, Naa'il shouted. "What is the meaning of this interruption?"

The guard grimaced and said, "I apologize for the interruption, Your Excellency. I bring you news. The Vizier escaped."

"What do you mean, 'escaped'?" Naa'il demanded.

"He overcame the guards when they reached the dungeon. All but one survived."

Naa'il closed his eyes and shook his head. "Where is my wife?"

"She is in a cell in the dungeon, but the Vizier disappeared."

Shoving the guard against the wall, Naa'il warned through gritted teeth, "Find him. I want him alive so that I can personally execute him for treason." He released the guard and said, "Go. Do not fail me, or I will execute you too."

"Yes, Your Excellency," The guard bowed to his master before making a hasty exit.

Rolling his hands into fists, Naa'il took several deep breaths to quell the anger churning inside him. He turned the knob to Tess's chamber and discovered an empty room. Furrowing his brow, Naa'il turned and walked away from Sarah's apartment. He got halfway down the corridor when he spotted Mamnoon approaching him from the other direction with a tray of food in his hands.

The servant carefully balanced the tray and bowed to his master. "Your Excellency."

"Why are Tess and her daughter not in their chamber?"

Mamnoon winced, "I was going to tell you...."

"Tell me what?" Naa'il snapped.

"Tess and Sarah had a disagreement yesterday. I thought it was best for Tess and her daughter to return to the harem."

"Oh?" Naa'il crossed his arms and tapped his toes against the floor. "Why did they quarrel?"

"You may remember that you assigned Tess to entertain Nathan Shelby."

"Yes," Naa'il's tone became more impatient.

"Tess fell in love with Captain Shelby. Sarah told her in confidence that Captain Shelby was her husband."

"Indeed." Naa'il's fist tightened. "Bring Tess to my private office."

Hassan stood on the quarterdeck of Claude Fornier's ship. He stared pensively at the Algerine fortress as beads of sweat rolled down his temples. Making the repairs to the ships was slow and arduous work. However, they made up the time on their journey to Algiers. The Persephone had a reputation for being a fast ship, and Hassan was pleased to discover that the rumors were true. He was equally grateful that his entire crew had volunteered for the next dangerous mission. He chose half of them, which included Tristan Thatcher and Luke Finch. Hassan promoted Adam Boyle to captain with orders to sail the Zafirah to a remote island off the Portuguese coastline with Claude and the French prisoners. If all went well, he, Sarah and the English prisoners would rendezvous with them by the end of the week. So far, his plan was working. At least a dozen ships filled the harbor, whose crews were busy loading and unloading their cargo. None of them seem to notice Hassan or his men.

The Persephone's cannon thundered, asking permission to come ashore. The Algerine fortress fired back, signaling their consent. Hassan was certain that the Dey's spies were looking for him. He hoped to elude them by taking a few precautions. While some of his crew prepared the captain's launch, Hassan instructed the ones going ashore to dress in European clothing. He then attached iron shackles on their wrists and ankles. The illusion was complete, yet the tension inside Hassan lingered.

"Permission to come ashore," Hassan called out as his jolly neared the dock.

"Permission granted," an Algerine soldier shouted back who signaled to one of the workers to secure the boat to the pier.

Hassan said nothing to the guards as he and his crew climbed out of the boat. They slipped inside the city unnoticed. After passing through the square, they ducked down an alley; Hassan unlocked the irons and handed them a bag. While his men changed into their Ottoman clothes, Hassan, Tristan, and Luke scanned the streets for possible danger. So far, he saw nothing of concern.

"Blend in. We will rendezvous tomorrow," Hassan said in a voice that only his men could hear.

"Finch and I are going with you, Captain," Tristan insisted. "You appointed us to protect you. We have no intention of abandoning our post now."

"Very well." Hassan nodded, hoping the bodyguards' large stature wouldn't call attention to them. He and his crew of six split into two groups, each heading in the opposite direction. No sooner had Hassan taken a step when a small army of soldiers plugged both ends of the alley. Drawing their swords, he and his men charged the Algerine soldiers, but for every soldier they killed, at least two more arrived in their place. Hassan saw one of his men falling to the ground from the corner of his eye. Just as Hassan raised his saber to counter a strike, he lost his balance after someone bumped him. His head hit the wall, and his world went black.

Tess trembled as she knocked on Naa'il's office door. She glanced over at Mamnoon.

He rested his hand on her shoulder and said, "Speak honestly with His Excellency. I promise that it will be alright."

Tess offered her friend a forced smile, which faded as soon as she heard Naa'il's muffled voice say, "Enter." Taking a deep breath, she turned the brass doorknob and went inside. Naa'il stood at the window with his fingers laced behind his back. "Your Excellency," the odalisque said as she fell to her knees.

Naa'il acted as if he hadn't heard her. "Rise. I understand that you and the Tahitian woman had a disagreement."

Tess's cheeks burned when she heard the coldness in his tone. "Yes, Your Excellency," She scrambled to her feet.

Naa'il turned his torso and aimed his face at Tess. "Mamnoon informed me that Sarah confided in you that she is Hassan Aziz's wife?" he stated in a casual tone.

"You mean Nathan Shelby," Tess frowned.

"Hassan Aziz and Nathan Shelby are the same person," Naa'il clarified.

"Then yes, that is what she told me, Your Excellency." Tess swallowed hard as Naa'il's eyes narrowed.

"What else did Sarah tell you?"

"Sarah does not speak good English. I knew by her demeanor that she is in love with him. That was all that was said before Mamnoon forced me to leave."

Naa'il nodded. "You may return to the harem."

Tess bowed and backed out of the room, closing the door behind her.

Naa'il picked up the chair beside him. "No!" he screamed as he hurled it against the wall. The chair made a loud crash and splintered into tiny pieces when it collided with the wall. Naa'il grabbed a small knife and tucked it under his belt before racing out of his office.

Several guards rushed towards him as he headed down the corridor. They stopped long enough to bow to the Dey. "Your Excellency, we captured Captain Aziz and his party."

"Where is he?" Naa'il sneered.

"We took Aziz and his men to the dungeon."

Naa'il followed close behind his guards through a series of corridors. They stopped in front of an unassuming entryway. Naa'il waited for his guards to unlock and open the door. They stepped inside and paused long enough to allow their eyes to adjust to the cave-like darkness. The stone walls leading to the dungeon were dark and dotted with black stains from the torches braced on the wall. Their footsteps echoed as they descended to the prison. Naa'il covered his nose with his hand to offset the stench when he reached the last stair. A guard removed one of the torches and led Naa'il through a narrow hallway. They stopped halfway and entered a large room. Hassan stood in the center with his outstretched arms chained to the opposing stone walls. His guards had already stripped the clothes from his body.

Naa'il picked up a whip and circled Hassan. Every part of the prisoner's body was muscle. There was no deficiency, no excess. The only imperfections to his physique were the thin scars on his back from previous floggings. After finishing one loop, Naa'il circled around to the front. "Do you know what I value the most?"

Hassan stared back in defiance.

"Respect and loyalty. My father used to say that you can possess all the riches of the world, but you are not a man if you do not command the loyalty and respect of others. You betrayed me when you chose to keep that Tahitian whore for yourself."

"What have you done with her?" Hassan demanded.

Naa'il looked Hassan in the eyes and said, "She is exactly where she should be, in my bed, willingly, I might add. Sarah never mentioned you. It was only through another person that I discovered that she was your wife. You must not have been important to her." Naa'il's smile broadened as he observed Hassan's face wrench in anguish.

"Keep her," Hassan calmly replied. "Your lover is the least of your problems."

Naa'il circled to the back of Hassan. "You *are* my problem." He cracked the whip.

Hassan screamed as the end of the whip sliced through his skin. "My government knows that you are enslaving our people. I am the only person who can stop England from declaring war on your country. There is a ship sailing for England, even as we speak. I am supposed to rendezvous with them in a few days. Their orders are to sail for home if they do not see me within the week. Understand that our countries will be at war if they reach England without me. You *will* lose everything that you hold dear."

"Your government will do nothing." Naa'il cracked his whip again. He struck Hassan four more times. The mighty corsair cried out each time the whip sliced through his skin. Naa'il raised his hand and stopped suddenly when he heard Cora say, *"Show him mercy."* Knowing that she would never forgive him, he couldn't continue. "You and the other infidels will die on the cross, like your savior."

"Your country will lose," Hassan mumbled.

"Your country will not defeat us. It is weak." Naa'il handed the whip to the guard and left the room. "Torture him, but keep him alive."

Hassan braced himself for more lashings, but none followed. All he heard was the sounds of a grunt and a thud. His outstretched shackled arms made it impossible for him to see what was taking place behind him. He also heard someone dragging something across the floor and the click of a lock a moment later. "Finish me!" Hassan shouted when he heard someone approaching him.

"It would be my pleasure to kill an infidel. I spared your life because I believe that we can help each other."

Hassan shifted his shoulders around enough to see Jamal standing behind him, except he was dressed as a palace guard. "Vizier?"

"Yes." Jamal handed the keys to one of the men standing beside him. Once the guard unlocked Hassan's shackles, Jamal passed a palace uniform to Hassan. "Put these on."

Hassan stuck his legs through each pant leg one at a time and secured the drawstring around his waist. "Why are you helping me?"

"I believe that we can help each other," Jamal replied as Hassan gingerly lowered the blue Ottoman shirt over his head.

"Help you, how?"

"I need your help, and you need mine," Jamal said in a low voice.

"Go on."

"I want you to assassinate Naa'il Dhar."

"Why would I do that?" Hassan crossed his arms.

"For weeks, members of my government whisperer that Dhar was becoming an apostate. Our worst fears were realized a few days ago. There is no greater betrayal than to turn away from our faith."

"Why not simply expose him?" Hassan challenged.

"Because Dhar is married to my sister. I love her too much to bring shame upon her and her daughters. For that reason, I would rather dispose of him discreetly than allow the news of Dhar's apostasy to spread through the kingdom."

Hassan pursed his lips. "Why not kill him yourself. You and your men have proven that you are equal to the task."

"I have my reasons. In exchange for your service, I will allow you and your men to go free."

"You are going to have to do more than that, Vizier. I don't know if you heard my conversation with Dhar, but I am the only person preventing England from declaring war on your country. You and the Dey have enslaved British subjects after taking tribute money from my government. The Prince Regent is demanding that Algiers free all British subjects. Anything less will result in a war with England."

"Does that include women?"

Hassan grimaced as he imaged Tess's naked body intertwined with his. "All Western women," he insisted after a long pause.

"I agree to your terms. You have my word that I will free as many as I can. Bear in mind that not all of the British subjects survived."

"Free as many as you can find. Know that I have spies who will tell me if you did not keep your word. Do not double cross me, Vizier. Your country's survival depends on my ship reaching the rendezvous point."

"You have my word; I will keep my part of our accord." Jamal angrily insisted.

"One other thing, I need to find the men who came ashore with me."

"We're here, Captain," Tristan called out from one of the other cells.

"I'm not leaving without them."

"I thought not." Jamal flipped to another key on the ring and led Hassan to the cell where his men were being held.

Hassan glanced at the trail of blood leading to a neighboring cell and spotted at least three naked bodies piled on top of each other through a small window. Jamal unlocked the door where his men were being held. Four out of the six crew exited the tiny cell. "Are you hurt, Captain?" Tristan asked.

"I will be alright." Hassan winced in pain. Glancing over at Jamal, he asked, "When do you want this assassination to take place?"

"This evening."

Naa'il returned to his apartment. As he had done so many times since Cora's death, he retrieved her Bible in hopes of finding an answer. Pacing across his reception room, he madly flipped through the pages for the answer he was searching for, but none of her notes provided the one he needed.

"That harlot made a fool of me," Naa'il shouted at the book. "I rescued her. I protected her. I gave her jewels and an apartment. I treated her like a wife. Still, Sarah loved that infidel dog and not me. You want me to forgive her, to show her compassion. I hate what you are asking me to do." Naa'il's face twitched in agony when he heard Cora's cries during the last night of her attack. He was wrong about her, and she paid a terrible price for his mistake.

Naa'il's debate continued for the next few hours. Back and forth he paced until his anger won out. "I am who I am, Cora. The people of my faith believe in 'an eye for an eye.' That was how I was born; that was how I was raised, and that is how I will die. I cannot change, not even for all the love that I feel for you." Naa'il threw her Bible into the fire. Tears filled his eyes as the book burst into flames. "Forgive me for what I am about to do." Wiping the tear from his eye, he rushed out of his apartment.

Sarah sat on the edge of her bench staring at her father's portrait. She knew something was very wrong when her father left her this morning. He was sad; he was angry, and she was unable to comfort him. A part of her worried that she caused his anger. The sun had set, and the call to the evening prayer echoed throughout Algiers. Still, there was no sign of her father. Pressing his portrait to her chest, Sarah stood and paced the floor, glancing at the door every time she turned to cross her apartment.

Moments later, the lock turned; Sarah spun around and faced the door with a fool's hope in her heart. Tears streaming down her smiling face, she released the portrait and bounded towards Naa'il. "Da, I was so worried about you," she cried in Polynesian as she threw her arms around his neck. Just then, she spotted the last person that she expected to see, and he was walking towards her. "Cattin," Sarah mouthed his name. She pulled away from Naa'il and ran towards her husband, but not before Naa'il grabbed her arm and pressed her back against his chest.

Sarah gasped as she watched Hassan glaring at her as if she were his enemy. She knew from the stiffness in Naa'il's body that he hated her husband too. "Da, this is Cattin, he is my husband. You wanted me to be with him. Remember?"

Hassan and her father shouted at each other in a language that Sarah didn't understand. She attempted to pull away, but Naa'il locked his muscular arm across her bare chest. She gave Hassan a pleading look when Naa'il brushed her hair back from her face and kissed her temple, all the while, with Hassan looking on with disgust. Sarah squirmed enough to elbow Naa'il in the ribs. The Dey grunted and backhanded her across her cheek.

She tumbled to the floor and lost consciousness when her head hit the marble tile. Her eyes fluttered open when she heard the sound of clanking. She gasped as she watched Hassan and her father fighting each other with sabers. Mamnoon was also fighting one of the tall men that guarded Hassan's door. "No," Sarah called out when Tristan thrust his sword into Mamnoon's abdomen. The warrior's eyes widened as he collapsed onto the floor. Wrenching in pain, Sarah pulled herself up and crawled over to her friend. Mamnoon comforted her with a peaceful smile as she held him in her arms. With an outstretched hand, the mighty Sudanese bodyguard looked past Sarah and whispered, "Cora," before his spirit left his body.

Her father gave Mamnoon a haunted stare. With a tortured look, he dropped his weapon just as Hassan thrust his saber through his heart. "No!" Sarah screamed. She carefully lowered Mamnoon to the floor and crawled over to Naa'il. *"Please, help Da. Give this to your father," said Emile as he handed her a tin cup filled with red liquid .... Da, please drink this. Emile said it will make you feel better." She held the cup up to her father's lips until he finished it. "Tell her!" Hassan shouted at Emile .... "This killed your father!" Emile bellowed, holding up the same cup. Her father looked at her with sadness in his eyes and whispered, "I love you with my whole heart."* Sarah winced in agony as her memories flooded her mind. Her chest rising and falling, she realized that her dreams were memories. "I'm sorry, Da, please don't leave me," she cried over and over again in Polynesian as she held Naa'il in her arms.

"It is alright," Naa'il whispered with a peaceful grin. "I am going to be with my daughter."

A guard poked his head through the crack of the door and spoke with an insistent voice.

"Come Sarah," Hassan barked in English.

Sarah was too stunned to move. She just kept pleading, "I'm sorry Da, please don't leave me."

Hassan threw a green paru over Sarah's shoulders. "Come Sarah, or I will leave you,"

Naa'il caressed Sarah's cheek and whispered, "Go."

Hassan locked his hand around her arm and pulled her to her feet.

Sarah stood up because she knew that she must leave. When she reached the exit, she looked back at Naa'il one last time before fleeing with her husband.

The corridor outside Sarah's apartment was eerily quiet. The guard who warned them was the only Ottoman in sight. He led them through the Palace's hidden corridors. Another guard was waiting for them at the exit, but this one held himself with a regal air. He and Hassan addressed each other as if they were acquaintances. They only spoke for a minute or so, and then they were free.

CHAPTER 33

Sarah struggled with every step that she took as they made their way through the city. Her temples pounded while her father's death replayed over and over again in her mind. It had been a dream, a small, benign dream. That all changed when Hassan came for her. Now, her memories were a great flood, and there was nothing that she could do to hold them back.

"Keep up, Sarah." Hassan barked as he pulled her through the narrow street.

You killed him. Sarah's knees buckled when they reached the first square.

"Oh, for God's sake." Hassan yanked Sarah to her feet and hoisted her over his shoulder. He and his men picked up their pace, Sarah grunting with every step he took.

Their running came to a sudden stop. Hassan stepped into the jolly and pulled her off his shoulder. Sarah landed on the wooden bench with a hard thud. Hassan took a seat in front of her while his men filled in around them. They rowed in silence on the way back to the ship. All but Hassan and Sarah showed outward relief to be leaving Algiers.

Jamal returned to his apartment and quickly changed out of the palace guard uniform and into his regular clothes. A fire was already burning in the fireplace. Concerned that he would be implicated in Naa'il's assassination, the Vizier tossed the uniform into the hearth. The flames voraciously consumed the blood-stained blue clothing as if it were its only meal. The small bonfire warmed his cheeks as it intensified before shrinking to a modest blaze. Within minutes, the only proof of his connection to the crime had been reduced to embers.

The Vizier's breath hitched when he heard men shouting to each other outside his apartment. Their excited voices warned him that they had discovered dead bodies, and it was likely that they knew about Naa'il's assassination too. For a moment, Jamal contemplated fleeing the Palace, but there was far more at stake than saving himself. If Hassan Aziz had told him the truth, Algiers' survival depended on his success in seizing power and shifting the blame away from him.

Jamal took a deep breath and exited his apartment. He only needed to reach the end of the corridor to find seven palace guards racing toward him.

"Do not move! You're under arrest for Dey Dhar's assassination," an older guard shouted with his sword drawn against Jamal.

Jamal squared his shoulders and stared down his nose at the guards while eying their outstretched sabers pointed directly at him. "I am the Vizier of Algiers, not a lowly subject. You will put away your swords, or I will have you beheaded." Only half the guards obeyed Jamal's command; the other half nervously glanced over at their leader for guidance.

"With respect, Vizier, His Excellency ordered your arrest earlier today, and he was found dead tonight," countered the guard who initially confronted Jamal. "You have been missing since you escaped."

"I have been in my apartment this entire time." Jamal sneered. "If what you say is true, then I am now the leader of Algiers. You will do well to remember your place. If you wish to keep your heads, you will put away your swords immediately."

The guard's Adam's apple bobbed up and down as he swallowed. "Put away your swords," he said in a shaky voice as he returned his own to his belt; the others obeyed their leader's command.

"You made a wise choice; I will overlook your transgression this one time. You said His Excellency was assassinated; calmly tell me what happened."

The guard told Jamal everything he knew about the events from earlier that day.

"Are you certain that Aziz was responsible for His Excellency's death?" Jamal challenged.

"No, Your Excellency, but it is a logical conclusion."

"Dey Dhar had other enemies," Jamal pointed out. "Burhaan Hakim, for example, had threatened His Excellency a few days ago."

The guard bit his lip and nodded. "Yes, that is true. I was with His Excellency when their confrontation took place." He paused. "They quarreled over the Polynesian girl after she was auctioned on the slave block. She is now missing from her apartment."

"Indeed. So the truth is, you do not know who is responsible for His Excellency's assassination. As of this moment, I am taking over this investigation, and it will lead to where I say it leads. It is safe to conclude that whoever was responsible for these deaths has already fled the Palace. It is doubtful that they will return to the city. Therefore, you will suspend your search immediately. Convey my orders to the other palace guards."

"Yes, Your Excellency."

"The late Dey's first wife was taken to the dungeon earlier today. Release her and escort her to her apartment at once."

"Yes, Your Excellency." The guards bowed and backed away.

Jamal headed to Sarah's apartment. The Palace surgeon and several guards had just placed Mamnoon's and Naa'il's bodies on litters and were getting ready to carry them out of the room. Jamal grimaced when he took one last look at the two corpses. Though he didn't know Mamnoon well, he respected this noble man, and Jamal was genuinely sorry to lose him. He swallowed hard when he glanced over at his brother-in-law. Naa'il was an apostate. It was better to kill him before his betrayal became common knowledge – at least that was what Jamal told himself. He still had no idea how he would explain Naa'il's death to his sister and nieces.

The Vizier scanned the apartment one last time when his eyes fell on a drawing lying in the center of the room. Jamal turned to leave because he still felt guilty about his part in his brother-in-law's assassination, yet his curiosity bade him to take a closer look at the drawing. He went over and picked up the portrait of the man petting the black and white kitten. The man had Naa'il's bald head, but the face and the thick beard wasn't his. He glanced up and spotted a stack of drawings sticking out of a turquoise bag. He sat down on the bench, pulled out the pieces of parchment and began flipping through the stack. Jamal marveled at the artist's ability to capture the characters of the Palace residents. One portrait depicted Mamnoon's regal demeanor. Another showed a little harem girl playing with a kitten. He grinned when he came to a picture of the same girl cuddling with a woman. The Vizier shoved Sarah's drawings and Sarah's parus into the bag. Just then, the kitten from the sketches jumped onto the bench and mewed. Jamal scratched behind the cat's ears when it occurred to him that he had found the perfect gift for his nieces. He draped the strap over his shoulder and tucked the kitten under his arms. The room was just starting to get dark. Jamal grabbed a lantern hanging outside the room and headed to Mariam's apartment.

His sister's residence was dark. No guards were posted outside her door tonight. The kitten mewed and squirmed to free herself from her captivity. "Go." Jamal lowered Poe' to the floor as soon as they were inside the room. "Mari," he called out and held the lamp in front of him in every corner of the apartment. All that he found was Mariam's furniture and belongings.

Jamal closed the door and ran to the dungeon where Mariam was being held. The guard he had sent to free his sister appeared at the top of the stairs. "Where is my sister?" the Vizier demanded.

"I am sorry for the delay, Your Excellency," the guard bowed. "I informed the first wife that she was free. She refused to leave."

Jamal groaned. "Does she know about the Dey's assassination?"

"I am not sure, Vizier. The first wife did not speak of it to me," the guard replied. "I did not think it was my place to convey this information to her."

"Very well."

"Your Excellency, someone removed the bodies of the dead guards when I arrived."

Jamal pressed his lips together when he heard the anger in the guard's tone. He knew the guard still suspected his involvement in these crimes, yet he was shrewd enough to keep his suspicions to himself. "Very well. Escort my nieces and their nurses here, but do not bring them down unless I send for them."

"Yes, Your Excellency," The guard's voice softened. "The first wife is in the last cell at the end of the hall. I left the door open."

"I shall not forget your service today," Jamal followed the torches to the bottom of the stairs, turned right and walked down a narrow corridor lined with doors on one side and lit torches on the other. Mariam's prison cell was at the end. The door was wide open, just as the guard described. Jamal swallowed hard when he spotted his sister lying on the stone floor. "Mari," he crooned as he entered her cell.

She sat up, balancing herself on one of her hands. "Is my husband dead?"

Jamal expelled a loud sigh as he stared at the stone wall directly above her head.

"I heard you talking earlier today. Answer me, did you kill my husband?"

He looked his sister in the eyes and said without hesitation. "Yes. Naa'il became an apostate. There was no mistaking it. You know as well as I that it was best to kill him now than to risk Naa'il's shame becoming common knowledge."

Mariam covered her mouth with her free hand and sobbed. Kneeling in front of her, Jamal held his sister in his arms. "I'm sorry," he whispered. "I will take care of you and your daughters." Nothing he said could hold back her tears.

"No!" Mariam screamed and beat his chest with her fists before surrendering to his tender embrace.

When her weeping subsided, Jamal stood and offered his hand to his sister. "Come, I will take you back to your apartment."

Mariam didn't budge. "No, I killed my child. I deserve to spend the rest of my life here."

Jamal hung his head and sighed. He squatted beside her. "Zeba's death was a tragedy. But it was an accident, not murder. That is why you must put this tragedy behind you and live for your daughters. Now that their father is dead, they will need you more than ever. I will leave you with a choice. You can live, or you can give up and die."

Mariam stared at her brother with a quivering lip and laid down on the floor.

"Very well. You can explain your decision to your daughters." He stood and headed for the exit.

Mariam sat up again. "What do you mean?"

"Bring my nieces down at once," He barked to the guard, standing at the bottom of the staircase.

"Yes, Vizier," the guard bowed.

Mariam gasped. "What are you doing? I am dead to my children."

"Then you will have to explain your death to your daughters."

Mariam jumped to her feet and rushed over to her brother. "You cannot do this," she pleaded as she rested her hands on her brother's chest.

"Mama," Laila called out.

Mariam retreated to the back wall and closed her eyes as tears streamed down her cheeks.

Jamal stepped aside to let his nieces join their mother. He grinned seeing the way his sister cowered in front of her children.

"Why are you here, Mama?" Yasmine asked.

Mariam looked at their little faces and then to her brother for an answer.

"Choose," Jamal said.

"What does Uncle mean, Mama?" Nahla asked.

Mariam glanced again at her brother then back to her children. She squatted and held out her arms to her daughters. "It means that we are going to spend a lifetime together. Come here, my darlings." The girls embraced their mother, each crying tears of joy. Jamal winked and nodded his approval to his sister.

Hassan's crew lowered the bosuns' chair for Sarah, but she didn't move from her seat. She just stared blankly at the water, rocking back and forth with her hands clutching her arms. "Get into the bosuns' chair, Sarah." Hassan shuddered at her disturbing demeanor. She didn't budge. He grabbed her arm and yanked her to her feet. "Get into the bosuns' chair; I will not ask again," he growled. He bit the inside of his lip when he spotted the fear in her eyes. Still, Sarah obeyed without accepting his assistance. While his crew pulled the ropes for the lift, Hassan scaled the lines as doubts about Sarah seeped into his mind. He couldn't understand how she could feel so strongly for a man that she only knew for a few short days.

Hassan reached the deck just as Sarah was being pulled over the railing. She toppled off the bosuns' chair and into Hassan's arms. Then the little food she had eaten that day came up and spilled all over Hassan. "What is wrong with you?" He placed his hands on her arms and straightened her. Holding her arm steadily, he forced her to walk with him. She took two steps when her knees buckled. Hassan wanted to grab her by the hair and drag her to his cabin. Seeing his crew's curious stares, he took a deep breath, scooped Sarah up in his arms, and carried her the rest of the way.

Luke opened the door and said, "We are here if you need anything, Captain."

"Thank you, Mr. Finch," Hassan replied as he entered his temporary quarters. Luke closed the door, and Hassan dropped Sarah in the middle of the floor. "I know you are a stranger in our world, but it is poor manners to wear another man's gifts," he said as he paced across his quarters. "Dr. Hyatt warned me about you. He said that the South Seas women were incapable of being faithful. But I defended you. I believed it was unfair to judge you. I hoped that your father had taught you about honor. What a fool I was. You are no different from a common whore," he said in a chillingly calm tone.

Sarah looked up at him with a slack jaw. "No, I keep promise," she insisted in a timid voice.

"Don't lie," Hassan shouted. "I know you were unfaithful!"

"No," she gasped. "I keep promise."

"I found you in Dhar's arms. Now you're mourning him as if he were the great love of your life!" Hassan shouted over her.

"No," she sobbed. "I keep promise."

"Stop saying that! We both know that it's not true."

"I keep promise!" Sarah repeated over and over again as tears streamed down her cheeks.

"Enough!" Hassan struck Sarah's face just as she pulled herself to her feet.

Sarah toppled to the floor and covered her cheek with her hand. She stared at her husband with a slack jaw and eyes round and dilated.

The expression on Hassan's face mirrored Sarah's horror. For a moment, he was too stunned to continue. "I guess that we're stuck with each other. And take off that bloody necklace," he said before fleeing their room. Hassan kept moving until he reached the surgery.

Peter covered his nose and looked up from his book with puckered lips. "You look as awful as you smell."

Do you have a spare shirt I can borrow?" Hassan asked.

"Yes, of course. I always carry at least one spare." Peter got up from the table.

"Thank you." Hassan pulled his shirt over his head.

Peter retrieved a peasant shirt from his bag and gasped when he spotted Hassan's bloodied back. "You're hurt!"

"I will live," Hassan chuckled. "This is the price of stupidity."

"At least let me clean your back before you bloody my shirt."

Hassan turned the chair around and took a seat with his chest resting against the chair back. He gritted his teeth as Peter cleaned his wounds. "You were right about her," Hassan said after a long silence.

Sarah remained still, long after Hassan had struck her. After a while, she moved enough to sit up and wrap her arms around her shins. When her memories had stopped spinning, Sarah was finally able to make sense of her cryptic memories. Her father died on the day that she met Hassan; Naa'il wasn't her father at all, but a friend, an angel who took care of her until Hassan came for her. Her father had ingrained in her at an early age that there are consequences for actions, specifically, punishments for wrong-doing. She was responsible for three deaths: her father, a man that she loved more than all the world, and her friends, Naa'il and Mamnoon. Sarah pulled herself to her feet and went over to a highboy in the dressing room. She rummaged through the drawers until she found a small knife. Sarah cried as she slit her upper forehead close to her hairline. She repeated until blood dripped down her forehead. That wasn't enough, she reasoned, not nearly enough. No one would punish her for her crimes. "You must be punished," she mumbled. Wiping the tears from her eyes, Sarah dropped the knife and ran to the door.

Hassan wandered up to the main deck after Peter had cleaned and dressed his wounds. Tristan, Luke, and a few others stood guard, scanning the harbor for potential threats. Laughing to himself at their devotion to duty, Hassan strolled across the deck and stood beside them. "Report," he said after scanning the city. The tan buildings had turned to a yellow hue from a line of torches burning on top of the city wall. Other than the firing of a cannon, the residents seemed unaware of Naa'il Dhar's assassination.

"The city looks so peaceful. Do you think the Vizier will release the English prisoners?" Luke asked.

"He had better. Algiers' survival depends on it. You're right Mr. Finch, the city does look peaceful from here. If I may, I have one more mission for you, but it can wait until tomorrow morning."

Tristan and Luke snapped to attention. "What are your orders, Captain?"

"I need you to return to the city to retrieve Captain Fornier's wife. I made a promise to him, and I intend to keep my word. Also, organize a party to buy food and livestock for our journey home. Buy as much as you can. We will need enough to feed the freed prisoners."

"We will take care of it, Captain," Tristan replied.

"Thank you, gentlemen. Continue your watch and contact me if there are any problems. Good work today." Feeling frustrated and helpless, Hassan wandered over to another part of the deck to be alone with his thoughts. He was sure that Sarah was different from Tess. He had spent most of his adult life wondering if he would ever know how it felt to feel loved, really loved, and not for his money, his family, or for his connections, but for him and him alone. Sarah made him believe it, and now he felt like a fool.

The activity on the ship was quiet. No one stood guard outside

Hassan's quarters that night. Even though she was only wearing a paru, Sarah slipped onto the main deck unnoticed. There were only a few crew members around, and none of them noticed her walking over to the ship's edge or climbing over the railing.

"Sarah, no!" Hassan called out.

Sarah could see him running towards her from the corner of her eye. She looked directly at him and said in Polynesian, "Goodbye, Cattin."

"Sarah, stop!" Hassan shouted. This time other men ran towards her.

Sarah closed her eyes and leapt, her stomach fluttering during her descent. Moments later, the cold, unforgiving water enveloped her. The wound on her forehead stung. For a moment, Sarah wanted to alleviate the pain by swimming to the surface. Remembering her role in her father's death was the only persuasion she needed to exhale the air from her chest. Just as she began to sink, she felt someone grabbing her arm and pulling her to the surface.

"What are you doing?" Hassan trod water with one arm and his legs while latching his free arm around her chest.

"Let me die," Sarah said as she fought to free herself, but Hassan wouldn't let go of her. "I killed Da, Mamnoon, and Naa'il. I deserve to die," she cried in Polynesian. Sarah confessed everything. "It is my fault that Da is dead."

"I don't understand you. You must speak in English. Please tell me why you believe that you must commit suicide."

Sarah wanted to tell Hassan what she did, but all she could say was, "Da dead. It was…" She stopped herself in mid-sentence when she feared that he would hate her more than he already did if she told him the truth. "Na na, Cattin," Sarah squirmed to break free.

"I am not going to let you die. Forgive me." Hassan pinched her neck with his free hand.

Sarah's eyes rolled into the back of her head, and her body went limp.

Hassan's crew lowered the bosuns' chair to the water. By that time, the pain from the salt penetrating his open wounds was excruciating. It took Tristan and Luke's help to secure Sarah to the wooden platform. Hassan was afraid to release her.

"Hold on to Miss Campbell, Captain. We'll pull you both aboard."

Cradling Sarah in his arms, Hassan nodded to his bodyguards. While his men pulled the bosuns' chair lines, he rubbed his hand across her stomach and frowned when he felt a wound. "What the devil?"

Tristan and Luke secured the lift when it reached the deck. Luke escorted Hassan and Sarah to the captain's quarters while Tristan retrieved a lantern.

Hassan laid Sarah on the berth and took the lamp from his bodyguard. "Thank you again for your help," Hassan nodded. Once he was alone with Sarah, he removed her paru and shined the light over her body. The wound on her belly had already scabbed over and was the size of a knife blade. It was a painful reminder that he didn't really know what happened to her during her stay in the Palace. Naa'il proved tonight that he wasn't opposed to striking her. Hassan scanned the rest of her body for wounds. He found another fresh wound on her forehead. He didn't remember seeing it when he rescued her. Then again, Hassan wasn't sure of anything after his whirlwind of a day. The only other wound he found was a minor cut on the back of her neck.

When Hassan moved to the window, he noticed a knife lying on the floor beside the highboy. He picked it up and gasped when he spotted fresh blood on the tip of the blade. Hassan knew that it was Sarah's blood, and he shuddered at the thought knowing that his actions drove her to harm herself. He had never struck a woman before. Up until this evening, he didn't think that he was capable of causing physical harm to a woman. Hassan's train of thought was interrupted when he heard Sarah's muffled cries. He looked back and found her curled into a ball, sobbing. Hassan sat down on the edge of the berth and rested his hand on her side. "Sarah."

She looked up at him with pleading eyes. "Let me die," she whispered before rolling back into a ball.

Hassan didn't know how to reply to her plea. All he could do was cover her with a blanket and let her rest.

Chapter 34

John woke from a deep sleep when he heard someone beating on his door. The windowless room made it difficult to ascertain how close the night was to the dawn. All he knew was that the morning felt earlier than usual. "One moment," he called out between yawns. He rolled off his cushion and pulled himself to his feet. John opened the door and stuck his head through the crack. "Yes?"

"The Vizier wants to see you immediately," The guard ordered.

"Of course. Permit me a moment to cover myself." John closed his door and frowned as he slipped on a pair of brown Ottoman trousers. He crouched on the floor and patted each surface until he found a tunic. Sticking his head through the opening, he poked his arms into the sleeves and wondered why Vizier Rahmani wanted to see him. In the years since the Dey employed him, never once had the Vizier spoken to him. Moreover, he had never even acknowledged his existence. John slid his feet into his slippers and rushed to the door. The guard escorted him down the corridors in silence. "May I inquire what this concerns?"

The guard just kept walking.

They turned down another corridor. The darkness in the courtyard had given way to the dawn's faint light. Tension continued mounting inside John. He knew something had happened to Naa'il when they stopped in front of the Dey's private office. The guard knocked and opened the door. John recognized Jamal from his royal blue, floor-length robe. He was standing in front of the window, staring out into the darkness. John stepped inside and bowed to the Vizier.

Jamal continued looking out the window as if he were alone. "Naa'il Dhar was killed last night."

John's lips parted when he heard the news, yet he wasn't surprised. "I am sorry for your loss, sir."

"His Excellency spoke highly of you," the Vizier said after a long pause.

"I served His Excellency as best I could, sir."

"I sent for you to inform you that you have earned your freedom."

"My freedom," John gasped. That was the last thing that he expected to hear.

Jamal swiveled around to look at the servant. "Yes, I think His Excellency would want that for you. I have two requests."

"Of course, anything," John said eagerly.

"I am releasing the infidels from the harem. I would like you to escort them to the dock. Hassan Aziz will give you passage to England."

"How can that be? He has a reputation for being one of the most ruthless corsairs on the Barbary Coast," John pointed out.

"Not everything is what it seems. Hassan Aziz is an English captain. His Christian name is Nathan Shelby."

"I trust your judgment, sir, and I will be happy to escort the women to the pier." John's voice trailed off. "Only, I do not know the way."

"My guards will escort you and the women."

"Thank you, sir. You said that you had another request?"

"Yes, do you see that bag lying on the desk?"

"Yes."

"It belongs to Aziz's woman. She has vibrant red hair. I would like you to return it to her."

John's trembling hand picked up the bag and draped it over his shoulder. Trapped between disbelief and elation, the servant could hardly stand still. "I will not fail you, Vizier."

"The guard will return you to your quarters. You will have a few minutes to collect your belongings."

"Thank you, sir. I wish you blessings upon your household."

Jamal just turned away and stared out the window.

Tess woke to someone shaking her vigorously. She sat up and glared at the eunuch. "Why the devil are you waking me during the wee hours of the morning?"

"Come with me. Gather your belongings and bring your daughter with you," the eunuch whispered.

"Why? What happened?"

"Do as I say, or you and your daughter will be sold at market. Cover yourself with this." The eunuch handed Tess a gray robe.

Tess pressed her lips together as she attempted to make sense of the change in the eunuch's demeanor. They had always been friendly to her. This morning, he looked at her as if she were his enemy. "Very well." She took the garment from him. Tess poked her head through the opening and studied the eunuch. "Will you at least tell me what happened?"

"The Dey was assassinated last night. The Vizier granted you, your daughter, and the other infidel your freedom."

"We're free?" Tess looked at him with disbelief as she finished dressing.

"You heard me correctly. Please collect your belongings and meet me at the entrance in a few minutes."

Tess scanned the room and wondered why Mamnoon hadn't delivered the message himself. Of all the eunuchs in the harem, he would have been the one to give her the news.

The eunuch had already moved on before Tess could ask him about her friend. She rolled the few clothes she owned into a ball and turned her attention to her daughter. Molly was still sleeping peacefully and would remain asleep for several more hours. Tess quickly wrapped her child in a blanket and cradled her against her shoulder. Abigail and the eunuch were already waiting for them at the entrance of the harem. She was dressed in a black robe with a look of confusion that mirrored Tess's.

"What is going on?" Abigail whispered to her friend.

"We've been granted our freedom," Tess whispered back.

"What does that mean?"

"I don't know." Still thinking about her friend, she asked the eunuch, "I would like to say goodbye to Mamnoon before I leave."

The eunuch winced. "Mamnoon was also assassinated last night."

Tess gasped as tears flooded her eyes. "What happened?"

"I do not know. You and the other infidel must leave at once," the eunuch said sternly.

John and two guards were waiting for them outside the harem. Tess recognized Sarah's bag draped over the servant's shoulder, but Sarah wasn't with him. Tess couldn't help wondering if she was also killed last night.

Tristan saluted Hassan. "Good morning, Captain. The night passed peacefully."

"Let's hope our time here will continue without incident." Hassan wiped the perspiration from his forehead. His night was anything but peaceful. He spent half of it listening for Sarah's cries, and the other half looking in on her after her weeping subsided for fear that she had found a way to take her life. Sarah kept breathing.

Hassan scanned the harbor, silently noting that it was still too early for the corsair ships to arrive. "Are there any signs of the prisoners?" The morning balanced on the tip of the night and the dawn. Most of the sky was black, spotted with glowing white crystals and a faint yellow hue lining the eastern horizon. The air was calm. Hassan also recognized the outline of Sarah's former ship, except there was no evidence that anyone was on board.

"Captain, there's activity ashore," Tristan said enthusiastically.

Hassan took the glass from him and held it up to his eye. The light from the torches held by people in the mob provided enough light to recognize Jamal Rahmani on the dock with a large group of people standing behind him. "My God," Hassan said when he spotted a few of his men. "Rahmani kept his word. Prepare the jolly."

"We're going with you," Luke insisted.

"I would be surprised if you didn't, Mr. Finch."

Hassan, Luke, and Tristan rowed ashore. All three were well armed in case they needed to defend themselves. Men were also standing by on the ship, ready to fire cannons. Jamal and his guards looked as anxious as Hassan felt, yet he knew that the Vizier wouldn't risk a war with England by breaking his promise.

"Your countrymen, Captain Shelby. Their numbers total 769. Take them, and never return to the Barbary Coast," Jamal warned after Hassan climbed onto the dock.

"And the women?" Hassan's voice trailed off when he spotted Tess holding a child.

"I have kept my word, Captain Shelby," Jamal insisted.

"Thank you. You have my country's gratitude. You need not worry about us returning so long as your government honors your agreement with mine." Hassan glanced over at Tristan and spotted the concern in his eyes. "Is something wrong, Mr. Thatcher?"

"No, sir ... it just, there are a lot of men, Captain. I worry that our ship is too small to accommodate that many people," Tristan blurted out.

"You're right Mr. Thatcher; there are a lot of people. We shall make due, for I have no intention of leaving anyone behind."

"You may take the ship that brought the Tahitian girl. Its crew has no use for it," Jamal offered. "I also took the liberty of providing enough food to feed you and your crew and passengers for the next few days."

"Again, I am grateful and curious. What became of the crew from that ship?"

"The captain died the night he brought the Tahitian girl to the Palace. He lived long enough to learn that his crew would spend the rest of their lives working in the quarries."

"I'll be damned," Hassan mumbled. "Please do not show them mercy. They murdered Sarah's father to profit from selling her."

"I have no reason to go against Dhar's wishes."

"You are a good man. I wish you a long and prosperous life."

"May you find peace, Captain Shelby." Jamal and his party turned towards the city and waded through the group of prisoners before Hassan could reply.

Hassan glanced over at Tess. It had been more than a year since the last time he saw her. He had forgotten how beautiful she was, but Sarah was exotic. Tess made him forget his troubled life whenever they were together, but so did Sarah. He approached the women and bowed his head. "Good morning, I am Captain Shelby. I was commissioned to take you to England," he said without taking his eyes off Tess and her sleeping child. Molly let out a little cry as she stirred and looked at the group with horror.

"Shhh," Tess said sharply.

Hassan studied the child and forgot what he was going to say next. Instead, he wondered if she was his daughter. She looked about the right age to be conceived during the first night he and Tess made love. The child's hair color was also similar to his. Hassan then wondered how well Tess and Sarah knew each other.

"I am Abigail Randall, Captain Shelby." Abigail curtsied.

"I am pleased to make your acquaintance, Miss Randall." Nathan bowed again.

Abigail glanced over at Tess, who shrugged and said, "We know each other."

"Of course," Abigail blushed.

"Ladies, please follow me," Hassan said after a few awkward moments of silence. He led Abigail and Tess to the jolly. Extending his hand to his female guests, he assisted Abigail into the boat. Tess passed Molly to Abigail. His former paramour offered Hassan a coquettish smile when she took his hand before stepping into the jolly. Once the women were seated, Hassan announced to the men standing on the dock. "I will take the women to the ship first. After that, we will begin shuttling you to my ships." He took a seat. The oarsmen rowed them to the Persephone. Even in Tess's presence, his eyes were still drawn to Sarah. His lips pulled back into a faint smile as he watched her climb to the top with the same ease as the seamen who tended the sails. There was no fear, no hesitation in her movements, only a determination to reach her destination. He was relieved to see that she had the sense to change out of her purple paru and into a pair of gray Ottoman trousers and a matching tunic. At a distance, Hassan felt her sadness as she sat on the round plank with her arms wrapped around her shins.

Hassan tore his eyes away from Sarah when the jolly reached his ship. An oarsman at each end of the boat threw the lead lines to the crewmen standing at the railing, who secured the jolly to the ship while another lowered the bosuns' chair.

"Miss Randall, I would like you to climb aboard first. Once you're aboard, my crew will lower a canvas bag for the child. Tess, you will ride on the bosuns' chair once your daughter is aboard," Hassan explained.

"Of course. I have ridden on a bosuns' chair before," Abigail replied.

Hassan helped Abigail onto the wooden plank. Once she was seated, he wrapped a rope around her waist to secure her to the lift.

"See you on deck," Abigail smiled to her friends.

"Captain, how long do you think it will take to load seven hundred prisoners?" Tristan asked.

Hassan tore his gaze from the bosuns' chair. "It could take the better part of a day, once you factor in the hour journey to and from the ship. We will make use of all the jollies that are available to us. If all goes well, we will be able to set sail this evening."

"Home." Tristan's lips widened into a toothy grin. "No word ever sounded so heavenly." He shook his head. "I never thought that I would set foot on English soil again."

"Weather permitting, we should arrive in Portsmouth within the fortnight." Hassan glanced over at Tess who grimaced when he said Portsmouth. The canvas bag had just been lowered to the jolly. "Tess, place your daughter in the bag, please."

Molly held onto her mother's neck and refused to let go. "Mama," she screamed as Tess attempted to place her small daughter into the bag.

Tess pried her daughter's arms from her neck. "Quit your screaming and get into this bag."

"I don't want to go," Molly screamed even louder as she clung to her mother.

"Riding in the bag is for your protection. You will only be inside it for a moment," Hassan said in a soothing voice.

"I want to go with Mama," Molly screamed even louder.

Tess slapped her daughter's cheek. "That's enough. Get into the bag and stay there, I don't want to hear another bloody word from you."

Molly's cries were reduced to a whimper as Tess placed her daughter into the bag. She didn't complain, even when the bag enveloped her completely.

"What?" Tess demanded when she spotted Hassan staring at her with a slack jaw.

Hassan held his arms at his sides with his fists clinched. "We'll discuss this in private," he said through gritted teeth.

"Fine." Tess turned her nose in the air and reached for the rope ladder.

"Wouldn't you prefer to wait for the bosuns' chair?" Hassan suggested.

"I can manage with the ladder."

Hassan shrugged and took a deep breath. "Do as you wish." He waited until Tess was half way up the side of the ship to start his ascent.

Abigail held Molly as she attempted to comfort the small child. Ignoring her daughter, Tess leaned over the edge of the railing and waited for Hassan to join them. Once he was aboard, Tess hooked her hand around her former lover's arm and said, "Shall we?"

Hassan escorted his guests to the quarterdeck. By this time, Molly's tears had been replaced with giggles as she skipped across the deck. "Miss Randall, may I trouble you to watch the little girl? I must speak to Miss O'Shea in private. I promise we will not be long."

"Of course, Captain Shelby. I would be delighted to watch Molly."

"Thank you. I will assign one of my officers to guard you. Bear in mind that the people on shore will be coming aboard shortly. I would advise that you and the girl remain on the quarterdeck. Do not wander around the ship on your own."

"I understand," Abigail said. "Captain Shelby," she called out just as Hassan and Tess turned away from her.

Hassan glanced over his shoulder. "Yes?"

"There was another woman. She had red hair, and her name is Sarah. She wasn't with us when we left the Palace," Abigail explained while ignoring Tess's glares.

"She's already aboard," Hassan grimaced. "Please excuse us." He extended his hand towards the ladder to the quarterdeck, "Miss O'Shea."

Tess batted her eyelashes and said in a playful voice. "Captain."

Hassan offered his former paramour an awkward smile. When he wasn't worried about Sarah, Hassan spent the rest of the previous night debating what he should say to Tess. Eight hours and a short walk to his make-shift quarters still wasn't enough time.

Tess had already dropped her bundle of clothes on the table and removed her robe by the time Hassan closed the door. His loins tightened when he spotted her enticing curves peeking through her nearly transparent uniform. Tess bounded towards him; her lips locked onto his, drawing him into their usual contest of wills.

Hassan pried her off him before she could lock her legs around his waist. "Tess."

"What?" Tess angrily demanded

"I just witnessed you striking your daughter, and you are acting as if nothing had happened."

Tess rolled her eyes. "She's *our* daughter, and you don't know her the way I do. She is always crying. I don't think I've ever heard her laugh."

"She just did a few minutes ago," Hassan countered.

"You're right; I shouldn't have struck me daughter." She sighed and bit her lip. "Molly makes me so angry sometimes."

Hassan crossed his arms. "When were you going to tell me that I have a daughter?"

"I would have told you, but I haven't seen you in over a year."

"Molly is not an infant either. You have had many opportunities to tell me about the child."

Tess's lip jutted into a pout. "I said nothing because I thought that you had enough concerns. I didn't want to give you another one."

"Why are you telling me now?"

"Because I thought you had a right to know."

Hassan jutted his leg out in front of him. "Tess, I know I wasn't your only lover in the Palace. How do you know that I am the child's father?"

"Because Molly was conceived on the first night that we were together. I swear it. I thought that we would reconcile if you knew the truth," she said, staring at the floor beside his leg.

Hassan let out a loud sigh. "Tess," he softened. "I'm married. We can't be together."

Tess pursed her lips. "Oh for God's sake. Do you think that you are the first married man to cheat on his wife? Men have been unfaithful since the beginning of civilization. What I don't understand is how you can marry that simpleton." Tess sashayed over to Hassan and wrapped her arms around his neck. "I doubt she can please you as I can. Cheating is allowed for the poor devils chained to witless women who can't satisfy their husbands." She rolled up on her toes and kissed Hassan's unresponsive lips.

Hassan pushed Tess away before he surrendered to his desire. "I'm sorry. I can't give you what you seek."

Tess arched her back and stared down her nose at him. "Can I assume that you will at least look after us once we're in England?" She crossed her arms. "You took me home and me livelihood when you rescued me this morning. All I have now are the clothes on me back."

"I cannot discuss this right now." Hassan made a hasty escape to the exit. "I must tend to my duties. We will talk about this matter later. In the interim, I would suggest that you withhold divulging my relation to Molly."

"Molly knows that you are her father. I talked about you for years."

"Of course you did, but does the child know that *I* am her father?"

Tess looked him in the eyes and said, "Aye. I told her in the boat. I would appreciate you having the decency to formally acknowledge her."

"I will send your daughter and Miss Randall to you momentarily." Hassan rested his hand on the doorknob and looked back at her. "Never let me see you strike your daughter again."

Hassan returned to the quarterdeck. The number of people on the main deck had increased by thirty. His crew had already set up three boats to shuttle the prisoners to his ships. Another three jollies had already begun shuttling prisoners to the Trésor. Tristan and several of his lieutenants stayed behind to direct the new crew to the surgery for an examination. Sarah hadn't moved from her perch.

"Captain Shelby," a man called out.

Hassan turned and spotted a man dressed as an Ottoman slave. Something about this man puzzled Hassan. He was a meek-looking man, who was too clean to have come from the quarry. On a quick intake of breath, Hassan realized that the man spoke with an American accent.

"Yes." Hassan frowned.

"Pardon the interruption, Captain. I am John Montgomery."

"What can I do for you, Mr. Montgomery?" Hassan said curtly.

"Vizier Rahmani asked me to return this bag to its owner. He said that it belongs to a woman with red hair. May I enquire if she is aboard the ship?"

"Yes, she is. Please give the bag to me, and I will see that she receives it," Hassan offered.

"Thank you, sir, and thank you for giving me passage to England."

"Mr. Montgomery, may I enquire how you won your freedom? I negotiated the release for British subjects only." Hassan called out as John walked away.

John turned back and replied, "I had the honor of serving Naa'il Dhar as his personal secretary. Vizier Rahmani granted me my freedom because he believed that Dey Dhar would want that for me."

"I see. You do understand that this ship is sailing to England. You will need to secure passage to America if you so desire."

"Thank you. Having my freedom is enough for right now."

"Contact me if you need anything." Draping the bag over his shoulder, Hassan turned and walked over to Tristan who was standing by the railing. "Report, Mr. Thatcher."

"Everything is proceeding in an orderly fashion, Captain. If all goes well, we should have everyone aboard by the end of the day." Tristan's lips curled into a lopsided grin. "Getting everyone settled may take a little longer. Mr. Finch and I still need to take care of that matter for you."

"Carry on with your duties. I will assign a lieutenant to make the sleeping arrangements. Please set aside four of the private rooms for the women. Post guards outside the wardroom at all times. Also, I want you to set up a security detail for the women whenever they are out of their quarters. Of course, we will need to rearrange everything once we move back to the Zafirah," Hassan ordered.

"Yes, Captain. I spotted Miss Sarah sitting on the top. Would you like me to send someone to bring her down?"

Hassan gave the platform a cursory glance and sighed. "Miss Campbell may stay up there for now. I surmise that she's safer up there than she is down here."

"I will keep a watchful eye on the lines so that no trouble reaches her."

"Thank you. I will take care of the matter in town myself."

"When would you like to go ashore, Captain?"

"I will take the next jolly. I must tend to a personal matter first. Do not hold the jolly for my sake," Hassan said thoughtfully.

"Judging its position, you should have approximately ten minutes before the next one leaves for shore."

"Thank you, Mr. Thatcher, I will be ready." Hassan stole away to the railing and propped his foot up on the lower rail. Placing Sarah's bag on his knee, he removed the cloths from the bag. Their size and shape were identical to Sarah's blue paru and were embroidered with gold thread, only each one was a different color. Hassan wanted to throw them overboard, but he couldn't bring himself to do so. He couldn't deny that Sarah looked beautiful in the purple paru. He was certain that she would look equally lovely in the other colors; so he hung them around his neck and returned his attention to examining the other contents in the bag. Hassan pulled out her portraits and quickly flipped through the drawings of the women and winced when he reached the sketches of the men. He recognized Mamnoon's portrait. Though he didn't know Mamnoon well. Hassan remembered that he was a good man, and he felt guilty about his death. Hassan didn't recognize the man in the other portrait. At a glance, he resembled Naa'il Dhar, yet it wasn't him. Moreover, his blue eyes were almost identical to Sarah's. Still, he couldn't remember where he had seen his face before. Hassan looked up when he spotted Molly skipping past him with Abigail chasing her from the corner of his eye. One of the Marines stood off to the side, watching over them. Hassan called out, "Miss Randall, may I trouble you for a word please?"

"Of course, Captain," she said as she approached Hassan.

"Do you recognize this man?" Hassan handed the portrait to her.

Abigail glanced at the sketch and handed it back to Hassan. "I'm sorry, Captain. I don't recognize him. I was only in the Palace for a little more than a month. I only knew two men during that time: Naa'il and my bodyguard. Perhaps Tess can tell you. She seemed to know everyone in the Palace."

Tristan smiled apologetically. Please forgive my intrusion, Captain. The jolly is ready for you."

"Thank you, Mr. Thatcher. Would you mind escorting Miss Randall and the little girl to my quarters?" Hassan requested. "Thank you for answering my questions," he said to Abigail.

"My pleasure, Captain." Abigail curtsied to Hassan and walked away, holding Molly's hand.

When Hassan stuffed Sarah's belongings into the pouch, he spotted something sparkling back at him. Tension billowed inside him when he discovered the diamond and emerald necklace and a ruby ring tucked inside a pocket. He was sure they meant nothing to Sarah, yet he couldn't deny that they meant enough to her to keep them. *The jolly was waiting for him*, Hassan reminded himself as he draped the bag over his shoulder. He climbed down to the boat. Not once did he look up at Sarah.

Chapter 35

No sooner had Abigail and Molly stepped into the captain's quarters when Tess charged towards them. Her eyes were round, her brows drawn together, and her lips were pulled back and curled downward. "Where the devil have you been?" she demanded in a panicked voice.

Abigail closed the door. A mischievous gleam flickered in her eyes as she spotted her friend's anxiety. "I was talking to Captain Shelby," she answered. "I can understand why you and Sarah are vying for his affections. He's quite the virile man. He's handsome too ... and kind ... and noble. My heart is all a twitter," she said, fanning herself while taking pleasure in tormenting her friend for all the times Tess made her weep.

"That's enough!" Tess raised her hand to slap her companion. Abigail stepped out of the way before she could strike. "What did Nathan say? Did he talk about me?" Tess pressed as she followed her friend around the room.

Abigail's smile broadened. "No, actually. He didn't mention your name, not once."

Tess bit her lip when it began to quiver. She turned away from Abigail to conceal the tears flooding her eyes. "What did you two discuss?" She asked in a faint voice.

Abigail looked at Tess and said in a compassionate tone, "Captain Shelby just showed me several drawings. That is it. I swear it." She studied her friend. "I trust that your meeting with him didn't go well?"

"He didn't want me," she whispered. "I spent all those years thinking about him, about us, about what our life would be like as a family." A faint smile formed on her lips. "We would live in the country, in one of those thatched-roof cottages. Perhaps we would live next to a lake. Nathan would farm the land, and I would tend a small garden and rear our children. We would be happy."

"But Tess, how can you expect Captain Shelby to marry you after you were with all those men?"

Tess's eyes darkened. "I did what I had to do to survive. Nathan was a slave once too. He understands what I did. That does not matter. He loves me. I know he does." Tess's face was a kaleidoscope of emotions. At first, her mouth snarled with anger; then her head drooped with despair. Her hand clutched her arm as she straightened her body. "I just have to help him remember." Finally, her lips blossomed into a toothy grin.

"What about Sarah? They are married, remember?"

"Aye, I know," Tess hissed. "I don't care about that as long as Nathan, Molly, and I are together." She scooped up her daughter in her arms and twirled around the room. "We're going to have a family after all," she said to her daughter.

"Mama, can we go back to our room. I want to play with my friends."

"We're never going back to the harem ever again. We're going to a better place, a beautiful place called England," Tess said, kissing her daughter's cheek.

"What about my friends?" Molly whimpered.

"You will make new ones. You will get to play outside. You will see your father every day. And we will take lots of long walks. We will be happy; you'll see," Tess assured her daughter.

The uncertainty on Molly's face faded and was replaced with an excitement that mirrored her mother's. "Can we go there now?"

"Aye, that is why we are on this ship. We will be there within the week."

"What about Papa?" Molly asked.

"He is already aboard this ship. You will meet him today."

"I will?" Molly said in a timid voice.

"Aye. Our lives will be perfect, you'll see," Tess said with a bright voice.

Abigail buried her face in her hand and shook her head.

Luke escorted Hassan on his errand. Though they had been up for hours, the low-lying sun hinted that the morning was still early. The shop-keepers were just starting to set up for their day. Hassan followed Claude Fornier's directions to his apartment. It was located in one of the many narrow alleys. All the buildings looked alike. "My apartment is on the third floor, above a Persian Rug shop," Hassan said as he read Claude's instructions scribbled on a small piece of parchment.

"There are a lot of Persian Rug shops," Luke complained.

"This is the right one. Fornier's wife is with child, and she is standing on the balcony above us." He pointed at a woman wearing a blue floor-length entari with a bubble protruding from her belly. They ducked through an arched door next to the shop and climbed the stairs in a hallway with walls adorned with yellow, brown, and cream mosaic tiles. They passed several doors on the second level and climbed another flight to the third floor. "Fornier said his apartment is at the end of the hall." Hassan knocked on the door. They heard rustling from the inside of the apartment and moments later, a woman said something in a muffled voice.

Hassan understood enough Arabic to recognize the word, "Yes."

"Mrs. Fornier, I am Nathan Shelby. May I speak to you on behalf of your husband?" Hassan said in French, hoping that she would understand him.

The woman opened the door wide enough to show her covered face. "What news do you bring from my husband?" she asked in French.

"He is alive. He sent me to take you to him. This is his ring." Hassan passed a gold ring with a ruby crest through the door's opening.

"Why should I trust you? How do I know that you didn't kill my husband?"

"This is the only proof that I can offer you. If you come with me, you have my word that you will be under my protection. You will be reunited with your husband in two, possibly three days."

"May I have time to consider your offer?" Janna asked.

"No, I'm sorry. You must come with us, or I will leave you here. You have five minutes to collect your belongings."

"My answer is no, sir. My husband spoke of you. He said that you are not an honorable man."

"It is true that your husband and I are adversaries. We faced each other in battle a few years ago, and we fought again last week. He lost and is required to leave the Barbary Coast. I came on your behalf."

"Mine, why?"

"Captain Fornier informed me that you are with child. It is a treacherous world for men. That is doubly true for women, especially those forced to raise their children alone. That is why I agreed to take you to him. You must decide if you can believe me. Know this, if I leave now, it is likely that you will never see your husband again."

The woman let out a faint cry. "What choice do I have but to come with you?"

"I give you my word that I will not give you a reason to fear me. You will have food and a private room that will be guarded at all times."

"I will trust my safety and my honor to you. I would rather die than live without my beloved Claude. May I collect a few belongings?"

"Of course. Please do not take long," Hassan replied.

Claude's wife closed the door to pack while Hassan and Luke waited for her in the hallway.

"I hope she doesn't pack too much," Hassan groused.

"We'll manage, Captain."

Janna appeared a few minutes later wearing a black and gold veil and a blue entari over her white tunic and green Ottoman trousers.

Hassan's lips puckered to the side as he stared at the small muslin bag draped over her shoulders. "Is that all that you want to take with you?"

"I don't need much," she said. "My name is Janna."

"I am pleased to make your acquaintance." Hassan bowed and offered her a sincere smile. "I shall call you Mrs. Fornier. That is the proper way to address a married woman. Shall we?" Hassan extended his arm towards the staircase.

The number of people in the streets had almost doubled by the time they reached the main square. Hassan and his party slipped through the crowds unnoticed, but that didn't stop Hassan and Luke from keeping their hands by their sabers. Janna stayed closed to Hassan during the rest of the journey to the pier. The better part of seven-hundred people was still waiting to be transferred to the ship.

"Captain Shelby," a man with a distinguished voice called out.

Hassan scanned the group until his eyes fell on a familiar face. "Ambassador Browning, have you come to see us off, or do you seek passage to England?"

"Regrettably the former," Ambassador Browning sighed. "My work here is not complete. May I ask how you succeeded in convincing Naa'il Dhar to release the British subjects? I had pressed him regularly over the past three years."

Hassan winced. "Ambassador, Naa'il Dhar was assassinated last night."

"Indeed." The ambassador frowned. "Poor devil, after all that had happened to His Excellency, and now this."

"Dhar could not be allowed to remain in power," Hassan said with a hint of anger.

"Yes, I agree. I still pity him."

Hassan's brow bumped into a scowl. "Why?"

"I saw Dhar about a week ago. He looked like a man who had lost his will to live. I understand that his daughter died a few days later. I hope for his sake that he is reunited with his child."

Hassan shuddered as he remembered Dhar comforting Sarah by telling her that he was going to be with his daughter. "I am afraid only God can decide his fate."

"Quite right," Admiral Browning agreed. "What's next, Captain Shelby?"

"Home, and hopefully a quiet life in the country."

"Well, I can't think of a more worthy man than you. I imagine that you will be the toast of England once your heroics are known."

"I don't need accolades, just a quiet life. I hope that you will have an opportunity to return home soon. Please don't hesitate to contact me if you need help escaping from this God-forsaken region."

"Thank you, I just may accept your offer. When I return to England, I hope that we will have an opportunity to share our stories with each other. Although, I imagine that yours are more interesting than mine."

Hassan laughed.

"May you have a safe journey home," Ambassador Browning bowed.

"Goodbye, Ambassador," Hassan answered in kind. He held out his hand to Janna. "May I assist you into the jolly?" The British subjects waiting for the next one stepped aside to make room for Hassan and Janna. He climbed into the boat first. Janna reached for his hand as she gingerly climbed down. Once she was seated, Hassan sat down beside her. A few more prisoners filled in the vacant seats. Hassan watched Sarah during the shuttle ride back to the ship. For as angry as she made him, he still couldn't take his eyes off her. She looked so beautiful sitting on her perch, and yet so sad.

Once his crew secured the jolly to the ship, they lowered the bosuns' chair for Janna. "Permit me to help you onto the bosuns' chair." Hassan offered his hand to his guest as she gingerly stood up; the former prisoners made room for them as Hassan and Janna moved to the stern. He held her arm securely as she took a seat on the wooden platform. After securing her to the bosuns' chair, Hassan continued, "I will climb beside you and will meet you on deck to help you aboard." He laughed faintly when he noticed Janna's knuckles turning white as she gripped the lines. "You have nothing to fear," Hassan assured her. Janna still looked terrified as his crew effortlessly lifted the plank to the main deck. Hassan had reached the top just in time to help her aboard. "That wasn't so bad, was it?"

"I have never been on a ship before," Janna said in a shaky tone.

"I regret that it may take time getting used to the ship's rocking."

"Welcome aboard, Captain, mum." Tristan saluted Hassan and bowed to Janna. "I see that your mission was successful."

"Yes, Mr. Thatcher. Thankfully, my errand was uneventful," Hassan said to his bodyguard. He glanced over to Janna and continued, "May I escort you to your quarters?"

Janna answered with a reluctant nod.

Freed slaves, caged chickens, goats, and a few other animals now filled the deck. Though the malnourished prisoners were dressed in tattered Ottoman clothing, everyone was jubilant. "Three cheers for Captain Shelby," one shouted.

Hassan tipped his hat to the crew before guiding Janna to the quarterdeck. He opened the door adjacent to the captain's quarters. "Your quarters are this way." He stepped onto a spiral ladder and extended his hand to Janna. Hassan kept a few steps ahead of his guest and stopped on every other stair to check on her progress.

By English standards, the Persephone and the Zafirah were both third rate ships. The Persephone was French built. This ship also had a few features that Hassan liked enough to want to incorporate into his own. He especially liked the spiral ladder leading to the wardroom, which provided his officers with their own private entrance to the quarterdeck. Like the Zafirah, six officers' quarters lined the hull, and a partially exposed window in the aft of the ship provided natural light to the wardroom galley.

Hassan's lieutenants had gathered around a table in the center of the wardroom. Several large Marines were already standing guard by the entrance to the officers' quarters.

"We cleared out our belongings, Captain," said a young lieutenant with sandy blonde hair.

"I appreciate your sacrifices," Hassan said.

"We're only too happy to give up our quarters for the women guests," said another lieutenant. This time there was sincerity in his tone.

"Send word to my other officers and the newly freed officers that I would like to meet with them this morning," Hassan said to the group.

"Yes, sir. I will pass your message, along, "the officer with sandy blond hair volunteered.

"Carry on," Hassan said before returning his attention to his guest. He led Janna to the cabin closest to the stern. "May I suggest that you stay in this one? I think you will enjoy having a chamber with a window."

Janna peered inside the door and bit her lip as she surveyed the room. Her new quarters were barely big enough to fit a berth, a chamber pot, and a small trunk. In spite of the cramped quarters, she liked having a room with a view of the ocean.

"I regret that I cannot offer you larger quarters." Hassan smiled apologetically. "Ships do not allow much personal space."

"This will suffice," Janna replied. "It is only for a few days, yes?"

"Yes," Hassan confirmed. "You are going to discover that our ways are very different from yours. You are welcome to walk around the ship. Please do not do so without an escort. That is for your protection. I will post security guards outside the entrance of these quarters."

"Thank you, the customs you described are not so different from our ways," Janna pointed out.

"That is true, but you are no longer required to cover your head and your face," Hassan countered smoothly. "There is a doctor on board. Would you like me to send him to you?" he asked, observing the color draining from her face.

"I am not accustomed to the rocking."

"You are experiencing seasickness. Regrettably, most sailors suffer from this ailment until their bodies adjust to the ship's movement. But that too will pass. Unless you need anything, I will let you rest."

"Thank you," Janna said, sitting down on her berth.

Janna still looked weary; Hassan was sure that she was more uncertain about her new living arrangements than she was queasy. Closing her cabin door, he headed back to the quarterdeck where he was besieged by officers waiting for his orders. Hassan hated leaving Janna alone, but he was even more anxious to bring Sarah down from the top. But his officers were right, he had been neglecting his duties, even if it was for a legitimate reason. He knew by the urgency of their requests that he couldn't ignore them any longer. Hassan spent the next hour tending to his duties which included sending food to the women. Once the demands on him ceased, Hassan climbed to the top.

Sarah nudged over so that Hassan could sit beside her.

He cringed after seeing Sarah's red puffy eyes. He knew that she was mourning the death of his mortal enemy. Hassan wanted to shake her and make her understand why he despised Naa'il Dhar. He wanted Sarah to hate him too, but her tears made it clear that he could not change her mind.

"You meet Molly?" she asked as she wiped a tear from her cheek.

Hassan gasped when Sarah broached the last subject that he was prepared to discuss with her, yet he was curious how much she knew about his history with Tess. He studied her. Sarah's tears made her sadness abundantly clear, but her somber expression made it impossible to ascertain if she was angry.

"What did Tess tell you about ...," his voice trailed off.

Sarah stared at her lap. "She say, you Molly's da," She raised her gaze to his eyes. "You like her?"

Unconsciously, Hassan's hand clutched the edge of his peasant shirt. He still didn't know how to answer her question, and Sarah had every right to know the truth about his history with Tess. His hand tightened around the fabric as he contemplated his dilemma. Sarah betrayed him when she was held captive in Algiers, yet she made him feel as though he betrayed her, even though his relationship with Tess ended long before he met Sarah. Hassan took a deep breath and looked her in the eyes. "I can't talk about this right now. Our ship is preparing to set sail for England. It is time for you to come down from the top. I do not want you to come up here again. That is an order, Sarah."

"Aye," she whispered with a sad nod.

"I have one more request."

Sarah swallowed hard and looked away.

"I am sure that you witnessed me bringing an Algerine woman aboard. I am taking her to her husband. She is with child and does not know anyone aboard this ship. I would like you to be her companion for the duration of the trip. We should reach her husband in two or three days. Will you do this for me?"

"Aye," Sarah replied in a quiet voice. She looked at him thoughtfully. "Is Tess not better with this person? She with people like her."

"No, I want you to be Mrs. Fornier's companion." Hassan stood up. "I will descend first. You will follow me; do you understand?"

Sarah nodded and stood up.

Hassan ducked through the top's hole, climbed down sever rungs of the ratline and waited for Sarah to join him. "Ready?"

CHAPTER 36

Hassan paused every few minutes to check on Sarah's progress during their descent. She moved with a confidence that he admired. Hassan glanced down when they reached the halfway point. Every person below them was watching their descent; Sarah didn't seem to notice. Onlookers cheered when his hands latched onto Sarah's waist and lowered her to the deck. That was the first time Hassan saw fear in her eyes, and he couldn't deny that she had a good reason. Every man seemed to leer at her. Hassan wrapped his arm around her shoulder and whispered in her ear, "You need not worry. I won't let them hurt you. Come, I will take you to meet Mrs. Fornier." Sarah remained close to him while they weaved their way to the quarterdeck. She followed him down the spiral ladder. Hassan knocked on Janna's door. "Mrs. Fornier?"

Janna opened the door and stuck her head through the crack. "Yes?"

"Forgive my intrusion," Hassan said in French. I would like you to meet …." His voice trailed off as he debated how to introduce Sarah. He hadn't told anyone on his ship that they were married, including Peter. Given their recent history, he was still too angry to admit that she was his wife. "I would like you to meet Sarah. I thought you might keep each other company."

"Hello," Janna said to Sarah in French.

Hassan continued in English. "This is Mrs. Fornier."

All Sarah could do was offer Janna a polite smile.

Hassan wasn't sure what else to say other than, "I will leave you two to get better acquainted." He felt each woman's uncertainty as he turned to leave them. He knew neither spoke a common language. In his heart, Hassan knew that Sarah didn't need words to make a person feel loved. He had just reached the long table in the center of the wardroom when he realized that Sarah's bag was still draped over his shoulder. Though Sarah looked at the bag as if it were an old friend, she never said a word about it. Hassan slid his hand under the strap, turned, and offered the bag to Sarah. "This might help you to communicate with each other. Inform the guards if you need anything."

"Thank you." Sarah took her bag from him.

Hassan returned to the quarterdeck where he found his officers assembled near the wheel. The lieutenant with sandy-blond hair approached Hassan and said, "We convened as many officers as we could find, Captain. Where would you like to meet?"

Walking with his officer, Hassan said, "The quarterdeck will do."

"Very good, sir."

Hassan and his officer approached the group. Many were standing near the wheel or leaning against the railing. All stood at attention when Hassan reached them. He silently scanned their faces, noting that he only recognized half of them. Out of his own officers, all but Peter Hyatt were present.

Sarah lunged towards Janna as she struggled to stay on her feet. Grabbing hold of her waist, she tore off Janna's headscarf and lowered her onto her berth. Sarah handed a bucket to Janna and darted behind her while Janna convulsed into the bucket. Janna offered her new companion a weary smile when she finished. Sarah shifted to the floor and ran to the

Marines standing guard in front of the hall where she was staying.

"Um." Sarah paused as she fought to summon the right words. "This woman … ill. Help, please."

"I will send for the doctor," said the Marine towering over her.

"Thank you," Sarah replied before returning to Janna's side.

Tess folded her spare pair of trousers and laid them on top of the stack of clothes sitting on the dining table. She glanced at the door and knocked the stack over. "Where the devil is he?" she said with a scowl.

"I don't know. I imagine Captain Shelby is busy preparing the ship to leave port," Abigail snatched a vest before Tess could grab it. "You don't need to keep folding these clothes."

"Nathan should be here with his daughter," Tess said fighting back her tears.

Abigail laid the vest on the table and covered Tess's hand with her own. "Give him time."

Tess slid her hand out from under Abigail's and crossed her arms. "I feel like a bloody prisoner. Let's explore the ship."

"Captain Shelby said that we should stay here for our protection."

"No, he wanted to put us away. Well, I will not be held captive," Tess shouted at the door.

"Will you keep your voice down? Molly is finally asleep after weeping for the past hour," Abigail whispered.

"You're right." Tess's tone softened. She covered her shoulders with a muslin robe and said, "Come on. Let's explore the ship."

"What about Molly?"

"Molly will sleep for at least an hour."

"What if she wakes up?"

"Then she will cry herself to sleep," Tess snapped. She held out her hand to Abigail and said, "Come, let's leave while we have the opportunity."

"Very well," Abigail conceded. "Shall we look in on Molly first?"

"Let's escape before she wakes up." Tess opened the door and gasped when she spotted the men standing outside their quarters. Dressed in Ottoman clothing, the guards towered over the two women. Though they both had tan-leathery skin, their blue eyes and light hair betrayed their European heritage. Tess offered them a coy smile and said, "Pardon us."

The guards exchanged concerned looks before returning their attention to the women. "Captain Aziz ordered you to stay in his cabin."

Squaring her shoulders, Tess stared down her nose at them. "We are Captain Shelby's guests, not his prisoners. We will go where we please. Come Abigail." She took her friend by the hand and trotted past the guards.

"Go with the women; I will stay and guard the captain's quarters," the Marine offered.

Tess and Abigail glanced over at Hassan who seemed too engrossed in his conversation to notice them. The women skirted to the main deck and headed to the gangway leading to the deck below.

"I've always hated ships. They are so dark and ... what is that foul smell?" Abigail's face puckered. She pinched her nose with her fingers to offset the stench. For a woman who had spent little time on ships, her sense of smell was extra sensitive, especially towards the men who looked and smelled like they hadn't bathed in months.

Tess's eyes gleamed as she scanned the men occupying every available space. Though the room was dark, the lanterns hanging from the overhead provided enough light to see their hungry stares. Tess leaned in and whispered to Abigail, "Look at them."

Abigail gave her friend a puzzled look. "What do you mean?"

"I was thinking of all the money I could make selling me services to them."

"Tess!" Abigail said with genuine shock.

"I didn't say that I would," Tess replied defensively.

"Well, I doubt they have any money."

The women laughed. "I suppose you're right," Tess sighed. "I wonder where the officer's quarters are."

"You sent for me?" Peter asked in Polynesian.

Sarah's back stiffened as she looked up after rinsing a cloth in a fresh bucket of water. "She is ill; can you help her?"

"Of course." Peter entered Janna's quarters. Sarah jumped up and skirted to the end of the berth so that Peter could examine her. "I am a doctor," he said in English to Janna.

His patient was too nauseous to answer.

Peter completed his examination in a few minutes.

"Is she and her bairn going to die?" Sarah asked after he stood up.

"Other than suffering from nausea, she is in perfect health. All she needs is rest." Peter motioned with his head for Sarah to follow him out of the room.

Sarah could tell by the concerned look on his face that he had more to say. She quickly covered Janna's head with a fresh wet cloth and left her alone.

"Sarah!" Abigail exclaimed, just as Sarah entered the wardroom.

Sarah ran over to her friend. The two embraced like sisters. She didn't know what to say to Tess.

"Captain Shelby informed us that you were aboard," Abigail said. "Have you been here all this time?"

"No, Cattin brought me here." Sarah looked past the two women. "Where Molly?"

"She's sleeping," Tess said coldly as she scanned Peter from head to toe. Peter stared back as if she and Abigail were intruders. "I see that we came at a bad time. If you will excuse us, we'll leave you to finish what you were doing, or did you already finish?"

Sarah's cheeks burned. For as poor as her English was, she understood the meaning of Tess's accusation. She knew that exiting

Janna's bedchamber with Peter looked bad. Peter's silence and smug grin only made her feel guiltier. "No, Peter, he help."

Peter still said nothing.

Tess in leaned and whispered, "I understand. You needn't feel guilty. Everyone cheats, *everyone*."

"No, I keep promise."

"We'll leave you to your reunion. Come along, Abigail."

Sarah wanted to chase after them if only to get as far away from Peter as she could. Still fearing for her charge, Sarah stayed behind. She glared at Peter and exclaimed, "Why didn't you say something to Tess and Abigail? You knew that I sent for you to help that woman. You let them believe that we were together."

Peter leaned in to caress her cheek. "You know that I came here for you. Captain Aziz told me what happened after you were taken prisoner. He feels betrayed by your infidelity. It's not likely that he will take you back. I can help you."

Sarah skittered away before his hand reached her face. "No!" she snapped, "I do not want your help."

"You don't know what awaits you in England. You will need a benefactor. I can help you. All I ask is that you submit to me."

"No!" She said more fervently. "Leave me, or I will scream."

"Very well. I will leave you, for now. Send for me should you need anything." Peter brushed past Sarah, pausing long enough to lean against her.

"Please leave," she whimpered.

Peter's hand had almost reached Sarah's breast, but he quickly lowered his hand when Sarah started to scream. He then walked away without saying another word; Sarah slipped into the room beside Janna's. Her knees buckled, and she collapsed onto the berth.

CHAPTER 37

Tess stepped onto the main deck and paused. Tilting her face to the sky, she spread her arms out and grinned as the sun warmed her face for the first time since her captivity. "I've dreamt of this moment," she said to her friend.

"We were just on deck not an hour ago," Abigail pointed out.

"Aye, but it was cloudy then; it's sunny now."

Abigail nudged Tess forward. But when her friend didn't budge, she complained, "Would you move over so I can feel the sun too?"

"Fine," Tess said, glaring at her friend. She scanned the quarterdeck for Hassan. There were men everywhere. Some were joking with each other and enjoying their new-found freedom, while others stood against the railing, staring at the city of Algiers in silent reflection. Hassan, Tess grinned, stood by the wheel, overseeing the activity on the main deck. Her heart fluttered as she admired his commanding presence. His tall stature and broad shoulders made him seem larger than life. Hassan also projected confidence by the way he stood with his legs splayed apart, and his hands clasped behind his back. "Come on," Tess said to her companion. Ignoring their admiring stares, she and Abigail pushed through the crowd. "Hello, Captain." She said, sidling up to Hassan.

Hassan studied the two women with a scowl. "I told you to stay in my quarters," he barked. "And how did you get past my guards?"

Tess's bottom lip jutted into a pout. "You promised that you would come and meet Molly."

"I apologize for my delay. I am on duty. My work requires me to oversee the activity on deck," Hassan's harsh tone softened slightly.

"What is so important that it requires you to stay? Your crew is doing all the work. Why don't you come and meet Molly?"

Abigail turned her head away and covered her mouth with her hand to muffle her laugh.

Hassan shifted his weight restlessly and let out a loud sigh. "Speaking of your daughter, where is she?"

"I think you mean *our* daughter."

"Where is the child, Tess?" Hassan growled.

"She is sleeping in our quarters." Tess snapped back.

"Never leave your child alone on this ship. Do you understand me?"

"Aye, I understand you. When will you come to us?"

"I will come to you after the ship's bell. Please, leave me to my work." He opened the door to his quarters.

"Very well," Tess conceded. "You will spend the evening with us, won't you?"

"I will be entertaining the officers at dinner tonight," Hassan stated.

Tess's thin lips broadened into a toothy grin. "Then Abigail and I can come too."

"What about the child?" Hassan challenged.

"You let me worry about that." Tess rolled onto her toes and kissed Hassan's lips. "We'll see you tonight."

Molly was still sleeping peacefully on Hassan's berth when the two women returned to his quarters.

Abigail stared at Tess's clothes. "Are you going to wear that tonight?"

"I would if I were having an intimate dinner with Nathan." Tess peeled off her robe and threw it onto the dining table. She looked down at her see-through trousers and frowned. "What am I going to wear? I haven't worn a dress since I left Ireland."

"Didn't you say that Captain Shelby was a pirate?" Abigail said, thoughtfully. "Perhaps he acquired a dress during one of his exploits."

Tess looked at her friend with a raised brow. "If I were a dress, where would I be stored?" She tapped her yellowed teeth with the edge of her fingernail.

Abigail went over to the entrance of the dressing area. "There are several trunks next to the highboy."

"I suppose that's a good place to start as any." Tess shrugged.

"Where should we look?" Abigail rested her hands on her waist and divided her gaze between the highboy and the two trunks.

"I suppose it doesn't matter." Tess knelt in front of the chest sitting in the corner and raised the domed lid. Her breath hitched when her eyes fell on a white cloth folded across the top. She reached for one end of the cloth. Her eyes lit up when she unfolded the dress. It was made out of fine silk. The edges of the high neck and puffy silk sleeves were adorned with the most delicate lace that she had ever seen.

"My goodness!" Abigail exclaimed. "This is exquisite!" She reached around Tess and pulled out the next dress on the pile; this one was made out of pink silk and white lace. "Did this trunk belong to a princess?"

Tess and Abigail removed and examined the chest's contents. It contained everything that a lady needed, including a hairbrush and firs. All that was missing were the undergarments. The two women spent the next hour trying on the dresses. Each one fit perfectly. They also found several pairs of shoes in the bottom of the trunk but quickly discovered that they were too small for their feet.

"Are there any colors other than white and pink?" Tess groaned.

"White and pale colors are very fashionable," Abigail said in a snooty tone. "What color are you hoping for, red?"

"And what's wrong with red?" Tess asked with casual interest.

"Nothing, I suppose. Ladies do not wear red, at least not at home," Abigail said, looking down her nose at Tess.

"That is why all of you are bores."

"Then wear your harem clothes. I doubt that the officers would mind. I like this one." Abigail held up the dress and admired how the pink fabric flowed to the floor.

Tess sighed and shook her head. She laid the other gowns across the dining table. Nibbling on her fingernail, Tess studied her choices. "What would a lady wear to a party?"

Abigail examined each dress and reached for the first gown that Tess pulled from the trunk. "Wear this one."

"White?" Tess sighed.

"Yes. All unmarried ladies wear white. The color symbolizes purity," Abigail said emphatically.

Tess looked at the gown with disgust. "If I must," she groaned.

Abigail bit her lip. "Do you think there are any jewels in this cabin?"

"Hmm." Tess tilted her head to the side. "Perhaps."

The women returned to the dressing room and discovered the second chest filled with more gowns. When they didn't find any jewels in the trunks, Tess began opening the other drawers in the highboy, but all they found were men's clothing.

Abigail hung her head when they didn't find what they were searching for. "At least we have something to wear tonight," she said in a tone laced with disappointment.

Tess continued looking at the bottom of the trunk sitting in the corner of the room. "Is it just me, or does the bottom look like it should be deeper?"

"Perhaps," Abigail shrugged.

Tess knelt in front of the trunk. She spotted a finger-size hole at the edge of one side and scrape marks on the inside panels. "I wonder." Tess poked her finger through the hole and exclaimed, "I knew it. It's a false bottom." She pulled up the bottom of the trunk and leaned it against the bulkhead beside her. The two women gasped when they spotted small-lumpy bags strewn across the lower part of the trunk. Tess's hand trembled as she picked up the bag closest to her. She reached inside and pulled out a gold and ruby necklace.

"Oh my goodness!" Abigail exclaimed. She reached for the bag closest to her and discovered a diamond broach inside the pouch.

Tess and Abigail removed bags of jewels from both trunks. They dumped the contents over the dresses and stared at the cache sparkling back at them.

"These trunks really must have belonged to a queen or a princess," she said admiring a diamond and sapphire necklace. "Do you think that we should give Sarah a dress to wear tonight? "

Tess glared at her friend with her lips pressed together. "That whore is not coming," she said with a snarl.

"But she is Captain Shelby's wife."

"Sarah is not coming! I'll make sure of it." Moments later, they heard Molly's muffled cries. "Why does she always have to ruin me fun?" Tess paused and stared at the table. "I have an idea." She marched into Hassan's bedchamber. By this time, Molly was screaming. Her nose was runny and worst of all, she smelled. "Oh, the devil," Tess picked up her child and held Molly away from her.

"Do you have a cloth that you can use?" Abigail asked, looking on.

"No, I was forced to leave the harem without any warning, just like you." Tess snapped at Abigail. "Stop your crying!" She shouted at her daughter. Molly's screams abated to a whimper. Holding her daughter at a distance, she carried Molly over to the door. "Take the robes and follow me."

The three ducked out of the captain's quarters and slipped past Hassan to the door leading to the spiral ladder. They looked inside each room they passed until they found Sarah. "Oh," Tess exclaimed when she spotted a pregnant woman lying on a berth in the same room that they caught Sarah leaving with Peter.

Sarah jumped to her feet and followed the women into the wardroom. "I pleased to see you," she said with a bright smile.

"Will you watch Molly tonight?" Tess demanded.

"Aye," Sarah answered without hesitation.

"Good." Tess handed her daughter to Sarah and walked away without saying anything to her child. She could hear Sarah whispering. Molly's tears had dried up by the time they reached the spiral ladder. Tess looked back and grimaced when she heard Molly giggle. She couldn't remember the last time she heard her daughter laugh. Tess kept walking as Abigail struggled to keep up with her.

The women's jaws dropped when they returned to the captain's quarters and discovered Hassan placing their jewels into a small chest. Tess didn't know what was more disturbing - losing her newfound wealth or seeing the scowl on Hassan's lips. "Now you return." Tess rested her hands on her hips and sashayed over to Hassan's side.

Hassan laid a diamond necklace in the chest and glared at the women. "I arrange for your freedom, offer you my quarters, and you repay me by stealing from me?"

Shivers shot up and down Tess's spine when she heard unmistakable anger in Hassan's calm tone. "We weren't stealing," Tess said, staring at the floor, "not exactly."

"But you would have taken them if you thought that I didn't know about the trunks' false bottoms," Hassan surmised.

Tess opened and closed her mouth without answering. She couldn't deny that she had planned to keep the jewels and use them to fund her new life in England. "Yes, I intended to take them, but you acquired them by stealing them too. Don't you dare judge me for wanting to give our daughter a good life in England?"

Hassan's knuckles turned white as he clinched the back of the chair. "I didn't steal them; I won them in a battle. My crew and I paid dearly for them with our blood," Hassan said, glaring at his guests. "You had no right rummaging through my belongings. This ship, my crew and everything in this ship belong to me. I will not tolerate stealing," he said with nostrils flaring.

"I didn't think you had any use for the dresses," Tess said innocently.

"The gowns were for Sarah. She doesn't own any western clothing."

Tess turned away from him and said in a hurtful voice. "Neither do we. We wanted to dress appropriately for your dinner tonight."

Abigail removed her necklace and the diamond brooch and returned them to Hassan. "I apologize; we meant no harm, Captain

Shelby. Wearing a dress made me feel normal again."

Hassan took the jewels from Abigail and dropped them into the chest. The anger on his face faded. "You may keep the gowns that you are wearing, but the jewels belong to me," he said in a softened tone.

Tess stepped back and spun around slowly. "Do we look appropriate for your dinner tonight?"

"You both look lovely."

"Then we may come to dinner? Tess confirmed.

"You need to tend to your daughter. Speaking of which, where is she this time?"

"Molly is spending the night with Sarah," Tess informed him.

"The devil she is." Hassan slammed the chest's lid shut. He threw a dress over his shoulder and stormed out of his cabin with the jewel chest tucked under his arm.

CHAPTER 38

A small group of seamen had gathered outside the wardroom. Each one leaned in as if they were standing outside a concert hall, hoping to hear the performance of a famous singer. Hassan paused at the bottom of the spiral ladder. Moments later, he heard a woman singing. Her voice was not operatic, but sweet and melodic. Giving into his curiosity, he followed the singing and found Sarah sitting on a berth with Molly perched on her lap. Holding the child close to her, Sarah rocked and serenaded her with a heavenly melody. Seeing the tenderness expressed by Sarah to this small child made him remember why he was drawn to this exotic creature.

Sarah's melody came to an abrupt end when she noticed Hassan leaning against the doorway as if he had nowhere to go. "Cattin!" she exclaimed in a bright tone.

Hassan didn't budge from his spot. "Don't let me interrupt you."

Molly wrapped her arms around Sarah's neck and buried her face in her protector's chest.

"Molly," Sarah said tenderly. "This your da."

Hassan hung his head and closed his eyes. He wasn't ready to reveal his relation to Molly because he still wasn't sure that he was her father.

Sarah stood up and went over to Hassan with Molly still clinging to Sarah's neck. "Molly, this your da. You no need be afraid. He good man."

This time Molly dared to look at Hassan all the while in the security of Sarah's arms.

Hassan had never been with a small child before, especially a little girl. He struggled to find the right words to say to her. All he could muster was, "Hello."

Sarah smiled apologetically. "Molly ..."

"Shy," Hassan offered.

"Aye, Molly shy." Balancing the child on her hip, Sarah took Hassan's hand and led him into the chamber. They both sat down on the edge of the berth; Sarah settled Molly on her lap.

Hassan observed that Molly couldn't take her eyes off the little chest. With a gleam in his eye, he asked, "Would you care to see what's inside?"

Molly stuck her thumb in her mouth and replied with a timid nod.

Hassan opened the lid. Molly's eyes lit up when she spotted the jewels sparkling back at her, but Sarah's knuckles turned white as she gripped the end of her tunic. "Sarah, what's the matter?"

"You wish me wear?" she asked in a small voice.

Hassan heard the dread in her tone. "Not if you do not wish. Please tell me what's wrong."

Tears filled Sarah's eyes as she pulled down her tunic neckline to show Hassan her necklace. "Naa'il put this here. I not take off."

"Why not?" Hassan frowned.

"I try. I not understand how." Sarah pleaded like a desperate woman.

"Come here," Hassan whispered. Sarah winced when his fingers rubbed against the cuts on the back of her neck. He could almost feel her desperation as she attempted to pull the necklace off, and her despair when she failed. After spending a few seconds fidgeting with the clasp, her jeweled shackles dropped into her lap.

"It off!" Sarah expelled a breath of relief.

Hassan studied the necklace. He had never seen its equal. The diamonds lining the string and surrounding the blue stone were stunning, but the sapphire was magnificent. As Hassan studied the royal blue stone, he wondered if it were a sapphire at all. Laying the small chest beside him, he stood up, went over to the lantern and scratched the glass with the blue stone. "My God," he exclaimed when the stone left a mark on the glass surface.

"Cattin?" Sarah said sweetly.

Hassan couldn't contain his excitement. He didn't even care that Molly was pulling out every jewel in the chest one piece at a time. "I had heard that Dhar acquired a very rare stone, a blue diamond. He considered this necklace his prized possession." Hassan looked at Sarah with disbelief and held the necklace up. "He gave it to you."

"You keep. I not like." Sarah insisted. Balancing Molly on her lap, she leaned over the berth and retrieved her turquoise bag. She pulled out her emerald and diamond necklace and handed it to Hassan when he returned to his seat. "You keep."

Hassan examined the necklace and held it up to her neck. Though the emerald and diamond string was simpler than the other one, it looked like it belonged there. Hassan laid the jewelry on his lap when he spotted the dread in Sarah's eyes. He chuckled as he envisioned Tess and Abigail cooing over Sarah's cache. He was equally sure that Tess would kill anyone who threatened to confiscate either one from her. But to Sarah, they were the equivalent to the slaves' iron chokers. Hassan caressed Sarah's cheek and offered, "I will keep them safe for you." He tipped his head to the side. "I suppose that you want to keep the ring."

"What is ring?"

"It is the jewel that you wear on your finger."

"Oh." Sarah retrieved the ring from her bag and handed it to Hassan. "You keep."

Hassan bit the inside of his lip when he heard her reluctance. "You like this ring, don't you?"

She replied with a reluctant nod. "I see Naa'il ... I fear him ... He kind ... He give me this .... I not fear him after. Naa'il friend, not husband."

Hassan pursed his lips. He wanted to believe Sarah, but the recent events cautioned him not to trust her.

"You keep," she insisted.

Hassan stared at the diamond and ruby ring. He knew she was trying to make peace by giving Naa'il's gifts to him. Sarah's offering made him feel as though he were stealing from a child because she clearly lacked the understanding of the jewels' value. He was sure that one day she would know their worth. Hassan looked back at Sarah and said, "I hate the thought of you accepting gifts from another man, but I am willing to compromise."

"What compro …?"

"Compromise. It's a concession."

"A what?"

"Never mind," Hassan sighed. "It is not important. The point that I am trying to make is that I would like you to keep your new parus; I will keep the jewels."

Sarah reached over the side of the berth and dropped her parus on Hassan's lap. "You keep. I want paru you give. I not want this."

Hassan smiled tenderly. "I am pleased that you like the one that I gave you, but I want you to keep the others. Even I have different shirts to wear." For as much as Hassan hated Naa'il Dhar, he couldn't deny that each paru that Naa'il had selected would be stunning on Sarah. Each one was a vibrant color. Her blue eyes, her peach and cream complexion, and her burgundy hair seemed to demand that she wear clothes made with brightly-colored fabrics. Hassan held up a lemon-colored paru to her face and grinned. "I think you would look lovely in this. I would very much like to see you wear the others."

"What is a paru?" Molly asked.

"It this." Sarah laughed and handed the yellow cloth to Molly. "I wear to sleep," she explained.

"Oh," Molly's frown deepened.

"Is our agreement satisfactory?" Hassan asked before Sarah could stand up to demonstrate how she wore her native costume.

Sarah took the ruby ring and offered it to Hassan. "Aye. You keep this."

"Thank you. I promise that you will have others." Hassan took the ring from her. "I appreciate your understanding."

Sarah nodded with a rueful smile as she took one last look at her ring. They returned their attention to Molly who had emptied the entire contents of the chest onto her lap. Hassan picked up a simple gold necklace and hooked it around Molly's neck; Molly's eyes gleamed. Hassan returned the jewels to the chest including Sarah's ring and necklaces without Molly uttering a single protest. She squirmed out of Sarah's arms and crawled onto Hassan's lap. Hassan closed his eyes as the child traced the outline of his face with her finger. When she finished, she turned around and snuggled against him.

Hassan marveled how light the child was, and how natural it felt to hold her. For the first time in his life, he knew how it felt to be part of a loving family, and he wanted that moment to last forever.

One of his lieutenants knocked on the door. "Forgive my interruption, sir," he smiled apologetically. "I was sent to tell you that dinner will be ready in an hour. What time shall I tell the others to arrive?"

"Have them arrive about fifteen minutes before dinner," Hassan replied.

"Very good, sir." His lieutenant saluted and left.

Hassan remembered why he came to the wardroom. He pulled the dress off his shoulder and offered it to Sarah. "I came to invite you to dinner tonight, and I would like you to wear this dress."

"But Cattin. That woman ill. I care of her. I care of Molly," Sarah insisted.

"Tess can care for her own daughter," Hassan said with a hint of anger. He paused as he thought about Janna. He couldn't see Tess or Abigail nursing a sick woman. Janna's customs forbade her from being alone with a man who wasn't a member of her family. Hassan also couldn't in good conscience leave a sick woman unattended. "Very well, I will excuse you this one time," he reluctantly conceded. He caressed Sarah's cheek with the back of his fingers. "You are my wife, and you belong by my side."

Sarah looked at him as if he bestowed a great honor upon her.

"Have you been attending to Mrs. Fornier this whole time?"

"Aye," Sarah answered. "Peter say she not ill. I no believe him," she said innocently.

Hassan grimaced. "You sent for Dr. Hyatt?"

"Aye. She ill; should I not?"

"Of course you should," Hassan softened. "Dr. Hyatt was correct. Mrs. Fornier is not ill."

Sarah frowned. "She not?"

"Not exactly." Hassan chuckled. "Did you feel ill when you first boarded the ship after you left your island?"

"Aye." She nodded vigorously. "It hard to eat."

"That is what we call sea sickness. It is very common for people's bodies to react adversely to the ship's rocking. It takes a few days for their bodies to adjust to the motion before the sickness goes away. That is the ailment from which Mrs. Fornier suffers."

"Oh," Sarah said thoughtfully.

Hassan lowered Molly to the floor and stood up. "Come, let us check on Mrs. Fornier." He reached for Sarah's hand. Molly protested with a whimper as she held her hands up to Hassan. "You may come too." He released Sarah's hand and picked up Molly.

Janna opened her eyes when she heard Molly chattering.

"How are you feeling?" Hassan asked in French.

"I feel useless," Janna admitted.

"Sarah informed me that you were still feeling ill."

"Sarah has not left my side except when I was sleeping. I am grateful for her kindness."

"Sarah insisted on remaining with you for the rest of your journey. Do you need anything?" Hassan asked.

"I am grateful for the opportunity to rest."

"I will have dinner brought to you," Hassan offered.

"Thank You, Captain Shelby." Janna paused and studied Molly. "What a beautiful little girl. Is she your daughter?"

"So I am told," Hassan winced.

"You are very fortunate to have such a beautiful family."

"Thank you. I will take my leave and let you rest. Should you need anything, please do not hesitate to contact my guards standing outside the wardroom."

"Thank you, Captain Shelby."

Hassan carried Molly and led Sarah back to their room. He wanted to spend every spare moment with his new family. Their time together was interrupted by an unexpected guest. Passing Molly to Sarah, Hassan jumped to his feet and bowed. "Miss Randall?"

Abigail blushed and froze like a person who had forgotten the reason for their visit. "Oh, um." Her face turned redder.

"Did you need something?"

Abigail glanced at her dress and removed a white gown draped over her shoulder. "I thought Sarah would enjoy wearing this tonight." She handed the dress to Hassan.

"Thank you, that is very thoughtful." Hassan glanced back at Sarah and stifled a laugh when he spotted the grimace on Sarah's face.

"Thank you," Sarah said. "I stay with Molly."

"I will look after Molly if you wish." Abigail offered.

"No, you go. I stay," Sarah insisted as she fidgeted with a lock of hair.

Hassan understood Sarah's reluctance. There was more to her insistence on staying behind to care for Janna and Molly. He recognized that Sarah wasn't prepared to attend a dinner party, let alone eat a full meal with a knife and a fork. The last thing he wanted to do was embarrass her. Hassan gently squeezed Sarah's shoulder and said, "Thank you, Miss Randall. You are very thoughtful. I agree that Sarah is needed here."

"Perhaps another time."

"Captain, dinner is almost ready," one of his lieutenants announced.

"Duty calls," Hassan sighed. He kissed Sarah tenderly. "I will return as soon as I can. May I escort you to dinner?"

"I would be delighted, Captain Shelby." Abigail grinned and tucked her hand under his arm. "I'm so sorry about this afternoon. I don't know what got into me. You must think I am the rudest person in the world."

"You've been through a difficult ordeal. I am certain that you needed to feel normal again," Hassan said as they ambled to his quarters.

"That's no excuse. What we did was wrong. I knew it, and I'm sorry."

"Give it no more thought. Thank you for bringing the gown to Sarah." Hassan patted her hand. They climbed the spiral ladder and stopped in front of his quarters. Hassan extended his arm towards the entrance and said, "Shall we?"

Hassan's guests were already being served wine from Claude Fournier's private stock. Other members of the dinner crew were busy setting up their meal in the background.

Though his guests were officers of the Royal British Navy, half of them looked like Barbary Coast corsairs; the other half like slaves. Tess and Abigail were the only ones who looked like they belonged at this elegant affair. Dressed in their new gowns and their hair twirled into buns, Tess and Abigail greeted his guests like perfect hostesses.

Tess sidled up to Hassan and Abigail. She handed a goblet of wine to Hassan while behaving as though her friend wasn't there; Abigail rolled her eyes.

Hassan pretended not to notice the women's exchange. "Would you care for some wine, Miss Randall?"

"I would love some," Abigail replied.

Hassan handed Abigail his goblet.

"Thank you," she smiled pleasantly at Hassan and turned her nose up at Tess.

"You both look lovely," Hassan said hoping to alleviate the growing tension between the women.

Tess wedged herself between Hassan and Abigail. "Thank you." She hooked her hand around his arm and gave every man in the room a look that said she was the captain's woman.

Abigail rolled her eyes and sipped her wine.

Peter was the first to approach Hassan and the two women.

"Good evening," Peter bowed.

Hassan's brows snapped together after he recognized a knife with a carved handle sticking out of Peter's belt. He gave it to Peter several years ago. What puzzled Hassan was why Peter wore it to dinner. He pursed his lips as he observed Peter and the women exchanging looks as if they were already acquainted. "Have you already met?"

"We passed each other earlier today when Abigail and I were exploring the ship," Tess replied coyly.

"Indeed." Hassan sipped his wine. "May I present our ship's doctor, Peter Hyatt."

Tess and Abigail curtsied to Peter.

Peter bowed back. "It is an honor to make your acquaintance."

John Montgomery was the next to approach them. Out of all the men in the room, he was the best dressed. His Ottoman clothes were clean and not torn, his beard perfectly manicured. John was also the only one who didn't look battle weary. "Ah, Mr. Montgomery. I am pleased that you could join us," Hassan said cordially.

"It's an honor to accept your invitation, Captain Shelby." John scanned the room and frowned when he didn't find what he was searching for.

"Is something wrong?" Hassan asked.

John's cheeks flushed. "I had hoped to finally meet the mysterious owner of that turquoise bag. I know that she is a real person because I watched her descend the lines with you."

"You are quite right, Mr. Montgomery. Miss Campbell is very real," Hassan paused. *Miss Campbell.* He knew that night that Sarah was the only woman for him, yet he still wasn't ready to announce to the world that she was his wife. Hassan glanced at Tess and remembered that Sarah didn't hesitate to tell her that she was married. "Not yet," he mumbled to himself.

"Will we have the pleasure of her company tonight?" John asked in a hopeful voice.

"Regrettably no. Sarah insisted on nursing another passenger, a woman who was not accustomed to the ship's rocking." Tess and Peter still looked at each other as if they shared a secret.

While the dinner crew set up their table, Hassan tapped his wine glass and announced, "I am pleased that you could be my guests tonight.

Shall we be seated?"

His guests lined up around the table and sat down at his invitation.

Hassan and his guests spent the evening exchanging stories about their captivity in Algiers. There were twelve different guests and twelve different stories, yet each tale was similar. They fell prey to Claude Fornier's unconventional attack. Once his ship was close enough, Fornier and his crew swarmed their ships. Instead of honoring a gentleman's code of conduct and releasing the crews, Claude sold them into slavery.

"How did you win your freedom, Captain Shelby?" one of the officers asked.

Hassan shrugged. "I swore my allegiance to the Ottoman Empire, while at the same time I searched for the people responsible for enslaving our countrymen. The Dey of Algiers refused to disclose Fornier's identity. We faced them in battle a few days ago. This time we prevailed. Claude Fornier and his crew will never sail under the French or Algerian flag again." Hassan tossed a glance at Peter, silently noting that he had finished his fifth glass of wine and held his glass up for another.

One of his guests raised his goblet and said, "To Captain Shelby."

The rest of the guests raised their cups and repeated in unison, "To Captain Shelby."

Shivers spiked up and down Hassan's spine when he felt Tess's hand rubbing his inner thigh. She had been rubbing his leg with her feet throughout their dinner. It wasn't until her hand reached for his inner thigh that her flirting began to affect him. Hassan jumped up from his chair and held up his glass. "Thank you, gentlemen," he said, silently wishing that Sarah was there to share this moment with him. At the conclusion of their dinner, Hassan's party adjourned to the quarterdeck to enjoy the festivities. The city of Algiers was behind them, and there were no corsair ships in sight. His crew informed them that the former prisoners were on the main deck, celebrating their freedom. All were singing a lively tune. Several members of Hassan's crew disappeared below deck and returned carrying their instruments. The musicians commenced with playing a jig. Abigail clapped her hands and moved her head to the beat of the music.

One of his lieutenants approached Abigail and asked, "Would you care to dance, Miss Randall?"

"I would be delighted," she replied. Taking his hand, his officer led her to a free space on the quarterdeck. The men on the main deck clapped and cheered as Abigail and her partner whirled around while Hassan, Tess, and his other officers looked on. Hassan was so engrossed in watching the dancing that he hadn't notice Peter stealing away.

Sarah closed the door to Molly's cabin as soon as she was asleep. Janna was also sleeping, and her half eaten plate of food was sitting on the floor outside her door. Sarah moved Janna's plate to the table in the wardroom and ducked into her chamber. She was about to turn her attention to straightening the room when she spotted Peter leaning against the doorway. Even at an arms distance, Sarah could smell the stench on his breath.

"Cattin is not here," she said in Polynesian, ignoring his hungry stares.

"Yes, I know. Your 'Cattin' is on deck with Miss O'Shea. I believe that they are dancing," Peter replied.

"What do you want?"

Peter swaggered into Sarah's room, "You broke my heart, Tiari; I'm going to make you pay for the pain that you caused me. The guards are gone, and no one is here to protect you."

Sarah yelped and backed away from him, but she couldn't escape from him pinning her against the wall.

Janna pulled herself to her feet when she heard Sarah's muffled cries. This wasn't the first time that she had heard a woman scream from being attacked. She stumbled into the wardroom and gasped when she didn't find the guards standing at the entrance of their quarters. Sarah screamed again; Janna ran to her friend's rescue. She expected to find Hassan or one of the sailors attacking Sarah, but not the benevolent doctor. "What are you doing?" Janna shouted in her own language, even though she knew that he wouldn't understand her.

As the doctor spun around and glared at the intruder, Sarah snatched his knife. Peter screamed when she slashed his arm.

Sarah shouted at him in a strange language; Janna stepped aside as the doctor stumbled out of the room. Once they were alone, Sarah dropped the knife and sobbed.

"You're safe," Janna said, wrapping her arms around Sarah's shoulders. Moments later, they heard Molly's muffled cries coming from the other room. Sarah pulled away and offered her friend a less than convincing smile. Janna nodded and stepped aside so that Sarah could go to the child.

The sixth song had ended, and Tess hadn't participated in a single dance. She had been asked by six different officers, but she refused each request in hopes that Hassan would ask her. He didn't. Not even her tapping foot could convince Hassan to ask her to dance.

"Are you going to ask me to dance?" Tess impatiently demanded after the beginning of the seventh song.

"It's not appropriate for the captain to dance," Hassan countered. He felt like a hypocrite for refusing Tess's request, but he didn't want to dance with anyone except with Sarah.

"Would you care to dance with me, Miss O'Shea?" asked the lieutenant with sandy-brown hair.

Glaring at Hassan, Tess reached for the officer's hand and said, "I would be delighted."

His crew cheered when Tess's dance partner led her to the floor. In her usual coquettish style, Tess leaned into her partner whenever they came face to face. Every once in a while, she glanced over at Hassan, who seemed too lost in thought to notice her.

As Hassan looked on, his thoughts returned to the night Sarah danced for him. He stayed for two more songs until he couldn't linger any longer. Like a bee drawn to a flower, he ducked down the spiral ladder. Sarah had just closed Molly's door when Hassan arrived. He was too focused on Sarah to notice that the guards weren't standing by the entrance. Reaching for her hand, Hassan led her into their private bedchamber. Hassan closed the door and kissed her tenderly. "I missed you tonight. Come to bed," he said in a throaty whisper before kissing her again. They took their time undressing each other, removing piece by piece between their kisses. Hassan lowered Sarah onto the berth. She held out her hand and welcomed her husband home.

Tess fought back her tears as she watched Hassan exit the celebration. She had used her entire arsenal to make him jealous, but he seemed not to notice her. She knew by his distant look that he wasn't thinking about her or the love they once shared. Moreover, his purposeful stride told her that he still wanted Sarah.

"May I have this dance, Miss?" asked a lieutenant with auburn hair.

Tess's whole body shook as she stared at the door leading to the officer's quarters. She glowered at the officer when he pressed her again. "No," Tess snapped and walked away.

Abigail froze and stared at her friend with a gaping jaw just as she welcomed a new dance partner. "Where are you going?"

"I have a headache." Tess turned back and glared at Abigail and to anyone else who attempted to approach her. She raced down the spiral staircase leading to the wardroom. Though Tess knew Hassan was with Sarah, she couldn't accept that her love affair with Hassan was over and that he had found love with her enemy. Her heart raced when she reached the wardroom galley. "Is Captain Shelby here?" Tess asked one of the guards standing by the entrance to the wardroom.

"Captain Shelby is indisposed, mum. You may request a meeting with him tomorrow," one of the guards replied as they blocked Tess from interrupting Hassan.

Tess didn't need to go any further when she heard moans and Hassan calling Sarah's name over and over again. She turned her head away and wiped a tear from the corner of her eye. "Where can I find Peter Hyatt," Tess asked with a forced smile.

Peter winced with every stitch he added to his arm. The wine clouding his senses wasn't enough to offset the pain from the wound, nor was it enough to make him forget the events from that evening. He remembered everything that took place that night, including attacking Sarah. All he could think about was how he would explain this attack to Hassan, which Peter was sure would result in his death. For as little time as Sarah had been with them, Peter had underestimated Hassan's feelings for her. Hassan was popular with the English ladies because they were drawn to his viral demeanor. He had always treated his admirers cordially, but he was different with Sarah. Hassan was always watching her whenever she was near him and usually with a subtle smile on his lips. It was much more than that. He was reserved whenever he was with English women, yet Hassan was gentle, attentive and almost excessively protective of Sarah whenever they were together. Every person on the Zafirah understood that she belonged to him.

"There you are," Tess said in a conversational tone. "I have been looking everywhere for you."

Peter winced as he looked up from his arm. His heart raced when he discovered Tess leaning against his doorframe, staring intently at him with narrowed eyes. Her head was slightly tilted to the side, and her pursed lips sucked on her finger.

"What happened to you?" she asked in a seductive voice.

"It's nothing," Peter said as his shaky hand attempted another stitch.

"If you say so." Tess invited herself to sit in the chair beside him. "You best let me help you with that."

Peter studied her. "Are you a surgeon, Miss O'Shea?"

"No, but I've been around enough wounds to acquire the skill to sew them up. May I?"

Peter passed the needle to her and sipped his wine as Tess sewed. She had a light touch, but it wasn't enough to sedate the pain. "What do I owe the pleasure of your company?"

Tess finished the last stitch. "I thought that we could help each other with a common problem."

Peter raised a brow. "What common problem do we share?"

"I saw the way that you looked at Sarah this afternoon."

"She means nothing to me," Peter grimaced.

"Really? Did Sarah give you that wound?"

Peter looked away without answering.

"It's no matter. My point is, you want Sarah; I want Nathan. I thought that we could work together to change Nathan's mind about his wife."

"They are not married," Peter interrupted.

Tess's lips parted. "Really? Sarah thinks that they are."

"The whore is either lying or gullible. I'm not sure which. The only thing that I know for certain is that Shelby and Sarah are not legally married - at least by English laws."

"Indeed. That will make our mission that much easier, won't it? Perhaps if we're lucky, we'll get what we want." Tess stood up from the table. "Where do you sleep?"

Peter winced again. "I have a cabin off the wardroom. Our captain asked us to make other sleeping arrangements until we rendezvous with the Zafirah. Happily, I have a small cabin off this room so that I can sleep here while taking care of patients.

Tess strolled around the table and scanned the bedchamber. Peter was right; it was only big enough to fit a small berth. She lifted the bottom of her dress to her knees and said, "Will you help me out of this bloody gown?"

"I thought that you wanted Captain Shelby."

"I do. This is recreation, not love," Tess said before slipping into the darkness.

His tightened loins reminded him that it had been years since he had been with a woman. Forgetting his pain, Peter rose from the table and followed his guest into his cabin.

CHAPTER 39

"Te pe'ape'a nei au, Da," she whimpered. Sarah sat up sharply from a deep sleep as sweat dripped down her temples.

Hassan sat up and wrapped his arms around her shoulders. "Sarah, you're trembling. What's the matter?"

"It bad dream. I sorry I wake you," she calmed herself by taking a few deep breaths.

"No, you're upset. Please tell me why." Hassan gently demanded.

"I dream about Da." Sarah forced a smile. "Cattin? You hold me?"

"Come here," Hassan whispered, coaxing her to lie beside him.

Sarah nuzzled against him with his arm locked around her chest. She had always felt safe whenever he held her, and yet Sarah still couldn't stop thinking about the night Hassan had struck her. He was angry, now he was kind, and she had no idea what caused him to doubt her love. "Cattin," she said softly.

"Yes," he whispered back.

"You still cross with me?"

Hassan let go of her and propped himself up on his elbow. "I don't know," he said after a long pause. "You've had numerous secret meetings with Dr. Hyatt. He confided in me that you had kissed him. You claim that you and Dhar were not lovers. It is hard to accept that you have been faithful to me after discovering you in his arms. You offer no explanation.

Now that we're married, I intend to make the best of it."

Sarah sat up and glared at him with her hand clutching the edge of the wool blanket. "Why I explain? I say I keep promise. You not believe. I say truth; you not believe. It not matter what I say; you not believe," she said bitterly. She climbed off the berth and threw her dress over her head.

"Where are you going?"

"Not here," she said before running out of the room.

"Sarah!" Hassan called out.

Sarah ran into a spare cabin on the other side of the wardroom. She threw herself onto the berth and cried herself to sleep.

Tess's face puckered when she felt her head throb. Her eyes fluttered open; all she saw was darkness. Her whole body stiffened when she heard Peter's soft breaths as he slept with his back pressed against hers. Tess had always hated waking up next to her lovers. This morning was no exception. She sat up and swung her legs over the berth. Resting her elbows on her thighs, she cradled her forehead in her hands as she thought about her betrayal to the only man she had ever loved. Knowing there was nothing she could do to undo her mistake, Tess knelt on the floor and felt around until she found her dress. After slipping it over her head, she glanced back at the sleeping doctor and fled like a thief.

One of her primary complaints about being on the ship was that it was impossible to tell if it were night or day below deck. The hammocks were still occupied with snoring crewmen. Tess climbed onto a bench in the galley and removed the lantern. Using the candle's light, she returned to the wardroom. "Can you tell me which room me daughter's in?" she asked the guards standing by the wardroom entrance.

"She's in the first room on the right, mum," answered one of the guards.

Tess nodded and passed by them. She shined the light over her sleeping child and marveled at her daughter's strong likeness to her father. Her mouth, her nose, even her wit were identical to her father's. Tess hung the lantern from the hook on the overhead and laid down, cradling Molly in her arms. She stirred an hour later when she heard a door open. Taking the utmost care not to disturb her sleeping child, Tess slid her arm out from under her daughter's neck and got up from the berth. She knew it could be anyone, but Tess gave into her curiosity and opened the door. "Good morning." She offered Hassan a warm smile.

"I didn't know you were sleeping in the next cabin," Hassan said with genuine surprise.

"I *am* Molly's mother," Tess reminded him.

"Yes, you are." Hassan laughed to himself.

"I trust you had trouble sleeping?" she asked after a few awkward moments of silence.

Hassan replied with a nod.

Tess knew him well enough to perceive that something was troubling him, but her profession had trained her not to pry. "Would you like some company?"

Hassan was reluctant to answer after glancing at the room across from him.

"Not that kind of company," Tess clarified. "A stroll up on deck would do me good."

"Certainly." He offered her his arm. The sky was still dark when they reached the quarterdeck. The half-moon had already set, and a splinter of an orange hue appeared on the eastern horizon. Sailing over the waters provided a gentle breeze across the deck. With Algiers behind them and no land in plain sight, Tess's life in the harem felt like a distant memory. The excitement of a new romance had deepened into a kind of love that two people shared in spite of knowing each other's deepest secrets.

Tess looked at him with a faint smile. "I dreamt about the night we met. Do you remember our first time together?"

"I shall never forget it."

Tess studied him. "You seemed troubled. Did Sarah upset you?" she asked before returning her attention to the black abyss in front of her.

Hassan refused to look at her. "I appreciate your concern, but I'm not going to discuss my marriage with you."

"Very well." Tess studied Hassan. "May I ask you another question?"

"You may ask, but I may choose not to answer."

"Fair enough. Mamnoon told me that His Lordship offered to give me to you. Why ... did you refuse his offer? I thought we ..."

Hassan tucked his fingers under her chin and swiveled her face towards his. "Tess." He caressed her cheek.

"I know you care for me, perhaps not enough to marry me."

"As you may recall, you ended our brief love affair first when you informed me that you had found love with Naa'il Dhar. Though you didn't say it, you made it clear that you intended to marry him."

"I didn't want to marry him," Tess insisted. "I wanted to be with him long enough to bare him a son." She glanced at the water swirling below with a haunted expression. "I was a fool," she sighed. "I learned later that I would never share his bed with him because I was impure. I'm sorry I hurt you."

"I'm sorry too," Hassan said. "I felt it was best for you to remain in the Palace because I couldn't give you the life that you deserve."

"I don't need a fancy life. I could face the most perilous dangers so long as we were together."

"Still, a ship is no place for a woman and a small child."

"You had no trouble offering that life to Sarah."

"The circumstances under which Sarah came aboard are different," Hassan said defensively.

Tess crossed her arms and glared at her former paramour. "In what way?"

"Again, I am not going to discuss my marriage with you."

Tears welling up in her eyes, Tess turned her back to Hassan and stared at the water swirling below. She marveled how he still made her tremble when she felt his strong hands resting on her shoulders.

"Tess," Hassan crooned.

She looked back at him with pleading eyes. "Please tell me that I meant something to you. Please tell me that we shared something special. Please tell me that we would still be together had I not hurt you, and you had not married Sarah."

Hassan spun her around. Resting his finger under her chin, he gently tilted her face towards his. "Tess," he said in a throaty whisper. He leaned down and kissed her slowly, tenderly.

His former paramour wrapped her arms around his neck. Hassan locked his own around her waist, pressing her body against him. Her lips fervently moved with his as her tongue encouraged him to deepen his kisses. She groaned when she felt him harden with desire. "Take me below," she said in a sultry voice as she silently relished the thought of Sarah seeing them together.

Hassan released her and pulled away without warning. "I can't do this. I accused Sarah of being unfaithful to me. Now I'm guilty of the very accusations I made against her."

"She's a bloody hypocrite," Tess snapped. "Sarah was unfaithful to you first. I saw it with me own eyes."

Hassan's lips parted. "What do you mean?"

"I saw Sarah with Dr. Hyatt yesterday afternoon."

"Sarah told me that she sent for him to look in on Mrs. Fornier."

"Did she also tell you that she and the good doctor were holding hands when they came out of the room? Afterward, they became intimately close outside their room. They seemed not to care who was watching them. Ask Abigail if you don't believe me. She saw their embrace too," Tess said angrily.

Hassan turned away from her and rested his hands on the railing as if he hadn't heard a word she said.

Tess touched his arm gently. "I'm sorry I hurt you. I thought you should know the truth. Sarah may seem sweet, but she is manipulating you by trying to make you believe that she is something that she's not. I know you're not married to Sarah. Perhaps you should end your relationship before it's too late. I love you; I always have. Molly will love you too. If you let us, we will be the family you deserve. I'll leave you to your thoughts."

Sarah was just leaving her quarters by the time Tess returned to the wardroom. The early morning sun was already streaking across the water.

Sarah looked away and wiped the tears from the corner of her eyes before saying, "Molly in here."

"I know where me daughter is," Tess snapped. "I came to talk to you - in private."

Sarah opened the door to her quarters and stepped aside so that Tess could pass her.

Tess was the first to break her silence. "I heard from a reputable man that you and Nathan are not legally married," she said with her arms crossed in front of her.

Sarah opened and closed her mouth without answering.

"So it is true. You are a bloody liar."

Sarah's cheeks burned from Tess's accusation. "No, Cattin and I made promise."

"Promises mean nothing where I come from. That's no matter; I'm not here to pass judgment on you. I came to talk to you, woman to woman. I understand that you love Nathan; he believes he's in love with you too." She paused and looked Sarah in the eyes. "I came here to remind you that Nathan has a daughter, a daughter that desperately needs her father." Her whole face crinkled. Tess covered her quivering lips with her hand. "You must understand," she whimpered, "Nathan will never be a proper father to her so long as he has you to distract him. I know what it is like not to have a father; not to know who he is … knowing that he would rather be with his family than with you. I don't want that for Molly. Can you understand?" Tess collapsed onto the edge of the berth. Propping her elbows on her thighs, she buried her face in her hands and sobbed.

Sarah sat beside Tess and rested her hand on her shoulder. "I understand," Sarah replied in a quiet voice. "Molly will have da."

Tess stared at Sarah with crying eyes, except her eyes were dry. "You would do that for Molly?" she asked in a small voice.

Sarah nodded.

Tess lowered her arms and straightened her back as soon as Sarah had left the cabin all the while staring at the door with a triumphant grin.

Hassan sneered as he watched Sarah approach him. She looked guilty by the way she hung her head. Her movements were slow and tentative. It hadn't occurred to him until that moment that Sarah had picked a fight with him so that she could slip a way to be with Peter. He still didn't know what to say to her until she reached him.

Sarah couldn't look at him. "Cattin, we not married. You da now. You love Tess. You be with her and Molly."

Hassan stared at the water swirling below. "Is that because you want to be with Hyatt?"

Sarah furrowed her brow. "What is Hyatt?"

"Peter Hyatt, your lover." Hassan said in a calm, but menacing tone. He was too angry to care that he was chastising her after sharing a kiss with Tess not fifteen minutes ago. "Yes, Tess confirmed what I suspected all along. She and Miss Randall saw you two together. So it appears that Mrs. Fornier wasn't the primary reason that you sent for him."

Tears flooded her eyes. Instead of pleading for his forgiveness, she kissed him on the cheek and whispered, "Good-bye, Cattin. I wish you happiness."

Hassan's hand gripped the railing as he watched Sarah walk away.

CHAPTER 40

Abigail stirred when she heard Tess humming as she entered the cabin. Crawling off the berth, she watched Tess whirl around the room as if she were dancing with her lover. Abigail crossed her arms and rested her shoulder against the divider. "So, the prodigal daughter returns. Did you leave Molly with Sarah or did you throw her overboard? Oh, I forget; you still need your daughter to ensnare the good captain."

Tess spun around and glared at Abigail. "I'll have you know that Molly is still sleeping."

"If you say so, but Molly awakes about this time every day."

"I am a good mother," Tess sneered, "especially now that I got Molly's father back."

"Oh," Abigail mouthed the word without making a sound. "I'm curious, does Captain Shelby know that you were unfaithful to him?"

"He knows that I was a slave, and I did what I had to do to survive."

"Uh huh."

"What do you mean by, 'Uh huh'? You know I had to do what I was told. It was either that or be sold at market."

"Yes, I understand, but you weren't a slave last night. What was your excuse for seducing Dr. Hyatt - exactly? Don't deny it; I followed you to the officer's quarters. I saw your disappointment when you learned that Captain Shelby was with Sarah. I should have returned to our quarters, but I was curious to discover what you would do next. It didn't surprise me that you sought another man's company," Abigail shrugged.

Tess's lips parted. "You're not going to tell Nathan are you? I just got him back."

"What do you mean by, I got him back? What have you done?" Abigail straightened herself and took a seat at the dinner table. Tess sunk onto a chair across from her friend. Abigail rested her elbow on the armchair, burying her eyes in her hand and shaking her head as her friend regaled the events that transpired during the past twelve hours.

"So you see; it's for the best for everyone," Tess said with a bright smile. "Molly gets a father; Nathan gets a family."

Abigail propped up her chin on her fist and looked intently at her friend. "And what does Sarah get?"

"Dr. Hyatt will look after her. He even said as much."

"Hmm. I got the impression that Sarah doesn't like him."

"Sarah and Peter care for each other. You saw them together."

"I saw relief on Sarah's face when we encountered them in the officer's quarters yesterday. Dr. Hyatt seemed pretty angry about our interruption." Abigail leaned towards her friend. "Now listen to a fellow schemer. The games, the lies, the schemes *never* work. The truth always finds a way to the surface. It's only a matter of time before Captain Shelby sees you for what you are."

"I am *not* a whore." Tess gritted her teeth as she enunciated each word.

Abigail leaned in until her chest touched the edge of the table. "I know how much you enjoy men's company," she said, looking her friend in the eyes.

"I told you, I was a slave. I was required to give pleasure to men; I did what was expected of me."

"Perhaps, but you couldn't leave Molly and the harem fast enough. Spending last night with Dr. Hyatt is proof that you enjoy your profession."

Tess pressed her lips together to form one thin line. "The only reason that I was with Peter was because Nathan was with that …"

"Captain Shelby and Sarah love each other. It was as clear as light when I saw them together."

"Nathan loves *me*," Tess growled. She lowered her gaze to the table. "He just needed to be reminded of that. Nathan's had many lovers, but he always comes back to me."

"Say what you want, but your scheme *will* fail."

Tess's lips twisted into a sneer. "If you do anything to sabotage my marriage to Nathan, I swear that I will slit your throat. Perhaps not on this trip, but one night you will not wake up," she said in a sinister voice.

Abigail shuddered when she spotted a killer's rage in Tess's eyes. "I don't need to say anything. Captain Shelby is an intelligent man. It's only a matter of time until he figures out that you are using your child, a child that you don't love, to ensnare him. Incidentally, Molly looks nothing like him, of course, Captain Shelby will figure that out too. If by some miracle you convince him to marry you, he will resent you for it, maybe not now, maybe not a year from now, but one day he will see you as the insidious schemer that you are. Believe me; I've played your games with hopes of winning the love of a man who loved another." Abigail wiped the tear from the corner of her eye. "It's hell loving someone who doesn't return your love. It's even worse when his indifference turns to loathing. That will be your fate if you continue on this path." Abigail jumped up from the table and ran to the berth.

"Good morning."

Sarah jumped when she heard the condescension in Peter's tone. She didn't need to look at him to feel him undressing her with his eyes. She spun around and glared at him. "Leave me before I scream."

Peter held his hands up in front of him. "I didn't come here to quarrel with you."

Sarah squared her shoulders. "No, you never do. If you lay one hand on me, I will scream. Please leave."

Peter hung his head. "I'm sorry about last night. I was drunk. I didn't know what I was doing."

"Last night was not the first time you touched me without my consent. Please leave and do not bother me again." Sarah attempted to push past him.

"Please let me finish what I have to say. I heard that you and Nathan parted company."

Sarah backed away from Peter as he reached for her waist. "Cattin believes that I broke my promise to him," she said bitterly. "He believes that we are lovers."

"What did you tell him?"

"I told him nothing. It does not matter what I say. He believes I did those things, and I cannot change his mind. Why would he think I would betray him like that?" Sarah said, pressing her hand against her middle.

Peter looked at every place in the room except at her.

Sarah bit the inside of her lip and whispered, "You made Cattin believe I did those things." Tears flooded her eyes. "Why, why would you say those things when you don't even know me?"

Peter shoved his hands in his pockets. "I want to help you, Sarah. Let me take care of you."

"You've done enough. Please leave." Sarah sighed when she heard Molly's voice. "Molly is crying; let me go to her."

Peter latched his hand around her arm.

"Let go of my arm," she said, trembling.

"Sarah, you don't know England like I do. It can be a very unwelcoming place. That is doubly true for strangers. England couldn't be more different than your island. It will destroy you if you try to live there on your own." Peter leaned in until his lips were almost upon hers. "I can help you," he whispered. "All I ask is that you submit to me, freely."

Sarah jerked her arm away, breaking free of his hand. "I must go to Molly. Do not come to me again."

"Please consider my offer." Peter stepped aside to let her pass.

Hassan hadn't moved from his spot since Sarah left him. Still reeling from the events from earlier that morning, he just stood there, resting his forearms on the railing as he watched the sun's rays dancing on the water. Instead of admiring the way the sun colored the nearby clouds with its pink hues, his thought remained on Sarah. He grimaced as her challenge replayed over and over again in his mind. She was right; he didn't trust her, and their marriage couldn't survive if he didn't find a way to do so. At the same time, Hassan's yearnings still churned inside him, screaming that he wasn't ready to let go of her.

Hassan tore his gaze away from the sunrise when he spotted John Montgomery strolling around the deck. Even at a distance, Hassan could feel John's inner peace radiating from his whole being. His movements were slow and unhurried.

"Good morning, Mr. Montgomery," Hassan said as John passed by him.

"Good morning, Captain Shelby. I saw you when I reached the top stair. I didn't say anything because you appeared deep in thought."

"You are not disturbing me." Hassan smiled politely. "You're up early."

"Morning is my favorite time of day. I use the peace and quiet to commune with God." John rested his arms on the railing beside Hassan.

"Does that mean that you were a man of the cloth before you were captured?"

"I was." John studied Hassan. "I can see that I interrupted you. I will leave you to your thoughts."

"Wait," Hassan called out just as John turned to leave. "I'm in need of your council."

"Of course." John returned to his spot beside Hassan. "How can I help?"

"How do you ascertain a person's true nature?"

"Is that all?" John teased.

Hassan remained unmoved by John's attempt of humor. He let out a loud sigh. "I rescued a woman and her father traveling from the South Seas. Her crew poisoned her father so that they could profit from selling her on the Barbary Coast. She was the most exotic woman I have ever known. I'll admit that I had preconceived notions of who this woman was. The first time that I was alone with her, I discovered that she was nothing like the wanton savage that I envisioned." The ends of Hassan's lips curled upward. "She was quite the contrary. Sarah was sweet … and curious." He chuckled, "and she's a bloody pickpocket. Most of all, she was the most innocent woman that I have ever met. The women on her island wear a cloth tied around their waist. Sarah called it a … pa … paru." Hassan laughed again when John raised his brows. "It's scandalous, I know. She was not the least bit sensual. She was naked, and yet she didn't know that she was naked. Above all, Sarah is the most loving person that I've ever known. She is always putting my happiness ahead of her own, even if it was a detriment to herself."

"She sounds like a truly lovely woman," John interjected.

"She is."

"What are your concerns?"

"A friend who spent time in the South Seas expressed concerns about my entering a romantic entanglement with a woman raised in that part of the world. He believes that Polynesian women are incapable of being faithful to one person."

"Infidelity is hardly exclusive to the people in the South Seas," John pointed out. "Regrettably, infidelity plagues every civilization throughout the world."

"True." Hassan reluctantly admitted. "My friend's warning was accurate. I walked in on Sarah's private meetings with my friend. Later, I discovered Sarah in Naa'il Dhar's arms on the night I rescued her. She insisted that she was innocent, but …"

"You don't believe her," John suggested.

"No."

"Then it appears that you reached a conclusion."

Hassan tore his gaze from the water and frowned, "Have I? I'm drawn to Sarah every time that I'm near her."

"What draws you to her?"

His lips curled into a distant smile. "I'm drawn to Sarah's love. She makes me feel as though she lives for me and me alone. I'm not ready to let go of her. How can you love someone that you don't trust?"

"Hmm. I wish I could give you a simple answer. Human relationships have always been complicated. I can tell you that I am doubtful that Sarah and His Excellency were lovers. Sarah's arrival at the Palace caused quite a stir - as would the arrival of any woman from an exotic land. She came during a particularly difficult time in His Excellency's life."

"I understand Dhar's daughter was killed recently," Hassan said.

"Yes. She died a few days ago. His Excellency also lost a woman he loved shortly before Sarah arrived. She was an American. I saw him almost daily. He shared his bed with a different lover every night during the four years that I served him. He stopped sending for his concubines several weeks after the American entered his life. To my knowledge, His Excellency and the American were never lovers, but he visited her daily. I believe she changed him for the better. It was evident to me that her death haunted him until the end of his days."

"Dhar boasted that he and Sarah were lovers. It was unmistakable that she cared for him by the way she wept over him when he died in her arms."

"I can't answer those questions, Captain. All I can say is that His Excellency never spoke of Sarah, to me or anyone else. Permit me to share Christ Jesus' council about sinning: 'He who is without sin, may cast the first stone.' If you genuinely love her, perhaps she is worthy of you giving her a second chance."

"I don't know."

"Perhaps you don't need to decide her fate just yet." John's voice trailed off as he stared thoughtfully at the water. "May I enquire what happened to her father?"

"He died on the night that we rescued them. Thank you for your council."

John offered him an apologetic smile. "I'm sorry that I could not help you resolve your dilemma."

"As you said, I don't need to decide our fates today."

Hassan felt the heaviness fall away. His uncertainty over his current circumstance was replaced by a calm that came from an assurance that the answer he needed would present itself when he was ready for it. The ship's bell rang, reminding him that it was time to report for his watch.

"Good morning, Captain," said the sailor as he nudged the wheel to correct their course."

"Good morning," Hassan replied as he took his place by the wheel.

"It's a fine day for sailing, sir. There's not a cloud in the sky. Do you think we'll rendezvous with the Zafirah today?"

"It's possible," Hassan replied with a slacked expression as he watched people filing onto the main deck. His crew and former prisoners worked alongside each other, swabbing the deck or taking care of anything else that needed to be done. Hassan was grateful to see the camaraderie between his crew and the former prisoners as they worked side by side. His knuckles turned white when he grabbed the railing in front of him as he spotted Tess, Abigail, and Molly approaching him from behind.

"Papa," Molly squealed once she was within arm's reach of Hassan. She let go of her mother's neck and reached for her father.

"Good morning, Molly, ladies," Hassan said in a stern tone, ignoring Molly's insistence for him to hold her.

"Won't you take your daughter?" Tess asked.

"I'm on duty, Tess. My duties do not include holding a child. You're welcome to stay on the quarterdeck if you wish. If you will excuse me, I must focus on my duties."

"Very well." Tess pointed her nose in the air and trotted off.

Hassan glanced behind him. Part of him expected to see Sarah sitting quietly on a bench, drawing in her sketchbook, but there was no sign of her. His hands tightened around the railing when he didn't see

Peter either. Scanning the quarterdeck, Hassan's gaze fell on Tess who balanced Molly on her hip as her daughter pointed to a bird flying above her. Tess was no longer an untamed lover, but a loving mother. A faint smile fell on his lips as he envisioned them as a family.

Chapter 41

The Persephone and the Trésor arrived at the rendezvous point during the early afternoon. Ships ranging from three-masted schooners to fishing boats filled the harbor. The Zafirah, Hassan grinned, was in the midst of the ships, just as he envisioned.

"We dropped anchor and lowered the jolly, Captain," reported one of his lieutenants. "A crewman is standing by to take you ashore whenever you're ready."

"Very good. I should be ready to go ashore within the half hour." Hassan headed down to the wardroom to retrieve Janna. His lips parted when he discovered Sarah sitting on the edge of Janna's berth. "Have you been here the entire time?" he asked Sarah.

"Aye," she quietly replied. "I not be here?"

His cheeks burned. "Of course you should," he said. "Mrs. Fornier," Hassan continued in French, "we dropped anchor and are ready to take you ashore."

Janna's cheeks were still pale, yet her face was radiant with joy when she heard the news. "I am going to see Claude?"

"Yes," Hassan confirmed. "I will wait for you in the wardroom while you prepare for your departure."

"Captain Shelby," Janna called out just as Hassan turned to leave.

"Yes?"

"I want to thank you for all that you did for me. You know that I was very reluctant to make this journey with you. I feared that your crew would harm me or force me to dishonor my family. Instead, you overwhelmed me with your kindness and your generosity. I never expected to be given a private room. And Sarah, she is one of the kindest people I have ever known. She has taken care of me ever since you introduced us. I shall never forget the care that you both provided."

"It was my honor to assist you." Hassan looked directly at Janna because he was too ashamed to meet Sarah's gaze. He had spent the better part of the day allowing his imagination to torture him with visions of Sarah in Peter's arms, or even worse, in his bed. She had been with Janna the entire journey. "I shall wait for you in the wardroom." He turned his attention to Sarah and continued in English, "Mrs. Fornier will be leaving us shortly to be reunited with her husband. Can you assist her or do you require my help?"

"Aye." Sarah jumped up from the berth and helped Janna to her feet.

Hassan marveled how well the two women communicated with each other in spite of neither speaking the other's language. Sarah steadied Janna, while Janna dressed. Hassan held out his hand and asked when Sarah reached for Janna's bag, "May I carry that for you?" Sarah handed Janna's belongings to Hassan. They stood on either side of Janna, each bracing her arms to steady her as she walked.

For as much as Hassan hated the thought of Sarah and Peter being together, he couldn't help wondering why Peter wasn't with them. A few minutes later, they encountered Peter heading to the quarterdeck. "Good morning, Doctor, I was just thinking about you." Hassan's voice trailed off when he felt Janna's hand squeezing his arm.

"Are you seeking fresh air?" Peter winced when his hand reached for his elbow.

"No, I'm taking Mrs. Fornier to her husband." Hassan shifted forward so that he could see everyone's faces. Though Janna's face was covered, there was unmistakable hatred in her eyes. Sarah sneered at him the same way she sneered at Emile after discovering that he had murdered her father.

"Well, I wish you all the best, Mrs. Fornier," Peter said, looking past them to avoid their gaze

Hassan pressed his lips together when he spotted blood seeping from the left sleeve of Peter's white shirt. "Did you cut yourself?" he asked with mild interest.

Peter held up his arm. "Oh, this. I did something foolish. It's no matter," he said in a casual tone.

"If you will excuse us, I must take Mrs. Fornier ashore," Hassan said, pretending not to notice Peter's refusal to make eye contact with him.

"I wish you all the best, Mrs. Fornier," Peter said, still refusing to look her in the eyes.

Hassan paused long enough to watch his friend slink away like a thief fleeing a crime. "Ladies." He held out his arm to the ladder leading to the main deck.

Luke and Tristan were already waiting for them by the bosuns' chair. "The bosuns' chair is ready for you, Captain."

"Thank you, gentlemen," Hassan replied. "Sarah, I want you to stay on the ship while I take Mrs. Fornier ashore. Say your goodbyes now if you wish." He said first in English. He then repeated the latter part of his message in French.

"Captain, would you please tell Sarah that I am grateful for her kindness," Janna said in French.

Hassan translated her message into English.

Sarah replied, "Say, she is ... my ... sister."

Hassan nodded his approval and translated her message into French. While the two women embraced, Hassan approached John Montgomery, who leaned against the railing admiring the scenery. Portugal's rocky coastline was very different from the City of Algiers. The stone buildings with triangular rooftops were a stark contrast to the Algerian white apartment structures. Instead of a call to prayer, bells rang from a small stone chapel perched on a hill.

Hassan tore his eyes away from the landscape and asked, "Mr.

Montgomery, may I trouble you with another request?"

"Of course, Captain."

"I was thinking about what you said earlier this morning. If you don't mind, I would like to introduce you to Sarah. Perhaps your unbiased opinion can help me resolve my dilemma."

"You don't need my help, Captain. I ascertained from our discussion that you are a man of high integrity and a keen judge of character. It would be my honor to speak with Sarah providing you still wish it."

"I do."

Hassan and John returned to the women. Luke and Sarah were busy assisting Janna onto the bosuns' chair. "I will meet you at the jolly," Hassan said to Janna. "Sarah, I would like you to meet John Montgomery. He brought your cloth bag from the Palace."

"La orana," Sarah said shyly.

"Mr. Montgomery, this is Sarah Campbell."

"Hello, Miss Campbell. I am pleased to make your acquaintance."

"I will leave you two to talk. I will find you when I return to the ship."

Sarah nodded.

Hassan reached for the lines and climbed down to the jolly. Luke and Tristan were already below assisting Janna into the boat. Hassan took a seat beside her and nodded to the oarsmen to start rowing. "Mrs. Fornier, I observed the contempt in your eyes when we were talking with Dr. Hyatt. Did something happened?"

Janna looked away from him and closed her eyes.

"Mrs. Fornier, please tell me what's upsetting you," Hassan pressed.

She looked at him with pleading eyes and said, "Please don't punish Sarah. It was my fault that he attacked her."

Hassan's lips parted. "What do you mean by, 'he attacked her?'"

"I ..."

"As Captain of this ship, it is vital that I be apprised of all that transpires on my ship. You have my word that if what you say is true, the only person that is in danger is Dr. Hyatt. Please, it is important that you tell me what happened."

"He is a horrible man …."

Peter stole away to an alcove to collect his thoughts. Leaning against the bulkhead, he cradled his forehead in this hand as his mind replayed his last conversation with his friend and captain. He and Hassan had spent every day together during the past two years. Peter knew that Hassan suspected something by the way he had divided his attention between him and the women. It genuinely surprised him that neither told him about the attack. He wondered if Hassan would act on his suspicions and force Sarah or Janna to tell him the truth. There was nothing he could do to stop them, he concluded, so he continued on his mission.

People filled the deck and kept busy by either working or enjoying the sunny afternoon. Sarah and John Montgomery were engaged in a conversation. Tess and the other woman stood next to the railing, keeping one eye on the shoreline and the other on a small child entertaining herself. Peter weaved around the crew until he reached the women. He bowed to them and said cordially. "Good afternoon, ladies. I trust that you are enjoying your day."

Abigail curtsied to the doctor; Tess pretended not to know him.

"It is a very pleasant afternoon," Abigail said with a wide grin.

Tess looked away.

"Miss O'Shea, may I trouble you for a word in private?" Peter enquired.

Abigail bit her lip to conceal her smirk. "I'll take care of Molly."

Tess glared at her friend before wrapping her hand around Peter's arm. "Certainly, Doctor."

Tess and Peter didn't say anything until they reached the surgery. He closed the door and turned and found her standing in the center of the room with her arms crossed and her foot tapping impatiently.

"What do you want?" she demanded in a tone laced with annoyance.

"I thought that we should discuss last night."

"What's there to say? We had a spot of fun. That's all. We can't do it again because Nathan and I are going to be married," Tess announced.

Peter pursed his lips. "Indeed. Does Nathan share this understanding?"

"Not yet, but he will. We talked about it this morning. Nathan's beginning to remember that we loved each other. I think we'll come to an understanding in a few days. That's why we can't be together."

Peter felt like a servant who had been unfairly dismissed after years of faithful servitude. Undeterred by her rejection, he advanced towards her, unhurried in his movements.

"I told you, it's over," Tess protested as he wrapped his arms around her waist.

"If you say so," he said as he nibbled on her ear.

"I can't do this," Tess groaned, wrapping her arms around his neck.

"You can be respectable tomorrow."

Tess jumped up, latching her legs around his hips. "This is the last time, do you hear me?" She kissed him hungrily.

Peter carried her into his chamber and lowered her onto his berth. "If you say so," he said in a throaty whisper before giving her a crushing kiss.

Hassan's knuckles turned white as his hand clutched the side of the wooden jolly. It was evident by his crewmen's blank stares that none of them understood his conversation with Janna. "Why didn't you inform me that the doctor mistreated my wife?" he demanded.

"Your wife? I did not know." Janna gasped.

"Please answer my question."

"I'm sorry. I feared that you would harm Sarah."

"I understand your concerns. The people in my country hang men for violating women. I will hold him accountable."

"What about Sarah?"

Hassan looked Janna in the eyes and said without hesitation, "I would give my life to protect her."

"I'm relieved to hear you say that. I do not know if it matters, but I believe that the knife is still under Sarah's bed."

"Thank you. That will help me," Hassan said as the boat reached the dock.

Claude Fornier and Adam Boyle were waiting for them on the dock. The oarsman tossed the line to Adam. Hassan's first lieutenant secured the jolly to the dock as Hassan helped to balance Janna when she stood up. Claude reached for her hand and together, Hassan and Claude pulled her ashore.

"Claude!" Janna cried with joy as she threw her arms around his neck. The two held each other as though they had been separated for a lifetime.

Hassan nodded when he spotted the tears of joy in Claude's eyes.

Claude released his wife's waist and bowed to the British captain. "You are a man of honor, Captain Shelby. I am in your debt."

"I did this for your wife and child," Hassan said sternly. "You should know that your cousin and Naa'il Dhar are dead. I would be lying if I said that I am sorry."

"I understand your sentiment; Gerard died when he abandoned me during our battle. I'm curious; were you successful in rescuing your woman?"

"I was." Hassan handed Claude a small pouch. "This is to begin your new life."

Claude opened the pouch and gasped when he found it filled with gold coins. "You're most generous."

"It's the least I can do since I'm commandeering your ship."

One end of Claude's lips curled into a lop-sided grin. "I suppose it's the price of losing the battle."

"Captain Fornier, allow me to speak plainly. If I hear that you returned to the Barbary Coast, you have my word that I will hunt you down and send you and your crew to the bottom of the Mediterranean Sea."

"You needn't worry, Captain Shelby. I have lost my desire for war. There is nothing I want more than to lead a quiet life with my wife and children. May I interest you and your officers in joining me for dinner tonight?"

"Thank you, no. I don't think it would be wise for our crews to dine together, considering they all want you dead," Hassan pointed out.

"Then I wish you well. Goodbye, Captain Shelby." Claude bowed.

"Goodbye, Captain and thank you again," Janna said.

Hassan offered them a curt nod.

"What are your orders, Captain?" Adam asked once they were alone.

"How are you progressing with the provisions?"

"We secured and stocked the provisions aboard the Zafirah. I also gave the crew shore leave with a warning that they will be left behind if they do not report back to the ship tomorrow morning."

Hassan lifted a brow, "How are they getting along with the French?"

"Peacefully, so far. The only thing on their minds today is getting drunk and enjoying a woman's company," Adam said with a sheepish grin.

Hassan handed Adam a sapphire necklace. "Sell this and do what you can to secure provisions for the other two ships. I was successful at freeing over seven-hundred British prisoners. Many of them are on Sarah's former ship."

"I thought I recognized her."

"I will task the other officers to shift people to the Zafirah for the journey home. You will take command of the Persephone; Sarah, several other women and I will return to the Zafirah. I will also give shore leave to my crew and the former prisoners with the same warning. I want the three ships to be well guarded in case Fornier and his crew attempt to commandeer my fleet."

"That is a wise decision, Captain."

"Make my intensions known to the Zafirah crew."

"I will, sir." Adam turned away and glanced back at Hassan. "Captain, I'm grateful that your mission was successful."

Still reeling from Janna's news, Hassan returned to the Persephone. He lingered on deck long enough to convey his orders to his officers before stealing away to the wardroom. The bloody knife was exactly where Janna said it was. Hassan retrieved the knife and pressed his lips together when he recognized its carved handle. Once he tucked the weapon under his belt, he marched to Peter's make-shift quarters and paused in the doorway when he heard moaning. Hassan glanced down at the poniard and burst through the closed door.

"Nathan!" Tess gasped.

Chapter 42

"Dress yourself," Hassan growled at Peter while paying little attention to Tess scrambling to cover herself. "You have a minute before I drag you off your berth."

Peter stumbled out of his cabin, tucking the ends of his peasant shirt into his brown breeches before closing the door behind him.

Hassan grabbed Peter by the scruff of the collar and pinned him against the bulkhead. "I just had an enlightening conversation with Mrs. Fornier, who informed me that you attacked Sarah last night."

Peter couldn't look at his captain. "I was drunk."

"Why did you need this?" Hassan used one arm to pin Peter's neck; his other hand removed the bloodied knife from his belt. "Again, why did you need this?" Hassan pressed the blade against the doctor's cheek.

Peter stared at his captain with bulging eyes and parted lips. "I forgot that I had it," Peter said in a tone that matched the terror on his face. "I would never threaten a woman. Sarah took it from me without my knowing it."

Hassan dropped the knife and grabbed hold of Peter's collar. "How long have you been harassing my wife?"

"I ..."

Hassan pulled Peter off the bulkhead and slammed him against it. "How long?"

Peter still couldn't look at Hassan.

"How long?" Hassan shouted.

"It only happened once - on the night you became ill. Sarah didn't kiss me; I attempted to kiss her, but I was unsuccessful." Peter's voice faded.

"And?" Hassan demanded.

Peter's chin quivered as he stared at the floor beside Hassan's foot.

Hassan kept the gaze from his narrow eyes on Peter. "And?" Hassan shouted with sneering lips.

"Sarah told me that she belonged to you. I tried to persuade her to submit to me, but she refused to listen," Peter whispered.

"So you retaliated by fabricating stories about Sarah and her people to turn me against her."

Peter looked Hassan in the eyes for the first time during their confrontation. "No. I told you the truth about my experience in Tahiti," Peter insisted. "I swear it."

"Why – why did you try to turn me against her?" Hassan's voice cracked.

"Because I believed that she was no good. You fell under her spell. I thought that if I could show you her people's true character, perhaps I could spare you from the same pain that I suffered. I swear that's the truth," Peter said with a tortured voice.

Hassan could tell by his tone that Peter believed what he said. "Did Sarah ever give herself to you?"

"No," Peter hung his head and whispered, "Do what you must."

"I'm not going to kill you today, but you *will* stay away from Sarah. If you look at her in a manner that displeases me, doctor or no, I will throw you overboard." Hassan released him and stormed out of the surgery.

Tess called out as she chased after him. "Nathan, can I talk to you."

"Not now," Hassan snapped.

Tess closed the distance between them enough to grab his arm. "It's important," she insisted.

"You have fifteen minutes.

"What I have to say won't take that long."

"We'll talk in my quarters."

Sarah hid in the shadows as she watched Hassan and Tess leave the surgery. She was happy and heart-broken at the same time. Sarah was glad that Tess and Hassan were finally reunited, yet her heart ached to give up the man she loved. It was the right thing to do, she told herself, and losing the man she loved was her punishment for killing her father. Once Hassan and Tess passed beyond her view, Sarah marched into Peter's quarters. He was still hunched over with his hand clutching his middle.

Peter gasped when he spotted her out of the corner of his eye. He straightened himself and glared at her. "What do you want?"

Sarah leaned against the doorway and said, "You called me Tiari the night you tried to hurt me."

"If you say so."

"She was your woman, and she hurt you. You blame me for the pain that she caused you."

Peter didn't answer.

"I am sorry she hurt you, but I am not Tiari."

Peter's lips contorted into a sneer. "But you're Polynesian."

Sarah was unmoved by his challenge. "What if I am?"

"Your people are savages."

"Your people are no different from mine."

"Our people do not smother their new-born children," Peter said bitterly.

"I cannot speak about how your people treat their children. It is true that some women kill their bairns, but I will not. I love children; I could never hurt them."

Peter rolled his eyes. "Is that what you came here to tell me, or did you come for another purpose?"

"No, I came to tell you that I would rather die alone than to accept your help. I love Cattin; I will not betray him by beholding myself to you. Stay away from me." Sarah stepped into the room and snatched the knife.

Peter gasped. "What are you going to do with that?"

"This belongs to me now. Consider it payment for attacking me. Goodbye, Peter." Sarah turned on her heels and ran away.

Hassan opened the door and extended his arm towards his quarters. Tess sat down at the table; Hassan took a seat across from her.

His former paramour stared at the table. "I don't know what to say. I never meant to hurt you."

"I'm not angry," Hassan said calmly. "I was sincere when I told you that I cared for you. You helped me through one of the most difficult periods of my life. I will always be grateful for all the times that you made me laugh. You also helped me escape from the hell in which I was trapped."

"But you don't love me."

"No more than you love me. Tess, I love Sarah. You gave me joy, but she gave me peace."

"Very well, I don't love you either. I was in love with the idea of you," Tess sighed. "You were the first man who was kind to me."

"Who is Molly's father? I know it isn't me."

Tess lifted a brow, "And how do you know that?"

"You reminded me several times of our first night together. I too will think fondly of that night. However, I have several memories of my own. For example, I distinctly remember tasting milk on your breast. I also remember waking up and finding you sitting in the corner of the room pumping milk from your breasts into the pot."

"Oh." Tess hung her head. "Why didn't you say something?"

"Because I sensed that you didn't want to discuss your past, and I didn't want to pry." Hassan looked at her with a thoughtful expression. "Where is Molly's father?"

"I killed him," she said without hesitation.

Hassan pursed his lips. "Why did you kill him?"

"Because he was an English gentleman and the cruelest blackheart I had ever known. Me mother sold me to him when I was but a wee child." Her lips curled into a lopsided grin. "His uppity wife wouldn't let him keep his pet in his home." She shrugged, "not that I minded." Her smile faded. "Me mum delivered me to him whenever he summoned me. I ran away often; he beat me every time after his henchmen found me." She bit her lip. "One night, I had enough, so I killed him, and I'm not sorry for it."

Hassan stared at her with dismay as Tess told him about her life in Ireland. She had always been fiercely protective of her past, and now he understood why.

"You can send me to the gallows for all I care, but I will never apologize for killing that blackheart. I only ask that you look after Molly for me."

"You know I wouldn't allow you to hang for that crime. If you ask me, he got what he deserved. Besides, I would have killed him if you hadn't. There is nothing more despicable than violating an innocent child." Hassan studied his former lover. "Am I endangering you by bringing you to England?"

"I don't know." Tess stared at the table. "Maybe, maybe not. Me master was a lord in England, and the chief magistrate for me town."

Hassan covered Tess's hand with his own. "You have my word that I will fight to protect you should anyone attempt to bring you to justice for this crime."

Tess leaned down and pressed a kiss to the back of Hassan's hand. "Thank you, but I can fight me own battles."

"I would like to help you get settled when we reach England. I've been away for a long time; I'm certain that I can provide a place for you and Molly to live on my family's property with enough money to help you start a new life."

"That is very generous of you, Nathan Shelby, but I don't need your charity," Tess said, holding her chin up high.

"You wanted my help before."

"Aye," Tess admitted. "I still hate accepting charity."

"Please, think of Molly."

"Very well, perhaps a wee bit of help - but only until I am settled and working in a proper job," Tess insisted. "Who knows, perhaps I'll catch the eye of a gentleman farmer."

"That won't be difficult. I think you can have any man you want."

"Except you," Tess teased. She leaned her head against the back of her chair. "Sarah *was* faithful to you. You're bloody lucky that His Lordship decided to keep her. He almost didn't, you see. He even went as far as having her taken to the slave block. Me friend, Mamnoon, was there. Sarah was almost sold, but His Lordship stopped the sale."

Hassan gasped. "What happened?"

"First, the fool threatened to kill herself after His Lordship attacked her …"

Hassan cupped his mouth with his hand as he listened to Tess's account of Sarah's captivity. Even though he had only heard part of the story, hearing the rest was a shock to his entire being. Now he felt even worse about confiscating Sarah's ruby ring.

"He was very sweet to Sarah after he brought her back to the Palace. He assigned Molly and me to keep her company because we could communicate in English. I can tell you for certain that Sarah and His Lordship were not lovers."

"How do you know that?"

"Because I didn't have to clean Sarah after His Lordship left her." A loud sigh escaped Tess's lips. "His Lordship also wore different clothes when I saw him the next morning. Besides, he was only with Sarah for a few hours, the one time he visited her. I think they were fond of each other, though – at least once they came to an understanding, but it was nothing more than friendship."

"Did you know Dhar's American mistress?"

"Aye. Cora was Abigail's cousin," Tess said with a haunted look. "I thought me life was hell until I heard what that blackheart did to her. Me life was pleasant compared to Cora's."

"What did Dhar do to her?" Shivers spiked up and down Hassan's spine as he listened to Tess's account of Cora's captivity.

"That very well could have been Sarah. His Lordship was a proud man. He did not take rejection well. I give Cora credit, though. She brought His Lordship to his knees when she died – at least that's what Mamnoon told me. He witnessed it, without His Lordship knowing, of course. I believe that Cora is the reason His Lordship changed his mind about selling Sarah. Cora is also the reason His Lordship was so sweet to your wife. Cora and Sarah were very similar, you see. They even looked alike, including having the same red hair. I think that they would have been good friends."

Hassan shot up from his chair and fled to the bulkhead. Facing away from Tess, he buried his forehead in his hand as he envisioned men lining up to violate Sarah.

Tess approached him and rested her hands on his arms. "Be comforted knowing that Sarah would have taken her life before she'd let any man touch her that way. She loved you too much to betray your love. Anyway, that's the reason I asked to speak to you in private. I figured that I owed you the truth after the way I cheated on you."

Hassan turned around and smiled at his former paramour. "Thank you for telling me about your life and the truth about Sarah's captivity. I do wish you well."

"And you."

Hassan kissed and embraced Tess one last time, but for the first time during their strange relationship, Tess was the first to let go.

Hassan released her waist and studied her. "Will you be alright?"

"You know me; I always find a way to survive. Who knows, maybe I'll ensnare one of your officers."

"Not the doctor?" Hassan challenged.

"He's alright, but he's not you. Now off you go. Sarah needs you."

Chapter 43

Hassan found John sitting alone at a table in the galley. He pursed his lips when he realized that he hadn't seen Sarah since he introduced her to John. Hassan sat down across from him. "How was your conversation with Sarah?"

"Good afternoon, Captain Shelby. I had a delightful conversation with Miss Campbell. I believe that your conclusions were correct. She is very sweet and innocent. Even though she spoke in broken English, her love for you was unmistakably clear. I have trouble believing that she would betray you. Above all, I sensed a deep sadness within her."

"Did you asked Sarah about her friendship with Dhar?"

"Yes, I did. The only thing she said about him was that he was her friend," John added. "But tears filled her eyes when I mentioned her father. She refused to discuss it."

"Indeed." Hassan nibbled on the inside of his lip. "It's strange. Sarah behaved as though her father didn't exist on the morning after his death. It wasn't until I rescued her that she became truly distraught."

"Hmm," John stared thoughtfully at the table. "I think I may have an explanation for her change in behavior. I counseled a man after he suffered an unimaginable tragedy. I won't bore you with the details, but what I will say is that he had no memory of that accident, even though he was at fault. Regrettably, he took his life after he remembered his part in his family's death. I think that's what happened to Miss Campbell."

Hassan turned his head away from John and squeezed his eyes shut in a feeble attempt to block the memory of the night he confronted Sarah. "She tried to drown herself after we returned to the ship. Her nightmares began that night. They have continued every night since then. I pressed Sarah to tell me about her dreams, but she refuses to confide in me."

"Perhaps Miss Campbell considered His Excellency as a father instead of a lover," John reasoned.

Hassan gasped when images of Sarah's portraits flashed in his mind. He jumped up from the table. "I will be right back." Hassan ran to the wardroom and retrieved several things from Sarah's cabin. On his way back to the table, he encountered Tess wandering through the deck. He grabbed her hand and said, "Come with me."

"Nathan, what is the matter with you?" Tess exclaimed as she ran to keep up with him.

Hassan handed one portrait to John and the other to Tess. "Do you recognize this gentleman?"

"He is dressed like His Excellency. However, I don't recognize his face. I'm sorry, Captain Shelby." John handed the portrait back to Hassan.

Tess studied hers a little longer. She tilted her head from side to side. "Well, I thought I knew every man in the Palace. This drawing proves that I was wrong. What puzzles me, though, is how Sarah met him. She was a prisoner in that apartment. The henchmen guarding her door prevented her from leaving, or from anyone going inside. Mamnoon, His Lordship, Molly, and I were the only ones allowed to enter the apartment. The only time Sarah left was when Mamnoon escorted her to and from the harem." Tess took the other portrait from Hassan and studied them side-by-side. "He looks a little like Sarah." She glanced up at Hassan. "Did she have a brother?"

Hassan stared at the portrait of the man petting the kitten when the drawings from Sarah's trunk flashed into his mind. Then he remembered where he saw the face. "This is her father," Hassan mumbled. He turned his head away from the group when Sarah's pleas to Dhar replayed in his mind. "Oh, dear God."

"What?" Tess demanded.

"She called Dhar 'Da' as she pleaded with him before he died. I thought she said Dhar, but Sarah referred to him as Naa'il whenever she spoke of him. No wonder she feared me. I made her relive her father's death," Hassan explained with a pained expression. "Her suicide attempt, her nightmares, her depression – they all make sense now. How could I be so blind?"

Just then Abigail ran up to the table, balancing Molly on her hips. "Captain Shelby, I have been looking everywhere for you," she said, struggling to catch her breath.

"What's the matter?" Hassan demanded in spite of the dread building inside him.

"Perhaps it's nothing; Sarah came up to me today and said goodbye. Then she walked away. I tried to follow her, but it was difficult keeping up with her while carrying Molly. Besides, the deck was filled with men waiting to go ashore. I'm sorry that I lost her. I've been looking for you ever since then."

Hassan spotted Peter standing in the shadows out of the corner of his eye. He looked as though he wanted to add something, but was afraid to approach them. "Do you have something to say?"

Peter approached the group with hesitant footsteps. "Forgive my intrusion, but I thought you should know that Sarah came to visit me after you left."

Hassan's lips parted. "What did she want?"

"Her reason doesn't matter. She took my knife and ran away before I could stop her."

"Oh God," Tess mumbled.

"Sarah must be somewhere on the ship," Hassan said with an authoritative tone. "We'll split up and search for her. Start in the usual places ..." He sent John, Abigail, and Molly to search the upper decks, while Peter and Tess searched the lower. Hassan returned to the quarterdeck. Abigail was right; men waiting patiently for a jolly to take them ashore filled the main deck. Sticking close to the railing, he scanned the water for signs of her red hair, but all he saw was blue water. Hassan crossed the deck to Luke and Tristan, who were overseeing the loading process. "Have you seen Miss Campbell?"

"I'm sorry, Captain. I have not seen her," Luke replied. "Did something happen?"

"I've been searching for her, and I can't find her anywhere."

Luke and Tristan joined the search. Another hour passed, and still there was no sign of Sarah. For Hassan, each passing minute was more tortuous than the previous.

Luke approached Hassan and the group after they exhausted their search. "This came from the acting captain of the Trésor." He handed the note to Hassan.

Hassan opened the parchment marked with his name and the word 'urgent" written across the cover. He unfolded the paper and gasped as he read the note. "Sarah is aboard the Trésor," he announced to the group. "Why would she go back there?"

"I will have a jolly prepared for you at once," Luke volunteered.

Hassan nodded to his bodyguard. Though the ship was only a few hundred yards away, the journey felt like a lifetime. His body trembled as he climbed aboard. The acting captain of the Trésor met him on deck.

"Thank you for coming so promptly, Captain Shelby," said the interim captain.

"You have news of my wife?" Hassan asked.

"Your wife?" the captain frowned. "I was not aware that you were married. I recognized her because I watched her climb down from the op with you."

"Where is …" Hassan paused when he realized that he knew the answer to his question. "Never mind; I know where she is."

"Captain, I should warn you; your wife was very distraught when she arrived. I posted a few guards outside her cabin in case their assistance was needed.

"Thank you," Hassan ran below. Sailors, clustered in groups, stood and whispered as Hassan darted past them. His heart raced when he spotted two over-sized guards standing outside Sarah's and her father's former quarters. Staring at the door, he paused, dreading what he would find. "Thank you, gentlemen, I will take it from here."

"Yes, sir." The guards saluted Hassan before leaving.

Hassan took the nearest lantern and opened the door. Sarah sat on the floor with rounded shoulders. She stared at the knife laying on the berth with her hands wrapped around her shins. Sarah seemed not to notice or care that her clothes and hair were dripping wet, or that blood streamed down her forehead. After hanging the lantern on the hook attached to the overhead, he wiped the blood off the tip of the knife, tucked the weapon into his belt and sat on the edge of the berth. "Did you cut yourself on purpose?" he asked softly.

"Aye," she replied in a haunted voice.

He took a handkerchief from his pocket and pressed it against her forehead until the bleeding had stopped. "Why did you cut yourself?" He wiped the blood from her forehead and laid the handkerchief on the berth.

Sarah lifted her gaze to his. "I sad," she replied.

Hassan wished that Peter were there to explain her cryptic behavior. His only comfort was knowing that she cut her forehead near the wound from several nights ago instead of on a part of her body that would have killed her.

"I try to die; I could not," Sarah confessed in a tone, just above a whisper.

"I'm glad." Hassan stood and scanned the room, wondering how Sarah and her father managed to spend a year in a room that could barely fit one person. He was sure that Sarah never complained about their cramped quarters because she never complained whenever she was with him, even when she had a good reason. Hassan covered her chest with a blanket and shifted around so that he could sit beside her.

"I not remember Da die. I remember now." She looked at him with tear-filled eyes. "How I forget he die?"

Hassan slid down the bulkhead until he was seated beside her. "Sometimes, forgetting is the only way a mind can cope with a tragedy such as your father's murder."

"I bad pers …?"

"Person," he offered.

"I bad person. I forget Da die."

Hassan looked her in the eyes and said, "You're not a bad person, Sarah."

"You say I am."

"I suppose I deserve that." He grimaced. "I wouldn't have married you had I believed that it was true about you." Hassan paused and smiled faintly. "You see, I made a mistake when I left you on our wedding night – our *first* wedding night." Hassan knew he owed her an explanation, a real explanation, and an apology. He hoped that his humor attempt would brighten Sarah's spirits.

She looked up at him with wide eyes. "Why you leave?"

"Because I didn't trust myself with you. You are the most beautiful woman that I have ever known. You overwhelmed me with your charm … your generosity …," he kissed her temple, "your curiosity … your strength. Those are only a few of the many qualities that I love about you."

"I not strong," she whispered, staring at her knees.

Hassan chuckled. "Sweetheart, you are the bravest woman I have ever known."

"No, I not."

Tucking his finger under her chin, Hassan swiveled her face towards his. "Yes, you are. If you were not strong, I would be holding your dead body and weeping because I had failed you. I thank you for sparing me from that unpleasantness."

"You not fail me."

"Yes, I did. I failed you when I doubted your love …." He paused. "I never should have struck you."

"You cross."

"There is no excuse for striking you," Hassan whispered as he shifted his gaze from this lap to her eyes. "I promise that I will never raise my hand in anger to you again."

"Cattin, you cross, you say I break promise."

"Yes, I did. You deserve to know why I doubted your love."

"You no have to say."

"Yes, I do." Hassan insisted.

"If you wish."

Hassan laughed faintly. "I wish." His smile faded. "I made the mistake of seeking an opinion from a person who was bitter about his experience in Tahiti. I should have challenged his views and trusted my judgment, but I allowed his beliefs to become my own. I understand that everything that Peter Hyatt said about you was wrong. I also know that he attacked you last night." Hassan's fingers wiped away the sweat dripping from his temples. "Why didn't you tell me that Dr. Hyatt mistreated you?"

"He your friend."

"Sweetheart, anyone who mistreats my wife is no friend of mine. I want you to confide in me when Dr. Hyatt or anyone else treats you inappropriately." Hassan paused and looked her in the eyes. "Tess told me the truth about your captivity. I understand that you and Naa'il Dhar were not lovers. I'm so sorry that I doubted you. So I sit beside you, humbled. Though I do not deserve it, I am asking you to give me another chance to prove myself worthy of your love."

"Cattin, you love Tess."

Hassan stifled a laugh. "No, most decidedly not. Tess and I are only friends."

"Why you not love Tess?"

Hassan sighed. "I cared for her, but I never truly loved her."

Sarah stared at him with rounded eyes. "Why? She beautiful and kind."

"Yes, Tess is pretty. There is a good reason that I do not love her." Hassan's hardened expression softened into a smile. "Tess is not you. You see, I knew I wanted you for my own from the moment you stood naked on the deck of this ship, surrounded by a mob. In spite of your humiliation, you fought back. You captured my heart when you bit Rochelle's hand."

Her lips parted. "Aye?"

"Aye," He kissed her temple. "I knew I could not part with you the first time you tied the blue and gold paru around your waist and sought my approval. My God, I wish you could feel my heart whenever I see you wearing your parus. My heart beats so fast that I fear it will burst."

"That good?" she asked in a timid voice.

"Aye," He kissed her temple again. "It may comfort you to know that Rochelle died on the night he brought you to the Palace."

"Emile say he give Gerard Da medicine," Sarah added.

"I'll be damned," Hassan mumbled. "You should also know that his crew will spend the rest of their lives doing hard labor as payment for their crimes."

Tears flooded her eyes. "I glad." She wiped a tear from her cheek. "Cattin, Tess say she love you."

"Sweetheart, what Tess says and what she does are two very different things."

"I no understand."

"Tess may declare her love for me, but she has never been faithful."

Sarah bit her fingernail as she looked at him through squinted eyes. "I no understand."

"Tess has given herself to many men, including Dr. Hyatt."

"Aye?" Her lips parted.

"Aye," Hassan chuckled.

"Tess and Peter together?"

"Uh huh, I discovered them in bed together this afternoon."

"She say she love you. Why she not keep promise?" Sarah asked with genuine surprise.

"In fairness to Tess, I did not expect her to be faithful to me."

"Why?"

"Because there is no formal understanding between us. In other words, we did not make promises to each other the way you and I did." Hassan studied Sarah's reaction to his revelation. Her furrowed brow and narrowed eyes made it difficult to ascertain what she thought as she stared straight ahead of her. Sarah's lips were neither smiling nor frowning, but pressed together, forming one straight line. "Sarah, do you understand what I just told you?

Her eyes widened, and her lips curled downward ever so slightly when she returned her gaze to him. "Aye," she paused. "Cattin, Molly, your daughter. You should be with her."

"Tess admitted this morning that I am not Molly's father. I think I knew it all along, but had forgotten until Tess reminded me of our first night together."

Sarah's face froze again. This time her eyes were wide, and her lips parted. "Tess not say truth?"

"No. It was a lie."

The muscles in Sarah's face tightened. "Da say I must say truth. Why Tess not say truth?" Sarah demanded, as her eyes flashed with fury.

Hassan grimaced. "Your father was correct; you should always tell the truth, no matter what."

"Why Tess not say truth?"

"Regrettably, not everyone does."

"Why not?"

"There are a lot of reasons why people tell falsehoods."

"You say truth?"

"I certainly try." Hassan winced before looking her in the eyes. "I will always tell you the truth."

"Cattin, why Tess not say truth?" Sarah pressed again.

"I surmise that Tess fears for her future." Hassan grimaced again. "That is my doing."

"What you do to her?"

"Tess had a very comfortable life when she lived in the Palace. She had food, servants, and a place to sleep. She lost all of it when I arranged for her release," Hassan explained. "Tess has nothing now." He paused when he spotted the concern on her face. "You need not worry about Tess and Molly. She accepted my assistance to help her start a new life when we reach England. They will have a home and all they require. They will never be in want."

"You good man."

"Thank you." Hassan pressed a kiss to her hand.

Sarah's bottom lip quivered as tears flooded her eyes. "I wish you knew Da. You be his son."

"I too regret not having the opportunity to know your father better." Hassan pulled her closer to him. "Sarah, I know you are in pain, but your wounds will heal in time. We will work through them together. Will you take me back?"

"Aye," Sarah whimpered.

"May I ask you to make another promise to me?"

Sarah looked up at him. "Aye."

"Please do not cut yourself again when you're sad."

Sarah bit the inside of her lip. "My people, they cut here when they sad."

"I see." Hassan kissed her temple again. "You don't need to harm yourself to express your sadness. Most people in England weep when they are sad. You may weep as often as you wish. Please do not cut yourself again." He grinned faintly. "I make this request for selfish reasons."

"What reason?"

"Sweetheart, I would hate for you to ruin your perfect face by cutting yourself. Will you promise me that you will never try to harm yourself again?"

"I promise." Sarah nuzzled against him.

"Thank you." She was still trembling. "Are you cold?"

Sarah nodded.

Hassan stood up and offered his hand to Sarah. "Come with me." He bundled her in a blanket, and they returned to the jolly. "Take us to the Zafirah."

"I'm sorry, Captain. Which ship is she?" the oarsman asked after scanning the harbor.

"It's the seventy-four gunship." Hassan pointed to the largest ship anchored in the middle of the harbor.

"She's a beaut, sir. I've been admiring her since we arrived."

Sarah was still trembling as she clung to the blanket during their short trip.

'We are almost there." Hassan rubbed her arms until they reached their destination. He grabbed the rope and threw it to the seamen standing at the railing above them. Once the boat was secured, he asked. "Can you climb, or do you need a bosuns' chair?"

"I climb." Sarah dropped her blanket and reached for the lines.

"Of course," Hassan laughed to himself as he watched her effortlessly scale the side of his ship. He threw the blanket around his neck and followed her. Sarah had already climbed aboard by the time Hassan reached her.

Sarah stared thoughtfully at the Persephone. "Cattin, we not go to Abigail and Tess?"

"Not tonight. I want you all to myself. You'll see them tomorrow." Hassan wrapped the blanket around her. "Come with me." He held out his hand to her.

There was only a quarter of his men left on the deck. Some were standing by the railing keeping a watchful eye for unexpected dangers, while others enjoyed the sunny afternoon. All of them stood at attention and saluted their captain as Hassan passed them.

"Welcome aboard, sir. It's good to have you back," said one of Hassan's lieutenants.

"Thank you," Hassan replied. "It's good to be home."

"Mr. Boyle informed us of your orders. We should be ready to set sail tomorrow."

"Very good. It's possible that we may need to delay our departure to rearrange all the freed prisoners. We're in no rush to get home." Hassan took a step and stopped abruptly. "Is there any fresh water aboard?"

"It's been raining for the past three days, sir. We collected at least ten barrels from the storm. Today is the first nice day we've had."

"Have some water boiled and brought to my cabin." Hassan glanced at Sarah who was still shivering from the brisk air. "Come, let's get you warm." Returning to his quarters felt like coming home. Everything had been returned to its proper place. His suite looked as if it hadn't been touched by battle. There was only one thing missing, and she was standing in the center of the room. Hassan went over to Sarah and kissed her tenderly as he slid the blanket from her shoulders and lifted the wet dress over her head. He wrapped the blanket around her and kissed her forehead. "Stay here, I will return shortly."

"You not be long?"

"No, I will not be long." Hassan kissed her again.

Sarah went over to her trunk. After removing her blanket from her shoulders, she laid it on the floor and knelt beside it. Sarah opened the lid. The island scents were as faint as her memories of her free-spirited life on her island. She removed her treasures, including her island paru and her drum. She shuffled through her drawings until she came to her father's portrait. "I miss you, Da." She kissed his picture. Sarah jumped when she spotted Hassan standing next to her.

Hassan squatted beside her. "Looking through your treasures?"

"I miss Da," Sarah whispered.

"I know, sweetheart. Your father loved you."

"I wish I could talk to him," Sarah said slowly as she carefully chose each word.

"It's difficult losing someone before you're ready to say goodbye. You don't need to talk to your father for him to know that you love him. Now you must do the hardest thing, live, and live the way he would want you to live." Hassan brushed her hair from her eyes. "Be a good wife; be a good mother. Above all, enjoy your new life. If you can do that, I am certain that you will make your father very happy." Hassan took the pictures from Sarah and returned them to her chest. "Now, I need you to sit on our berth," he said with a playful gleam in his eye. "And no peeking."

"Cattin, what?" Sarah offered Hassan a curious look.

Hassan stood, pulled her to her feet and wrapped the blanket around her shoulders. He spun her around, pointing her towards his berth. "It's a surprise. Now off you go." Hassan gave her bottom a loving pat before escorting her to his bedchamber.

Sarah sat on the edge of the berth and stared out the window. It was difficult resisting the temptation to peek while listening to the mumbles, the scuffs, and the swishes. The only words Sarah recognized were, "Thank you, gentlemen."

Hassan peered around the divider moments later. "I'm ready for you," he announced with a proud grin.

Sarah followed him into the main part of the cabin. The table and chairs had been moved to the side, and a large barrel with steam rising from its center was sitting in the middle of the room. Hassan slid her blanket from her shoulders and lifted her into the barrel.

"I'm afraid this is the best bath that I can offer you,"

"No, it good." Sarah sank into the warm water until it covered her shoulders. Every rigid muscle in her body relaxed, especially when Hassan massaged the back of her neck.

"Are you enjoying your bath?"

"Umm. Baths on island cold. I like hot water."

"I will convey your sentiments to all the men who carried the buckets of water."

"They carry much?"

"More than they expected, but they didn't complain too much."

Sarah dunked her head. Hassan lifted her out of the barrel and wrapped her in a blanket. "You bath too?"

"I thought that I would. I can't let this fresh warm water go to waste." Hassan pulled his peasant shirt over his head.

Sarah gasped when she spotted the bloodied slices in his back. "Cattin, you hurt!"

"It's nothing, I assure you." He kissed her forehead. Hassan slid his breeches off and climbed into the water. Instead of sinking the whole way, Hassan leaned forward to avoid getting his back wet.

Sarah sunk into the chair beside him and stared at his back. She was surprised and ashamed that she hadn't noticed the fresh marks before. "Cattin," she said breaking her silence. "How you hurt?"

Hassan leaned over and kissed her again. "It's no matter, sweetheart."

Sarah's gaze dropped to her lap.

Hassan caressed her cheek with his finger to get her attention. "Why so somber?"

Sarah forced a smile. "I sad you hurt."

"Sarah, look at me." Hassan waited until he had her attention. "You need not worry about me. The wounds on my back will heal, just like the others. What matters is that we are together."

In spite of Hassan's cheerful demeanor, Sarah knew that he had suffered greatly when he risked his life to rescue her. There was so much that she wanted to say to him, but her command of the English language prohibited her from expressing her thoughts.

Hassan climbed out of the tub and dressed. After tucking some food, wine, and cups into a bag, he pulled her off her chair and asked, "Would you care to join me for a picnic dinner on the top?"

"Aye," Sarah replied with subdued enthusiasm.

It was a perfect evening for a picnic. The clouds surrounding the sunset were ablaze with pink and yellow hues. Instead of pulling out their dinner, Hassan retrieved two rings from his pocket.

Sarah's breath hitched when she recognized Naa'il's ring. "Cattin, I gave you," she protested when he slipped it onto her right hand's middle finger.

"I understand that you regarded Naa'il Dhar as a friend." He paused as he stared at the sunset before looking back at her. "Tess told me how he rescued you from the slave market. No matter how I feel about him, Dhar did both of us a great service that day. I doubt that I would have found you had Dhar allowed the sale to go through. I want you to keep this ring as a remembrance of your friendship with him."

"You certain, Cattin?"

Hassan offered her a smile. "Yes, I am certain."

Sarah spotted another ring in Hassan's hand. This gold band wasn't as fancy as Naa'il's ring, yet she was drawn to its simplicity. "What is?"

Hassan held up the ring between his fingers. "This?" he said with a twinkle in his eyes.

"Aye."

"This is a wedding ring. In my country, it is a tradition for the groom to give his bride a ring after they exchange their marriage vows. You see, wedding rings symbolize eternal love. I regret that I didn't have an opportunity to give this to you on the night we exchanged our vows. I want you to have it now." Hassan reached for Sarah's left hand and rested the ring at the tip of her fourth finger. "I offer you this ring, my beloved Sarah, as a symbol of my unconditional love."

Sarah trembled when he slid the gold band onto her finger. She stared at it as if he had bestowed a great honor upon her as her finger traced the outline of her band. Sarah glanced over at Hassan's hand and removed her ruby ring from her finger when she realized she didn't have a ring for him.

Hassan's eyes narrowed when she reached for his left hand. "What are you doing?"

"You wear."

Hassan chuckled. "Thank you, Sweetheart, but men don't wear wedding rings."

"Why?"

"Well," Hassan bit his bottom lip. "I don't know the reason. Men simply don't wear wedding rings in my country. Besides, I think it would please Naa'il Dhar if you wore his ring."

"It not please you."

"As I said earlier, I behaved like a jealous fool. I'm sorry for that."

"I not blame you."

"You are very kind." Hassan kissed the back of her hand. "I'm sorry for doubting you."

Sarah got quiet. Ever since her bath, her mind had been in a desperate search for the right words to express her thoughts. It wasn't until that moment that she knew what she wanted to say to him. "Cattin." She stared at her lap. "I not stop think about you. Every day, I hope you find me; we be together. Naa'il friend. Peter, not friend. I choose you, Cattin. I *always* choose you."

Hassan caressed her cheek. "I know, sweetheart, and I choose you too. I want you to understand that you are the very best part of my life. You make me feel loved in a way that I have never felt loved before. I feel alive when we are together. More importantly, I feel hope for our future. It has been a long time since I felt any of those things." He leaned in and kissed her. "That is why I would sail to the far reaches of the world to get you back."

Sarah rested her head on his shoulder. "Ua here vau ia oe," she whispered.

Hassan lifted her head and swiveled her face towards his. "Would you care to tell me what you said *in English*?"

Sarah blushed. The word she wanted was on the tip of her tongue, but for the life of her, she couldn't remember what it was. "I forget word."

"Try."

Sarah stared at the faint moon then looked back at Hassan. "I … feel …" her hand patted her heart, "this for you."

Hassan crinkled his forehead and bit his lip. "Sarah Shelby, are you trying to tell me that you love me?"

"Aye, love."

Hassan kissed her forehead. "I want you to repeat after me," His lips curled into a playful grin, "I love you, Nathan. Now, you try."

Sarah mimicked Hassan's impish grin." I love you, Cattin." She paused and studied his response. "I say wrong?" Sarah knew by his pursed lips that he was disappointed that she still couldn't address him by his Christian name. Though he was Nathan Shelby in his world, to her, he would always remain, "Cattin."

"No, it's close enough – for now." Hassan sighed.

She winced when she heard the disappointment in his tone. Sarah rested her head on his shoulder and whispered, "I love you, Natan."

Closing his eyes, Hassan whispered back with a blissful smile on his lips, "I love you too, sweetheart."

The following day was hectic for Hassan and his crew. Everyone who went ashore returned to their assigned ship. Hassan, Molly, the women and most of his crew transferred over to the Zafirah. It took the better part of the day shifting the crew around so that everyone had a place to sleep. That night, when the tide was favorable, they weighted the anchor and pointed the bow towards home.

CHAPTER 44

April 2, 1814

Hassan leaped off his berth when he heard the drums beating to quarters. Sarah lifted her head and looked at him for an explanation. "I'm not sure what the drums mean," he said tersely. "I want you to stay in the cabin until I return."

Hassan quickly dressed and headed to the quarterdeck. He found one of his officers staring at the horizon through a spyglass. He could see two ships battling against one with the naked eye. "Report."

His lieutenant handed the spyglass to Hassan. "It looks like two Frenchie ships are preying on one of ours, sir. I thought we had seen the last of the fighting when we left Portugal."

"It appears that the French are not ready to concede defeat. Let's show them a little Barbary Coast hospitality," Hassan said with a menacing grin.

"Yes, sir!" His officer snapped to attention.

Hassan glanced over at the Persephone. He could see that Adam was watching the battle through a spyglass. Hassan signaled his intentions; Adam signaled back that he had the same idea.

"Prepare for battle," Hassan shouted, sending his officers and crew into an organized frenzy. He returned to his cabin to warn Sarah about the upcoming battle.

Wearing only a paru, Sarah paced the floor. She bounded over to Hassan soon as he closed the door. "Cattin." She flung her arms around his neck.

Hassan hugged her back. "All is well, sweetheart." He pulled away and looked her in the eyes. "Remember the loud noises that you heard on the beach?"

"Aye, they frighten me."

"You will hear them again soon. I want you to dress. You are not to leave this cabin for any reason. I will return as soon as I am able."

"Cattin, please no go," she pleaded.

"I don't have a choice. I promise that I will return. Until then, I'll have Molly, and the other women brought to you." Hassan pressed a kiss to her lips and left her standing in the middle of the cabin. "Remain at your post. Guard Sarah with your lives," he said to Tristan and Luke.

"We'll keep them safe, sir," Luke vowed.

Once his fleet of ships was closer to the battle, Hassan gave the orders to hoist the Algerian flag. He grinned when he spotted Adam's ship flying the same colors. The Trésor displayed their French flag because it was the only one they had, or so Hassan surmised. He hoped that this small merchant ship would be their Trojan horse. Instead, it looked like a toddler chasing after its parents.

Every officer and seaman in Hassan's fleet were ready for the fight. No one flinched when they heard the cannon fire blasting in the distance. Armed with swords, knives, and pistols, Hassan and his corsairs hid out of plain sight of the French and British ships. A group of former slaves assembled below deck and prepared the cannons to fire. As soon as they were close enough to smell the smoke from the guns, Hassan gave the order to fire one shot towards the nearest enemy ship. That was sufficient to get the French ships' attention. The corsair captain and his men showed themselves to the enemy, every one screaming like Banshees. Both the French and English sailors stared in horror at the sight of the Barbary

Coast pirates. Hassan signaled the order. With knives clenched between their teeth, he and his men swarmed the British ship.

Hassan grabbed a line and swung over to the battle. "We are here to assist you," he said to a British officer who had just killed an enemy.

The officer stared at Hassan as though he were a figment of his imagination. "I don't understand," he exclaimed.

Hassan and his soldiers fought alongside their countrymen. Adam led another group to seize the other French ship. The French fought back, but they were no match for Hassan's trained corsairs. After a long and bloody battle, the French surrendered.

"We're very grateful that you came to our rescue; we feared that our cause was lost." The British captain bowed to Hassan.

"We're happy that we could assist you." Hassan bowed back to the fair-haired officer wearing a blood-stained uniform.

"I'm Captain Samuel Trent."

"Captain Nathan Shelby, at your service."

"Judging from your attire, I imagine that you have quite a story to tell."

"Indeed I do, but that will have to wait," Hassan replied.

"May I impose on you to meet Admiral Rowley before you return to your ship? He is below deck; he will want to meet you after the service you provided today," said Captain Trent.

"Of course, but I cannot stay long," Hassan insisted.

Admiral Rowley wandered below deck surveying the casualties among his men. Dressed in a British Admiral's uniform, the Admiral looked like a shadow of a distinguished gentleman.

"Admiral Rowley, may I present Captain Nathan Shelby," said Captain Trent. "Captain Shelby, this is Admiral Rowley." The captain bowed before leaving them alone.

The Admiral's hazel eyes narrowed as he surveyed Hassan from head to toe, then back again. "Why the devil are you dressed like a ruffian?" He pursed his lips. "Wait, I've heard your name before. It was whispered that you were on a special assignment on the Barbary Coast."

"You were well informed, Admiral. I concluded my mission only a few days ago," Hassan answered.

"And was your mission successful?"

"Yes, and I'm hopeful that the new Dey of Algiers will honor Algiers' accord with England."

"And were you successful freeing British subjects?"

"Yes, sir," Hassan said proudly. "I freed over seven-hundred men and women, and one child."

"Jolly good," Admiral Rowley replied with a wide grin. "Captain Shelby, will you and your officers do us the honor of dining with us tonight? We should have this mess cleaned up by then."

"We would be honored, Admiral. My crew and I will be happy to assist you with disposing of the bodies."

"Splendid. We will talk after dinner."

"If you will excuse me, I must return to my ship to tend to an urgent matter." Hassan bowed.

"Until tonight then."

Sarah was still pacing when he returned to check on her. Tess and Abigail looked on as Molly played with a doll made of stockings.

Sarah ran into Hassan's arms. "Cattin."

"You are trembling," Hassan pressed her against him.

"I thought," she whimpered as tears spilled onto her cheeks.

"I know. I promise that the worst is over. Are you alright?"

Sarah nodded as she clung to her husband.

Hassan was the first to pull away when he spotted the pained look on Tess's face. "Are you two alright?"

"We are well, Captain Shelby. Thank you for your concern," Abigail replied.

"I'll have some food brought to you. I came to inform you that you will be dining together without me."

"You not eat with us?" Sarah asked.

"I am sorry, but my duties prohibit me from being with you tonight. I'll return as soon as I can." Hassan leaned down and kissed Sarah on the cheek. He gently squeezed her hand and said, "I'll see you later tonight."

Sarah replied with a dejected smile.

Hassan returned to the battle scene and was pleased to discover that there was only one fatality among his crew. A few others sustained minor injuries, but there was nothing about which to be concerned. The other British ship had sustained some damages, but their crew wasn't as lucky. They had lost half of their officers and almost a third of their crew. It was speculated that they would have lost more had Nathan and his small fleet not arrived when they did. The crews of the four ships made quick work of the clean-up duties. Later that night, Hassan and his lieutenants joined the Admiral and his officers for a celebratory dinner.

"The sight of you and your men gave us quite a start," said Captain Trent.

"Please forgive our attire. My men and I have been detained in the Barbary Coast for the past few years. I regret that our Ottoman clothes are the only ones we have," Hassan explained.

"Would you care to regale us with your tale?" Captain Trent pressed.

"Certainly, I commanded a ship that provided convoy protection near the Iberian Peninsula. We sustained heavy fire from a French ship. It was a long and bloody battle, which we ultimately lost. The French captain sold all of us into slavery in Algiers," Hassan explained.

"I don't understand how the Algerian government could enslave you when our government pays them tribute money to leave British ships alone," Captain Trent reasoned.

"That is true. The French captain that captured us had made a secret accord with the previous Algerine Dey. They both profited handsomely from enslaving crews from British ships. I was fortunate to escape. Once I was reunited with our navy, I was given a secret mission to put an end to enslaving British subjects."

Raising his glass, the Admiral stood and said, "Well done. I would like to propose a toast to Captain Shelby, and his band of privateers."

After dinner, Admiral Rowley and Hassan met in the Admiral's quarters. It was one of the few places on this ship that hadn't been touched by the battle. The reception room was large enough to fit a desk, a few chairs, and a small cabinet.

"Please sit." Admiral Rowley closed the door. Hassan took a seat in front of the desk; the admiral went over to the cabinet and pulled out a crystal decanter and two matching glasses. "Would you care for some port?" He held up a crystal decanter. "I keep it for special occasions."

"Yes, please. I haven't had port in years."

The Admiral handed a glass to Hassan and sat in the chair behind his desk.

"Thank you," Hassan said before taking a sip. Closing his eyes, he swirled the syrupy liquid around his mouth to savor its sweet flavor and the spirit's bite just before he swallowed. "It's good, thank you."

"So, what is next?"

"Home, sir. It has been almost five years since I've been on English soil. Even then, I was there for only a few weeks," Hassan answered with hesitation. A knot formed in his stomach when he spotted the grimace on the Admiral's face.

"I was not completely honest with you when we met. I have heard of you. I know of your family by reputation. I also understand that you served under Lord Nelson."

"Yes, sir, I was a young lieutenant who had the good fortune of being assigned to his ship."

"You are too modest. Lord Nelson chose you himself. He would not have done so had he not seen your genius. You proved today that Lord Nelson made a wise choice."

"You are too kind, sir."

"I understand that you have been away from England for a long time. I also recognize that you may not be aware that England is still at war with the French, although I heard whispers that we are close to defeating Napoleon."

"I am relieved to hear that. Our war with France has gone on much too long," Hassan said.

"What you may not know is that America declared war on England two years ago. They did not approve of us seizing their ships and pressing their crew into duty."

"Yes, I took a few American ships myself, sir." Hassan chuckled. "Of course we were all sold into slavery a few months later."

Admiral Rowley's demeanor remained stoic. "Now that our war with Napoleon is coming to a close, His Highness intends to turn his attention to ending the war with the Americans. If all goes well, we should put down the rustics once and for all and take back all the territory that they stole from us by years end." Admiral Rowley took a sip of his port. "Shelby, I regret to inform you that I cannot release you from His Highness' Navy. As of today, you and your crew will join our fight. Where you will be sent, still remains to be seen."

"Sir, I understand His Highness' need for my ships and my crew. I was recently married, and it is vital that I take her to England," Hassan insisted.

"I give you permission to take your new wife to England, but you must report for duty within a fortnight."

"Sir, it is not that simple. This woman was raised in a primitive culture on an island in the South Seas. It will take time to acclimate her to the British way of life."

"How the devil did you acquire a South Seas wife?"

Hassan told the admiral about how Sarah came into his life. "So you see, Admiral, I must have time to immerse her into British society."

"Your family lives in England. Why can't they acclimate your wife?"

"It's complicated, sir. More importantly, I'm not so cruel as to bring Sarah to England, only to abandon her a week after taking her to my family home," Hassan maintained.

Admiral Rowley jumped to his feet. "You have a duty to serve the Crown during our hour of need!" he shouted.

"I have served England for most of my life. I sacrificed my freedom and my duties to my family – all in the name of serving my country. My service is over!" Hassan shouted back with nostrils flaring. He took a deep breath and calmly added, "My wife lost her family when she sailed here. I am all she has now. She needs me."

"I understand your predicament. Now you must understand mine. Every officer and sailor in the Royal Navy made the same sacrifices that you did. England is at war. We cannot afford to lose you or your crew. As a token of my gratitude for your service today, I will give you a little time to settle your wife in England. You will be expected to report for duty exactly five weeks from the day. Fail to report, and I will have you hung for treason."

"Yes, sir." Hassan stormed out of the Admiral's quarters and returned to his ship. Not wanting to upset Sarah any further, he stole away to the hold. His mind and body felt numb as he reflected on leaving Sarah with his family. It wasn't until he was faced with this dilemma that he fully understood Peter's warning. The doctor was right; Hassan's family and social circle would reject Sarah because she has no money, no family, and no social connections. He feared how they would treat her after they learned of her exotic heritage. The shore-leave that was given to him wasn't enough time for him to find a suitable alternative.

Jamal had arranged for Mariam and her daughters to live in their family home while he assumed his duties as the Dey of Algiers. Mariam was glad to be home and to be free of the trappings from the Palace intrigue. That night, she wandered through the rooms of her spacious home. After looking in on her daughters, Mariam found herself counting her blessings. She was grateful to Jamal for fighting for her freedom and reminding her of her reasons for living. She was equally thankful that he kept his word that he would provide for her and her children. Jamal even found a suitable husband for Samina. As the new Dey of Algiers, he ensured Mariam and her family of a lifestyle suitable for royalty. The former first wife of the Dey of Algiers leaned down and kissed her eldest daughter, who slept beside her sisters. She looked tenderly at each child, thinking how fortunate she was to have them in her life. Mariam was equally grateful to Naa'il for giving them to her. After kissing her other two daughters, Mariam wandered out to the garden and sat on a stone bench. Her new kitten jumped onto her lap and purred as Mariam stroked its black and white fir.

"Good evening, Cansu. Could you not sleep either?" Mariam grimaced when her pet's sharp claws poked through her green salvar and into her leg.

Cansu yawned, turned around several times before curling into a ball on her mistress' lap. "Oh, I see. You were looking for a comfortable place to sleep." Mariam mused as she stroked her pet's soft fur. She too was grateful for her brother's gift, who brought laughter to her daughters during an otherwise miserable few weeks. As she continued counting her blessings, Mariam's thoughts drifted to her unsuspecting heroes that sacrificed their lives to save her family's honor.

"My lady." Bashira bowed as Mariam entered the bathing room through her private entrance. She leaned in and whispered. "Can you send your attendants away? Someone has requested an audience with you. It concerns His Excellency's marriage to the infidel. She is privy that you are against this union, and is offering a solution."

Mariam offered the valide a subtle nod. "Leave this room and do not return until I send for you." She barked at her attendants.

Once they were alone, Bashira helped the first wife undress and wrapped her body in a muslin cloth. The valide opened the door to the steam room. The hot rocks sizzled when they entered. All Mariam could see through the thick layer of steam were outlines of the blue and white tiles on the wall and a petite woman standing on the far side of the twelve by twelve-foot room.

"Bashira, would you please translate our conversation?" An American said, stepping into plain sight.

"Of course," Bashira replied in English.

Mariam's whole body stiffened when she recognized Cora Bradley.

"Your Excellency," Cora curtsied to Mariam. "Forgive me for not addressing you correctly. I'm still ignorant of proper Algerian protocol. I regret that I don't know your title. Please allow me to introduce myself. I'm Cora Bradley."

"I know who you are," the first wife snapped.

"Of course you do. Thank you for meeting with me. I understand the risk you're taking."

"What do you want?" Mariam demanded.

"His Excellency asked me to marry him this morning."

"Yes. My husband informed me," Mariam said bitterly. "I trust that you agreed."

"No. I asked for a few days to consider my answer. I wanted to talk to you before I gave His Excellency my reply. Of course, he doesn't know about our meeting. I doubt that he would want us to consult with each other."

Mariam laughed faintly. "You understand my husband well for only knowing him for a short time. He forbade me from interacting with you. I must admit; I wanted to meet with you too." She held out her hand, inviting Cora and Bashira to sit. Mariam was the first to sit on the wooden bench; the other two women took seats adjacent to hers.

Cora rested her elbows on her knees. "May I enquire about your concerns?"

"I believe that your faith will destroy my family," Mariam replied.

"I understand."

Mariam jumped up from her seat. She stared at Cora as if she were a plague. "No, you do not understand. We come from two different worlds. And in my world, my people live by strict rules that were set forth by our ancestors. My people can be executed if they deviate from any one of these rules. My husband changed after meeting you; I fear that he is turning from our faith. You must understand that my husband's actions affect my entire family. My daughters and I will lose everything if my husband becomes an apostate. My children will never marry, and I will have no means for providing for them. We will have no home and no money. We will spend the rest of our days living as objects of ridicule. That is why I am against your marriage."

Cora stood and approached the first wife. Standing face to face, she looked Mariam in the eyes and said, "Thank you for your candor, but I'm not your enemy. I would rather go to my death than to bring shame upon your family."

Mariam's lips parted. She rubbed her arms and studied Cora. "You must marry my husband; you have no choice."

"Then I will try to change his mind."

Mariam laughed to herself. "You stupid girl, you will not change my husband's mind. Once Naa'il makes a decision; you must obey."

"Then I will persuade him to see that I am not a suitable wife for him."

"And what if you fail?" Mariam challenged.

Cora stared at the floor, then back at the first wife. "Then I will take my life, but it must look like a murder, and it must be done in public." Cora went over and added a log to the stove before pouring more water on the hot rocks.

"Are you mad? His Excellency will execute all of you for this conspiracy."

The three women jumped when they spotted Mamnoon standing in the doorway. None of them saw him slip into the room.

Cora ushered her friend into a corner and whispered in a voice loud enough for everyone in the room to hear her. Bashira continued translating. "Please, say nothing. This is my choice. I was never meant to live in a cage, even in one as beautiful as this."

Mamnoon stared at her with dismay. "Why would you do this?"

Cora glanced back at Mariam and said, "Because it is the right thing to do. Mamnoon, I'm Anglo-Saxon. Though I respect your people, I will never convert to your faith. My own faith forbids me from being part of a polygamous marriage. I love my god too much to betray Him that way. You know this, my dear friend. More importantly, I couldn't live with myself knowing that I destroyed the lives of these noble people." Returning her attention to her friend, Cora rested her hand on his arm. "Please, I beg you to respect my wishes this time."

"What about your cousin? You have sacrificed yourself to protect her. Why leave her now?"

"I must do what I should have done all along; I must trust her to God's care. Please, will you help me?" Cora pleaded. "This is best for everyone."

"It is not best for me, and it is not for you," Mamnoon angrily countered.

"How can it not be when I will be reunited with my family again?"

"How do you know that you will not spend eternity in hell for this?"

Cora answered with a faint laugh. "Who knows what really happens after we die. In my eyes, I'm willing to sacrifice my life so that innocent people can live. That must count for something," Cora paused. "Will you help me?" With pleading eyes, she whispered to Mamnoon, "Please, I need peace."

Mariam gasped as Cora's countenance changed before her eyes. The American captive began this meeting as the epitome of a strong woman. Standing with her shoulders pulled back, and her head held high, Cora gave the impression that nothing could defeat her. In less than a minute, she removed her mask revealing a defeated soul who had endured the worst kind of hell. It was clear to everyone in the room, including Mamnoon, that Cora desperately wanted to be set free from the bonds of her mortal existence.

The bodyguard answered Cora's plea with a faint nod as tears spilled onto his cheeks.

"I can provide the poison," Mariam offered.

"No, my lady, the risk is too great for you," Bashira insisted. "I will get it."

Cora straightened her posture, and once again she transformed into the confident woman that everyone was accustomed to seeing. "I don't want any of you to die for me," she countered. "When I said that I was willing to give my life to protect you, I never said that I was willing to sacrifice the lives *of the people in this room. If my plan is truly endangering your lives, then I will find another way."*

"There is no other way, Cora," the first wife interjected. "My husband is in love with you. Of that I am certain. Your death may be the only way to stop this unholy marriage."

Cora crossed her arms and stared at the floor. "I still don't want anyone to die for me," she protested in a quiet voice.

"I appreciate your concern, but everyone in this room became part of this conspiracy when we agreed to meet." Bashira pointed out. "Although, I hope that you will be successful at changing His Excellency's mind."

Mamnoon glanced over at the women sitting on the bench and said, "I agree with Cora. Bashira, my lady, your sacrifices are not necessary. I will acquire the poison."

"That is very generous of you, but I am perfectly happy to sacrifice myself for the first wife and her children." Bashira countered. "I will get the poison, just as I promised."

"You need not bother; I brought some with me," Mariam said with a sheepish grin. "I was desperate."

"Give it to me, my lady. I will keep it safe should it be needed," Bashira offered.

Mariam bowed her head and said, "Thank you all, I am humbled by your desire to protect my children and me." She slipped a green vial into the valide's hand.

"Let's hope that I will be successful at changing His Excellency's mind," Cora said.

Mariam approached Cora and rested her hand on her arm. "I heard what my husband did to you. I am so very sorry; it should never have happened. I would have ended your life then, but ..."

"Your husband forbade you from interfering," Cora surmised.

"Yes," Mariam confirmed. She leaned in and whispered to Mamnoon, "I understand why you and my husband love her."

Mariam looked up at the night sky. With tears of gratitude filling her eyes, she said to Bashira, Mamnoon, and Cora, "Thank you again for your sacrifices. Please watch over my husband and Zeba, and may peace and joy be with you for all eternity."

The remainder of the journey home was mercifully uneventful. Sarah gave into her hunger for sunlight and joined her husband on the quarterdeck. Tess, Molly, and Abigail were already enjoying their day. While her friends kept a watchful eye on Molly, Sarah retreated to her bench and kept herself busy by drawing in her sketchbook. Hassan and his crew halted their duties to admire the green-capped rocky coastline rising from the blue water. The gray sky softened the glare that the sun would have otherwise created. Sarah admired the thin rods of sunlight streaming through the clouds onto the tiny houses dotting the cliffs.

Laying her sketchbook on the bench, Hassan took her hand, led her to the portside of the ship, and sandwiched her between him and the railing. "This is my island. Its name is England." He wrapped his arms around her and pressed her against him.

"England." Sarah looked up at her husband as a warm salty breeze caressed her cheeks. *It was a beautiful island.* Sarah bit her lip as she observed Hassan's and his crew's reaction when they saw their home. Regardless of whether they were young or old, the sailors were silent, and a few even wiped tears from their eyes. Sarah thought of her island and wondered if she would ever see her home again. Hassan's strong embrace gave her hope that she would find a new and a better life in England.

BEFORE YOU GO

Dear Friend.

I hope you enjoyed reading *A Maiden's Honor*. Your feedback is important to the success of this story. Not only will it help other readers to decide if this story is right for them, it also will help me improve as a storyteller. All you need to do is click on the link below, scroll to the bottom of the page, and click on Write a Customer Review. Thank you.

ISBN 978-1-939625-64-9

CPSIA information can be obtained
at www.ICGtesting.com
Printed in the USA
LVHW032326250319
611839LV00001B/86/P